"The Sooner I Am Wed,
the Better,
For Until I Am,
My Mother Has the Right
To Dispose of My Property."

Laurie had practiced over and over what she would say.

"I know that you have come to England for the purpose of finding a young woman of good family, good reputation, and some means to marry you and return with you to the West Indies. . . . I am virtuous and possess a modest fortune. If you will meet certain conditions which I will explain, I will marry you. . . ."

"You do understand, Miss Stepney, that I seek a real wife? A woman to grace my home and bear my children?"

Laurie looked down at her whitened knuckles gripping the plaid reticule and wished herself elsewhere. But, the only alternative was . . . She lifted her chin.

"I do understand. And I will do my best to please you."

Silversea

Jan McGowan

A TAPESTRY BOOK
PUBLISHED BY POCKET BOOKS NEW YORK

This novel is a work of historical fiction. Names, characters, places and incidents relating to non-historical figures are either the product of the author's imagination or are used fictitiously. Any resemblance of such non-historical incidents, places or figures to actual events or locales or persons, living or dead, is entirely coincidental.

An *Original* publication of TAPESTRY BOOKS

A Tapestry Book published by
POCKET BOOKS, a division of Simon & Schuster, Inc.
1230 Avenue of the Americas, New York, N.Y. 10020

ISBN: 0-671-54282-6

First Tapestry Books printing October, 1984

10 9 8 7 6 5 4 3 2 1

Chapter One

A TIME OF BELONGING WAS AT AN END. LAURIE Stepney watched her beloved moors drift past in a soft mist, seeming to swing up and down with the motion of the great London-bound coach in which she rode. In the dawn light the moors breathed, like some recumbent, mossy monster upon whose back they traveled, and the monster's breath was the scent of heather, of wild sea, of Scotland—sighing in farewell.

Laurie had dreaded this ending. A year ago, when Old Hugh had stopped tramping the moors with her and had huddled, silent, by the fire, her heart had told her she would lose him soon. In her memory her grandfather had forever been as strong as the handhewn gray stone of his great manorhouse, but then he had begun to sag and crumble with the weight of his years. Still, he had endured the summer and the work with the sheep, though when fall came he left it all to Breen. Laurie's heart had lifted in February, when Old Hugh came out with her to laugh at the antics of the newborn lambs. But then had come the wild winds and rains of March, and suddenly, like one of the weathered stones of the cliff that cracked without warning and fell into the sea, her grandfather had fallen into death, carrying with him all the warm and happy years when she had known his encompassing love.

"Laurie!"

She turned and looked with fresh wonder at the woman beside her. A curious, charming creature, feminine and honey-sweet, yet with a shrewd look in her pale

1

blue eyes. Her face was colorfully enameled with various ointments and paints, her yellow hair elaborately curled. She wore a lovely high-waisted, flowing column of thin, wine red wool that clung to her slender body. There were small, soft slippers on her feet and a tiny bonnet perched on her coiffure. It seemed impossible to Laurie that this pretty stranger could be her mother, the Lady Desirée of Mayfair.

"I do not believe you have heard a word I have said." She had such a light, lilting voice. "And I do so want you to listen. It is important to plan how we shall use your inheritance."

That seemed a private matter, and Laurie glanced involuntarily at the tall, bony woman opposite them. Middle aged, with the long nose and sharp features of a provincial Frenchwoman, she accompanied the Lady Desirée as a personal maid. She wore a proper maid's uniform, and, Laurie noted, a proper expression of disinterest, as if she were stone deaf.

Desirée—it seemed easier to Laurie to think of her as Desirée rather than as her mother—saw Laurie's quick glance and laughed lightly.

"Thérèse is privy to all my secrets, my dear child. We may speak freely in her presence at any time. Now, attend to what I say! It is most rude of you to ignore me." For a moment the enameled face was haughty, then Desirée smiled and tapped Laurie's hand forgivingly with her long fingernails. "And do curb that quizzing gaze of yours, my darling, for it will never charm London society. No one cares to be examined like a butterfly on a pin."

Blood rose in Laurie's cheeks and she looked away. She had been staring at her mother, trying to see through the colorful coating to the woman within, and she well knew her stare could be disconcerting. Old Hugh had told her that her eyes, an unusual blue-green, were like her father's eyes. He had sworn that Young Hugh could see beyond time, that eyes like these had second sight, could foretell the future and catch a thief. Laurie had thought it nonsense, yet a thieving housemaid had confessed and then left the manor, stating plainly that Miss Stepney was a witch. It had astonished Laurie, who had not suspected the girl, though for some reason she had disliked her intensely.

"I am sorry," she said now. "I was deep in thought of Grandfather, of the lands I am leaving—and of Annie and Breen."

"Oh, you must not be grieving! Death has ended Old Hugh's dominion over you and, indeed, you should be glad. As for the servants, I am afraid it is a mistake to have allowed them to stay at the manor. It will be much harder on them when it is sold and they must leave."

"Sold?"

The Lady Desirée smiled brightly. "Oh, yes. It will bring a very good price. Enough to dress you like a princess, my sweet, and still provide a dowry to tempt any young nobleman contemplating marriage. When that time comes, of course." She hesitated, running her eyes over Laurie, whose small figure was hidden in the folds of her best woolen tweed. A bulky skirt and a long voluminous cape of the tweed covered a plain blouse, high-necked and long-sleeved. Desirée sighed as she added, "Decent clothing will make a difference, and Thérèse will know what to do with all that black hair; you certainly cannot continue to pull it back into such a large and unsightly bun. It will take all her skill to make you presentable."

"That will be unnecessary," Laurie said gently. "I care nothing for fashion or society. But, as to the manor and lands of Stepney Downs, they are mine. I will keep them."

"No, you will not," her mother said, her smile deepening. "That barren old monument of stone is much too far from London for our use. We will dispose of it, and the lands around it. I promise you, you will much prefer London. Even your father—God rest his soul—

would want you there now that you are grown." She reached into the embroidered satin bag tied to her wrist by its ribbons and brought out a wisp of linen to touch to her dry eyes. "Had he not insisted on going to that terrible war in Portugal he would be here to welcome you back." She appeared, Laurie thought, to be more irritated than sorrowful. "In truth, you should have remained with me all these years. Then you would not be as ignorant as any Scot peasant, trudging the muddy moors after sheep."

Ignorant? Laurie veiled the indignation in her turquoise eyes with long, black lashes. Old Hugh had brought excellent tutors to the manor, and at seventeen, almost eighteen, she was better educated than most of the young men of the day. But her mother could mean only that she was unversed in charm of manners, of fashion and parties and, indeed, she was ignorant of those.

"Surely you remember how lively life is in London," her mother was saying, "You were six or so, weren't you, when Old Hugh took you from me?"

"It is very dim," Laurie said, wondering why she lied. She kept those memories locked away, but they were sharp and clear nonetheless, and now one came forward, the same one as always, that of her father's face as he carried her, exhausted, from his carriage through the big door of the manorhouse and thrust her into Old Hugh's warm embrace. Her father's voice, forcing words out said, "She is yours. Make sure of it. Her mother is not fit to touch a child." He had turned away, choked. "My lady wife can now be said to rival the greatest of the London courtesans—both in the number and variety of her bedmates. Withal, she has little time to attend my daughter."

It had been the last time she had seen her father, a time of great emotion which kept the memory very clear. She would always remember him as he had looked that night. The blazing blue-green eyes, the thick, tousled black

4

hair, the black beard that set him apart from the pink-faced dandies that thronged the Mayfair house when he was absent. She was aware that her resemblance to her father was startling and this was a comfort to her, since it seemed to mean that some part of him would always be with her.

Old Hugh had made himself her legal guardian. Laurie had accepted that gladly, but she had not understood it until this past week, when she went through his documents. There had been an agreement, signed by the Lady Desirée, in which she gave her parental rights to the Laird of Stepney Downs, promising never to visit or communicate with the child Laurie Stepney from that day forward. In return, Desirée was to receive annually a thousand pounds sterling. But proud Old Hugh had put out a story in the village that Young Hugh's wife had been devastated by his death in the Peninsular War, had become an invalid unable to care for her child. He would have no scandal in his family.

Laurie came back from her memories, realizing that her mother was still talking.

"And, in a year or two, when you have attended the Academy, you may come out. One of the patronesses of the Harwick Assemblies is a dear friend of mine, and . . ."

"Please!" Her interruption brought a flash of irritation to the pale blue eyes, but Laurie continued. "Do not trouble yourself. I prefer a quiet life."

Desirée shrugged. "You will change. London has reached a height you cannot imagine, for with the poor King at last confined in his madness, the Prince of Wales is Regent. And Prinny, for that is what we all call the Prince, is much in favor of enjoying life to the fullest. It is a mad whirl . . ." She laughed, the same brittle tinkle of sound that Laurie remembered from childhood. "I shall say no more. When the time comes, you will be swept up in it. No one could resist such pleasures."

Relieved, Laurie sat back, looking again from the

coach window. They were descending a narrow mountain road, and far below there was a blue glitter of tarn, a small meadow where sheep grazed beside the water. Three years would change her no more than it would Annie and Breen, and they all must be together again. She must keep Stepney Downs.

If only Old Hugh, who had loved her so well, had trusted her as much. But he was not a man to think a young female could manage a fortune. He had left her everything, house, land and monies, but he had stipulated that two guardians be appointed by the village magistrate. One to be a man of God, the other a trustworthy person chosen by the magistrate. Control of Laurie's inheritance was to be left to them until she was twenty-one, or until, with the consent of both guardians, she married. Laurie had been content, knowing Old Hugh wished to protect her. But no one could have foreseen that the Lady Desirée, hearing of his death, would come apace to Scotland to tell the magistrate that her health had improved mightily and she stood ready to give Laurie the love and care of a mother, was indeed anxious to make up for the years when she had been too ill to do so.

Of course the magistrate was impressed by the lovely widow of Sir Hugh Stepney, pleading so sentimentally for the guardianship of her own daughter. And when the Lady Desirée suggested that the other guardian be her own spiritual advisor, the bishop of Wight, the magistrate had thought it wonderful that young Laurie should have a bishop as her mentor.

Firm in his conviction of mother love, the magistrate had ruled it so. Laurie had thought that the earth in the churchyard near Old Hugh's grave might tremble. How he would have hated it! For one rebellious moment she had stepped forward, ready to tell the whole sordid story. But who would have believed her in the face of the story that Old Hugh had told? The agreement was nothing, for it mentioned no misbehavior.

She had stepped back, sighing, telling herself that she could stand it for three years as long as she knew she could come back again. But now she was cold with fear. She had not imagined that a guardian could sell off a ward's property without the ward's consent, but her mother seemed very confident.

"Now," said Desirée exultantly, "we will see the world fly by."

They had reached the bottom of the mountain and turned on to the macadamized toll road, stopping at the bar which was lifted only after the coachman had paid.

The Tally-Ho coaches were famed for their speed, and once away from the bar Laurie discovered that their fame was justified. The four sweating horses galloped wildly beneath the coachman's long whip, pulling the heavy coach at a marvelous twelve miles an hour. Laurie felt a sharp pity as they rounded a curve and she could see the lead horse's bloodied back. Her grandfather had said that England was now a hell for horses and she could see that it was true. But her mother's next remark drove all else from her mind.

"I do wish," Desirée said, "that I had thought to put Old Hugh's legal papers aside, so that I could have studied them during this journey." Her light voice was again irritated. "It is so dull to ride along." She glanced at Laurie questioningly. "I wager they are in the bottom of your trunk, or some other inaccessible place."

The documents were in the reticule that lay between Laurie's small feet. And amongst them, she knew, were the title deeds to Stepney Downs. She struggled for only an instant with her conscience. Raising well-shaped dark brows in simulated surprise, she said, "The bottom of my trunk? Oh, no. I left them in safekeeping."

"Left them! I am sure I told you to bring everything of importance. Those are valuable papers, not meant for the prying eyes of servants."

"Annie and Breen do not pry," Laurie said coldly, "and in any event I did not leave them at Stepney

Downs. There is a large strongbox in the magistrate's offices, and Grandfather has always kept them there.''

Her conscience, Laurie noted with satisfaction, did not hurt at all. Any method of delaying a sale seemed more important than deception. But the words seemed to upset Desirée even more.

''The magistrate's office? Why, he may . . .'' She reddened beneath her paint, and Laurie surmised that her mother might wonder what proof against her was contained in those papers. ''Documents,'' Desirée added crossly, ''are private matters. I will write immediately and have them sent to me.'' She looked at Laurie sharply. ''You appear to have a mind of your own. Please remember that your notions are now subject to my judgment.''

Laurie said nothing, but her eyes went involuntarily to the long, harsh face of the maid Thérèse and surprised a glimmer of sympathy there. Odd, she thought. But as Thérèse looked away immediately, she could not be sure. She sat back, her slim ankles burning as they pressed against the reticule that held her only chance of ever returning home.

At Edinburgh there was a fine inn where they spent the first night. To Laurie's surprise, Thérèse divided her attentions between her mother and herself, managing hot water for baths and other amenities with quiet efficiency. In the morning Thérèse came to dress her hair, braiding the shining, waving mass into a coronet around her head.

''It is not in fashion,'' she commented dryly, setting Laurie's bonnet at a becoming angle, ''but more comfortable for traveling. It will not slip so easily.''

There was no trace of expression in either the long face or the voice, yet Laurie felt a consoling warmth.

In the four days that passed before they reached London the weather changed markedly. A chill pervaded the coach and a dreary fog lay along the road, muffling the shouts of the driver and the crack of his whip. The Lady Desirée spoke only to complain of boredom and discomfort and Thérèse spoke not at all. An elderly couple had boarded the coach at Edinburgh to sit wedged with Thérèse. It was plain that they had correctly evaluated the rank and class of the Lady Desirée but they showed no pleasure in traveling with such a fine lady. They also ignored Laurie, except at one of the stops when the old woman spoke to her, asking the destination of her mistress.

"London," Laurie had answered politely, concealing her surprise at being taken for a servant. She had looked around at the various stops and had seen only one other person wearing clothing such as hers, and that had been a rotund peasant woman with a kerchief tied around her fat, red face. Reluctantly, Laurie decided to buy more fashionable clothes. She was a Stepney and should look the part.

But the thought didn't cheer her as they galloped on. It seemed her heart grew as dreary as the fog, and on the fifth day when they entered London it was to her only a confusion. Towering buildings, a jumble of horses, carriages and street sounds, and then the bedlam of the huge Bull and Mouth Coaching Inn. It was cold for mid-March, and all through the city families warmed themselves by sea-coal fires, so that the smoke lay dense and choking in the still air.

Stepping from the coach on legs unsteady from lack of exercise, Laurie looked up and saw the famous church spires of London thrusting through the low-lying smoke, their sides gilded by the sun in the clear air above. She felt she should be filled with admiration for these works of man's genius, but instead a wave of homesickness assailed her. She could think only of the moors, and the fresh wind from the sea that swept over them.

"My Lady!" Laurie turned. A young man in livery, well-built but coarse-looking, was hurrying through the crowd toward them. He spoke, of course, to the Lady Desirée, but his eyes, bold and contemptuously amused, were on Laurie.

"I brought your barouche, My Lady, in the hope you would arrive today."

From the glaze in his eyes and the odor that accompanied him, Laurie thought it more likely that he had driven to the inn for other reasons. But Desirée looked quite pink with pleasure.

"How accommodating of you, Hervey. My daughter and I will refresh ourselves in the inn while you see to the baggage." The smile she wore held unmistakable intimacy. Age, Laurie thought, has not changed her, except that it seemed her taste had worsened. In the past, Lady Desirée had confined her favors to gentlemen.

The house on Grosvenor Square, its Palladian facade soaring gracefully to overlook the center gardens, brought a sharp and painful memory of the solitary hours Laurie had spent staring from those high windows, confined to the nursery while her mother entertained guests below. Climbing down from the barouche, she promised herself she would not again be imprisoned in loneliness.

At the door she turned to look back. Her mother was holding her skirts coquettishly, exposing her slim ankles and a good part of her legs as she leaned on Hervey's arm. Stepping down slowly, she looked him full in the face, her eyes sparkling and red lips parted. As for Hervey, the arch of his neck and the swaggering stance of his thick legs reminded Laurie irresistibly of the fierce ram at Stepney Downs, let in amongst the ewes at mating time. It had not mattered to the ram if the ewe was young or old—only that it was female and not unwilling. She was repelled by the scene and she saw that her expression revealed it, for her mother caught her glance and the red mouth drooped.

"My dear Laurie, do not stand staring! Ring the bell. Hervey will need assistance with our baggage." Gaining the sidewalk, she shook down her clothes with an angry twitch, and then forced a smile.

"Welcome home, my dear. It must be so exciting for you—the beginning of a marvelous new life."

In that moment, Laurie knew she could never bear three years with her mother.

Chapter Two

"OH, SADLY LACKING IN GRACES, HARRIETTE, AND SO very provincial. I can scarcely credit her a daughter of mine. Nor, for that matter, of Hugh's."

A loud chuckle drowned Desirée's voice for a moment and then it came again, lightly laughing. "Oh, no. I am not implying that her paternity is in question! Indeed, I am quite sure she is Hugh's get. Her eyes—do you not remember the frightening way he had of looking through one?"

The voice faded as Laurie went on toward her own bedroom, wincing. Even after days of listening she had not become accustomed to the open acceptance of affairs and lovers shown by London's upper class. To hear her own paternity decided only by her resemblance to her father was shameful. And yet she must dress and go into her mother's sitting room to be again presented to some of Desirée's friends, forced to sit listening to recitals of extravagant shopping, lurid gossip and plans for parties.

"It is only Madame Smith-Alderly and her daughters," her mother had said carelessly. "You need not worry about your manners. Harriette is quite commonplace and jolly." Her eyes had swept Laurie critically. "But do ask Thérèse to dress your hair. She has a great skill with the new Grecian modes."

Thérèse was waiting, a gown laid out, when Laurie opened her door. Quickly, Laurie stepped out of her heavy linen dress. The gown was a delicate green muslin, trimmed with dark green ribbon that outlined the

12

extremely low decolletage and formed tiny bows on the wisps of puffed sleeves. Directly below her half-exposed breasts another ribbon was threaded through the thin material. When Thérèse drew it tight and tied a bow with streamers, it allowed the material to flow down gracefully in a long line that floated free, barely touching her slender curves. Looking down at herself, Laurie compressed her lips but held her silence. The dress was in the newest fashion, and her mother expected her to appear in it. She allowed herself to be led to a chair before an oval mirror.

Managing a smart coiffure with the heavy mass of wavy black hair was far beyond Laurie's skill, but Thérèse's long fingers were sure as she worked it into a thick twist on the top of Laurie's head, teasing forth a curl or two to dangle like black silk against the white neck. She topped it with a small green lace cap and stood back, surveying the result.

"It is—quite nice," Laurie said, surprised as she studied herself in the mirror, and then waved a hand in dismissal as Thérèse brought out a pot of rouge from a drawer. Thérèse's lips twitched.

"You are quite right, Miss. You do not need it."

"I do not like it, that is all," Laurie said, and stood, looking down at the gown again. The material was so thin she could see the lace of her petticoat through it. "This gown is nothing! The halls are draughty and I will be cold."

Thérèse nodded. "It is correct, however. A swathe muslin, very much in style. Happily, it has a wrap." She went to the tall, mahogany wardrobe and brought forth a length of heavy, dark green silk. "You wear it so, Miss, with the material gathered to fall over your arms, the fullness in folds . . .''

"Ridiculous."

"It is correct."

Laurie sighed. "So be it. Thank you, Thérèse." She

went to the door, feeling a fool, but as she opened it Thérèse spoke again, which was quite out of character.

"The style is perfect for you, Miss."

Her mother's small sitting room seemed overpowered by billowing bundles of lace in every corner, and the sound of chattering and laughter was enough for a crowd. Desirée came forward and took Laurie by the hand, leading her around in a flood of introductions. The bundles of lace took form as Madame Smith-Alderly and her three daughters, all of whom were very large females, made tremendous by their bedecked finery. The daughters were Jane, the eldest; Claudia, who seemed near Laurie's age, and Adele, no more than thirteen yet dressed as elaborately as the others.

"My dear, you are indeed late, for you have missed a most entertaining tale," Desirée said gaily. "Harriette, you must tell it again, with more detail. It is too amusing . . ." She gave Laurie a flick of glance as she guided her to a fragile Hepplewhite chair and gave her a cup of tea. Interpreting the glance correctly, Laurie smiled mechanically and said, "Oh, yes, do tell."

The big woman, tightly bound in brown satin beneath swirls of ecru lace and wearing a soaring, ribbon-trimmed bonnet on graying red hair, shook with laughter.

"It is past belief," she said, "but pray believe it in spite of that. Today I received offers of marriage for both my older daughters—within the space of a few minutes, imagine! And then, my dear, imagine further—both offers from the same man!" She was off again in a spraying laugh that threatened to burst her strained seams. "And *then,* when I regretfully declined on behalf of both Jane and Claudia, the gentleman did not sigh, but only remarked that it was a pity Adele was so young, for in truth he liked her the best of any!"

Laurie gazed at her in wonder, and then at her

daughters. Jane, a pretty pink-and-gold version of her mother, was smiling calmly. Claudia, freckles plain beneath a heavy coat of powder, was frankly laughing. But Adele had tears in her eyes.

"*I* would have married him gladly, Miss Stepney," she burst forth, "if I were but old enough. Mama is cruelly rude to laugh so, when he—he is so lovely!"

Her words sent the rest of them into more spasms of merriment, but the child seemed truly upset.

"Perhaps," Laurie said gently, "when you are older he will offer again."

"That cannot be," Adele said dolefully, "for he needs a wife now, and in any event he will be leaving for his home across the ocean."

"Ah, an American rebel," Laurie said, now trying to distract her. "I have heard they are most bold."

"Oh, no, no, no! English to the core," Madame Smith-Alderly was wiping her streaming eyes. "And a wonderful match if only he lived in England. He has no title, though he may in time, since he is Lord Oldenburgh's nephew. And he is quite wealthy. But unfortunately he lives in the Indies on an isolated plantation. A ruinous life for a woman, my dear. No one of sensitivity could bear it. His own mother, I hear, sickened and died at an early age."

Halfway through this outpouring of personal information, Laurie had seen her mother stiffen, and now Desirée spoke sharply.

"Nephew to Lord Oldenburgh? Surely, you are mistaken. I have not heard a word . . ."

Amazement turned rapidly to malicious enjoyment on Madame Smith-Alderly's round face. "You truly did not know? Why, Desirée, he has been here a fortnight, visiting in Lord Peter's home. He is seeking an English wife of good family to join him in Barbados. I have heard that his father insists on pure British blood for his grandchildren, and evidently young Covington is obedient. He has offered for at least a half dozen eligible young women. Of course it is quite natural, but it is amusing because he is so peculiarly blunt about it. As long as the girl is of noble blood and virtuous, he seems not to care which one he claims.'' Her eyes sparkled with mischief. ''I am amazed that you, of all people, did not know.''

Chagrin was plain on Desirée's face. ''I have seen Lord Peter constantly since my return from Scotland, but of course we have many more interesting things to talk about. However, I share your amazement. Considering Jane's age and lack of offers, I am completely surprised that you did not snap him up.''

''Indeed!'' Anger reddened Madame Smith-Alderly's face. ''Send my daughter to live on a lonely, cannibal-infested island? Have you not heard of the slave riots, the terrible things those savages do to white women? Oh, I know the planters have found it a veritable gold mine, but even that advantage will be gone when the Quakers and Wilberforce have their way. More than one English investor will lose a fortune when the slaves are freed.'' Her smile as she stood up was not pleasant. ''I am afraid we must be leaving. It has been such a pleasant visit, hasn't it, girls? Come, now.''

Only Laurie seemed embarrassed by this exchange. The others rose and moved to the door in a swishing wave of skirts and a twittering of compliments. Laurie could think of nothing to say, but was warmed by a small hand touching hers.

''You were lovely to me, Miss Stepney. Truly, they are awful to laugh at him. He is so very nice.''

The door closed behind them and Desirée turned to Laurie, her small mouth hissing words like an enraged cat. ''That fat bore! She came here only to taunt me. I am sure that she and those great lumps of girls greatly enjoyed my discomfiture. Well, she will regret refusing a bona fide offer for either of them. The man must be mad

16

indeed to consider the connection." She swept back to the tea table and flung herself into one of the delicate chairs, leaning back and closing her eyes.

"Oh, exhausting. Please, my dear, fetch the brandy from the top of the chest. I must have a drop after such an experience."

Laurie brought the decanter and found a glass, then poured for her mother since the pale eyes were still closed. She thrust the glass into the small, outstretched hand and sat down with her, curious in spite of herself.

"Is Lord Oldenburgh a relative of yours?" She had seen the man often and heard his name when the maid announced him. A tall, gray-haired man who invariably waited in the entry hall dressed in evening clothes, silent, with an aquiline, impassive face. But Desirée, who hurried down to meet him, had never introduced him, nor even mentioned him.

Now, as Laurie covertly watched, a flush rose beneath the paint on Desirée's face. Her eyes were open, but she kept her gaze on her brandy glass, twirling it thoughtfully. "A friend," she said at last. "A very dear friend. If it were not for Lord Peter I would have found myself in straitened circumstances many times since your father so inconveniently gave his life for England in Portugal." She downed the rest of the brandy in an unladylike gulp and set the glass down, looking at Laurie indignantly. "A thoughtless sacrifice, brought about by high-nosed pride and foolish ideals."

Laurie's turquoise eyes darkened angrily, and Desirée hastily thrust the brandy glass in her direction, indicating more. While Laurie poured, her mother began another subject.

"And Harriette felt forced to pique me by speaking of that infernal Wilberforce and his efforts to abolish slavery! She well knows Lord Peter's fortune is heavily invested in West Indies sugar, and if Wilberforce wins he may lose all." She sipped the brandy thirstily. "Still,

17

Lord Peter has told me that the slaves on his and his brother's plantations are well treated and happy. He believes they would stay even if freed.''

"That couldn't be," Laurie said, her voice low with intense conviction. "I have read of the burnings, the lashings. Punishment meted out horribly, even to children. To be a slave must be the worst fate that could befall a human being! I know that I, if a slave, would do anything to escape!"

The Lady Desirée gazed at her in surprise, and then her eyes crinkled in amusement. "But of course you would feel so! Any civilized person would. But the slaves, you understand, are like domesticated animals. They were wild savages in jungles, and now live in a world far better than they could have imagined. Protected, fed and clothed, even provided with medical attention when needed. If they were human, they would know how fortunate they are.''

"No!" Laurie rose. "Nothing can make up for the lack of freedom, ma'am. Nothing!" Her silly wrap having fallen from her, she bent to pick it up, knowing she must leave before she said too much. She turned and left the room. Walking down the chilly hall she felt the call of Scotland and could almost smell the sweetness of heather on the moors. *I am no more than a pampered slave myself,* she thought, *and if Desirée has her way, I will never see my home again. But how far worse the fate of those black Africans, cruelly abused and overworked, without ever a chance of going home, even to their own country.*

The next morning, quite unexpectedly, Laurie made the acquaintance of the bishop of Wight. Twice since they had arrived in London her mother had mentioned him casually. Once, when writing to the magistrate at Stepney Downs she had wondered aloud if she should require the bishop's signature on the letter, but had decided it wasn't necessary, and once she had yawned and remarked that perhaps they should attend chapel occasionally to please the bishop. Laurie had been secretly anxious to meet him in any way she could, hoping to make an ally of him. Her mother's frequent references to selling the manor and lands frightened her, and she was desperate enough to hope that the bishop would help her to keep them. So, when the maid informed her that the bishop of Wight was waiting in the drawing room below, she rushed down without preparation, wearing one of her old, high-necked gowns and with her hair in the usual careless knot.

Standing at a window and looking out over the Square, the bishop turned at the sound of her footsteps and smiled, advancing to take her hands. Short, stocky, with a thickening waistline, the bishop was dressed in a fashionable morning suit of dark brown, with a camel-colored waistcoat and flowing silk cravat knotted beneath his heavy chin. He looked like no churchman Laurie had ever seen, but his face, his candid eyes, inspired confidence. *He is kind,* she thought instantly, and smiled back at him.

"Dear Miss Stepney," he said, still holding her hands, "even though late, let me offer my condolences. I knew your grandfather only slightly, but by his reputation I admired him greatly. His death was a loss to us all."

"Thank you, sir. I mean, Your Eminence . . ." Laurie blushed, wondering just how to address a bishop.

" 'Sir' will do nicely, child. One cannot stand on ceremony with one's ward, eh? I have come to discuss your future with you, to be of assistance if I can."

He spoke rather absentmindedly, for it seemed his eyes studied her, his thoughts not on what he said, but on what he could make of her by examination. He took the chair she indicated and watched her as she sat beside him on a small couch.

"You are not at all like your mother, my dear."

Laurie agreed quickly. "I am afraid I am a great trial

to her, sir. I do not fit into her life." She hesitated and then plunged on. "I truly believe both of us would be happier if I could be allowed to return to Scotland."

"But you have no family there, do you? I seem to recall . . ."

"I would have Annie and Breen," Laurie said eagerly, "and they are like family. Annie was Grandfather's housekeeper, and she raised me as a mother would. Breen, her husband, manages the lands, and he is all the protection anyone would need. My grandfather trusted him as a son."

He stared at her sadly. "I see you are homesick, and I remember the feeling from my own youth. But you are the heiress of a rather large fortune. It would not be proper for you to live alone with servants in such a wild, out-of-the-way place. You will wish to marry well, as all ladies do . . ."

"Not I!"

"In time, my dear, in time. And it would be difficult to find a suitable match in the Scottish Highlands. Besides, your mother would never hear of it. She wrote of the future with such enthusiasm, and I know she mentioned that Stepney Downs was to be sold. Has she changed her mind?"

"She has not," Laurie said bitterly. "But, sir, the property is mine! I wish to keep it. Even if I were never to see it again, I would wish it mine. Were I to die, I would wish it given to Annie and Breen. Please, can you persuade my mother not to sell it? *Can* she sell it without my consent?" She had leaned toward him with the fervor she felt, and now she saw him draw back, saw his eyes shift away, his round face holding both regret and embarrassment.

"The only signatures necessary would be your mother's and mine," he said reluctantly. "Please do not ask me to withhold my approval. I would have to assume she was acting for the best, since she is your mother."

Laurie's disappointment was intense, and she lashed out wildly.

"My mother! Uncaring, immoral and greedy! She will keep me, pretending affection, until she manages to gain Old Hugh's fortune for herself. Then, when I am no longer of use to her, you will see at last that she has no love for me at all!" She stopped abruptly, as stunned by her own words as the bishop appeared to be. His face had gone white and pained, still avoiding her eyes.

"You may be right, Miss Stepney. I have been among the nobility in London long enough to become inured to their habits, their lack of morality. But I do remember your father, and just now you reminded me of him. You are scarcely large enough to contain his strong spirit, but it is there." He rose and paced away, strangely tense. "I very much wish I could help you, but there are reasons . . ." He turned, his heavy shoulders slumping, a look of defeat in his eyes. "I cannot cross the Lady Desirée, Miss Stepney. I am sorry."

In some way, her mother controlled this important man. *I should have known*, Laurie thought bleakly. *Otherwise, she would not have chosen him as the other guardian*. Suddenly full of both disgust and pity, Laurie rose from the couch. "I am sorry also—for both of us." She did not bother to add the "Sir," and was halfway to the door when he spoke again.

"You could marry, Miss Stepney."

She almost laughed as she turned to answer him. "Exchange one master for another? Under English law, a husband has as many rights as any guardian—and other rights as well."

"Still, it is the only way out of your predicament, my dear. And all husbands are not the same. Perhaps you might find one like your father."

In spite of her anger Laurie was softened by his effort to help her. *Help her*, she thought wryly, *without getting himself in trouble*. But she felt his shamed sincerity.

"Thank you, sir. But you have forgotten—in order for me to marry my mother would have to give permission. Until she bleeds me of my inheritance, do you think she would?"

He was shaking his head sadly as the door opened and Desirée, her freshly made-up face a study in surprise, stepped in.

"Why, it is you, Charles! When the maid told me Laurie was entertaining a gentleman in the drawing room I could not imagine who it could be. You have not come to thunder at me, have you, Charles? I do know I have been remiss. I should have brought Laurie to you weeks ago . . ."

Laurie left, going quietly up the stairs, unable to bear more of her mother's falsely sweet, flattering talk.

That night at dinner Laurie was congratulated for her thoughtfulness. Desirée patted her hand as she spoke.

"It was so wise of you to leave the room, darling. The bishop and I talked concerning your future, and your presence might have put a constraint on our conversation. As it is, you will be glad to know he approves of all I have done and the decisions I have made. But he wishes us to attend chapel regularly."

Laurie nodded, silent, and waited. In a few moments Desirée gave a little trill of laughter.

"Can you imagine—Charles felt you might wish to be married! I reminded him of the year of mourning for your grandfather and told him that even when it ended, I might delay allowing you to come out until you are more mature."

Laurie stared at her, at the triumphant amusement in the pale blue eyes. *She knows how I feel,* Laurie thought, *how desperate—how helpless. And she is* enjoying *it.*

"The year of mourning," she said quietly, "applies only to the spouse of the deceased. However, it is heartwarming to find that you believe it should be observed. Tell me, did you find it very lonely staying alone in your home during the year following my father's death?'' She fastened her eyes on her mother, their turquoise depths burning with penetrating light. And Desirée's face wavered, changing, and came clear again, the paint smeared, the mouth stretched grotesquely in a silent scream, the eyes rolled back and glazed. Still as death.

Horrified, Laurie jumped to her feet as her mother laughed.

''Truly, Laurie, there may be hope for you . . . that is the first bit of wit that has come from your too-innocent lips.''

Desirée's face was again perfectly normal, more amused than ever as she continued, ''You know very well your father and I were estranged, I could hardly hide it from you, who heard most of our battles. Of course I was not lonely—I was free at last.''

With what poise she could muster, Laurie nodded and left the room, still horrified, but now at herself. How could she hate her mother enough to wish her dead? For that could be the only reason for such a vision . . .

Chapter Three

THE WEATHER BRIGHTENED, AND LAURIE FOUND A WAY out of her prison, even if only for a few hours a day. When the constant fogs lifted she discovered Hyde Park, only a short walk away. Fortunately, she also discovered that Thérèse enjoyed walking in the fresh air, so every morning they walked west on Upper Grosvenor Street then north to the Gate and the Park, both of them wrapped warmly against the chill of the morning.

They walked briskly, faces growing pink, while Laurie revelled in the memory of freedom. Of course, the small pools were poor substitutes for mountain tarns, the cantering horses with their fashionable riders were poor substitutes for lambs, but still, she thought, how much better than the stale air inside, with windows fast-closed and hung heavily with damask and velvet.

At first they talked little. Thérèse seemed determined to keep her proper place, walking slightly behind Laurie and never speaking unless spoken to. But Laurie spoke, more often every day, and they soon walked together and chatted. But when they went back to the house on Grosvenor Square they fell silent again by unspoken agreement.

The Lady Desirée was annoyed and perplexed by it all. "Hyde Park in the morning? No one of any consequence goes then. Later, when you have come out, we will ride there in the afternoons. It is all the style, though we will need a new barouche and a fine pair of matched horses to come up to the mark. But why ever do you wish to *walk?*"

Laurie knew that her mother's irritation was at least partly from another source. Desirée had had a letter from the magistrate at Stepney Downs. Not the parcel of documents she had expected, but a terse note that informed her that if he was to go through his strongbox and extract anything concerning the Laird's property which now belonged to Miss Stepney, he would expect a request that had been signed by both of her guardians.

Desirée had been furious, but Laurie knew that in the end it would make little difference, since the bishop would sign when Desirée commanded it. But Laurie also was grateful for the delay—and surprised. The magistrate knew she had the papers, for he had given them to her himself. Yet he had not said so. She wondered hopefully if he had regretted his decision to appoint the Lady Desirée guardian. Perhaps some rumors had reached him. Perhaps he could even help her! In the meantime, she did not wish to give up her walks, for they would give her the opportunity to post a letter to the magistrate.

"I walk for my health," she told her mother. "And I think you should join us. The fresh air is most invigorating." She knew her mother would shudder at the thought, for she never stepped her slippered feet on anything but stone, abhorring the feel and dampness of grass.

"*I*," said Desirée scornfully, "was not raised as a peasant." She turned away, clearly disgusted. But not even her clever mind could come forth with a reason for denying Laurie's wish to be strong and well.

Even posting a letter to Stepney Downs the next day brought Laurie's yearning for home to a peak. She was unhappy and rebellious as she and Thérèse turned toward the walk home.

"I would like to keep on walking," she said to the maid whose lanky body hesitated, slowing the pace, while she looked at her questioningly.

"Oh, no," Laurie said, laughing, "I do not mean

now, for a few more minutes. I meant—oh, Thérèse, I meant all the way to Scotland! Do you never long for France?''

Thérèse smiled her small smile and resumed her steady walk. ''Within a year or two I will go home. I have saved for many years to make it possible.''

''I am happy for you.'' But Laurie felt desolate. Thérèse was now a valued friend. ''Yet I envy you. I would do anything . . . anything! . . . that would allow me to escape this life. I would even marry, since that is the only legal way to break my mother's hold on me. But it is certain she would never give her consent, even if an eligible man should offer for me.''

The white cap bobbed in understanding and they both fell silent as they approached the house. But as they neared the steps Thérèse spoke suddenly, keeping her voice low.

''What of Lord Oldenburgh's nephew? He badly wants an English wife. If he offered for you your mother would be forced to agree. She could not risk his lordship's displeasure.'' She went briskly up the steps and opened the door, standing aside for Laurie to enter. ''Though he might not please you, Miss.'' Her lips were folded primly, but a glint in her faded eyes surprised Laurie into laughter.

''Thérèse! How impossible!'' A quick glance around showed the entry deserted. ''We have never met, nor ever shall. The Lady Desirée does not wish me to be in the company of young gentlemen.'' She knew it could never happen, yet she felt excited by the daring of Thérèse's suggestion.

Thérèse smiled calmly. ''Accompanied by an elderly maid, it would be proper for you to call on him as a friend of the family,'' she said. ''Unusual, perhaps, but not unheard of.''

Laurie was amazed. Strict Thérèse, holding such a notion. But as she left her she touched her arm with affection, thinking how much she was trying to help. ''I will seriously consider it,'' she said, without the least intention of giving the matter another thought.

But later, alone in her room, she could think of nothing else. She removed her pelisse and bonnet, hung them away, and sat down to brush her hair without once knowing what she was about. Her mind alternated between wild hope and the conviction that both Thérèse and herself had taken leave of their senses. Approach that odd, blunt man who went about Mayfair offering marriage to any young woman of good family, without even a pretense of proper feeling? How could anyone consider it?

But what Thérèse had said was true. Desirée would not dare to offend Peter Covington, Lord Oldenburgh. Laurie had never faced the thought, but she knew it was his wealth that provided the upkeep of this house, paid the servants, bought the expensive clothes and food. Even all of Old Hugh's fortune would not make up for the loss if Lord Peter withdrew his support. She had noticed Desirée's fear of any sign of lessening interest from Lord Oldenburgh, and Thérèse had told her the affair was of long standing, explaining that Lord Peter's wife was an invalid and had been so for many years. And so it was entirely possible that if My Lord's nephew asked Desirée for her daughter's hand she would be forced to agree. And very likely it would be the only chance Laurie would ever have to escape and save her home.

Laurie sat still, brush in midair, aghast at her own thoughts. Annie had said marriage was difficult even with love. Men, she had said, were most demanding. And women must please them, must subject themselves to them. She had said it was easier to give in to their desires if you loved them. Then, Laurie thought, since I do not love, my situation might well be much worse with him than with my mother. She put the brush down with a thump, determined to forget such nonsense.

Still, sleepless in the middle of the night, she thought

of it again. It came to her that she *did* love—not some unknown man, but Annie and Breen, and the home they all loved. To think of losing it and them broke her heart. Madam Smith-Alderly had said the man was wealthy, so he might not insist on selling Stepney Downs. And Adele had said he was nice. She laughed at herself for considering a child's judgement and knew she was grasping at straws.

She would have to live in those far islands, and might never see Scotland again. Unless . . . unless they could strike some bargain . . .

She sat up in her bed, galvanized by the thought. He did badly want an English wife, but all the prospects he had approached were too frightened of the infamous islands to accept. It might be possible!

Noiselessly, she climbed from bed and went through the dark halls, up the flight of steps to Thérèse's room.

It took the remainder of the night to make plans. Thérèse professed to be horrified by Laurie's decisions of what to say and what to do. Only, she explained, because surely a young girl would not have the courage.

Laurie scoffed. "I am a daughter of lions," she told Thérèse grandly. "My courage is phenomenal, my grandfather often told me so. I can do it all, for the sake of Annie and Breen and our home." She gave Thérèse a final, confident smile and left, creeping down the stairs with shaking knees.

In less than a week a chance arrived to put their plan into action. Desirée and Lord Oldenburgh left the city for Hampshire, where, with half of the city-bred nobility, they were to attend a countryside fete. They would be gone the better part of three days.

Thérèse and Laurie spent the morning choosing appropriate clothing for her. A fashionable blue silk dress, high-waisted, with tiny puff sleeves and low cut, but not so low cut as to appear wanton. No bonnet, for Thérèse chose a darker blue pelisse with a hood trimmed in fur.

"If we are seen entering Lord Oldenburgh's home," she explained, "the hood will hide your face from curious onlookers."

"But they will recognize you," said Laurie, troubled. "So, with Desirée out of the city, they shall know who I am."

"No one recognizes a maid," Thérèse said, "for they do not notice them." She busied herself with Laurie's hair, taking infinite pains, snipping an overlong dangling curl here and there, softening the line of her forehead with tiny wisps. "I foresee only one difficulty. My Lord's butler is a formidable man, and he will know we are not expected. You may have to use a good deal of charm to get past him."

In spite of Thérèse's expectation, entrance to the Oldenburgh mansion was surprisingly easy. The door was not opened by the butler, but by one of the largest men either of them had ever seen. A Negro, dressed in an impeccable morning suit instead of servant's livery, which made Thérèse uneasy. But his manners were correct, and, since he informed them immediately that Mr. Covington was at home and in the library, Thérèse calmed her fears and followed Laurie into the huge entry hall, where they waited while the servant announced her.

Opening the library door, the man spoke in a booming, resonant voice that seemed to fill the house. "Miss Laurie Stepney is calling, sir," he said, and for a moment Laurie considered a quick flight, a leap into the barouche, huddling in Thérèse's arms as they rushed home. She had wondered for two days how anyone could approach a man with such a proposal, sure that she would die of embarrassment, particularly if he laughed. But she had told herself to be prepared, for undoubtedly he *would* laugh, possibly as long and as hard as Madame Smith-Alderly had laughed at *him*. But she must change his mind, must show him that the marriage would be advantageous to them both. She expected an odd-looking person, pockmarked or otherwise ugly, and hoped that would make him more amenable.

Now, as the heavily carved door swung wide, she saw how mistaken she had been. He was as tall as his uncle, but bigger, broader of shoulder. He was dressed informally in a striking double-breasted riding coat, tight breeches and leather boots, his hair as black as her own, thick and shining like a raven's wing. Above the white linen stock wound round his neck was a black beard so like her father's that it made her heart stop. He had risen from a writing table and now stood staring at her, an expression of surprise and suspicious reserve on his uncommonly handsome, strong face.

"Miss Stepney," he acknowledged, sounding only faintly surprised. His eyes swept her in a quick but thorough appraisal as he added, "Please come in." He nodded at Thérèse to include her in the invitation, and Laurie went forward with a great deal more confidence than she felt. His eyes were a dark, liquid brown, but very cold. Wishing he were not so excessively handsome and assured, she forced herself into speech.

"We are strangers, Mr. Covington, so perhaps you will think my visit improper. However, my mother, the Lady Desirée Stepney, is a . . . a close friend of your uncle, Lord Oldenburgh. I have come on a matter of great importance to me, to speak to you privately . . ." She faltered, seeing a wary flicker in his eyes, and then added, "If it is convenient . . . ?"

"Of course." He glanced at the large Negro, who withdrew, shutting the door behind him. The brown eyes went to Thérèse, but Laurie hastily removed her pelisse and handed it to her, motioning her to a chair to show that she meant her to stay. Covington's thick brows rose, but he said nothing, only drew up a chair for Laurie and, without waiting for her to be seated, took a chair himself, crossing his booted legs and leaning back. The suspicion in his face had been lightened by wry amusement, and as Laurie set her plaid reticule on the floor by her chair she saw his eyes go toward it and his lips twitch.

"My papers," she said, though he hadn't asked. She felt more vulnerable than ever with her bared neck and shoulders, the high-waisted gown emphasizing her round breasts. Fashion or not, she would have much preferred to conduct this talk in one of her usual linen gowns, high-necked and long-sleeved, thick enough to disguise her femininity. As for the reticule, she could hardly blame him for wishing to laugh. Thérèse had fussed over it, and surely it was not a charming accessory to the fine gown. But the old bag and its contents were her only source of courage, and even so she was frightened, staring at her hands and wondering how to begin.

"I am at your service," Covington said finally, sounding impatient.

Laurie had practiced over and over what she would say, and his impatience opened the dam.

"I understand that you have come to England for the purpose of finding a young woman of good family, good reputation and some means, to marry you and return with you to the West Indies. I am the daughter of Sir Hugh Stepney, lost in action in the Peninsular War. I am the granddaughter of the late Laird of Stepney Downs in Scotland. I am virtuous and possessed of a modest fortune. I have come here to say that if you will meet certain conditions which I will explain, I will marry you . . . that is, if . . . if you have no objection."

He didn't seem at all surprised. In fact, he was perfectly relaxed in the chair, looking down his aquiline nose with half-closed eyes, a faint smile on his broad mouth.

"A masterful maneuver, Miss Stepney. Since it has become fashionable to be one of the young ladies who can say they have turned down young Covington, I have been approached by several flirtatious aspirants, but none so enterprising as you. May I have your proposal in writing? I should like to take it along when I make my offer to your family. Perhaps then they will not consider it quite so hilarious.''

Laurie was stunned. She could feel blood burning its way up her bared neck. He actually believed she was dallying with him, hoping to fool him into making an offer, so that Desirée, too, would have a story to tell amongst the social gatherings. It seemed it was now a point in favor to be one of the families approached by Lord Oldenburgh's nephew.

''You mistake me,'' she said, her voice trembling. ''I did not come here to cause you embarrassment. I will be glad to put my proposal in writing—if I can add to it my own conditions, which you have yet to hear.''

In spite of his sarcasm and her own discomfiture, Laurie felt instinctively that Covington was an honorable man; perhaps not very pleasant, but possessing integrity. She met his eyes steadily until he laughed and suddenly sat forward.

''Conditions under which you will accept me, if I decide to accept you?'' His tone was acid, his expression did nothing to sweeten it. ''How interesting. And amusing. Since I have nothing better to do, I will listen.''

Laurie took a deep breath. There was a cruel streak there, so perhaps it was unwise, after all . . . but what else would save Stepney Downs? She reached for the reticule, fumbled and dropped it, spilling her hoard of title deeds, agreements, leases and accounts. Hastily, since he made no move to help her, she knelt and gathered them up, feeling his hostile amusement as he watched her. She settled back into her chair with the title deed to Stepney Downs in her hands, where the feel of the thick parchment was like a touch from Old Hugh's rough fingers. She hesitated, and then leaned forward and put it firmly into Covington's hands.

''I have brought this,'' she said, ''and these other

documents, both for proof of what I say and to keep them from the grasp of my mother, the Lady Desirée.'' She saw his eyes change, become surprised and sharp. ''I will explain . . .''

For a half hour he listened without saying a word. At the end, emotionally exhausted from putting her fears into speech, Laurie asked if he had understood. He nodded, straightened the papers he still held, and handed them back to her.

''You have made it quite clear, Miss Stepney. You wish to marry me to preserve your wealth. Why, though, did you pick me? Anyone would do.''

''No one else would do,'' Laurie said tiredly. ''For only your uncle could persuade my mother to agree to my marrying. You are my only chance.''

He smiled wryly. ''Then I take it you would not expect to be courted, nor require a period during which we would become better acquainted.''

Laurie was much too distracted to notice the change in his voice, or the dawning interest in his eyes. ''The sooner I am wed, the better,'' she said firmly, ''for until I am, my mother has the right to dispose of my property. If she had these papers to hand, she would have done so before.''

He looked at her thoughtfully. ''Perhaps I deserve your businesslike approach, Miss Stepney. My own recent proposals, which have brought so much merriment to Mayfair, were not made in the throes of passion either, but simply for convenience.'' His tone was casual, but his gaze had become searching. ''I think I should tell you my reasons. I am my father's only son and he is a widower. He wishes to see me married to an English woman of quality so that I can carry on the line.'' His smile had disappeared, he looked serious. ''At thirty-five, it is time I married, I admit. But you are young, and appear fragile.''

''I am strong,'' Laurie said shortly, ''and country-bred. You need have no fear, there.'' For the first time she was curious about him. ''Were there no English ladies in the Indies?''

He frowned. ''Not many, now that the riots have frightened them off. Only a few of unmixed English blood, and none of the nobility. And,'' he added carelessly, ''there is no one there whom I wished to wed who also wished to wed me.''

Laurie nodded, realizing that he could well mean there was someone he had wanted but who had refused him. But that was nothing to her. She was silent, waiting for what else he might say.

''I would have no objection to you retaining full title to your property,'' he said slowly, and Laurie's heart lurched. He was actually considering her proposal! ''But, your other condition, that you be allowed to visit Scotland periodically, rather troubles me. I am of the opinion that a wife's place is with her husband and children.''

Laurie studied her hands again. Then, without knowing why, she compromised. ''Perhaps I could lengthen the time between visits, and we . . . we might come back to Scotland together, as a family.'' She raised her head and looked at him directly. ''But as for giving up the visits entirely, I cannot. My home is there. If I can but know I will see it again, even though seldom, I can be happy.''

Covington was silent for some time, his impassive gaze wandering over her face, the tightly drawn bodice, the slender arms below the tiny sleeves. She could tell nothing from his expression, so when he spoke his words were a complete surprise.

''It is little enough to ask, I suppose. Travel agrees with me. If permission is forthcoming from your guardians, we will marry.''

In the very moment of gaining her purpose, Laurie felt again a strong urge to bolt and run. Silently she cursed her Scots heritage that had given her such delicate skin that reddened so easily. It was one thing to plan how to win her battle with Desirée, another to suddenly realize she would be sharing a wedding bed with this very masculine stranger. She hoped her voice would be steady.

"Very well. Then if you will supply me with pen and paper, I will write out my proposal and the conditions immediately, if you do not mind."

"That will not be necessary. I no longer doubt your sincerity."

"On the contrary," Laurie insisted. "I think it a very good idea. You may take it along when you offer for me."

He looked at her quizzically, his brows rising again. "You would have me take it to the Lady Desirée? If what you tell me is true, the fact that you are to keep Stepney Downs will enrage her."

"I would have you take it to my other guardian, sir. The bishop of Wight. I wish you to sign it in his presence, indicating that you accept the conditions, and then leave it with him. Following that, you may approach my mother, with your uncle's approval beforehand. You will need Lord Oldenburgh's intervention if your suit is to be successful."

The brown eyes were suddenly cold again. "You plan exceedingly well," he said, and rose abruptly, to pace away from her and then come back, standing before her with his booted feet apart, his hands grasping the wide lapels of his coat. "Perhaps you plan *too* well. Intelligence in a wife is a virtue. But a lack of feminine graces . . . a lack of softness . . ." He stopped, rocking on his heels, the corded muscles of his powerful thighs clearly discernible beneath the smooth, fawn-colored breeches. Why must he remind her, as Hervey had, of the fierce ram at Stepney Downs? He was very large, and appeared tremendously strong . . . She struggled to pay attention as he continued.

"You do understand, Miss Stepney, that I seek a real

wife? A woman to grace my home and bear my children?''

Laurie looked down at her whitened knuckles gripping the plaid reticule and wished herself elsewhere. Misgivings crowded her mind. But, the only alternative was to lose . . . and Annie and Breen would lose, too. She lifted her chin.

"I do understand. And I will try my best to please you."

He nodded shortly and went to the desk, found paper and pen and laid them on the polished surface. Steeling herself, Laurie rose and went to the desk and sat down. She felt his eyes on her as she wrote, but when she handed him the paper he took it without comment. She was standing, looking toward Thérèse, still sitting silently in her corner.

"Your mother will ask where we have met," he said, folding the paper and slipping it into a waistcoat pocket. "What will you tell her?"

His question filled her with alarm, for she hadn't thought so far ahead. "Why, I do not know . . . I am not allowed to attend social functions . . ."

Thérèse's voice startled them both. She had come forward quietly with Laurie's pelisse. "Perhaps, Miss, you could say the park."

Laurie looked at her with gratitude. "Yes!" She turned to Covington, smiling for the first time since they had met. "We, Thérèse and I, walk in Hyde Park early each morning. I can say we met there. I do not lie very well, but perhaps she will believe me."

He was looking at her parted lips and white, even teeth with interest. "It will not be a lie. I will see the bishop this evening and meet you in the park tomorrow to tell you the outcome of my visit."

"Thank you. That is very good of you." Laurie turned to allow Thérèse to place the cloak on her shoulders. "We shall be there at eight." She followed him as he went to open the door, and in the doorway she stopped again, looking up at him. ''Oh! How ridiculous I would feel if my mother asked me your given name and I did not know it. Please do tell me . . .''

''David,'' he said absently, staring down at her upturned face. They were quite close, and she could see his eyes changing, sense the sudden stillness of his muscular body. She looked down quickly, submissively, and hurried through the door. Turning, keeping her gaze down, she said she hoped the meeting with the bishop would go well.

''I shall see that it does,'' he said, his voice arrogant. ''You need not worry that he will refuse me.''

Outside, climbing into the rented barouche Thérèse had obtained, Laurie gave the Frenchwoman a wild glance. ''What have I done?'' she whispered.

''Perhaps you have acquired a man,'' Thérèse said, amused. ''Not an easy task in London these days. Thank *le Bon Dieu* that Lord Oldenburgh's nephew is not a silly fop such as we see daily in your mother's home.'' She gave Laurie the little smile that Laurie had once thought frigid and now loved. ''You managed it all very well, Miss. But it may be the last time you will be permitted to manage something yourself. If he had not been entranced with you from the beginning, I believe he would have shown us the door.''

''*Entranced?*''

''Oh, la!'' Thérèse rolled her eyes expressively. ''Could you not see it? From across the room I noticed the look in his eyes. It is a very good thing you are, as you say, strong and country-bred. Otherwise, I am afraid you would find the first weeks of your marriage exhausting . . .''

''*Thérèse!*''

Thérèse chuckled and was silent.

Chapter Four

THREE DAYS LATER, AT NOON, THE LADY DESIRÉE retired to her boudoir with a raging headache, leaving Laurie in the spacious drawing room downstairs with a group which included the distinguished Lord Peter Oldenburgh. It was quite uncharacteristic of her to leave such a gathering, but His Lordship, the bishop of Wight and David Covington all excused her behavior with perfect, if unspoken, understanding.

Desirée had left them with a forced smile, her light eyes full of tears of anger. She had not looked at Laurie at all, for which Laurie, frozen in fear and embarrassment, had been very grateful. In the space of a very few minutes Desirée had signed a paper giving Laurie permission to wed David Covington, and, under the frosty glance of Lord Oldenburgh, had congratulated Laurie and David without once meeting their eyes. Then she had handed the paper to the bishop of Wight and watched, trembling with rage, as he dipped his pen in the inkwell.

"Are you quite sure, Charles," she had asked venomously, "that you won't regret this in the future? So young a girl. . . ."

The bishop had looked at her blandly. "My dear Desirée! How could I regret it, with your signature leading mine? What would you think of me if I ignored a mother's judgment?" He had signed with a flourish, his wide face wreathed with smiles.

Desirée had rung for Thérèse to help her up the stairs, saying her headache had become blindingly painful.

Lord Peter and David had nodded to her with identical, impassive faces, but as the door closed the bishop turned to Laurie with a shamefaced but happy grin.

"And now to the court," he had said, "where I have much more influence than I have ever had in Mayfair. If David wishes a special license, I can promise he will have it."

They were on their way out when Laurie saw a crumpled letter lying near her mother's chair, and recognized the writing that spelled out "Miss Laurie Stepney" on the envelope. She picked it up hastily and, once they were in the carriage, read it. It was for her, and from the magistrate, but Desirée had opened it—and now knew everything. The magistrate had discovered the Lady Desirée's reputation and knew that she had offered Stepney Downs for sale. He was excessively angry. He advised Laurie to put the documents in a safe place until he could find a way to have her mother discharged as her guardian. Laurie handed the letter to David.

Reading it, his broad mouth twisted. "Excellent advice," he said, "but very poor judgment—sending it to the Lady's house." The way he said "Lady" accented his contempt. "You were quite right to insist on an early wedding."

Laurie flushed, tucking the letter away in the plaid reticule, which never left her hands these days. She wished he had not mentioned her unladylike insistence, though both Lord Peter and the bishop knew all the circumstances. But how fortunate that David had arranged to meet her again in the park this morning, before the four of them descended on her mother. If she had been at home when that letter arrived, what a bitter tongue lashing she would have received!

The visit to the court was not long. A word from the bishop and a clerk smilingly made out a special license. Laurie was conscious of the power of wealth and position. These men spoke, and it was as if the king himself had asked a favor. She wasn't at all sure she approved, but, she reflected, she had tossed caution to the winds the day she had called on David Covington, and it was now too late to gather it up again. She stole a look at him as they left, wondering at his reserved expression. He appeared to take this day as something to be endured.

Back in the carriage they went immediately to the bishop's manse, where the wedding would take place. Here, the time spent was much longer.

It was not to be an elaborate wedding, the bishop said, but he meant it to be a true marriage. He took the time to explain the full meaning of the sacrament to them, and the duties they were expected to fulfill. He spoke of God, a Personage Laurie had not considered overmuch lately, and of God's Will. He sounded, she thought, a trifle rusty but very sincere.

Following these instructions, the bishop insisted on serving what he called a light repast, with chilled wine, since it was wearing late into the day and none of them had eaten since breakfast. Laurie watched David's eyes light up as the servants brought in a shoulder of lamb, Cornish pasties, fruit from a hothouse and cheeses. She forced down a pasty and drank a glass of wine to chase away the chill of apprehension as she remembered she would have to go back to her mother's house for her baggage, which even now Thérèse must be packing.

At last the bishop donned his robes and fetched his Bible. With Lord Oldenburgh attending David, and the bishop's motherly housekeeper smiling beside Laurie, they made their vows. When the bishop pronounced them man and wife Laurie felt a trifle lightheaded, which she put down to the wine.

Then they were back in the carriage again, only three this time, since the bishop remained at home. Laurie felt dazed. The marriage did not seem real. It had been only words, which had fled in the haste of their leaving. All that seemed real, in fact, was the knowledge that now she truly owned Stepney Downs, that she would always, always own it, that Annie and Breen were forever safe, as she was, too. She could not stop smiling.

David, who even through the ceremony had preserved his impassive air, glanced at her and remarked that from her appearance she was a happy bride.

"All brides are happy," Laurie said carelessly. "And I most of all." She was still glorying in thoughts of Scotland. "I am amazed at how simply you managed everything."

"I?" David asked wryly. "Your plan was most explicit. All that was needed was to follow it. But my plans must now take over. You must bid your mother good-bye quickly and see that your maid has finished your packing. You must remember that we go to the Isle of Dogs tonight, and board the brig."

"I shall be ready," Laurie said submissively. That part of the plan had not seemed so important. Only the marriage, her release from the Lady Desirée, had seemed paramount. She glanced at David beneath her lashes. What a stubborn man he was. With so much to do today he was still determined to sail at dawn for the Indies! She was startled as his hand touched her chin and raised her face so he could stare at her intently.

"Your eyes," he said with sudden interest, "actually seem to gather light and send it forth again. I do not believe I have ever seen eyes exactly that color before."

It was the first personal remark he had made to her, and Laurie, acutely aware of his warm fingers and the closeness of his strong face, said the first thing that came into her head.

"They are my father's eyes, I am told. Grandfather said eyes like mine are able to see into the future, that I would have what he calls second sight."

David smiled patronizingly. "And do you?"

Laurie laughed and shook her head, breaking his hold.

"I cannot foresee anything, or surely I would not be forever in trouble. The power didn't come with the color in my case."

Across from them Lord Oldenburgh smiled grimly. "Perhaps that is fortunate. Though I hope if you ever see your future, Laurie, it will be a happy one. Had I seen mine at your age, I would have been unpleasantly surprised."

"But then you could have changed it," Laurie answered gaily, still full of happiness and a feeling of great good luck. "I have discovered that a life can be changed, with the help of others like yourself. I must tell you I shall be forever grateful to you, My Lord. David and I could not have married had you not convinced my mother."

"That was not difficult," Lord Peter said cynically, and lapsed into silence until they arrived at the house on Grosvenor Square, when he took Laurie's hand and wished her Godspeed and a happy life.

Impulsively Laurie leaned forward and kissed his spare cheek. "You have made my future bright," she whispered, "no matter what I may see."

At the door David reminded her again of the need for haste, and asked if she wished his company when she spoke to her mother.

Laurie refused, knowing how she would hate it if David saw the inevitable scene that would take place when her mother learned they were married. "There can be no real trouble," she said with more certainty than she felt. "There is nothing she can do. Our farewell will be brief, I am sure." Then he was gone and she was flying up the stairs to find Thérèse.

The scene that greeted her in her rooms was terrible. Thérèse, white and angry, was finishing the packing, but Laurie knew she couldn't be responsible for the conditions. Clothes, books, and every kind of personal possession had been flung to the floor, drawers from the chest pulled out and overturned, even the mattress pulled from the bed.

"Has my mother gone mad?" Laurie could hear her own voice trembling with fright.

Thérèse shrugged. "She has been looking for the title deed to Stepney Downs," she whispered. "Do not go near her, Laurie. She is in a terrible state."

"I must," Laurie said, her heart sinking. "I cannot go without some word, some explanation." Still in her bonnet and cloak, she went to her mother's room. Even in the dark of closing twilight she could see that Desirée's pretty face was swollen and distraught, her eyes glazed and red-rimmed. An empty brandy decanter still sat at her elbow where she lounged on a long chair, and when she spoke her voice was thick.

"So you have come home at last. I suppose it is useless to ask you what new improprieties you have committed, for you would only lie to me."

"I have done nothing improper," Laurie said, feeling both anger and pity. "It is only that the bishop had so much to say, and everything took so long . . ."

"I also have much to say!" Desirée pushed herself to a sitting position, staring at Laurie with hate in her eyes. "First, light this lamp beside me, and then go and fetch your grandfather's documents from wherever you have hidden them. Do not be surprised, you—you peasant! I was bound to find you out sooner or later."

Laurie sighed. "I was sorry to have deceived you, ma'am. It is true that I have them, and have always had them. But I wanted so much to keep Stepney Downs, and to provide for Annie and Breen as Grandfather would have wished me to do. I could not bear to lose my home and the lands."

"But you will bear it," Desirée said with grim satisfaction. "I have a buyer. A merchant from Edinburgh, who is most anxious to own the place. He has promised the full sum in my hand as soon as I can give him the title deed. And, though you may be betrothed, until you are married you are my ward and I have the power to sell. Fetch me the papers, now!''

''I am no longer your ward,'' Laurie said stiffly. Even at this pure evidence of her mother's greed she regretted having to tell her so bluntly. ''David asked for and obtained a special license. We were married an hour ago by the bishop of Wight.'' She watched the terrible fury rise in her mother's face as Desirée realized that the impossible was true, and her own anger rose to meet it. ''So,'' Laurie added sharply, ''Annie and Breen are safe in spite of you! They will always have a home. The house and lands are mine forever, for David has signed a paper to make it certain.''

Desirée screamed, her small, smudged mouth stretched and ugly. Frantic, she grabbed the heavy lamp beside her and threw it toward Laurie, bursting into tears as it fell short and smashed at Laurie's feet, spreading a creeping pool of oil over the delicate carpet.

''Get out! Get out of my house! I promise you, I will make you regret what you have done to me! Your heart will bleed . . .'' She tried to rise, to fling herself on Laurie, the small hands curved like claws. But her drunken body would not hold her, and she collapsed on the floor, weeping wildly.

Laurie fled, finding a pale Thérèse coming rapidly along the hall.

''Are you all right, Miss?''

''Yes. Thérèse, come with me! I need you, I will need you always . . .'' Laurie fell into the thin, bony arms and felt them close around her protectively.

''You will have maids aplenty,'' Thérèse said gently, ''and you have your husband.'' She stood back, smiling her tiny smile. ''It is a good match, I believe. You will be happy.''

Laurie wiped tears from her eyes that she hadn't realized were there. ''I do hope so. I will try very hard to gain his respect. But I would still wish you with me.''

"Sh-h-h. I cannot go. And he is here, waiting in the hall and growing impatient. I have just sent the coachman and Mr. Covington's manservant to fetch your trunk. Go down, before he grows angry . . ."

Laurie nodded, tightlipped. Nothing seemed real. She could still hear the hysterical sobbing in the room behind her as she turned and ran down the stairs.

David was indeed impatient. He grabbed her arm as she arrived and led her outside immediately. "We have very little time," he said. "Are they bringing your trunk?"

Laurie nodded breathlessly as David thrust her into the carriage and sat down beside her, glancing back at the house with knitted brows. He had handled her with a different manner, an assurance of possession that startled her into realizing that she was, indeed, his. By law, she was little more than a chattel. She remembered, suddenly, that he could beat her if he wished, though he was allowed to do so only if he used a stick no heavier than an inch thick. Looking at his broad shoulders that now filled the window of the coach as he watched for the men, she considered the rule poor comfort. But why such irrelevant thoughts! She sank back into the far corner of the luxurious seat with a sense of being carried along by events that were not under her control, though she herself had set them in motion. Busy with fearful imaginings, she barely noticed the thump and sway as the trunk was placed on the rack behind, nor the movement as the coachman mounted into the box. Only when they began to move did she realize that the manservant hadn't entered the coach. She glanced nervously at the bearded profile beside her.

"Your servant sits outside?"

David settled into his own corner, and she saw the white gleam of a smile in the black beard. "We must travel the lawless section of London to arrive at the Isle of Dogs. Ham is wonderfully able with footpads, and the coachman asked for his help."

"Oh." Laurie had heard about that. Prudent souls avoided certain down-at-heel parts of the old city at night. Cutthroats were said to await fine carriages that entered the rough, cobbled streets. When horses were slowed for the uneven paving the thieves ran to grab the reins and killed and robbed the passengers. It was said that even the stout Charleys—watchmen who patrolled newer London streets and called out the hours of the night—always avoided those streets. She sank back into her corner again, her heart thumping heavily.

"There is no reason for fear," David said, amused and patronizing. "I am armed. And it takes a brave man indeed to start a mill with Ham."

Ham, then, was the name of the manservant, that huge black man who had opened the door at the Covington mansion. No matter his size, it seemed an unconscionable amount of trust to put in one man. And it would be one man, for Lord Peter's coachman was elderly and small. Laurie wondered suddenly if Ham were a slave. If he were, how anxious would he be to save his master, now that he was in a country where black men were free? She twisted uncomfortably in the soft seat and attempted to put such thoughts from her mind. Sitting straighter, she looked out at the passing scene.

They were traveling as fast as the crowded streets allowed, but the pace gave her time to wonder at the brilliance of the new gas lights and to see numbers of sumptuous carriages, with jeweled and coiffed ladies seen in laughter with gentlemen in evening clothes. David gave the streets only a casual glance. Either he was used to such grandeur or bored by it. Laurie kept silent until they had progressed into the darker streets beyond.

"How do we manage to board the ship before dawn? I have heard that the docks are tightly secured at night, to prevent thievery."

Again the smile flashed in the dimness. "You have heard aright. But the captain of this brig is a friend of mine, and has put his ship off and anchored in open water. A small boat will pick us up from a shore nearby.''

Laurie was quiet, thinking of stopping, defenseless, on an open beach. Beginning the voyage in a small boat rowed to the side of a ship in darkness. And then, the open Atlantic. She shuddered. If only they could have begun their life together in some ordinary way—or in Scotland. She glanced again at David and saw that he now sat forward, his face turned toward the window, a hand resting on his knee with something gleaming . . . she concentrated on the gleam until it resolved itself into the long barrel of a pistol. Hastily, she turned away and shut her eyes, leaning back and considering the consequences of her own daring, improbable actions.

She had married a stranger. It was not his fault, however, that she had expected him to be more . . . more ordinary. She thought of how she had parroted those marriage vows—''For better or worse''—without thinking of the meaning at all. What *had* she thought of? Why, Annie and Breen and the land, and, worst of all, of triumphing over her mother's greed. Still, she had given her word and Old Hugh had taught her that promises must be kept. She drew a deep breath and sat up again.

Now the narrow streets were lit only by a few flaring oil lamps, leaving menacing patches of darkness between them. It was just as well, she thought, for there was nothing lovely to see. The streets were lined with decaying hovels, with buildings where walls were tumbling and doors hung drunkenly beside gaping black holes that spoke of poverty and desperation. Their pace slowed as the carriage lurched into a number of holes. There was movement beside her and she saw that the barrel of the pistol now rested on the edge of the window.

''You would not shoot someone, David?''

''Only if necessary,'' he replied coldly. ''I do not kill men for sport, if that is your meaning.''

Laurie saw he was offended, but before she could say more she also saw that his caution was justified. A ragged figure broke from the shadows at a corner and ran swiftly beside them for a moment, to vanish with a jeering laugh and rude gesture when the smoky light from an oil lamp illuminated the carriage and the shining barrel of the pistol. She sank back into her corner again, her breath caught in her throat.

Outside, the coachman had seen the running figure and was laying on the whip in spite of the potholes. Laurie forced herself to breathe deeply as the carriage swayed and jolted. They seemed in danger of overturning yet their speed did not slacken. She could hear a note of fear in the old coachman's harsh shouts.

"Look!" Laurie could not help her sudden cry. This time figures had appeared at her window, two or three of them, dodging in and out among the dark buildings, running beside the coach like shadows, darting away and reappearing, their coarse laughter rising. David leaned across her to put his pistol in plain view on her window, and his thick shoulders shielded her from view. But Laurie felt a rising, choking tide of dread. They looked so—so dirty, so evil. Not quite human. She kept her eyes on the wide, strong body angling across her until the figures fell behind and David sat back again.

"I do not believe they plan to stop us," he said calmly, "or they would have made their attempt by now. They may, however, gather others and follow to our destination. It must be plain to them that we are heading toward the river." He laid the pistol down and took her hand, his fingers casual but warm. "Do not be afraid. If they rush us when we stop, stay in the carriage until I tell you it is safe to descend."

She nodded, speechless, certain that she could not gather strength enough to leave the carriage in any event, for her veins seemed filled with ice water. She wondered at his confidence. One pistol, a manservant and a terrified old coachman—against what might be a mob of cutthroats! What chance would there be? Her throat dry, she finally managed to speak.

"Might we turn back?"

"The ship would leave without us, my dear."

Let *it!* She wanted to scream the words wildly. *Let it go . . . let us find safety, lights, warmth and comfort!* She clamped her teeth together so her cowardice would not be evident, clung with what strength she had to the edge of the seat as the carriage swung alarmingly in a wide curve and thundered down another black street.

"Ah." His voice held satisfaction. "We are nearing the river. If the small boat arrives, there may be reinforcements. Perhaps they will not attack at all."

Immediately, silently, Laurie prayed that the small boat awaited with a huge crowd of sailors, all armed. Then fear rose to choke her again, for the carriage slowed perceptibly and she was sure she heard running feet behind them. There were no buildings here, only a straggle of broken stone, shrubby trees like specters in the dim glow of the carriage lights. Then the sound of the horses' hooves were muffled by damp ground, the wheels dragged, and there before them was the swirling Thames, darkly gleaming, and in the distance the light of a boat lantern.

Laurie stifled a cry as they slowed further and came to a lurching stop. David, pistol in hand, was out, springing through the door as wild yells broke out at the rear of the carriage. She could see a swarm of tattered figures around them, grasping at the horses, could hear them tearing at the straps that held the baggage on the rack, hear furious cursing. She cowered, pressing frantically into the deep cushion. Then came the heartbursting report of a pistol, and at that moment the door beside her jerked open and hands grabbed her, wiry arms going around her. A gutter smell filled her nostrils and she fought against the arms, screaming as a wild-haired, snarling man dragged her from the carriage, his hands going to her throat. A new shape, a massive shape, blocked out the sky. A man, all black, black as the night, was there and the wiry arms holding her loosened suddenly. She fell to the ground, her head striking something hard . . . the carriage wheel . . . and she was dazed, seeming to see the wild-haired man fly up away from her. He was screaming as she had screamed, there was the sickening sound of bones breaking, and against the dull gleam from the river she saw him rise further, hurtle through the air, limp and lifeless, to land amongst other figures that were snatching at the baggage they had pulled from the rack.

Laurie scrambled to her feet, shaking, her head throbbing, to lean against the carriage and watch without believing as the towering black man ran, sure and silent, to catch another of the thieves. Once more there was a desperate, dying shriek before that man, too, was flung after the now fleeing others.

"All right, Ham." It was David's voice, faint but clear through the buzzing of her ears. He came from the other side of the carriage to Laurie, to look at her in the light of the small carriage lamp. She leaned there, panting, feeling a clot of mud on one cheek, aware of dizziness, of what seemed to be a dark hovering cloud threatening to close over her. David touched her forehead gently and drew away bloodstained fingers.

"I am sorry. Are you badly injured?"

Laurie shook her head, increasing the dizziness. He turned his attention to the huge black man still standing at the rear of the carriage.

"You were slow, Ham," he said with a faint note of reproof.

"He were not slow!" The quavery voice of the old coachman, still frozen in the box, contradicted him. "One come at him with a cutlass afore we stopped! Look down here!"

Near the front wheel, a body like a crumpled rag, one outstretched hand loose around the dark handle of a shining, great knife.

"He thought to be rid of me quickly," Ham said in calm explanation. "The time it took me to dispose of him made me late to aid the mistress."

"I see," said David. "These five will not run coaches again. One shot, one clubbed for me—and three to your hands, Bonebreaker. You have improved since the Grenada riots, though I would not have thought it possible."

Though his words were still clear, their meaning escaped Laurie, and his voice was still faint and fading. She could not rid herself of the dizziness. The dark scene slid and tilted before her, and the feel of the carriage at her back was the only reality in a world of death and huge, black men . . . there were more figures, coming now from the river, voices . . . the carriage began to slide upward behind her.

Chapter Five

SHE WAS SMALL AGAIN, QUITE SMALL, CURLED COM-
fortably in Annie's capacious lap, dazzled by the flickering flames of the woodstove and warm and peaceful.
They often sat so, rocking as they were now, until the
creaking of the old oak rocker made Laurie sleepy and
Annie carried her off to bed.

But she was sleepy now, and they were still rocking.
She opened her eyes and watched the yellow glow of a
lantern swinging overhead, casting a moving circle of
light on dark varnished boards. It was a lantern she had
not seen before. She looked around curiously, discovering more unfamiliarity. A chest, with an odd, tiny railing
around its top, held a basin and ewer of water. Cabinets
of the same dark wood as the ceiling and walls. A very
small room, made smaller by a clutter of baggage.
Baggage? She jerked upward, sat clutching the clean,
coarse sheet and rough blanket. Fully awake, she remembered.

"So you have wakened at last."

It was David, appearing around the solid end of the
bunk she lay in. He was dressed amazingly in an open-
necked, homespun linen shirt, in gray pantaloons tucked
into loose boots. With his hair caught at his neck and his
black beard, he looked very much like a pirate. A faintly
smiling, arrogant pirate. Laurie clutched the covers
closer. There was something in his eyes that reminded
her that beneath the covers she wore nothing at all.

"We are on the ship!"

"You were hoisted aboard like a sack of meal, my

52

dear. That bump on your head was harder than I had thought. Are you in pain?''

''My head aches, that is all.'' He moved closer, and she watched him as a mouse might watch a cat. ''My clothes?''

''Torn and muddy. Set aside until we are home and they can be properly cleaned and repaired. You must choose something else from your baggage when you feel well enough to rise.''

''You . . . removed them, David?'' From the heat of her face she knew it was flaming.

''Naturally. There is no lady's maid aboard.'' His dark eyes gleamed in the swinging, golden light. ''I *am* your husband, if you recall.''

Beneath the covers Laurie's skin seemed to shrivel with embarrassment. ''Naturally,'' she repeated his word, choking over it and then forcing her voice to a more normal tone as she saw the amusement in his face. ''It was . . . very kind of you, I'm sure.''

That brought his white flash of grin. ''Pray do not thank me,'' he said with exaggerated courtesy, ''for performing such a pleasant task. I was agreeably surprised by what I discovered.'' He came closer yet, bent and touched her forehead gently, his fingertips exploring a painful lump. He sighed and straightened.

''I will bring you food. You have slept the clock around and more. We are at sea.''

''In the Atlantic?''

He smiled again, and she supposed him amused by her frightened awe. ''It is much the same as any sea. The winds are favorable.'' Then he added that the air was mild and that once she had eaten she might feel well enough to go up on deck. Then he left, evidently to find food for her.

She lay back, feeling for the first time the pangs of hunger, the aching limbs from her struggles with that figure of horror in the night. She shuddered with the memory of fear, but a new apprehension drove the dim remembrance away. She burrowed her naked body deeper into the bed. David, when he stood beside her, had had that same tensed look, the same arch of neck that she had seen in Hervey—the fierce ram among the ewes . . .

Was it, then, that mating for men was the same rough, terrible, driving force? Into her mind came the pained, frightened bleating of a newly chosen young ewe. She had always been so sorry for them, had wondered why they did not run away . . . she threw back the covers hurriedly and swung from the bunk, wavering on weak legs, her bare skin cold from the damp air. Her trunk was nearby and she opened it hastily and snatched the first clothes she saw. She dressed, though her head spun with dizziness and hurt much more than it had at rest. When she made her way to the small steel mirror over the basin she saw a great, spreading bruise on her swollen forehead, with a small cut in the center. She dabbed it away and brushed her hair, setting her jaw. It was Stepney blood, and it would heal.

If David was surprised to find her up and dressed when he returned he made no sign of it, but gave her the tray of food and left, saying he would be on deck. Later, coming up from the faint light below to the sparkle of sun on sea, warmed by hot food and comforted by being dressed again in clean clothing—for after she had eaten she had bathed and found a light wool gown, high-necked with elbow-length sleeves—Laurie found David lounging near the companionway. She clung to his arm and looked up, filling her eyes with the beauty of the fat clouds of sail. The soft leather slippers she wore were suitable for the slanting deck and she went without fear or awkwardness to peer over the rail at the blue water running swiftly past. Behind her, David laughed.

"There's a sailor somewhere in your family's past," he said, "for you were born with sea legs."

"I sailed the tarns as a child," Laurie said absently, for her senses were busy with the sea and the ship, the hum of braces, the snapping sails. "But, oh, it was nothing so grand as this!"

"Sailed?"

He sounded so incredulous that she laughed aloud. "Sailed, and rowed, and fished! Old Hugh had no grandsons, so he made do with me. You look so odd, David! Do you consider such activities unladylike?"

"Unlikely, rather, for a Mayfair beauty. I would have expected fine embroidery, perhaps painting or poetry . . ."

Laurie sighed. "Then I must learn. There must be many things I will have to study before I am a proper wife. I hope you have patience."

"Very little." But he was smiling. "Perhaps I will learn to appreciate the qualities you already own."

"That would be much simpler." Demurely, Laurie turned, suddenly lighthearted, to lean against the rail. "I am well versed in ordinary household duties. Living in the country, a daughter of the house joins in work with the servants. I can bake, and sew, and . . ."

"That interests me not at all," he said, interrupting. He had that intent look again, his brown eyes darkening as they traveled from her face to linger along her body, outlined now by the breeze that flattened the thin wool gown against her. It was as if he remembered that same body without the gown, and when he lifted his gaze again Laurie averted her face and turned again, leaning against the rail, strangely upset by what she saw in his eyes.

After a long moment he spoke again. "The services you will perform for me will not be quite so domestic," he said, with that hated amusement plain in his tone. "House servants I have aplenty." His hand closed over her arm, his dark face gleaming with both humor and an arrogant anticipation. "Your injury," he added, lowering his voice because of the seamen working near them, "has delayed the consummation of our marriage, so I am very glad to see you have recovered so quickly." He drew her away from the rail, tucking her hand into his arm. "Now, my dear, I will introduce you to Captain Martin and First Officer William Burdick. Then you will either find a seat midships, where you will not be in the way, or below in our cabin." He took her rapidly along the deck, adding, "As a courtesy, you will thank Mr. Burdick for the use of his cabin. He gave it up gladly when he learned there would be a bride aboard."

Laurie went with him silently, wondering if it would have been better, after all, to have lingered in bed and pretended to be weak. And wondering, too, if she would ever get over the fright she felt when his eyes darkened like that, and swept her with that compelling look.

In the captain's quarters Laurie endeavored to be gracious, and succeeded as far as she could see, for the captain's cool appraisal soon warmed to friendliness. Meeting William Burdick proved to be no trial; she was at ease with the young man from the beginning, for he glowed with admiration and told David he was a man to be envied. Burdick was a sensitive-looking man, with golden hair that waved back from a high forehead and eyes as blue as the sea. He hastened to hold the door for Laurie as they left, and his glance down at her would have flattered any woman.

Out in the breeze again, avoiding the scurrying sailors as they went about trimming the sails, Laurie said nervously that she thought she would go below. Her head was aching, she added, and rest might be advisable. Arching his brows, David smiled.

"It may not be only the blow that is causing your head to ache," he said. "I have heard that headaches are a common malady among reluctant virgins and ill-suited matrons. Fortunately, I will be able to cure that for you tonight."

Laurie stared at him, for the first time realizing that he was actually—actually *teasing* her! He had sensed her fright and was making sport of it. Her chin shot up and her turquoise eyes blazed into his.

"How very kind of you," she said frigidly, "to inconvenience yourself for my sake."

They had neared the companionway, and she pulled her arm from his and swept down it, hearing his low laughter behind her. Furious, she entered the small, neat cabin and shut the door behind her. Sitting on the one chair, she considered it.

She fully intended to live up to her bargain, that was the first point. She would submit to him without argument or delay, and bear what unpleasantness might ensue. But it was most unkind of him to rag her about it! And, just when she had begun to feel quite companionable. Were there no more men in the world like her grandfather? So much had disappeared with Old Hugh's death. Kind men, her loving Annie, the peace and serenity of the moors.

At least, she thought, dabbing her eyes, it is still there, even if I am not. It's waiting for me. And that I owe to David Covington. My payment will be doing what I must to be a good wife.

Standing, she removed her cape and looked for a hook to hang it on. She found that the cabinets opened to reveal both drawers and a hanging space already filled with her own gowns. The baggage had been emptied, even the trunk, and every item had been placed neatly in either drawer or hanging cabinet. The bunk had been made up neatly and fresh water stood in the ewer. She had planned to neaten the cabin herself following her turn on deck, and she wondered who had done so. Perhaps, in spite of what David had said, there was a maid of sorts on the ship. In any event, someone had left her nothing to do. She lay down to think and in moments was fast asleep.

Later, a knock on the door wakened her and she padded to it in stocking feet, opening it to encounter again the huge Negro. She stepped back involuntarily and he seemed to know that he had unnerved her, for he smiled very gently. Held in one big hand was a small table, in the other a dinner tray, with savory odors floating above it. He was not, Laurie saw, nearly as dark as she had remembered from that night. In fact only his hair and eyes were that midnight hue she had recalled. His skin was light brown, fine textured, and the expression on his regular features, which she had visualized as heavy and contorted, was in fact quite pleasant. Slowly, she smiled back at him.

"You are Ham, are you not? I owe you my gratitude. I well know you saved my life. Come in."

Bending to step through the low doorframe, he flicked a puzzled glance at her and then set the table before the small chair and placed the tray on it.

"Your dinner, Mistress. In an hour, I will return for the tray. Is there anything else you require?"

Laurie extended her small hand. "Only that you accept my heartfelt thanks. Without your quick action, I would not be here to dine at all."

For a moment she thought he would not accept her handclasp, for he stood motionless, staring at her. Then his huge hand came forward and enveloped hers, but only for an instant.

"My action was not quick enough, Mistress. Otherwise, you would not wear that bruise. I will be quicker in the future." He bobbed his head and left, leaving her wondering how a man that size could move so like a cat. She could not hear his footsteps even on the creaky risers of the companionway. She sat down rather weakly, for in spite of her genuine gratitude, the sight of him had reminded her of how quickly, how ruthlessly he had killed, with only his bare hands. She thought of his remark about the future and quailed at the thought that he would ever have to use his tremendous strength again on her behalf.

In the twilight she went up again to the deck and found a seat amidships. The winds had dropped and become variable, and sailors hauled at the tackles, turning the sails at the foremast to catch the best of the breeze.

Glances came her way often. She heard whispered remarks and low laughter, but though it made her uncomfortable she kept her seat. David, she was sure, was in the captain's quarters and she thought it likely he would come out soon and inquire how she felt.

The ship's lanterns had been lit before she rose to go below again. There had been no sign of David, nor of the captain, though William Burdick had come to sit beside her and ask about her recovery. He had been most gallant, and she had talked and smiled willingly, but if David had been watching it had not brought him out. Finally she wished Mr. Burdick a good night and went slowly toward the companionway, pulling her cape tightly around her, for the air was getting cooler. Her foot was on the first step when she saw a huge figure leaning on the forward rail. She hesitated, and then went to his side.

"Ham, will you please tell your master that I wish his company in our cabin?" She could feel pride stiffening her face as she tried to conceal the searing embarrassment she felt. It was truly demeaning to be forced into such a request. But Ham did not smile.

"Yes, Mistress. Right away."

"Thank you." She thought his tone most proper, and walked away with what she thought was great dignity.

A few minutes later David stepped into the cabin and closed the door behind him. A faint odor of rumbullion accompanied him, but his eyes were clear, his step sure as he came to the table where she sat.

"You sent Ham for me," he said, unnecessarily, she thought. "Is there something you need?"

She looked up at him. He was still wearing the open-necked linen shirt, the pantaloons and boots—clothing that clung to his broad, heavily muscled body, accenting his thick shoulders and strong thighs. He seemed to fill the small cabin with his presence, and it was suddenly very difficult to say what she had planned. Nevertheless, she stood up and put a hand on his arm.

"I lack nothing. It is only that I am going to bed, and I thought . . . I thought you might like to join me." She saw the thick brows arch in surprise, and before he could speak, she gave him his own words back swiftly. "You are my husband, if you recall."

Then he did fill the small cabin—with laughter—as he bent and picked her up in his arms.

"No man I know, husband or not, could refuse such an invitation! I have only been teasing you, Laurie—I fully intended to give you another day or so to recover from your experience. But, God! If you are truly willing . . ."

Laurie was amazed by the softness of his beard, the warmth and gentleness of the broad mouth covering hers. Then he had set her on her feet and turned her around, his hands busy with the buttons that were so hard for her to reach. "This time," he was saying, his voice growing hoarse, "you will be awake for the unveiling of this tender beauty . . ."

Speechless, quivering, Laurie stood like a statue as David's nimble fingers finished the row of buttons, moved warmly beneath the thin wool and slid the gown from her shoulders. It slithered to the floor, leaving her wearing the assortment of underthings that included the long, thin cotton petticoat, the chemise that confined her breasts and torso, the knee-length, lace-trimmed cotton drawers that she insisted on wearing in spite of Desirée's contention that they were unnecessary. But she felt naked already, frightened but resolute. His hands were still on her shoulders, caressing, his warm breath on the back of her neck.

"Skin like Highland cream," he murmured, and a hand moved to lift her loosening hair. She felt his mouth, hot and moist, sliding over her nape and sending a sensation down through her that centered, burning, in her belly. Then the mouth went away and the hands turned her gently to face him. She met his eyes helplessly and saw that the look she feared was there, hot and shining in the brown depths. She dropped her gaze and then hurriedly brought it back up to his shirt front. Even in the loosely fitting pantaloons his arousal was evident, and astoundingly large. She drew a long, shaky breath as his fingers began on the bows of ribbon that held the chemise tightly around her breasts.

"You look frightened," he whispered, expertly twitching the bows apart. "You have nothing to fear, Laurie. I know what I'm doing . . ."

In spite of his confidence his deep voice was unsteady, and as her breasts swelled free of the chemise his fingers shook. "Lovely," he said hoarsely. "What treasures you hide beneath those high-necked gowns of yours . . ." His hands pulled down the lacy straps of her chemise, letting it drop to her waist, then rose to cup the breasts, his thumbs moving back and forth across the small, rosy nipples.

Laurie, her face flaming, refused to look at him, staring determinedly at one broad shoulder. But that same sensation moved deep inside her again, insidiously warm and inviting. Then her breath caught in her throat as his hands went to the tight band of her petticoat. Even with the chemise draping down over it, he seemed to know precisely where the string was tied, and where the buttons were that fastened the knee-length drawers. In minutes she stood nude before him, with a pool of swirled white underclothes around her ankles. Silent, intent, with his hands resting just below her waist, warm but motionless, he let his gaze travel over her slowly and then back up to her face.

"You have known no other man?"

Her drooping head snapped up, her blue-green gaze met his in angry pride. "None! Have I not told you I am virtuous?"

He smiled and drew her to him gently, reaching to take the rest of the pins from her already loosened hair, letting it fall over her shoulders, trail down her back in a shining black mantle. Pressing her stiffening body closer yet, he buried his face in her hair.

"It is only that I cannot believe my luck," he said, muffled. "This beauty, untouched by any other . . ." He swung her up suddenly, out of the nest of crumpled clothes, and put her down in the bunk. Extinguishing the lantern, he took his clothes off in the dark and slipped in beside her.

Lying on her back, her jaw set and every muscle tensed, Laurie waited for his crushing weight, for the driving thrusts that would tear through her flesh. She was determined that she would not cry out, no matter what the pain. All women, she told herself, must stand this if they marry. Am I less courageous than they? She felt the thick mattress move, and in the faint starshine that came through the porthole she could see his shoulders and head hovering over her. She shut her eyes, bracing for his onslaught.

A hand slid beneath her shoulders, lifting her, settling her again with her head cradled on a thick, warm arm. The other hand touched her cheek and a finger traced her stiffened jaw, moved to her lips and drew their shape slowly, pressing them apart. "So temptingly soft," he whispered. "Let me enjoy them . . ."

The hot mouth within the soft beard was amazingly seductive, alive with sensual movement. It warmed her lips, sucking them in, worrying them with teeth and tongue until heat spread deep in her tense body. She drew in her breath in sharp surprise and his tongue followed softly, searching the recesses of her opening mouth, finding places to probe that immediately yearned to be touched again. Then he had moved away, leaving her lips parted and panting, and she felt his head settle beside hers on the pillow while the hand that had caressed her face moved down her neck and over her shoulder, pressing tight muscles into softness with a circling thumb, smoothing down the slender arm.

She was silent except for her rapid breathing, filled with the insidious warmth that had come from his deep kiss. Her senses concentrated on the wandering hand, which carried a penetrating heat that flowed through her flesh wherever it traveled. The hand seemed unerringly aware of what it should do to increase that subtle, deep pleasure, and as it encircled a breast and began slowly kneading, Laurie moved involuntarily to allow it more freedom.

"Yes, my sweet darling," he breathed, bending over her. "Give yourself to me . . . offer me love . . ." His mouth closed over the breast, his beard a soft, enclosing cloud as he suckled, and Laurie felt her body tremble and twist, felt his hand move again, soothing. Her own hand wavered up, touching his thick hair, pressing him closer as dark flame bloomed and spread inside her.

"David," she said huskily, "This . . . this feeling is sweet beyond reason . . ."

He answered by moving again to her lips, and she opened her mouth eagerly, wanting the thrust of his tongue again. This time he covered her with his broad chest and when she felt his warm skin, the mat of hair against her breasts, she strained upward, her arms going around his shoulders.

David's breathing sharpened, the wandering hand gripping the soft curve of her waist and then becoming gentle again, circling the smoothness of her belly. "Like fine silk," he whispered, and his hand caressed the curve of hip and thigh.

Burning, Laurie searched for his retreating tongue with her own, sliding the tip between the broad lips and coaxing for another thrust. She was hardly aware of the hand sliding between her thighs, kneading the soft inner flesh, but when he began pressing her legs apart she widened them obediently. In moments she was still, immobilized by wonder, by the aching delight of the skillful, deceptively gentle fingers that had parted the soft folds between her thighs. They had found the moist velvet and were trailing a smooth path through dark curls, sliding upward to circle, featherlight, around a tiny, fiery point that made her hips rise from the soft bed. He pressed her down again with a hot palm, then moved the fingers down and probed inward, careful and slow. Taking his lips from hers, he buried his bearded face in her neck with a long, shuddering sigh.

"A true virgin," he whispered, and circled her with an arm. Pulling her beneath him, he settled cautiously between her slender legs. "There will be pain, my darling, but soon over . . ."

The heat of his loins was scalding, the hard pressure became frightening as it increased and increased and then . . . she cried out, her fingers digging into his shoulders as he broke through the tender barrier and pushed upward into her. Panting, he pressed on until he had entered her fully and then lay still, pushing the tangled hair back from her damp face, his hand soft as a woman's.

"That is all," he murmured. "No more pain, my darling. The rest will be far, far different . . ."

Still clutching his shoulders she lay throbbing beneath his big body, wondering at the growing, delicious feeling radiating from the thick hardness within her. But when he began to move she moved with him instinctively, picking up the sinuous rhythm, her arms going around him, her hands clasping the rolling muscles of his powerful back.

Pacing himself carefully, keeping a strict control over his passion, David smiled in the darkness, watching the pale oval of the face below his. The brilliant eyes were closed, the soft lips parted and moist. Her warm breath fanned in and out, ever more rapidly, making small sounds very like purring . . .

Waking, knowing in her country-bred heart that it was close to dawn, Laurie felt deliciously relaxed, almost boneless. David, she thought contentedly, did not mate like the ram. She would remember forever how gently he had taken her, how, at the end, her whole heart and body had opened to him eagerly, had melded with him in a glorious blaze.

How quickly the pain had been forgotten. How wondrous a thing it was, after all, a man and woman together. A pleasure so great as to be indescribable. Her body still lay close to his, and she did not want to move. But in a few minutes a thought entered her mind that made her laugh, and though she muffled the sound with the blanket, still David heard her. He turned, a heavy arm settled over her, his bearded face pushed into her neck.

"A cheerful sound," he drawled lazily. "But for what reason?"

Laurie swallowed laughter and told him. "I have discovered why the ewes do not run away."

He sat up as the greenish glow of first light at sea stole through the porthole and glinted in his dark eyes. "What ewes? What are you speaking of?"

"The young ewes at Stepney Downs. When the ram goes amongst them, so fierce and bold, and seems to punish them." Laurie had no way of knowing how tenderly childlike she appeared to him, her brilliant eyes large and trusting, her love-swollen lips parted in her young, happy face. But she saw his eyes soften, staring down at her.

"And you thought I would be the same."

The tenderness of the night welled up in her. "If I did, I was wrong. From the tales I have heard, a first joining can be a terrible experience. How did you know so well what to do?"

He smiled, a trifle cynically, she thought. "I was fortunate enough in my early youth to meet a French Creole woman who knew more of lovemaking than she should have known, perhaps. She was an excellent teacher.'' He watched the soft lips droop, some of the brilliance fade from her eyes. ''It was years ago, Laurie. Does the thought annoy you?''

''I am not sure,'' Laurie said slowly, considering it. ''Did you . . . did you love her very much?''

The cynical smile was still on his face as he turned away and looked out at the increasing light of dawn. ''She was not the kind of woman one loves,'' he said. ''Only the kind a young man learns from.''

''Then I am not annoyed,'' Laurie said, smiling again. ''Perhaps I am even grateful. You were wonderfully nice . . .''

David laughed softly and lay down again, gathering her into his arms. ''I am wonderfully fortunate,'' he said. ''The fearful child I married has turned into a beautiful, passionate woman.'' Holding her tightly, he pushed the blanket and sheet down, exposing an ivory and rose breast, then covered it with a possessive hand. ''But do not count on such patience each time I take you, my sweet. Right now, I could eat you alive . . .''

Laurie wound slim fingers around his thick wrist and lifted the hand, inspecting the breast beneath it, the hard, jutting rosiness of nipple. ''It would appear,'' she said wonderingly, ''that part of me is willing . . .''

Chapter Six

IT WAS STRANGE, LAURIE THOUGHT, TO FIND THAT HER husband was two different men. One, who walked with her on the decks and sat beside her at the meals they took in the wardroom with the captain and Burdick, was a man gifted with exquisite courtesy, a cool wit, and a reserved demeanor. The other man, present only when they were alone in their cabin, was passionate and hungry, reveling in their lovemaking. He taught her more and more, tuning her young body like a fine instrument, until it took but a touch from him to make her melt into desire. That second man became more beloved every day, and she turned to him with eager joy when he entered the cabin. But the man she knew in the company of others was distant and rather frightening. No matter how often she glanced into the brown eyes she could never find a hint of her lover. Logically, she decided that David preferred to keep their love a secret, and after a day or two of practice she managed the same distant courtesy when they left the cabin.

But she did sense an odd curiosity on the part of Captain Martin and William Burdick. It was natural, she supposed, that they would wonder. They knew that she and David were newly married and undoubtedly expected some small display of affection, if only a touching of hands. Mr. Burdick in particular seemed puzzled, his blue eyes often going from one to the other at table, his fair skin flushing pink when he saw she had noticed his interest.

Only Ham seemed to know, without doubt, what fires burned within them. He too kept a proper distance and expression around the others, as a servant should. But when he happened on them alone his pleased smile and softening eyes made his knowledge evident. And David did not appear to mind.

Standing with them one early morning at the bow of the boat, when all of them were marveling at how the good weather had held, Ham remarked that one of the old sailors on board was mystified by such excellent fortune and was still expecting a bad blow.

"But he has expected it daily," he added. "Because there is a lady aboard. He has told me the only worse luck is to carry a minister."

David laughed shortly. "And we are close to having both. I understand this is William Burdick's last voyage —he is to be ordained as a minister soon after we arrive at Barbados."

Laurie smiled. "Is he? He will look the part. With that golden halo of hair and those innocent blue eyes, a clerical collar is sure to make him appear angelic."

David frowned. "I would say few men are angelic. As for Burdick, he is overyoung to make such a decision. He is barely twenty-one, and there is much foolishness left in a man at that age."

Twenty-one seemed quite old enough for wisdom to Laurie, but she smiled agreeably and turned to address Ham.

"And do you believe in the sailor's superstition? Has he convinced you?"

Ham's slow smile lighted his black eyes. "Not in this case, Mistress. The lady aboard this ship is a fair wind home."

David laughed, looking at Ham with amusement. "Yet you were the one who groaned loudest at the thought of a Mistress at Silversea. I had thought you spoiled by our free bachelor menage."

"Yes," Ham admitted, still smiling, "but you have found a Mistress who will grace even Silversea. The old Master will clap you on the shoulder."

Laurie was startled by his praise, but David, still laughing, looked down at her teasingly. "Ham has not yet discovered how wilful you can be," he said. "Not to say stubborn . . ."

She knew he was referring to an unfinished argument about his father, Bartram Covington. David had mentioned casually that his father was refurbishing an older house on the plantation, one long unused, and would move into it when they arrived, and would henceforth live alone.

Laurie had objected, immediately and strongly. It was traditional to her that elders who were widows or widowers lived with their children, cared for and loved, part of the family. She had reminded David that her grandfather had raised her, and added that she wanted to know and love his father in the same way.

"He will be cared for, very well," David had said wryly. "He is taking Molenga, our housekeeper, with him. And she would have been a great help to you."

"That is of no great account," Laurie had said. "But having him lonely, thrust from his own home, does not suit me. You must help me persuade him to stay with us."

David had looked amused. "If you think to change Bartram Covington's mind, you have my permission to try," he had said. "But I will not attempt something so certain to fail. My father is a determined man, and he has his reasons for wishing to live apart from us."

"But he does not know me," Laurie had said. "How can he be so sure he would not be happy with us?"

David had looked away. "There are certain attitudes that are common to all English gentlewomen," he had said. "Attitudes that may not suit his way of life."

She had lost her temper at that. "You must help me to show him that my attitudes will not interfere," she had said, her turquoise eyes sparkling with anger. "I *have* no attitudes!"

69

He had laughed indulgently and pulled her into his arms. "Then I suggest you develop one. Such as a fervently passionate attitude . . . toward me."

That, she reflected now, had not been difficult. The memory made her smile, perhaps too openly for public view, so she left the two men together and went back to the cabin.

Closing the door behind her, she reflected that here, at least, she could do something useful. She had discovered a week ago that it was Ham who had cleaned and straightened their cabin, and had run him out with mock ferocity.

"Am I to fold my hands and look at the ocean all day?" she had asked him. "I am well able to take care of this tiny place and our clothes. Go! Find something more amusing to do." And since then she had spent an hour or so every day in the cabin. It was neat and clean, and there wasn't a button missing on their clothing, nor a small rent that she could find. The brig was a fine ship, but walking the deck didn't absorb her young energy. Idle hours were always endless.

She had finished her cleaning and was picking up the ewer to go and replenish the water when the cabin door opened and David came in.

"Ham tells me," he said, shutting the door carefully behind him, "that you have insisted on taking over his duties."

He sounded, she thought, faintly critical. "Yes, I have," she said, putting the ewer down again. "I prefer to have something to do."

David sighed and sat down in the little chair. "Ham expects to look after us, Laurie. He is the only servant of ours here. When we arrive home, I hope you will not run the maids from the rooms nor the cook from the kitchen."

"I will make friends of them," Laurie said, smiling at the thought of being in David's home. "And very likely will assist them."

"No, you will not, my dear. Even your orders to them will be issued through Ham. Only Molenga knows English, and she will be gone. The rest of them will not understand you. My father is well versed in their languages and has no trouble. But Ham is invaluable there. He speaks several tribal dialects."

Laurie stared at him. "Your house servants are *slaves?*"

"Naturally. There are no more than two or three white servants in all of Barbados. But don't let it disturb you. They try very hard to please and are quite competent. It is considered a privilege to work in the house instead of the cane fields."

Laurie sank down on the edge of the bunk, miserably conscious that she should have known—she *had* known. Desirée had mentioned the slaves on the Covington estates, saying they were happy and well cared for. But she had been so immersed in her own concerns that she had not even considered that now her clothes, her food, all her needs would be bought by the labor of humans captured and forced into submission.

"I *hate* slavery," she whispered, looking at her hands.

"You know nothing about it," David said firmly. "When you do, you will understand. We treat our laborers well, and most of them are happy."

"Most? And what happens when one is not happy? Does he run away, to be brought back and beaten?"

His mouth was a straight line. "I see you have been reading the pamphlets put out by the Quakers and that mealy-mouthed Wilberforce. Yes, our runaways and malcontents are punished. Would you have it otherwise? Men are hanged in England every day for breaking unimportant laws. At least, Covington justice is not that severe."

"It is true that English courts are too harsh, especially with the poor. But an Englishman is free to choose the

71

kind of life he wishes to lead. These Africans— Oh, David, can't you see? No man should own another man.''

He shrugged. ''The slaves are better off than they ever were in their jungles. Wait, Laurie, until you have been in Barbados for a time. Then tell me if you think they should be sent back to savagery.''

''I will still think the same,'' she said obstinately, and David, exasperated, clamped his jaw shut. But later Laurie brought the subject back, for she had a question she thought was important.

''Is Ham a slave?''

David sighed. ''He was born a slave, but my father freed his mother when Ham was born and later, when I was born, his mother gave him to me.''

Laurie was completely puzzled. ''Gave him to you?''

''It is a custom,'' David said casually. ''Life on a plantation is lonely for an only child, and many times the child is given a slave near his own age as a companion. Ham is a few years older than I, but we grew up together. He is educated as well as I am, for the same tutors taught us both.'' He smiled. ''I freed him, out of friendship, as soon as I was old enough to do so.''

''Then he is like a brother!''

David looked amused. ''Not quite. But he is a friend as well as a servant.'' He rose, stretching, and put out his hand to Laurie, pulling her up beside him. ''And may I point out that he is free and yet remains with me? Does that begin to change your mind?''

''I don't know,'' Laurie said slowly. ''I suppose it is true that I really know very little about it . . .''

''In self-doubt lies the beginnings of wisdom,'' David said, laughing. ''I have told you—wait and see.''

Laurie thought deeply about that conversation for several days. If a man born of a savage could become as educated and contented a being as Ham, there might be some argument in favor of importing the Africans, even against their will. Perhaps within a generation or two a great change for the better would be evident. She tried hard to believe it, for in her heart she wanted nothing more than to believe in David and to please him. Still, in the deepest recesses of her mind there was the persistent conviction that freedom was the most valuable right of man.

Barbados was sighted on the twenty-first day, its low contours misty blue in the distance, looking no more than a larger wave oddly stationary in the rolling sea. David brought Laurie to the bow to see it, and Captain Martin joined them.

"You are welcome aboard my brig any time," he told Laurie genially. "You have confounded the most superstitious of my sailors, all of whom admit that we have had wonderful weather, a fast crossing and a perfect landfall. Who could find better luck?"

"It has indeed passed quickly for me," Laurie replied. "I cannot believe it has been three weeks since—as my husband said—I was hoisted aboard your ship like a sack of meal. I am almost sorry to have the voyage end."

It was true. She sensed that the world of the brig, in which David and she had no real part, had given them time together that they might not have again. She had used that time to fall in love with him, and she knew it was real and lasting. She hoped that David had at least begun to value her, though he never spoke of his feelings. But when they landed there would be another world in which he had great responsibilities to occupy his mind. And she would have a home to run for them—and for their children! As she gazed at the indistinct outline of the island a rising excitement swept away regret. It was a new world, and Laurie Covington would have a place in it.

Captain Martin told her that it would be another full day before they came upon the island, for they must run with the sea along the rocky windward coast and then around the southern tip, beat up against the strong winds to the harbor at Bridgetown. But the island was still a magnet to her eyes, and she leaned on the rail for hours, watching as the small bit of land in the immensity of ocean grew nearer, seeming to float across the waves toward the brig. She was there again on the final day, excited and eager.

"I had heard," she said to William Burdick who had appeared beside her as he always did when he found her alone, "that the West Indies were mountainous islands, sometimes rising to great heights straight from the sea. A traveler's tale, I suppose, since I see no mountains."

He moved closer, smiling. "Do not doubt your travelers, Laurie. All other islands of the chain are indeed mountainous, offering breathtaking views. But they have worse climates, being subject to deluges of rain on one hand, and sections too arid to cultivate on the other. On Barbados, the trade winds sweep over without obstruction, keeping the land cool and dropping their rains gently."

His use of her given name startled her, but she had never stood on ceremony and after a minute she addressed him as William and asked for more information, adding that she supposed he knew all the islands well.

His handsome face grew eager at her interest. "Yes, but Barbados is my home. I am very happy to be returning this time, for I am leaving the sea to stay here." He hesitated and then went on with increasing enthusiasm. "I am to be ordained! I studied for the ministry at Codrington College on this island, and hope to find a place where I can teach Christianity to those who need it most, the descendants of slaves."

He had caught Laurie now. She turned a bright smile in his direction. "How wonderful. You mean to work among the slaves—to teach them!"

His own smile dimmed. "I wish you were right. That was my dream, but it is impossible. The planters will not hear of it, saying such understanding is past the powers of the slaves and would only agitate them. I may work only among the freedmen. But, if I can bring them an understanding of Christianity and the sacrament of marriage, I will feel my time well spent. Many of them are now setting up homes, having children . . .''

He went on, describing the small farms the freedmen were allowed to own, their daily lives, while Laurie puzzled over what he meant by the term. Ham, she supposed, would be called a freedman. But she had considered him a rarity. It was heartening news that so many Africans had been freed that they constituted a class of their own.

"I did not realize," she said when he paused in his talk, "that so many slaves had been freed by the planters."

"Oh, yes." He was thoughtful, staring at the island. "All of mixed blood, you know. Usually the child and the mother are freed as soon as it becomes apparent. It would never do to have a slave with white blood in his veins." He straightened. "I consider it a wonderfully fertile field for a minister. I think them the unhappiest on the islands, for they sit between the two classes, ignored by both the whites and the blacks, victims of their two heritages."

Laurie was silent, knowing William had not realized how saddened she was by knowledge that white men could be so base as to take advantage of a female slave and then ignore their own progeny, setting them free to starve or live according to chance. Ham at least had been rescued from such a fate by being chosen as David's companion. Now, she knew the reason for his almost European features, the lighter brown of his skin. Half of his heritage was white, yet he was considered fit only for a servant's role in spite of his intelligence and education. She turned away from William, saying that she must see to her packing.

David met her at the companionway and followed her

into the cabin, reserved and silent. He shut the door behind them and sat down, looking at Laurie critically.

"For a married woman you seem overfond of another man's company," he said slowly. "Especially one who shows his interest in you so plainly."

"Why, William is to be ordained," Laurie said, protesting. "A man of God is not likely to permit himself interest in someone else's wife, even if I were inclined to flirt, which I am not!"

David's face softened. "I did not mean to imply misbehavior on your part, Laurie. Only ignorance. Man of God or not, Burdick is more than a little attracted to you. Had you been older or more experienced you would have realized that yourself, and taken pains not to encourage him."

Laurie was silent, taking off the plain dress she wore, putting on a silken wrapper to wear while she finished the packing. Perhaps she was young and inexperienced, but she had, after all, sensed William's warm feelings. She had even enjoyed the admiration in his blue eyes! She went about the packing with a flurry of activity, thinking that she had, perhaps, deserved the rebuke. She folded clothes carefully, leaving aside one of her favorite gowns, and also the tailed riding coat, fawn breeches and leather boots that David had worn the first time she saw him. She smoothed the linen stock with her hands, wishing out loud for a heated iron. David laughed at her.

"Would you have me mistaken for a London dandy? I believe I will be comfortable in plain clothes. We land at midday and the heat will be considerable."

"A dandy? You?" Laurie looked at him teasingly. "Where are your silk kneebreeches, your figured waist-coat? Even if you managed the fancy clothes needed, that great beard of yours would destroy your pretense."

His hand went up defensively to his beard, his dark eyes quizzical. "You disapprove of my beard, Laurie? Would you like it gone?"

She straightened from the trunk she was filling and

gave him a slow smile. "I very much like your beard. It is so delightfully soft against my skin."

He rose, laughing, and swept her up into his arms, pressing his face into the opening of her wrapper, nuzzling her breasts. "I will wear what you have chosen for our landing," he said, muffled, "or walk naked on the dock if you prefer." He lifted his head to look into her eyes. "If the truth were known, there is little I could refuse you . . ."

His face in her bosom had darkened the turquoise eyes, parted the soft lips. Her body was warm and yielding in his arms. He watched as the tip of her tongue moistened the corner of her mouth and then he swung abruptly to sink down into the bunk with her. Struggling out of their clothing, they moved to the inner side of the bunk and lay panting in each others arms.

"I pity Burdick," David said hoarsely, "who can only look at you and yearn . . ." He traced a dark, winging brow with one finger and kissed first one eye shut, and then the other. "Your eyes alone could drive a man wild, cause him to fling caution to the winds . . ." His mouth moved to hers, his tongue thrusting possessively, and she felt his strong body move involuntarily, arching symbolically against her side. For the first time, David was not in control of his passion, and she knew it when his arms went around her, crushing her to him so tightly she couldn't breathe. Pushing against his broad chest, gasping for air, she felt him drag her beneath him, and then he had thrust into her, with a hoarse, triumphant sound, straining his hard loins against the soft cradle of her thighs. "Mine," he said, staring down at her, "You are mine . . ." The words seemed to take away his urgency and he held her more gently, burying his face in her neck, his teeth closing in a soft bite, his tongue tasting her flesh as he began the slow arching rhythm of mating. Beneath her, his hands moved down her back and cupped her buttocks, long fingers kneading the soft flesh. "Come with me," he whispered, his hot breath in her ear. "Come with me, my darling, my love . . ."

Closing her eyes, Laurie sighed and turned her head, making room for the bearded face. She felt fluid, without will, part of his body, her heartbeat a counterpart of his. Rippling with motion like the ship they were on, she could feel the first rolling beat of pleasure beginning . . .

Later, as Laurie slipped from the bunk and hurriedly finished their packing, David dressed and came to her before leaving the cabin. Holding her, he smoothed back her hair tenderly.

"Truly, Laurie, I did not suspect you of encouraging Burdick. But you are so young and beautiful, with no knowledge of men. You are vulnerable, and must be very careful."

She wound her arms around his neck and kissed him. Instinctively, she knew he *had* doubted her. It was the reason for his rough, uncontrolled passion, his assertion of ownership. "I will never want anyone but you," she whispered. "You are my true mate."

His arms tightened, and he smiled. But deep in the brown eyes Laurie thought she could still see a shadow.

When the brig, close hauled, ghosted into harbor, David and Laurie stood in the middle of their pile of baggage and watched. The harbor was clogged with vessels, a forest of tall masts stretching to the sky and small fishing boats dotting the calm, protected surface. Two small boats rowed by shouting Negroes came to pull and shove the brig to a berth at the merchandise docks. Standing there, watching the ship, was a man in soiled, loose pantaloons, a flapping shirt and a kerchief tied around his head. His face was split by a grin, and as the brig slid along the pilings he shouted up at them.

"What have you for me?"

Captain Martin stepped to the rail. "All you could want except credit! Open your warehouses if you can pay!"

The grin grew wider. "*If* I can pay? I can load you

with sugar enough to sink you, or rum enough to float you!''

A wave of laughter from bystanders ended the exchange, but there were more calls as the laughter died down. Laurie was too fascinated by her first sight of Barbados to listen. It was so flamboyant, so colorful. The Negroes, laughing and shining with perspiration as they rowed the small boats, were clothed in rags of red and blue, bright yellows that served as shirts, their wiry black legs protruded from baggy pants torn off at the knee. And on the docks were the same vibrant colors, seeming so natural under the brilliant sun. Beyond the line of warehouses she could see the town rising as the land sloped steadily upward from the harbor. There were lines of solid buildings on streets bowered by an astonishing array of flowering shrubs and large trees. But, except for that tropical growth, it looked completely familiar. She turned to David in surprise.

''The settlers brought England with them. The buildings, the houses . . . I will feel as if we are living in our own countryside.''

''Wait,'' he said. ''There are miles to go to our home.'' His eyes were on the dock, watching someone in the crowd. ''There is one of our neighbors,'' he said in a lower tone. ''Not the pleasantest, by far, but the closest, and, since he has seen us, the first one you will meet.''

Laurie followed his gaze, picking out a thick-bodied, short-legged man who was wearing a heavy coat and black knee breeches as if angrily defying the heat. He was standing and talking with the man who had called out to them. As well as Laurie could see, his face beneath his wide-brimmed hat was stern, with a thin mouth set in disapproving lines. As she watched he turned and went back into the shade cast by the warehouse behind him. Mopping his face with a large handkerchief, he stared toward the brig, his gaze finding David again.

"He means to wait for you," Laurie said softly. "Perhaps he has a reason."

"A lecture, no doubt. A continually contentious man, who believes we need much instruction in running our plantation. I am glad I have an excuse to leave quickly." David grinned down at her, his face suddenly boyish and happy. "Even Prentiss Bailey should understand my haste in taking my bride home."

They had scarcely set foot on the dock and dispatched Ham for a carriage when Prentiss Bailey approached. Laurie studied him during the brief greeting and introduction. He removed his hat to acknowledge her and hastily replaced it against the sun, but not before she had seen the dirty patches of grey hair on an otherwise bald head and the bulging eyes. He repelled her, and she employed woman's prerogative and did not offer her hand but merely nodded. He turned immediately to David.

"I am glad you have finally returned," he began, with an air that said plainly that young Covington had been negligent. "For I trust you have more influence with your father than I have. Bartram is again indulging your slaves and I cannot reason with him."

David's only answer was an arch of thick brows, but that seemed sufficient encouragement.

"He has given them even more new provision grounds, ten full acres, mind you! And, even more foolishly, an extra day each week to tend the crops. Furthermore, the acreage is just on our common boundary and my slaves have seen it. They are grumbling to their overseers, wanting the same treatment! He has increased my problems immensely, for my slaves are a troublesome lot at best."

"You would be wise to give them new acres," David said calmly. "Your great gang, like ours, is busy finishing up in the boiler houses, but the second gang is idle, and may as well be working for themselves. It will save on buying food when the work grows heavy, for they much prefer their own fresh produce. I am surprised you have not thought of it yourself, Prentiss."

"Entirely unnecessary," Prentiss said contemptuously, "since I do not feed my workers in the lavish, wasteful manner you practice. That ten acres will be more profitable in cane."

David shrugged. "You will spend that profit and more some night on a dark beach, buying contraband slaves. It seems advisable to keep your crews healthy now that England has forbidden us to buy more. But I will not argue further, sir, for I see Ham coming with our carriage. I am anxious to introduce my wife to my father."

Bailey's bulging eyes returned to Laurie sourly. "The lady appears delicate," he said, in a tone that made it no compliment. "It is to be hoped she will not find the climate here debilitating, as so many English ladies do." He turned away, adding with an exaggerated, false piousness, "Both the climate and other conditions in Barbados can be fatal, as your father well knows."

"The devil's own whelp," David muttered, his face grim. "I would like to call him out, old as he is, but he is too clever to give a direct insult."

Laurie was silent, watching David and Ham load the baggage onto the carriage rack. She was appalled by Bailey's coarseness, which amounted to cruelty. She had learned that David's mother had lived only a year after coming to Barbados. She had died as David was born, and his father, David had told her, had never married again. There had been no woman in the family at Silversea since then, and Laurie had wondered more than once how she would be received.

But now, climbing thankfully into the carriage, for the sun bore down with an intensity she had never before experienced, she was not thinking apprehensively about her welcome. There was too much excitement, too much to see in this little island in the great ocean, to bother with dreary thoughts.

Driving through Bridgetown the echo of England grew stronger. There were more teashops than one could imagine, and familiar names on the signs swinging over typical English establishments. Even the streets wore signs like Broad Street, Lightfoot Lane, Trafalgar Square. On the outskirts of the town were several new wooden houses, large and fine, built in the latest of English architecture. Set back from the road in groves of trees, they looked grand indeed.

But, as David had intimated, once they had left the town the familiarity was gone. The land rose gently, yet the roads they traveled were in shallow ravines, at times far below the level of the fields around them. Occasionally they passed over a sturdy stone bridge or went suddenly down into hollows where a dripping profusion of strange, thick underbrush and massive trees pressed in on either side. Then the road would rise again, until they could look across acres of silver gray, sword-shaped leaves.

"Ratoons," explained David as Laurie stared. "The second growth of cane. It produces sugar, but not of the quality or quantity of the first growth, which will be planted in late fall." He smiled. "You will not believe its height. When full grown it is well over Ham's head."

It was hard to imagine such a giant crop, especially on fields which seemed unending, rising and falling on either side, gradually growing higher in the distance on the right, dipping lower on the left, the leeward side of the island. Only an occasional windmill, turning in the breeze, or a tall spinney of mahogany trees broke the monotony of the view.

Once, far from the road, Laurie saw a group of laborers in the fields. They moved slowly back and forth in the sun, all ages and sizes, from stooped old men to children, brightly dressed in the vivid colors they preferred. Slaves. She said nothing to David, remembering she had promised to wait and see, and in any event they seemed no different from field laborers in England, though perhaps better suited to the tropical sun. The visions she had had of cringing, naked savages constantly belabored by long whips held by snarling white men seemed childish now. Still, she thought, they cannot leave the field, cannot seek out a better life . . .

In an effort to forget the thought Laurie asked questions about Silversea and David's father, who still didn't know that David was bringing home a wife. She wondered if he would be surprised.

"Indeed not," David said, wryly. "Since he sent me to find one, he would be surprised only if I came home alone."

Laurie smiled uncertainly. "I do hope he approves."

David took her hand. "You amaze me. You must know you are the answer to his prayers. A lovely, healthy, English daughter-in-law, possessing the blood of heroes. But, you must be prepared to find him watching you constantly, with eyes like a hawk, searching for signs of approaching motherhood."

Laurie laughed. "With your assistance, I hope to oblige him. Which would he wish first, a granddaughter or grandson?"

"He will never be satisfied until you bear a son," David said. "So perhaps that is what you should plan for your firstborn." He was looking at her with amused tenderness and Laurie thought that it was indeed possible to plan or do anything as long as they planned it together. She sighed and leaned back against him.

"Very well. A son first, and then a daughter. Why are men always so set on a boy?"

"As you may have guessed," David said, "in his case it is thwarted ambition. My father sets great store by nobility, and he dreams of a time when either I or my son will succeed Lord Peter in the House."

For a moment Laurie was back in England, in Mayfair, among the ambitions, the petty jealousies, the immoralities and overweening affectations of the nobility. "I hope Lord Oldenburgh lives forever," she said vigorously. "I would hate to return to London as the wife of a lord."

"Perhaps we can avoid it," David said, laughing, "and in any case, it is not imminent, and your first sight of your new home is. As we top the next rise you must look to the east . . ."

Laurie sat forward eagerly, her hands clasping the edge of the window. As the horses trotted up the last of the rise she saw the great house of Silversea in the distance, its wide windows glinting in the late afternoon sun. Surrounded by immense mahogany trees, it sat high on a knoll like a ship in an ocean of silver green waves.

But the fields before it—the broad avenue that led to it—all, all were filled by an army of running black bodies, whose bare backs gleamed in the light of the torches they carried, whose knives flashed bright as they drew them. Faintly, the hoarse, rolling rumble of an angry mob came to her ears . . .

Crying out, she turned and flung herself into David's arms. "The slaves! Hundreds of them! Attacking the house . . ." Shuddering, she buried her face in his shoulder. "What shall we do?"

David grasped her shoulders, pushing her away to look into her terrified eyes. "Laurie! There is nothing there, nothing but the house and the fields. It is only the waving leaves. Look! Look again . . ." He forced her around, his own face pale with sympathy, jolted by the expression in her eyes.

She looked, and thank God he was right. She sank back into the seat as the carriage jostled down the other side of the rise and the house was again lost to view. She breathed deeply, trying to rid herself of the fear her own imagination had conceived.

"I would have sworn . . ." She looked at David, shamefaced. "I even thought I could hear them . . ."

He put an arm around her again. "You are over-wrought, and your mind always seems to be on slavery, on the terrible lot of our workers. You will soon see how

much worry and pain you have expended over nothing.''
He smiled and touched her chin with a finger, tilting her
downcast face to his. "And never a word about your new
home. Didn't you like it?''

Laurie laughed, and the laughter dispelled her fear.
"The queen herself would envy me, living there," she
said. "It is as beautiful as any castle.''

"We will be happy there," David said, like a promise.

Chapter Seven

As they turned into the avenue that led to the great house Laurie leaned on the open window and watched in wonder. The avenue was lined with trees of orange and tamarind, with shrubs brilliantly green of leaf, flaming red with blossoms. And ahead, past Ham's muscular thigh and dusty boot, his long whip waving over the horses' plump backs, their nodding, tasseled heads, was the most amazing of mansions.

Like welcoming arms, a double flight of steps curved outward, leading up to a pillared portico. The base of the house was rough native stone and above it the three storys of white painted wood blazed with wide windows, each with dark blue shutters laid open. A mansard roof, like a dark gray bonnet trimmed with red chimneys, lay over it all protectively. A green lawn, dotted with magnificent trees, sloped away in each direction, making the imposing structure seem higher yet, imperious and commanding. She dropped back into the seat and looked at David, half frightened.

"*I* am to be mistress of such a home? Truly, David, it overwhelms me. I will not be able . . ."

"You will have no trouble," he said abruptly, not turning his head from his window. "Do not concern yourself. They have seen us. There is Father, coming out on the portico, and the servants gathering behind him." He had stiffened, the hands resting on his knees were tense, his voice sounded flat, and Laurie gazed at him uncertainly. Only a moment before he had been warm and indulgent, but now he seemed hardly aware of her presence. She turned again to look toward the house.

Bartram Covington was easily identified, even in the shade of the portico roof. Tall and bulky, with an air of authority, he stood gazing toward the carriage like an emperor, his high-held head emphasized by a mass of snow-white hair and beard. Dressed in a light linen coat and tan breeches, he overshadowed the smaller, dark figures around him.

"Your father . . ." In spite of the distance, Laurie was half whispering, "David—he looks like Moses."

David laughed wryly. "How discerning of you, Laurie. I truly believe he thinks he *is* Moses, with his own Ten Commandments tucked under his arm." He turned and looked at her with a thick eyebrow cocked. "But that need not worry you, my dear. I imagine he will inscribe your slightest wish on his Tablet, as another immutable Covington Law."

She laughed lightly—how else take such a ridiculous assumption?—but his tone shocked her. There was that bitterness that always seemed to be present when he spoke of his father. She was certain, somehow, that he didn't realize it himself. Perhaps it came from some old trouble between them, and was now only a habit, and the trouble long forgotten. She wanted to touch him comfortingly, but there was the carriage block before them, and they were stopping . . .

Stepping out, her hand on David's arm, Laurie watched the striking old man come down the steps, followed closely but respectfully by a veritable flock of uniformed black women. They arrived just as she and David stepped from the carriage block and Bartram Covington grasped his son's hand. But his eyes ignored the blackbearded face and centered on Laurie, raking her with a searching gaze. David laughed and dropped the welcoming hand.

"It is not often that I follow your orders so closely,

Father. But as you must realize, this is my bride. Formerly Laurie Stepney, daughter of Sir Hugh Stepney, granddaughter of the Laird of Stepney Downs, Scotland. Pure, noble blood, Father, straight from the shores of Great Britain.'' David's voice was tight, his head high, his half-closed eyes looking down the strong arch of his nose arrogantly.

Laurie glanced at him in amazement. It was unlike him to be so utterly disrespectful, she thought, and then forgot the thought, for as she put her slim hand in the strong, wrinkled fingers of Bartram Covington, David slipped an arm around her and added, ''Strangely enough, I find her well nigh perfect. And I am certain you will, also.''

It appeared that Bartram Covington ignored his son's words and attitude completely. His faded blue eyes were moving over Laurie in a kind of possessive delight. ''I remember your grandfather well, my dear. And his son, too, in his youth. One is not likely to forget Young Hugh's eyes, especially when repeated in the face of a beautiful woman.''

Laurie's heart warmed immediately, she was delighted that he had known Old Hugh and had even remembered her father. ''Thank you, sir,'' she breathed. ''You are very kind. . . .''

''*You* are the one who is kind,'' Bartram said expansively, ''to have graced Silversea with your presence . . .'' He hesitated, again sweeping her with a glance that seemed to note for the first time precisely how small she was, and how slender. She could almost read his thoughts. The Stepneys had been very large men, and it was possible that he had never seen Desirée. Tiny Desirée . . . His eyes came back to her face, questioning.

''You are . . . strong, my dear? Able to stand our debilitating climate? And the rigors of plantation life?''

A memory flashed through Laurie's mind: Her grandfather's measuring glance as he chose which young female lambs would be kept as brood ewes, which would be sent to the butcher. She could feel the blood rising in her face, the spurt of indignant anger that caused it. She raised her chin and looked him in the eye.

"I was raised on Scotland's moors," she said shortly. "You need have no fear that I will sicken." Her pleasure in the meeting was gone. It seemed so very clear that her role here was decided long before she arrived. Her importance was to hinge solely on her ability to bear a child. Her father-in-law had not been able to resist questioning her before she was even in the door!

Behind her, she heard David laugh and then felt his arm tighten around her waist. "Don't doubt the lady's stamina," he told his father. "On the brig she was as comfortable as any sailor, and her appetite never flagged."

Laurie watched Bartram's questioning gaze go past her to Ham, as if for corroboration. Ham nodded solemnly, and as Bartram's glance came back to her it eased into warm acceptance. She fought a hysterical impulse to laugh and inquire to which butcher she would have been sent without these testimonials.

"Come, daughter," Bartram was saying, reaching for her hand. "I will present your staff to you. They will be anxious to know your status here." He drew her to the group of brightly turbaned women behind him and proceeded to present her as the "Mistress". At least, that was what she supposed, since he spoke an odd mixture of slovenly English and an incomprehensible dialect, with the word "Mistress" the only clear note. The women's faces beamed on her with a childlike curiosity and the pleasure that comes from new company. They were not at all intimidating, though they seemed confused and uncertain as she insisted on shaking hands with each of them. A round dozen of maids! And Bartram explaining on the side that the kitchen maids and cook were not present, since they were hard at work preparing a dinner.

"When we saw your coach turn in," he added, "I sent word to the kitchen. You can be assured that they are doing their best at this moment." He hesitated. "You will have difficulty at first, understanding them and giving them orders, but I shall be at your command to interpret."

"It will not be necessary for you to trouble yourself," David broke in smoothly. "Ham will supervise the servants until Laurie can make herself understood." Without waiting for his father to answer, he turned to Ham. "Put our baggage in the master suite, Ham, and see that it is made ready for us immediately." He swung back to look at his father's startled face. "I trust the other house is ready for your occupancy, Father? Good! Now, if you have completed your greeting, I will escort my wife into my home."

Her hand on David's arm, Laurie mounted the steps with a clear impression that the house before her had just changed ownership, rather more suddenly than Bartram Covington had expected. It was like a game, with two contestants and one pawn. Herself. And she seemed to have given David a decided advantage, but certainly without intention, for she still felt, in spite of his measuring looks and doubts, that David's father should be a member of their household.

Inside, her thoughts were swept away by awe. The immense entry hall would have encompassed the entire lower story of her mother's Mayfair home. Paneled in mahogany, the curving walls soared twenty feet or more over her head, and a broad staircase led up to a most impressive curving gallery, edged with a railing of intricately carved balustrades. It served, she could see, as a passageway to the second-floor rooms, for halls and doorways led from it. She dropped David's arm and stood still, looking around at the expanse of shining wood floor, Oriental carpets and benches, chairs and tables enough to fill an anteroom for the queen. It might well be a monumental task to manage such a house, to handle so many servants. And, most importantly, to raise a family in the midst of it. But surely, if it could be done, a Stepney could do it. She smiled at the two waiting men.

"It is very beautiful," she said graciously, "and most luxurious."

Bartram's face brightened. "You have only begun to discover the charms of Silversea House," he said, taking the lead again. "Come into the drawing room, my dear, and rest while your rooms are prepared. I'll call for some sherry . . ."

Seated in a low-backed, comfortable chair, sipping the sherry, Laurie was glad of the strong, warming wine that eased her sinking heart. It was such a very large room, filled with a bewildering array of furniture and a profusion of art objects. There were huge paintings on the wall, Ming vases, crystal vases, bisque figurines. There were great crystal bowls that held roses and then more crystal, hanging in fountains of prisms from chandeliers. And all of it polished and shining, lighted by wide windows that were draped with embroidered linen but open to the sunshine and air. It was possible to understand why there were so many servants, and also why David had spoken regretfully of losing the housekeeper with such an odd name . . . Molenga?

She sat up, finishing the last of the sherry in one gulp as she considered that now she would be responsible for keeping the servants up to the mark. And this was only one of the rooms! She glanced at the other end of it, where David and his father were pouring yet another glass of brandy and talking in low tones.

Suddenly tired and yet restless, Laurie rose and wandered to the still-open door, seeing two of the maids trotting up the wide staircase with boxes and her bonnet case in their arms. Passing them, on his way down, was Ham with a large but unfamiliar trunk balanced on a shoulder. It took but a moment to realize who the trunk must belong to, and why it was leaving. Laurie turned back into the room and set her full skirts swaying with the quickness of her steps toward David and his father.

"Father Covington!" She laid a hand on Bartram's arm, looking up at his startled face imploringly. "David has told me of your plan to leave us and live apart, simply because he is now married. I understand you believe it is a generous gesture, and so it is, perhaps, but it would grieve me. To think of you living alone and lonely, when . . . when there is so much room here . . ." Her voice trailed off as she saw the two faces staring down at her and seeming, for once, to share the same thought. David's hand closed over her arm, pulling her fingers from Bartram's arm, drawing her to his side. But it was Bartram who spoke.

"A lovely sentiment, my dear Laurie, and I appreciate it. Yet I must disagree." The light from a nearby window glinted on the white hair and beard and gave him a prophetic appearance. "David is now master here, and there is never room for two masters on a plantation—nor in a house." His smile was both wry and indulgent. "I will be quite comfortable, my dear. I have many set ways, many likes and dislikes, and my housekeeper knows them all. Molenga and I will settle together quite well."

"But . . ." She stopped again, for David's grasp had shifted to her waist and now it tightened painfully.

"You seem distraught," David said coolly. "Fatigue, very likely. And we have dawdled long enough over our brandy, Father. Surely the maids have readied our rooms by this time." He tossed down the remainder of his brandy and set the glass down. "If you will excuse us . . . ?"

"Indeed, and my apologies to you both. Naturally you are tired, I should have remembered the long sea voyage and dusty trip from Bridgetown." There was a hint of irony in Bartram's faded eyes as he added: "I shall make my farewells at dinner tonight."

In spite of mixed feelings Laurie was wise enough to be silent as David took her up the staircase and along the grand gallery at a pace that had her trotting to keep up with his booted stride. He opened the farthest door on the right and peered in.

"It is ready and they have gone," he announced. "And now I will have a word with you." He pushed her inside and shut the door, leaning against it and looking down at her. "I tried to dissuade you on the brig when you talked of keeping my father here, and I thought I had you convinced. It is embarrassing to find out so awkwardly that you meant to interfere."

His injustice made anger flare in her turquoise eyes. "You gave me permission to try! You said—"

"I know what I said," he interrupted coldly. "But certainly I thought you listened as I explained my reasons. Nor would I have expected you to mention it again without consulting me."

"Am I not to have thoughts or feelings of my own? Are you so used to ordering slaves about that you consider me in the same light?" Laurie's independence, so submerged as she followed his lead on the ship, rose full and strong. "I am your *wife!* My wishes should be as important to you as your own!"

She had drawn herself to her full height, which did not quite come level with his shoulder. Her eyes blazed brilliant blue-green in a pale face, her breasts heaved beneath the tight-buttoned bodice of her traveling suit. He gazed down at her for a full minute before he opened his mouth, and then it was to laugh uncontrollably. He reached and scooped her stiff body into his arms, holding her across his chest, and he was still laughing, his eyes gleaming above the black beard.

"You have much to learn, little spitfire. And I do believe you have forgotten your bargain, have you not?

You are my wife, yes—for the sole purpose of providing me with an heir and gracing my home. There was no mention of needing your help in conducting my other affairs, was there?''

She struggled, though the feeling of his arms and his body against hers was weakening. "But some of your affairs are mine, also, and your father is now part of my family! If I want him in our home . . ." She stopped, staring into the eyes so close to her own. "This *is* my home, too, isn't it?"

"Is it?" he countered, his voice dry. "I thought your home was in Scotland."

She shut her eyes in quick pain, rebellion seeping from her. It was true, she had forgotten the bargain. She had forgotten everything but the glorious fact that she was married to the man she loved and beginning a new life. "Yes," she said, half strangled by her reluctance to admit it. "My home is in Scotland and ever will be. You have lived up to your part of our bargain and I am overstepping my part. So . . . if you prefer that your father live elsewhere, then . . . then I should not interfere."

"Now you are being sensible," he said gently, and put her down on her feet. Smoothing back a lock of hair, he cupped her face in his large palms and kissed her, a quick, light caress that barely touched her lips. "Look around your new domain, my dear, and rest. I believe you will find a bath drawn and your clothing close at hand. Put on a pretty gown for dinner, for my father will enjoy seeing the latest fashions from London."

She watched him leave, his air that of a man who has solved a trifling problem and must now be about more important affairs. If there was anything that could put her in her place, it was that attitude. *No wonder*, she thought dully, *that his father examined me so oddly. Here, I am no more than a breeding ewe. I have contracted the use of my body and what household skills*

I can learn. And, as David has just pointed out, what charm and fashion I can lend his establishment. He has no use for my mind . . . or my heart. I was a fool to think he might learn, at least, to respect me.

She turned, noting with surprise but little pleasure that the master suite took up the whole south side of the house. She was standing in a lovely sitting room, her feet deep in a cream-colored Persian rug with a pattern of pastel roses, twining green stems and artfully delineated leaves. The furniture here was quite delicate, a combination of French and Oriental designs, with inlaid wood and ivory, and much gold decoration. The wide windows were dressed with sheer silk draperies, blowing gently from the fresh sea breeze, giving everything a light and airy look. To the east, a wide arch led her to investigate the rest of the apartment.

In here, the bed, canopied in pale rose silk looped back with golden cords, a lace coverlet spread on the wide, thickly stuffed mattress. Immense chests, a large, ornate armoire—the horde of maids must have been very busy indeed—her clothes and David's unpacked and inside, folded or hanging, with small bags of sweet-scented herbs.

She went on, feeling travel-stained and weary, and opened a wide door to find a dressing room and bath, where a huge tub was filled with sparkling, cool water. Her spirits lifted, gazing at it. Perhaps this was not her true home, but certainly she was expected to make herself at home in it! Her head rising, she went back and selected a silk dressing gown.

It is not possible, she thought firmly, divesting herself quickly of the traveling suit, the petticoats and lace-trimmed drawers, *that a Stepney can live here and not make her presence felt! No matter how they think, I am not a nonentity, nor a brood ewe. David may never love me, and indeed I have no right to expect it, but he will know I am here . . .* Naked she went to the tub and got in, sinking beneath the cool water with a gasp of pleasure, her black hair floating around her face in a gleaming, wet cloud. I will, she thought with more bravado than confidence, make my mark on Silversea . . .

Later, wrapped in the silk robe, her hair toweled almost dry and the sweet smell of soap and rosewater adding to the delicious languor she felt, she found the wide, soft bed irresistible in spite of the beginning twilight outside that told her it was time to dress for dinner. She turned down the lace coverlet neatly and climbed in between soft sheets. A short nap would restore her flagging spirits, and oh . . . this was so much better than that narrow bunk on the brig . . .

Lips touched hers, and then a hand slipped beneath her shoulders and lifted her into a half-sitting position. She opened her eyes and looked, dazed, at David's dark face, the brown eyes amused, his grin white in a freshly trimmed beard. He was pushing pillows behind her and the room was dim around them, only the glow of a few lamps coming through the pale rose draperies of the bed. She sank back on the pillows and stared at him in surprise.

"I have brought you a late supper," he said, and pulled a small table to the side of the bed, sitting down beside her and indicating a tray on the table. "You would have been starved before breakfast."

Her eyes went to the windows, black squares of night outside the glow of the room, and then back to him, guiltily. "Why didn't you wake me? Your father will think me unpardonably rude."

"My father thinks you are beautiful and very kind. When I told him you were fast asleep he heartily agreed with my decision to let you rest." David was taking covers from dishes, the silverware clattering on the tray. Shaking out a big square of white linen, he laid it across her lap. "In all honesty, he also thinks you too young and weak for life in Barbados, and asked me quite pointedly why I did not pick a sturdier mate." His smile widened as she gasped in angry surprise. "I told him I had offered for several young ladies who were sturdier by far, but that they lacked your courage."

"I can see," Laurie said stiffly, "that it is fortunate I did not come down for dinner. My presence would have dampened your interesting discussion." Her eyes sparked. "And, did you tell him of our agreement, and how I proposed to you?"

"I did not. That is a matter between us and no one else. Now, stop talking. I intend to feed you, and I want no messy droppings on our sheets." He was now holding a silver bowl of steaming, savory seafood and rice in one hand, a laden fork in the other, and as the fork advanced Laurie's mouth opened automatically.

"Ummmm . . ." The fish, or whatever product of the sea it might be, came in small and tender pieces, covered with a delicious sauce flavored with curry, and the rice beneath it was fluffy and hot. She chewed and swallowed and opened her mouth eagerly as the fork approached again. Several bites later, with sips of white wine between, she asked David if he thought her too young and weak to feed herself.

He laughed and handed her the stemmed wine glass. "You may attend the drinking. But I find an odd pleasure in giving you your food." His big body relaxed as he placed the bowl on her stomach and stretched himself across her thighs, propping himself on one elbow while with the other hand he continued to bring forksful to her waiting lips. His eyes were shining, his firm mouth half smiling . . .

He truly did seem to be enjoying himself, Laurie thought, feeling helplessly childlike as she accepted and chewed obediently. He was nurturing her as gently as any woman might do, just as she had decided he was a heartless wretch. A wretch who would exile his father from his home and treat his wife as no more than a receptacle for his seed. A wretch she happened to love, though surely he had never requested love from her, so she couldn't blame him for that. In the half-shadows of the canopied bed she studied him covertly, thinking how handsome he was with the trimmed beard and freshly washed, curling black hair. He had dressed for the evening in a fine silk shirt and gray satin breeches, and even the easy movement of his arm as he scooped up food and presented it to her brought a fascinating rolling and rippling of sinuous muscles beneath the sheen of the clinging cloth. He seemed a splendid and powerful animal, full of vitality and dangerous strength, and her stomach, already warmed by the heat of the silver bowl that sat atop it, grew warmer by far, licked by desire. Her eyes glistened, the accepting lips grew softer yet as he fed her, and beneath the silk robe her breasts swelled with an alarming sensitivity. The bowl was nearly empty when she waved it away and handed back her empty glass.

"I have never dined so well with so little effort on my part," she said rather shakily. "Though I still cannot see why you find it pleasurable to feed me."

He had sat up to replace the bowl and glass on the tray and push the table out of sight. Now he swung back across her and flicked the napkin away, tossing it toward the table. His hand slipped into the loose closure of the robe and found a swollen, taut breast, closing softly around it. "Because your appetites continually astound me," he said huskily. "You are so eager for life . . . for food and lovemaking . . ." he stared at her, his eyes darkening. "So young, so small and delicately made, yet burning with great desires . . ."

She wanted to tell him that what he said was true, but had not been true until he himself had wakened her to joy, that she had been no more than a prim child until his magic touched her. But she was dizzy with the slow caressing of his hand, with the look in his eyes, and she could think of nothing but lessening the distance between them. She curled her legs back and rose to her knees, swaying toward him, untying her robe to allow his hand freedom, winding her arms around his neck. The sweet scent of her warm body rose around him, the cloud of her hair enveloped their faces as she kissed him. "Feed me more." she whispered. "Feed me love . . ."

He rolled backward as smoothly as a great cat, lifting her as she went with him so that his face settled between her breasts, his hands sliding sensuously over her back. She gasped with pleasure as the beard and hot mouth moved slowly, biting and licking until she throbbed with exquisite pain. Then, holding her, he turned until she lay beneath him, naked in the silken crumple of the open wrapper, and sat up to look at her.

She watched him, watched the dark eyes rove from her panting mouth to the damp, thrusting breasts, the handspan of waist. He laid a hand, dark and masculine, on the soft whiteness of her belly and stroked slowly downward over the black curls to close on the soft inner flesh of a thigh. Then his eyes came back to hers with an indescribable look of triumph, like some savage king with a captive. "Here," he whispered, "you are mine. How I hated those days on the brig . . ." He leaned down to her parted lips and took them, his tongue gentle but inexorable, slowly searching her mouth with deep thrusts of symbolic possession while his hand roamed, skillfully teasing.

Her body quivered and arched, her hands softly frantic, sliding over the silk shirt, feeling the heat beneath yet unable to find an opening and slip within. She moaned in frustration and he laughed hoarsely, sliding from the bed to disrobe.

"Be kind," she whispered as he came back to her. "Don't make me wait . . . I am aching for you."

Hovering over her, immense in the dimness, dark with the mat of hair that covered his chest, he eased into the tender clasp of her thighs, incoherent sound rising from his chest as he took her. "Never have I felt so welcome," he said, delight rippling through his hoarse voice, "Nor so graciously received . . ."

She laughed softly, twisting, tipping her slender hips to allow him full entry. "Never have I been so happy to have you . . ." Her hands, free at last on bare skin, smoothed down the thick muscles of his back to circle silkily on hard buttocks as they began to contract and relax. "Oh, David . . . Oh, darling . . ."

And they were suddenly one, a rippling, fiery being that made soft sounds and groaned, moving blindly upward, rising to a height of passion she had never found nor imagined before. Shaken by the force of completion they descended slowly, still surging in repeated shocks of intense pleasure that were sweeter yet, because unexpected. In the end she was gasping for breath, half-smothered by his panting weight but not minding, thinking dazedly that it might be a glorious way to die.

He rolled on his side, taking the weight from her yet leaving a possessive thigh across her legs.

"You may have driven me out of my mind," he said, softly and wryly. "I have an ungodly urge to lock you in this room where no one else can see you or touch you." He laughed raggedly. "I would tend you carefully, Laurie. Bathe you and feed you, and most tenderly caress you . . ."

Her half-closed eyes opened fully and sparkled up at him, delighted by his nonsense. "I will be here for you when my more practical side has finished overseeing the business of this great house you have saddled me with." She studied his flushed face, her eyes growing soft. "Here, I will lie always in your arms, open always to your caresses . . .'' She drew him down again until his bearded face was in her neck, and then closed her eyes in a different kind of ecstasy. In this dreamy state it seemed possible that this big man, so strong and unreasonably cool at times, might some day be as much hers as she was his . . .

Chapter Eight

IN THE WEEKS THAT FOLLOWED LAURIE STRUGGLED TO learn the ways of the household, for though Ham was at her service to explain, to translate her orders to the servants, she knew he was needed elsewhere. David would ask her if she could spare Ham for an hour or so, and take him off, down the long slope to the far fields or to the barracas—long, communal living quarters for the field slaves. Some of the slaves, Laurie learned, had their own cabins. Small wooden buildings painted bright colors, with a fruit tree or two for shade and invariably a plot of sweet potatoes. These were the high-ranking laborers, those trained in carpentry or running the mills. There were often women and children about those cabins, though David had told her that family life was not encouraged and that most of the slaves were not interested in forming ties, but simply copulated and bred much as farm animals. Pregnant females were excused from field work and brought to bed at the time of birth in the dispensary, a building set aside from the rest and with a midwife in charge. Occasionally a doctor came from Speight's Town, which lay to the north, and treated any ill or injured.

All this Laurie either saw from a distance or heard from David, for he had expressly forbidden her to go near the barracas or the other cabins, or even to wander near the fields where slaves might be working. The overseers, most of them freedmen, came up to the house often, but aside from hastily snatching off a hat and executing an awkward bow, they simply stood, silent, and waited for David to appear and take them off to talk.

And, as Laurie leaned on the garden wall, for the slave community was within sight though not within hearing distance there, the scene below seemed busy and peaceful. Idyllic, at times, when the young children were out rolling and playing in the wide-trodden paths around the barracas, the women set to tend them gathering in knots as women do anywhere to gossip and laugh. Without deep thought Laurie began to accept slavery, if not as an ideal state, then as a practical custom. A custom mostly beneficial to the workers and certainly convenient for the planters.

In any event she had little time to consider it, with the myriad things she had to learn. Food, she discovered with relief and then delight, was never a problem. There were so many choices. Seafood included both fish and shellfish foreign to Laurie but delicious. There was lamb and mutton from their own sheep. Fowl was a staple, and pork, also. Vegetables were plentiful from their own garden, and there were wines and liquors kept on hand as if for a banquet. And the fruits! The overseers brought basketloads to the kitchen. Mangos and mangosteens, bananas and wild limes, citrus and Barbados cherries and a kind of rough textured, misshapen fruit that when cut yielded a custardlike filling both sweet and tart. The fruits were paid for. By custom all the produce from the fruit trees was considered the property of the slaves.

But when it came to the running of the house Laurie often regretted that Father Covington had taken the housekeeper with him. She had never seen the woman Molenga but she knew the shining perfection that had been Molenga's mark, and now there was dust in the corners, dull crystal, tarnished silver and even spots and stains on the rugs. Yet the round dozen of maids always appeared busy. Hating to bother Ham with small details, she fretted silently and then took action. Her hair tied up, an apron covering her gown, she started in on the small jobs herself.

"Mistress."

She turned, almost dropping the pan of vinegar-water in which she was rinsing a crystal vase. Ham had appeared as he always did, as silent as a genie rising from the center of the Persian rug. She gazed up at him, still a bit wary of the gigantic man. He held out a hand for the pan and without hesitation she gave it to him. It didn't seem wise to refuse.

"It is not proper," he said gravely, "for the maids to leave work for the Mistress. Give me a list of what has been neglected and I will take measures."

She bit her lip, knowing the criticism was as much for her as the maids, and then made out the list and returned the apron to the storeroom where she had found it. Half angry, she still knew he was right. She was supposed to act with authority, not knuckle under and do the work herself. But it irked her not to be able to communicate properly. The cook and two of the maids had a smattering of English, and it occurred to her that it would be easier to teach them English than it would be for her to learn three or four different dialects. She began simply with the two maids who had a few English words at their command, and lost no opportunity to add to their vocabulary.

"They learn quite rapidly," she said to David and his father. "It's surprising. But the most surprising part is that the effect doubles and triples. One maid tells another, and in the last two weeks all of them know the phrases and terms I have taught to just two."

They were sitting at dinner, with Bartram as a guest, and both men had been surprised by the alacrity with which a maid had followed one of Laurie's orders, issued in English.

"I suppose," Bartram said, "I could have taught them long ago. But since I had learned the dialects . . ." He stopped, smiling, his white beard lifting into bunches on his cheek. "It is possible I didn't consider them intelligent enough to learn."

Laurie raised her delicate brows. "But, with Ham as an example? He learned! David told me once that Ham learned from the same tutors as he, and was just as well educated." She sat back, waiting for one of them to say that Ham was half-white, and that gave him an advantage. David had never mentioned Ham's parentage or the fact that he was a half-breed, and she had wondered. Of course, she had never told him of William Burdick's illuminating explanation of freedmen, either. But she was curious . . .

"Ham is . . . different," Bartram said, his eyes sliding from her face. "Some of them are, you know. There are many different tribes in Africa. Some are much more advanced than others, more organized . . . possibly more intelligent." He coughed. "Certainly more aggressive."

"This is not a particularly entertaining subject," David said coolly. "If you wish to teach the maids English, Laurie, by all means do so. In the meantime, let us talk of something more interesting."

She was not puzzled by his coolness. David's attitude here was the same as it had been on the brig. In their suite he was ardent, open and companionable, a lover any woman would have adored. But in the presence of others he was distantly courteous. No one, she was sure, would ever guess he had the slightest regard for her. Remembering their bargain, she didn't complain, but followed his example. She never touched him nor said an affectionate word, and was completely unaware that her expressive face gave her away when she looked at him.

And there was one other place where David let down his guard, and in the silence that followed his remark she toyed with her food and smiled unconsciously, thinking of it. Southeast of the house, and out of sight, a long, gentle slope of thick grass ran down toward a precipice with a ravine below. The first sunlight touched this slope, drying the dew, and they often breakfasted there, with a picnic basket from the kitchen. The view was lovely, and in the deep ravine was a group of huge, oddly shaped rocks that particularly interested Laurie. The slanting rays of sunrise played with the shadows of the rocks, creating moving shapes of animals and beasts, filling the ravine with a miraculous population.

David laughed at her imagination, preferring to lie back in the grass and let her ply him with chilled fruit and cold fowl, and bits of the long loaves of bread wrapped in linen to keep them warm and buttery. Since the first night in the house the act of feeding each other had become sensual, and in this isolated spot their caresses were warm. Only this morning he had taken her, half-naked, the sight of her white thighs exposed in brilliant sunlight seeming to bring out his most primitive feelings. He had taken her fiercely, with deep sounds in his chest like the growls of a lion. Warm with the memory, she looked up, startled, as David spoke her name. He smiled faintly.

"Daydreaming, my love? Father asked you if you would like a party."

Laurie looked at Bartram, confused. "A party?"

"It's time, my dear. You have settled-in well, and will soon be lonely without friends. It's customary to have a reception to introduce a new family member to the other planters and their wives. There will be only a small gathering, and with help, I'm sure you can manage it."

"Oh! Oh, yes! I would like it very much."

David frowned. "I suppose we should, it's expected. But I, for one, find such affairs very boring."

"I ignored your mother's need for friends," Bartram said heavily, "and I am sure that loneliness added much to her illness."

David's brows shot up, his gaze roved critically over his father's wine-flushed face, as if he considered loneliness the least of his mother's problems. "Perhaps," he said shortly, and then turned to Laurie. "Have I been selfish, then? Would you like a party? Do you think you could manage it—the planning of food and the serving, the seating arrangements and other fol-de-rol?'' He sounded as if he were quite doubtful, and Laurie quailed inside. Formality was beyond her yet, and she knew it. Then she was suddenly inspired.

''Why not a garden party? Late afternoon in the garden is quite the coolest, nicest part of the day.'' Her imagination leaped as she warmed to the idea. ''We could set a long table with an abundance of food. We could put benches about, and light chairs—perhaps a shelter of palm fronds in case of rain. And, we could put the wine to cool in the stream that feeds the duck pond!''

Both of them stared, and then Bartram slapped the table with an open hand and began to laugh. ''Leave it to the young to think of frolics! Of course, a dinner *al fresco*. It will surprise our guests, but I wager they'll enjoy the cool air and the appetite that comes from eating out-of-doors . . .''

''So you would, indeed, like other company,'' David said slowly. His face was more somber yet, looking at Laurie's sparkling eyes, the flush of pleasure on her cheeks. ''You should have mentioned it . . . In any event, it shall be done.''

In the days that followed there were difficulties. The cook, whose name was Octavia, was frightened and confused by the plan, since she had never done anything like it before. But Ham understood, and Laurie left it to him to convince the cook while she consulted with David about a guest list.

Due to the distance between plantations the list was very short. David warned her immediately that it would be necessary to invite Prentiss Bailey, whose plantation adjoined theirs. He explained that parties were so few that it was considered an unpardonable insult to be left out if one lived within a day's ride.

''You will take some consolation in providing amusement for his daughter, Grace,'' David added. ''She has been alone there since her mother died many years ago. A gawky, mousy creature she is, but with a sharp wit.''

Laurie was unconvinced that any Bailey would suit her, but wrote the invitation. Also to receive invitations were Richard Allyn and his wife, Martha, who managed Lord Oldenburgh's plantation to the northeast of Silversea, and John Edrington and his wife, Vanessa, who owned a small plantation to the west. From David's description she looked forward to the Edringtons, whom he had said were in their early thirties and had two children. Vanessa, he had added, was a beauty and always cheerful, though she talked overmuch of her children. Laurie did not think she would mind that, particularly since in recent weeks she had begun to suspect that the subject would soon be of great interest to her.

And that was all. Even with the two children it was only eight guests, but Laurie thought that after the solitude it would seem a great crowd. The invitations went out, David carrying them on horseback, since he visited the other planters often. When the answers came back all had accepted. Others, Laurie decided, were lonely, too.

She threw herself into preparations, upsetting everyone from the cook to the gardeners. The latter were forced to build the shelter which went up quickly, however, being nothing more than a framework of giant bamboo thatched with palm fronds. The sight of it, fitting in so well with the tropical garden, inspired Laurie to further endeavors.

Ham worked with her on the menu. He was to go himself to select the crab claws and crayfish she chose as a first course, and supervised the selection of a suckling pig for a roast. He knew the trees that bore the best fruit and saw that the older slave children dug sweet potatoes to roast with the pig. Then he went to the stone cellar and brought forth so much wine, brandy and rum that Laurie was taken aback.

"There will be only a few guests," she protested. "Surely they will not consume all of that?"

Ham smiled, a rare occurrence that Laurie watched for, since it brightened his brown face charmingly and made him seem gentle. He set down the cases in the pantry and flexed his great shoulders to ease them. "That and more, Mistress. The planters pride themselves on it. A party in Barbados is a failure if you can sit your horse when it is over."

Later, Laurie asked David if what Ham had said was true, and David laughed. "Quite true. At times even the older ladies must be helped into their carriages when they depart. They will expect unlimited amounts of food and drink, Laurie. It will not do to stint."

"I shall not stint," Laurie promised. "But I do think we have some odd customs here." She went off to supervise the maid who was washing the crystal, determined that there would be enough goblets to use in all the drinking these Barbadian barbarians would do!

The party was on Sunday, the guests invited for two o'clock. By eleven Laurie was dressed in one of her prettiest gowns, a white gossamer silk with lace around the low, square neckline—lace that did not quite hide the enticing swell of satiny breasts. A blue-green ribbon that matched her eyes was threaded through the absurdly high waistline, and the fall of filmy skirt moved and flowed about her slender curves before brushing the top of soft leather slippers. In England the more daring coquettes made gowns like these even more revealing by dampening their petticoats so that they clung to the body and showed every line through the gossamer, but Laurie considered that not only scandalous but uncomfortable.

It had taken her an hour to dress her hair as Thérèse used to do, with the thick twist smooth on top and the lock or two that hung like black silk question marks against her white neck. But, looking into the mirror before going down, she felt it had been worth it. David would not be ashamed of his young wife today.

The garden scene was set, with the long table sparkling with silver and crystal, the chairs and benches and tables disposed conveniently around in shady spots. And flowers were everywhere, not just the ones so plentiful on the shrubs, but others cut and placed in tall vases. Laurie was there in a final consultation with Ham, when David strolled out to announce that the Allyns were driving up the avenue.

"So soon?" Laurie stared in sudden fright. "But we are not ready . . . the food half cooked . . ."

David yawned. He was not long out of bed. "They will all come early, my dear. Parties are rare, and they will not want to miss a word of the talk. And, I should have told you, there may be extra guests. It is common for those invited to bring along anyone who has happened by their homes. And I do see a rider following the Allyn coach." He smiled at her, for once his eyes tender, even with servants around. "I'm sure you will do well . . ."

She smiled back, relaxing. "If the number doubles, there will still be enough food." Hooking an arm in his, she added lightly, "Let us go to greet them."

The Allyns, escorted by a maid, were rounding the corner of the house, looking with wonderment at the decorated garden. Richard Allyn was a square, hearty man with a country look and a rolling accent that brought Scotland with him, brightening Laurie's smile. Then Martha, a buxom, graying woman in beruffled silk who kissed Laurie's cheek with vigor and wished her happiness with this "handsome dog." But aside from the flutter of greetings the conversation came to an abrupt halt as the "extra guest" came hesitantly forward.

"William!" Laurie cried, and flew to take both his hands. "How nice that it is you!"

William Burdick, his golden curls and handsome face

more angelic than ever over a clerical collar, blushed and stammered that the Allyns "had insisted, but if I am at all in the way you must tell me immediately . . ."

"Not at all in the way," Laurie said eagerly. "We are so happy to have you, aren't we, David?" She turned and looked at David, glowing. "Can you imagine? Our shipboard companion, now a dignified clergyman."

David came forward to shake William's hand. "I suppose we must now call you Reverend," he said lightly. "But Reverend or First Officer, my wife and I welcome you to Silversea."

"As a matter of fact," William answered, still with a slight stammer, "I cannot stay long. I have a hard ride ahead of me to my lodgings in Speight's Town."

"Oh, no," Laurie said confidently, clinging again to David's arm. "We cannot countenance that. This is our first celebration and you must stay. We shall put you up for the night and you can make the ride tomorrow. That would be best, wouldn't it, David?"

"By all means," David said, his voice colorless. He disengaged her arm gently. "Now, perhaps you should see that Mistress Allyn finds a comfortable seat and has a glass of wine. The other guests will be arriving shortly."

Within an hour the guests were all there. First Father Covington, splendid in bright blue breeches and coat, with a figured yellow waistcoat that gave him a festive air. Then Prentiss Bailey, still in black with no concession to frivolity. He brought his plain daughter, Grace, to introduce her to Laurie with an air of conferring a favor. The Edringtons arrived and were precisely what Laurie had expected. A tall, laconic man, quiet and pleasant, and the beauty, Vanessa. Dressed in palest lavender muslin, she was tall and slender, with red-blond hair and emerald eyes that glowed with appreciation of the garden scene. They had brought only one of their children, a three-year-old charmer named Barbara Lee. Laurie, now secretly sure of her own pregnancy, felt her heart turn over in anticipation as she watched John

Edrington pick up his daughter and hug her with absent affection. It was not hard at all to imagine David with a child in his arms . . .

The hum of conversation rose as the wine bottles emptied, and then Vanessa trailed her lavender skirts across the grass to stand beside Laurie, saying she was much impressed by her first visit to Silversea and would very much like to see the interior of the house.

Pleased, Laurie said it was a perfect time to do so, since everyone was occupied with talk.

"Except for Grace Bailey," Vanessa said softly. "It might be a kindness to include her."

Laurie looked quickly and saw that Miss Bailey was sitting off to the side, gazing morosely into the distance. Embarrassed that she had ignored her, she nodded and went to invite her to accompany them, noticing for the first time the warm, quizzical eyes that illumined the plain face. Smiling, Grace rose immediately.

"I would enjoy that. I have never seen the inside of the mansion, though my father has mentioned it as—full of treasures."

Going toward the house, Laurie was sure Prentiss Bailey's words had been changed to suit the occasion. Undoubtedly, he had mentioned Covington extravagance. Her pride was tempered by humility as they wandered through the rooms. *Her* home was in Scotland. But still it was nice to see Vanessa's appreciation as she touched a Chinese vase lightly, stroked velvet upholstery. Grace, though she seemed to enjoy the company, was absentminded until they entered the library. There she was soon engrossed in studying the book spines.

"How lucky you are," she said, "to have such a selection of literature. Are you fond of reading?"

"Indeed I am," Laurie said. "Though I have little time for it now. Once I learn to manage the house I am sure I will spend much time here."

Vanessa laughed. "Do so quickly. When your children arrive you will have less time for everything." She looked around and sighed. "How I would love to have such a nice house. But I am sure I will, for John is making a great success even though our plantation is small. In any event, I could not manage it now, for we have only fifty slaves and they are needed in the fields. Except for a cook, I have no servants."

"Only fifty?" Grace looked interested. "My father said you must have many. Passing by, he saw a dozen or more children in your garden, some of them old enough to be in the fields. He wondered it took so many to weed it."

"They were not workers," Vanessa's face was suddenly pink. "They are members of my school. Do not look so startled, Grace. I must teach my own, and John and I agree it is well to teach them, also."

Grace was staring. "But—do they learn? My father says they cannot retain abstract ideas . . ."

"Your father is wrong," Vanessa said simply, and then gave Grace a quick smile. "However, I hope you will not tell him I said so."

Grace laughed aloud, a rich, warm sound, surprising from the thin body. "I certainly won't. For if I did, he would try to keep me from visiting your school, which I intend to do with your permission. I have often wished that education was possible for the slaves, and only my father's firm belief has kept me from attempting it."

Laurie had listened with a growing sense of wonder. Had not David said that the white mistresses never had anything to do with the ordinary slaves?

"Does David know of your school?" She asked the question carefully, not sure she wanted to hear the answer.

Vanessa smiled. "He does, but he does not approve of it. His advice was to send the boys of eight or ten to the fields to replace their mothers. Then, he said, I could bring the mothers in as maids. I was tempted, but in a very few years I will have taught them all I know, for I am not highly educated like Grace, and then perhaps I can have maids. In the meantime they are learning to read and write and do sums.''

Laurie gasped. ''They learn all that?''

''Certainly. Once they learn the language, they learn as fast as my son. And what is more, their mothers are learning the language very rapidly from the children.'' Vanessa turned, her skirts fluttering. ''Why, here is John. Have we been dallying too long, dear?''

''Your daughter believes so.'' John laughed as the small child released his hand and ran to her mother to be picked up.

Conscious now of neglecting her other guests, Laurie moved toward the door. But as they went through the great hall, she spoke quietly to Grace.

''When you go to the Edrington plantation, Miss Bailey, I would very much like to accompany you, if you don't mind.''

''I would enjoy your company,'' Grace said in her abrupt way. ''I will send you a note to tell you the date.''

Laurie nodded, and then they were outside, and there was Ham bringing a number of empty bottles back from the garden. The rum, she noted, had begun to flow, and she excused herself and went toward the kitchen. She meant to speed the serving of the food, for it was said that rumbullion on an empty stomach was twice as potent. She entered rapidly, looking for Octavia, and stopped short as a black woman completely strange to her turned from the huge iron stove.

Laurie gaped. The woman was so tall, so slender and long-boned as to appear attenuated. Her gown, if that was what one could call the length of vividly colored silk wrapped around her, was strikingly becoming. She was not young, yet her small head was erect on a long neck. Her features were clear and sharply delineated; her expression proud to the point of arrogance. She was entirely different from any of the slave women Laurie had seen, with their rounded bodies and soft, smiling faces, yet her skin was ebony black. For an instant

Laurie felt an odd jolt in her mind, as if the edges of reality had cracked and then come together again, and in that instant she saw the woman differently, facing her, with the long arms wrapped around a bundle, the head high with that same proud look, the jet eyes staring into hers. She shook her head to rid it of such fancies.

"I am looking for Octavia," she said, wondering if the woman understood any English at all. "Do you know where she is?"

"I have sent her to the pantry for spices," the woman said, shocking Laurie anew with the cultured perfection of her voice. "She had forgotten to season the roast pig correctly." She continued to look at Laurie, a spoon held motionless in long fingers, a faint smile on her chiseled lips. "I am Molenga."

"Oh." Laurie smiled involuntarily. For some moments she had been conscious of a feeling of great happiness, which she did not understand at all. "How very nice of you to come to help."

The woman turned back to stir a large pot on the stove, but not before Laurie saw the look of amusement cross her face. At that moment Octavia hurried in, packets in hand, gave Laurie but a passing glance and went to Molenga, handing her the packets as she might have presented offerings to a god.

Laurie turned and left the kitchen. She did not know why, but it no longer seemed important if the guests were drunk before they dined, or after they dined. She felt completely relaxed, and ready to enjoy the party herself.

Chapter Nine

IT WAS A LOVELY PARTY, ALMOST TO THE END. THE mood of the guests changed from the first slight uncertainty caused by the unfamiliar mode, relaxing into a gay, picniclike informality. Conversation grew louder as the level of rum in many bottles dropped lower, and there was much laughter.

The day was perfect, with a steady sea breeze cooling the garden, and the food was more than perfect. Laurie had thought Octavia a good cook, but with Molenga's touch the flavors became sharper, more delicious than she could have imagined. And the three maids who served from the long table did not giggle amongst themselves as they usually did, but were sedate and quick to note when a guest required service.

Laurie realized fully where credit was due, and sought out Father Covington in a corner of the garden, waiting while he finished a conversation with Richard Allyn. She took him aside to thank him for bringing the housekeeper to help.

"It was very thoughtful of you," she began. "She has taken over completely and I have such a feeling of relief. I know everything will go well."

Bartram regarded her uncertainly, his faded eyes sliding from her face. "Yes. Well . . . she said it was time for her to offer you her aid. Now, tell me what you think of your neighbors."

Laurie smiled. "It is early for decisions, surely. But I can say I am much impressed by Mistress Edrington and I like Grace Bailey very much. She is not at all like her

116

father." She took Bartram's hand impulsively. "And thank you, sir, for suggesting the party. I *was* quite lonely."

He nodded and wandered off to speak to Prentiss Bailey while Laurie turned to rejoin the other guests, thinking that he had changed the subject of Molenga rather quickly. But perhaps he was averse to accepting gratitude.

"A lovely occasion, which one might expect from the loveliest of hostesses."

Laurie turned, and of course it was William Burdick, flushed and warm with liquor, his dazed, sea-blue eyes resting on her in helpless admiration. His gaze traveled from her brilliant, black-fringed eyes to the ebony curls against her white neck, then to the swell of her breasts in the low-cut, gossamer gown, back to the soft fullness of her lips and stayed. The tip of his tongue touched his own lips nervously before he spoke again.

"I am very . . . very grateful to you, Laurie, for allowing me to attend your first gathering. I have thought of you so often . . . constantly, I promise you . . . since those days of our companionship on the brig. And I have been so very lonely . . ."

Laurie was both flattered and touched. His youth, and his admission of loneliness that followed so closely her own admission to Father Covington made her feel very close to him. And he did not have her advantage—a loving mate to fill the evenings with happiness. Remembering his kindness to her on the brig, she took his arm to stroll through the far reaches of the garden, to talk to him of his prospects of finding a church to serve, and to make him, for a little while, feel less alone.

They had not gone far before she realized her action had been foolish. William did not want to speak of his chances in the future, but to talk of a chance he had already missed. He was much more inebriated than she had thought, but he was still shrewd enough to wait until they were behind some large shrubs before he grasped her in his arms. Laurie struggled—silently, because they were still within earshot of the party, but ineffectively, since he proved surprisingly strong.

"Only let me hold you for a few moments," William said emotionally. "I know you are lost to me, my darling Laurie, but if only I could have met you before you were wed . . ." His rum-laden breath assailed her nostrils as he tried to kiss her, his frantically clutching hands disarranging the soft gown, pulling the tiny puff sleeve from one shoulder as she pushed away from him with all her strength.

"You forget yourself, William, and where you are," she hissed, low and furious. "What do you think David would say if he saw you now?"

"He would say," David broke in from behind her, "that the beauty of my young wife tempts even an ordained minister." His voice was icy, dripping with scorn, and when Laurie whirled and looked up at him the brown eyes were full of contempt.

"Straighten your clothing and hair," he said roughly, "and go back to your guests. I will have no scandal aired here."

Laurie's face flamed. She was stunned and then angry with him. "There is no scandal, David! It is only that William is drunk on your damnable rum!"

"Only that?" The question was deceptively easy. "Are you sure, my dear, that you are not engaging in a bit of flirtation with your willing victim? I thought you'd bear watching when you greeted him so enthusiastically . . ."

"It is my fault alone, sir . . ." Shocked into partial sobriety, William had found his voice. But the rest of his words were lost on Laurie, who had whirled, furious, and left the scene. She went back to the unnoticing, noisy guests. And just in time, she noted through the red mist in front of her eyes, since more food was arriving and more drink, which she was sure was unneeded. She moved among them, urging desserts of fruit trifle and flaky pies on stomachs she knew were already stuffed, until she caught Vanessa's eyes on her, completely understanding and full of pained sympathy. The sympathy unnerved her, her own eyes filled with tears and she hastily excused herself and hurried into the house.

"Wait!" Vanessa's voice caught her as she dashed up the staircase, and she stopped and looked back, tears running down her cheeks.

"How *could* he?" She had completely forgotten that the woman advancing on her was a stranger she had only just met. "He actually thought I was encouraging William's attentions!"

"Sh-h-h . . ." Vanessa's warm arms enclosed her, led her upward and toward her rooms. "Let us bathe your eyes and set you to rights. He will come to his senses eventually . . ."

Laurie allowed her to lead her on, to soothe her hot face with a damp cloth and to neaten her hair, repinning it where it had loosened. Calming somewhat, she sat down in the dressing room and stared at Vanessa disconsolately.

"You will think me a fool. But how could he think it? I assure you, there's no other man in the world . . ."

"You don't have to assure me. I have seen you look at David. But you have hit a sore point. The slightest hint of friendly interest in another man will set him off, I promise you."

There was conviction in Vanessa's voice. Laurie stared at her, wondering. "Why did you say that?"

Vanessa sighed. "I can tell you, for everyone knows, and that is part of the problem. David was badly fooled by a woman he thought he loved, and was made a laughingstock by her cruelty. He saved her life during a riot in Grenada and became infatuated with her. He brought her here, intending to marry her. She was a lovely girl, beautiful, charming, and witty. But she refused to marry him in the end, and went back to Grenada. He went with her, and we heard he stayed with her long enough to find out he was sharing her favors with a large number of older, wealthier men. She laughed at him, and so did half of Grenada, since it was well-known there how she had amassed her fortune.'' She looked at Laurie's stricken face with sympathy. ''He never looked seriously at another woman until he fell in love with you.''

Laurie was dizzy with pain. ''Who is this woman? Where does she live now?''

Vanessa sighed again. ''I see you are not immune to jealousy either. It was so long ago; David was perhaps nineteen, and the woman older. But remember, David had no mother, and this woman was his first experience with feminine ways. He was very bitter, and I am sure will always be suspicious. Put the woman from your mind, Laurie, and just be sure never to give him cause to doubt you.''

It was excellent advice, but impossible to follow. She had a question that must be answered. ''What was the woman's nationality?''

Vanessa looked at her in surprise. ''Does it matter? French Creole, as I remember.''

Not a woman one loves, he had said, only a woman a young man learns from. But what he had learned was bitter; jealousy, suspicion, faithlessness. And he had loved her, or thought he did . . . She stood up, smoothing her gown. ''Thank you for telling me. Let's go back to the others.''

They found everyone standing, startled, looking off to the north, and Richard Allyn calling to David: ''It is spreading. Surely, your slaves are not burning off trash on a Sunday . . .''

Fire. A widening column of smoke in the blue sky, and all at once David had turned and was running down to the stables and the barracas, down the long slope from the gardens, his silk coat shimmering against the sun-struck emerald of the grass. Then Ham's huge form flashed by without a sound with John Edrington behind him. Richard Allyn started off purposefully to his carriage, one hand dragging along his twittering, expostulating wife. And William Burdick ran staggering to his horse and flung himself into the saddle, cantering haphazardly down the slope. But Prentiss Bailey, still staring expressionlessly at the smoke, only remarked that it might possibly sweep his north fields as well, and walked to his carriage with Grace following silently.

Then there was only Laurie and Vanessa, the latter holding her daughter, frightened and quiet, in her arms. Bartram Covington had gone to the garden wall and they joined him, peering down at the distant settlement of the slaves, where they shortly could see men and women pouring from the barracas, heading out in groups toward the smoky sky. David, Ham, Edrington and Burdick, all on horseback now, were leading the way.

"It is not a bad fire, my dear." Bartram was consoling her. "Soon out, I am sure. I believe it to be the new provision grounds, for the smoke is not the smoke of cane."

Laurie was cold with apprehension and Vanessa seemed half angry as she spoke.

"How could it start, Mr. Covington? The provision plants are still green, are they not? Ours are. And, it has not been dry . . ."

He wagged his leonine head, staring at the sky. "It is puzzling, indeed." He sounded grim, but his tone brightened as he added, "There will be plenty of help to put it out. Allyn will have his slaves rushing from the north to join in, and undoubtedly Bailey will see that it is put out along his fields at least." He turned to Laurie. "But it is not a fitting way to end such a delightful occasion. Your first social event was a great success, I believe."

"Thank you." Laurie was fearful and impatient, forcing her smile. "Shall we all go in? There is nothing we can do here."

His gaze had turned toward the house, and she

followed it, seeing the tall, slender woman wrapped in silken brilliance, skin like polished ebony, walking toward his carriage.

"I think not, my dear. It is time for me to return home." He set off at his dignified pace, crossing the deep grass to his carriage. As it moved away, Vanessa broke the silence.

"Who was that striking woman? Surely not one of your slaves?"

Laurie laughed, feeling hysteria close to the surface. "Molenga," she said, the name an exotic flavor on her tongue. "She is Father Covington's housekeeper, and yes, I suppose she is a slave. But, I have met her for the first time today . . . and, if there is such a thing as nobility in the jungles of Africa, then I believe she must have been Queen!"

The men were not gone long to the fire. Only long enough to ruin their clothes, blacken their faces and hands and parch their throats. They came in and sat around the long dining table, all of them quiet and David almost completely silent, his bearded face grim. They drank, though William Burdick confined himself to water. Slowly, through John Edrington and William answering Vanessa's questions, the story came out.

It had been the provision grounds, as Father Covington had thought. Five acres, all that had been planted so far. It was a great loss, borne by the slaves, for by custom the produce was theirs both to eat and to sell. Of course they would be provided with food, but they counted on the money to buy their small luxuries and to pay for the bright clothes they wore on holidays. They were very angry and despondent, John Edrington said, and with good reason because the fire had been set. Bundles of dried hay had been placed between the rows, scattered over the green tops of the thriving plants, stacked around the corn. The charred torches which had been used to ignite the hay were still there, thrown down carelessly at one side of the field.

"I cannot see how it was managed." William Burdick's voice still held fright. His clerical collar was loose, one end stuck upward, nearly to an ear. His blue eyes were red-rimmed from both alcohol and smoke, his fair hair grimed and tousled. "There is not time in a half day to carry and place one-third of those bales."

"It was not one person," David said, breaking his silence, his deep voice heavy. "It would have had to be a great gang, all young, strong men, to accomplish it so quickly. It had only been two hours since the slaves who were tending it had left."

"But why?" John was puzzled. "Jealous slaves, who were not to share?"

"I do not know," David answered, and for the first time since he had come in his eyes swept to Laurie, icily warning her not to speak of Prentiss Bailey, a signal she understood. She remembered Bailey's grumbling about the new provision grounds, but she knew also that there was no proof. At this moment she was more worried about the ice in David's eyes than anything else. She had been sure that by now his temper would have cooled, he would have seen the error of his thoughts. She was prepared for a lecture on foolishness, but not for his anger. She shifted uncomfortably in her chair and his eyes came back to her again.

"You may retire, Laurie," he said stiffly. "I will see to our guests."

"I am not weary," she said quickly. "It isn't necessary—"

"I believe it is quite necessary." Pushing back his chair, David rose. Taking her arm, he pulled her from her chair. "I am sure you need rest after such a hectic day." He escorted her to the dining-room door and opened it. "Do you require help? I will send a maid . . ."

She stared at him in astonishment, and then glanced back into the room, finding Vanessa's glance cautiously sympathetic. "Not at all," she said lightly. Then, smiling, she said, "Good night. I will hope to see you again, soon, Vanessa."

"You will . . ." Vanessa's answer came faintly through the closing door.

Going up the staircase, Laurie wished she had embarrassed him thoroughly by simply refusing to leave. He had certainly embarrassed her! But, she thought wryly, it was still better than being dragged, kicking and crying, from the presence of their guests. And somehow she was quite sure David would have been capable of doing just that, had she balked. His grip on her arm had been bruising, cruel, and when she considered the time when they would be alone again, she found she was more frightened than angry.

Alone in her room, she was able to think it all through for the first time. She felt instinctively that Vanessa had been right in saying David was unusually suspicious, and having once been publicly laughed at for his devotion to a woman, it was also undoubtedly the reason he was so uncaring in the presence of others. But he did care. She was suddenly sure of that, and just as sure that he knew she cared for him. Her spirits lifted, and then fell again. He *was* angry. Very angry.

She paced the room, reconstructing the scene. David had come upon them suddenly, but surely he had seen that she was struggling to escape from William, not leading him on! Surely he had heard her tell William in no uncertain terms to leave her alone . . . Suddenly stricken, she realized that she hadn't said that, she had only meant it. She had said something else entirely—she had told William he was forgetting where he was, and asked him what he thought David would say if he saw them! Her heart sank, realizing how different an interpretation could be made of that . . .

Slowly, she began undressing, brushing her hair out, preparing for bed. He would simply have to take her on faith, that was all—although he had very little of that . . . She put on a light gown and got into bed, leaving a dim lamp glowing.

David was taking a very long time to say his farewells to the Edringtons and settle William Burdick into his room for the night. At least he had been sensible enough not to call poor drunken William out, nor offer him physical harm of any kind. That, she thought, showed David's innate fairness. The thought gave her hope. Comforted, she sat up and began braiding her hair for the night.

"Leave it down." David, opening the door, was still grim and tired, still stained by ashes and smoke. "It suits you much better, my dear, when it is loose and uncontrolled."

Laurie stared at him as he stalked toward her in his ruined clothes. There was a glittering hardness in his dark eyes, an insulting sarcasm in his deep voice. He had waited until they were alone to unleash the full force of his anger and suspicion. For a moment terror gripped her and then her own anger rose, bringing courage. She swung from the bed and stood up in the thin silken nightdress she wore, shaking back the loosening hair and meeting his eyes with a brilliant look of pride and challenge.

"You have no right to speak to me in that manner," she said quietly. "I am an honorable woman and I have done no wrong."

"I have every right known," David said contemptuously. "I have the right to beat you if I wish—to bruise that white skin so it is less attractive to a man you fancy. I am quite aware you have done nothing wrong, and I also know why—you have lacked opportunity. Was it to begin tonight, dear wife? When I was asleep, and young Burdick waiting breathlessly down the hall? Isn't that why you insisted that he stay the night at Silversea House?''

Shocked, she stared at him, her anger draining away. His eyes were glazed, flat brown stones she hardly recognized. "You can't believe that," she whispered. "Not of *me!*"

"Can't I?" He began to laugh softly, jeeringly. "It doesn't matter, now. Young William is much too frightened. I doubt even your tender hands and soft mouth could raise his passion. In any event, you will not have another chance. There will be no more parties here, nor will you attend others. You will stay in this house and I will watch you. When you bear children, I wish to be certain they are mine.''

It was past belief, past anger. But she should have known . . . That first night here, when he had spoken of keeping her locked away, where no one could see her or touch her. Beneath his suspicion and fury, he was tortured, but not by her. Another woman, faithless and laughing, was twisting his mind and his heart. After all those years the French Creole woman was still a rival to be reckoned with. But *he* was a fool, not to see past his ancient hurt and know that she was different!

"At least," she said bitterly, "you need have no doubt of the first child. I am two months and more pregnant—and as you remarked, I have had no opportunity to betray you.''

It was neither the time nor the way she would have chosen to tell him, but as his face paled beneath the smokestains she was grimly glad that she had. She had shocked him out of his obsession, for his eyes changed, and for a moment he looked vulnerable and deeply hurt. Then he had turned on his heel and was gone. In the other room she heard the outer door open and close behind him.

Heartsick, she went back to bed, lying in the darkness with her eyes open, feeling the great, echoing house close around her like a prison. She was as much a slave as she had been in her mother's house. As much a slave as any African held in the barracas. She had told Desirée once that nothing could make up for lack of freedom, but, lulled by pleasure and love, she had forgotten it.

She would not forget it again.

Chapter Ten

AT BREAKFAST, THERE WAS ONLY ONE PLACE STILL SET, so David had preceded her, and was already riding the fields. She sat down with a feeling of dull relief, but when the maid brought her melon and small pot of freshly brewed tea, she bore also an air of importance. She was one of the maids who had spoken no English at all, and her face shone as she straightened and imparted a message.

"When you through, Mistress, the Master to see you in liberwerry."

Startled, Laurie nodded. "Thank you, Rose." Then, seeing that the maid still stood there expectantly, she added, "Very good. You are doing well," and watched the maid leave with a satisfied air.

It was likely, Laurie thought, that they wanted to learn even more she wanted to teach them. Caught here and helpless, unable to communicate with their captors, they were struggling to find a sense of belonging, of worth. She tried to keep her mind on the subject, avoiding the thought of the coming interview with David. No doubt it would be a reiteration of his opinion of her character and his rules for her future behavior. He would be cooler after a night's sleep, perhaps, but the very fact that he had chosen the library for the conversation was chilling. There they would be subject to interruption and that meant he would be cold and distant.

She shrugged, toying with the melon and taking her time with the tea, putting off the moment when she would have to join him. Her heart felt frozen, though below the ice there was pain, waiting for its chance to overwhelm her. She still loved him, though now it seemed but a weakness . . .

Finally she rose and went out. She had dressed this morning in the most dignified gown she owned, a dark blue silk with a high neck and elbow-length sleeves that hid the faint bruises on her arm where he had grasped it. The skirt sprang from her small waist in ponderous folds that quite hid her figure, and the fact that she looked fragile and childlike by contrast had not occurred to her. She felt tired and mature as she swept through the open door of the library.

This room, on the southwest corner of the house, was cool and dim in early morning. Lined with books, furnished with leather chairs, it was like a retreat. The drift of air from the west windows was sweet with the odor of jasmine, alive with the humming of bees in the blossoms. For a moment she thought how comforting it would be if it weren't for the tall figure rising from a chair.

David was a trifle pale. Dressed in a worn shirt and old tan breeches, Laurie guessed that they were clothes that had been left behind in his old rooms when he moved into the Master's suite. Undoubtedly, that was where he had spent his night. Silently, she went forward to a chair beside him and sat down.

"First," he said, still standing, "I wish to apologize for my actions and words last night."

The words shocked through her with their unexpectedness, but instead of feeling vindicated and righteous, her eyes filled with tears. He sat down heavily and stared at her.

"Please, don't cry."

"I am not crying." She wiped her eyes and looked at him. "Do not apologize to me unless you mean it."

"I do mean it. I believe I was wrong."

She wanted, very much, to be in his arms. But he made no move toward her, and he seemed to be considering his next words thoughtfully.

"I was angry beyond reason, or I would have known you would do nothing dishonorable, Laurie, no matter what your feelings toward Burdick. You will respect our bargain because of your character, if nothing else. And I am more than pleased to discover . . ." He stopped, drawing a deep, ragged breath, ". . . that you have managed to begin fulfilling it."

She glanced at him and then turned her gaze to the window, staring out. Could there be a colder way to acknowledge the fact that she was bearing his child? No happiness . . . no word of how miraculous it was. No touch. Pain had broken through the ice and was raging inside. She hardly heard his next words.

". . . Time will come," he was saying, "when you will want more. You are a very passionate, loving woman, Laurie, and you will want a lover like yourself —young, romantic and full of delightful illusions. A marriage of convenience will not satisfy you long."

"Marriage to you satisfies me." She hated the quiver in her voice.

Surprisingly he smiled, his eyes sweeping her face in wry acknowledgment. "In ways, I know it does. But there is more in your heart than a bed and two bodies, though I admit we do well together in that respect. But you want more, and I cannot supply it."

There was only one thing he had ever denied her, and she knew immediately what he meant. Somehow he had divined that she loved him, and wanted his love in return. And he *couldn't* supply it. She waited until she knew she could speak calmly.

"I understand, David. It is not . . . not something that can be forced. But still you can be assured that I will never shame you." An easy vow, she thought bitterly, since she could want no one else. And it was time, now, to stop this conversation—before she broke into tears

130

and shamed herself. She stood up, avoiding his flung-out, detaining hand.

"Wait," he said, "there is more . . ." He broke off as Ham spoke from the doorway.

"Master, we are needed at the barracas."

David was on his feet, going toward the door. "They are planning an attack . . . ?"

Ham nodded, and Laurie gasped involuntarily, her hand at her throat. "The slaves! David! What does he mean?"

"It is all right," David said quickly. "It is only that they are angry at Bailey's men. You are in no danger here at Silversea."

"But . . . a riot?" Laurie had heard that riots, once begun, spread like wildfire, senselessly . . .

"There will be no riot. Ham and I will see to that." He took Laurie's arm gently, leading her to the door. "Though I do not blame them for wishing revenge."

"They can't know it was Bailey's men," Laurie said wildly. "They may be wrong . . ."

"They are not wrong, Mistress." Ham stood aside, allowing her to pass. "There are many footprints, all leading the same way." He looked at David. "We should be there."

Nodding, David released Laurie's arm. "Stay inside. You will hear when it is over."

She watched them leave, and then, perversely, went back into the library and shut the door, even though it was time to begin her day's supervision. She curled herself in the chair where David had sat, imagining a faint warmth still lingered. And, also perversely, she was now more irritated than sad. If he cared nothing for her, why had he bothered to apologize? Why had her feelings affected him? Of course, now she was valued. Now she might be carrying the Covington heir . . .

A knock, tentative and then repeated more strongly interrupted her thoughts. She uncurled herself and stood, smoothing her gown. "Come in."

The door opened to William Burdick's reddening face and Laurie looked at him astounded; she had forgotten that William was in the house. He came in hesitantly, leaving the door wide-open behind him.

"I am leaving, Laurie, but I could not go without making my apologies to you."

"There is no need." She thought she could become quite bored by apologies.

"But there is! I made a fool of myself and caused trouble for you, and I am most heartily sorry. I have shamed my calling . . ." He stopped, biting his lip.

Laurie felt a remote pity, saying, "Truly, William, it is of no consequence. David and I have . . . have a great understanding."

"Oh, I know! He made that quite clear to me." William looked suddenly awed. "He could have called me out. Many men would have done so and with less provocation. And I would be dead, today. Your husband was most generous. He said . . ." William turned red. "He said stronger men than I would find you irresistible, and of course that is true . . ."

He was only a boy. Older than she by years, but only a boy. Laurie wondered why she hadn't realized that before. "It is all right," she said firmly. "Just so it doesn't occur again."

"It won't," he said, turning away, "ever. No matter what my feelings . . ."

"Very well. Now come into the dining room and have breakfast. The ride to Speight's Town is wearing enough without attempting it on an empty stomach." She urged him toward the door, still talking, wondering if she were going to laugh or cry. Here was the epitome of what David thought she wanted. A young, handsome and romantic man, with a head full of illusions. How little David thought of her taste!

When William left, following a substantial breakfast, Laurie went to the kitchen and planned the day's menus with Octavia. She had finished and was starting for the drawing room to inspect the work done when the kitchen door opened and David came in.

"Come, and we'll finish our discussion," he said, taking her arm. "It's cooler in the gardens."

"I thought that you wanted me to stay inside." she said, still perverse.

"It is safe enough now," David said. "Ham is talking to the leaders we found to be stirring up trouble. They will listen to him if they will listen to anyone."

A bench had been placed in the shelter, and that was where they sat, with the wind rattling the drying fronds over their heads. David settled himself against the broad back of the bench and then took her hand. She looked at him in utter surprise. In the garden, where anyone might come by, he was showing affection! And he didn't seem to think it unnatural, simply sat there, staring down at her hand lying in his large palm.

"The dangers of childbirth frighten me, Laurie. It is likely because of my mother . . ."

"I will be fine, David."

He looked serious, older than his years. "But you are rash at times. And, you are so small." He circled her wrist with his fingers, frowning. "I have heard that small, weak women . . ."

"*Weak!*" Laurie snatched her hand from his. "I am not *weak!* I am a daughter of lions, I have strong Scots blood. I may be small . . ."

His stiff face relaxed into an unwilling smile. "*May* be small? Have you bothered to look? And—a daughter of lions? If that be true, what cub must I expect?"

It was almost pleasant to hear him teasing her, and some of her anger fled. She smiled back at him, just as unwillingly. "A son," she said, "as handsome and strong as his father. But not a planter. He will make his own way, and not grow rich on the backs of others . . ." She stopped, almost frightened at what she had said, at the implied criticism she had given him. But he did not look angry at all.

"I pray God you are right," he said slowly. "I know I will not insist, as my father has, that he follow my footsteps. I have never liked this life, and as I grow older I like it less . . ." He sighed. "But that is not what I wished to speak about. I want to talk of your future."

She had a presentiment of sorrow; why, she could not tell. "What of my future? And, please, do not look so forbidding . . ."

"You are fulfilling your part of our bargain," he said, ignoring her words, "But I have only fulfilled part of mine. You have your home in Scotland that you love so dearly, but there was more that I promised, and so I wish to tell you this. When your child is born and weaned, old enough to stay with a nurse, then you may go back again. Back to the moors, and your Annie and Breen." He turned and looked at her shocked face. "That will please you, will it not?"

She was on her feet, trembling, staring at him, then turning and running, running anywhere away from him, until she saw Ham's head and then his shoulders, rising, coming slowly up the slope from below. She stopped, her heart pounding, trying to settle herself and forget what David had said. How could he think she could leave her child, and never see him again?

Coming closer, Ham looked at her uncertainly, and then past her as David came up.

"I do not believe they will attack," Ham said, but his voice was not calm. "I told them it is impossible to say if the fault lies with Bailey or his slaves. There are men amongst them who wish to fire Bailey's fields, but I believe I have convinced them it would be unwise."

Laurie had turned away stiffly, intending to leave. But David's hand closed on her arm gently and held her, though his attention was still on Ham.

"The men have asked you to lead them, haven't they? The Bonebreaker would be an admirable leader— Bailey's slaves would break and run." There was a strange sympathy in his voice.

Ham straightened, his head stiffly erect on his power-ful neck, and Laurie wondered where she had seen that arrogance before, that look of an eagle. His big body was tense.

"They asked. I believe they had the right to ask, to hope for my help. They have been badly used." He stared at David with his face still and hard. "Yet I answered that if they tried to go they would find me waiting, and that their deaths would be swift and merciful because they are my friends."

Laurie shuddered because she remembered, and there-fore she believed. And she saw something more than the lethal danger in Ham. She saw his heart, torn between two heritages.

"I will wait with you," David said. "By nightfall they will have talked others into anger." He held up his hand as Ham shook his head. "Do not refuse, unless you can prove you have grown an eye in the back of your head. I remember a cane knife wielded in Grenada . . ."

Ham's arrogance faded into a grin. "Yes, and so do I. The fellow wished to scratch my back for me, and you changed his mind, as I recall. I will welcome your company tonight."

Back in the house David followed Laurie to their rooms and shut the door behind them. She had grown calmer, though her conviction persisted that David wanted nothing from her but the child. Why else would he attempt to send her away when the bargain was completed? She stared at him impassively as he sat down.

"Now, tell me what I said that disturbed you so. I thought you'd be delighted to visit Scotland."

"Visit?" She looked away, her voice faltering. "I thought you meant me to . . . to remain there."

"Not unless you prefer it," he said. "Of course, I was raised without a mother in attendance, but if you feel you want to be near our child, then I would heartily approve.

Later, you could stay in Scotland with good reason. He should be educated in England."

"Yes, of course." Laurie's voice was dull. She turned from him and went to the window, looking out unseeingly. When would she learn he cared nothing for her—at least, not as she cared for him. "That is an excellent plan."

He sighed and got up. "It is far in the future, certainly. But I have come to realize that I have taken advantage of your desperation, and I wanted you to know that you will have your freedom later. It would be cruel to hold you, Laurie, only because you were forced to find a solution to your mother's greed."

She was silent, her head pressed against the window. In a few moments she heard the door open and close again. He was gone, very likely relieved to have gotten this over, his mind now back where it belonged, with his problems and his sentinel duty with Ham. The thought brought a flutter of fear, but she put it from her mind and went downstairs purposefully, to begin again the duties she had neglected.

At dusk, David left to join Ham. Wandering the quiet house, hearing only faintly the chattering of the maids in the kitchen, Laurie went into the library and tried to read, an exercise in will that soon failed. Nothing could keep her from thinking about David, out there on the far boundary of the provision grounds, facing what her imagination supplied as an army of angry slaves. She had read in England long ago of how the repressed hatred for whites could take over, and the most subdued and obedient of slaves could form mobs which poured like waves over whatever and whomever stood in their path. Stories of atrocities they committed in dealing with the planters and the planters' families would chill the blood of the bravest, and Laurie felt herself far from brave when danger threatened someone she loved. The murderous acts meant certain death to the slaves who rioted, for they were invariably hunted down with dogs and horses and killed when found, often by torture. But even the knowledge of certain death did not stop them when their anger burst out of control.

Both lonely and anxious, Laurie went to bed with her fears, trying to comfort herself with the memory of Ham in that London night. David had said it took a very brave man to start a mill with Ham, and these slaves, unlike the London thieves, knew what the Bonebreaker could do.

Lying alone in the wide expanse of the canopied bed, she thought it quite likely that she might have many a lonesome night. There was no reason now for David to bed with her; she was already carrying the child he wanted. And with his fears for her, he might consider it safer to leave her alone. She thought again how clear it had been that he thought they should part.

Yet he was a passionate man. *Why* did he want her to go? In spite of her faithlessness, did he still want the French Creole woman? Perhaps he longed for her skillful ways of love, and comparing them, one with the other, found his wife's awkwardness too uninspired.

That thought depressed her and she resolutely shut it out of her mind. Whatever he wanted, he would still have to wait until the child was born and then weaned. She tossed restlessly, plumping the pillow, finding a cooler spot for her cheek. The baby, she thought grimly, might find himself forced to the breast until he could walk!

She settled herself for sleep a dozen times without success, and as the eastern sky began to lighten she heard him come in. He undressed in the sitting room, trying not to disturb her, and then eased into bed. Laurie hardly dared to breathe. Then he had not, after all, chosen to sleep in another bed. Finally, when he seemed to be asleep, she slid carefully to curl within his warmth.

He yawned hugely and put an arm around her. "I thought you were sound asleep," he said, and pulled her closer.

"Did the slaves attack you?" She was still fearful.

He gave a small laugh. "Nothing quite so exciting. A few of them came, scurrying along the edges of the fields, disappearing at once when they saw Ham moving toward them. The sight of him cooled them instantly." He touched her face with a long finger, tracing her features in the dim light. "You should not be worrying now, my dear. It will be better if you remain calm and happy."

"I am very happy," Laurie said, wriggling even closer. "I had thought—I had feared—you had left our bed entirely."

"What?" He held her away from him, trying to see her expression. "Why would I be so foolish? You are my wife, and I expect you to gratify my needs, though of course not at present, in the early months of pregnancy. But surely a communal bed is a part of marriage."

"Oh, *yes,*" she sighed, and relaxed against him. "Indeed it is . . ." Her hand, resting on his thick chest with fingers threaded through the crisp hair, moved caressingly downward, following the narrowing dark trail to his flat belly, where it circled and roamed and then drew away the sheet that covered him. Returning, the hand crept down the crease of his groin, studiously avoiding the lively change occurring beside it. From the warm groin the hand stroked a muscular, hairy thigh as far down as it could reach, then crossed to the other thigh and trailed upward, the slim arm arching high to clear a quivering obstacle in its path. The hand settled again on the belly, quiet and warm.

"Laurie . . ." The deep voice held half plea, half threat, and Laurie, rising on one elbow, looked down into his bearded face and smiled. Leaning down, she kissed him, her tongue sliding along the inner part of his lips. "I have needs, too," she murmured. "Even now. I want you as much as ever I did, though you have given me a child to bear."

"But the first months," David said, his voice ragged. "I have heard they are the most dangerous."

"Then we shall be most careful." She sat up, pulling her nightdress over her head. In the slowly brightening glow from the windows her skin was pearly, luminous, her turquoise eyes gleaming like jewels. She knelt beside him, caressed him intimately, stroking and kissing and watching his eyes close with the pleasure, his face soften into sensual delight.

She could no longer breathe properly, nor stand the tingling skin of her own body, the swelling, throbbing ache that wanted him so badly. Panting, she slipped over him, arched above his narrow flanks, and lowered herself gently, slowly, until she had enclosed him entirely. David's eyes were still closed, but perspiration had beaded his forehead.

"Be still," he said hoarsely, "or this will . . . will end too quickly . . ."

In answer, Laurie squeezed her hips together, drew them slowly and tightly upward, and was rocked by the arching explosion of his body beneath her. Closing her eyes, letting out her breath in a long, shuddering sigh, Laurie slid down into his arms, holding him while the force of completion shook them both.

At last, breathing easily again, David drew her up and turned to hold her beside him, her head in the hollow of his shoulder. "So young, and in ways so wise," he murmured, his mouth against her cheek. "Your instinct leads you more surely in pleasing a man than years of experience could do. You are a pure delight, my Laurie . . ."

The unexpected, extravagant praise thrilled her as much as the lovemaking, her heart swelled as though it would burst. "When I am with you, I am very full of love," she whispered. "Too much to hold . . ." She could feel his lips curving against her cheek. "You are full of love wherever you are," he said indulgently. "Like a happy child. I am fortunate to share it. If only . . ." His deep voice trailed away, his mouth moved from her cheek as he turned to stare upward. In a moment he climbed from the bed and went to draw the curtains, standing at the window for a time looking out over the rolling land in the long shafts of light.

Laurie watched him, her brilliant eyes tender as she let her gaze travel his magnificent physique with its proud, dark head and strong column of neck above powerful shoulders, down the muscles of his tapering back, the hard, tight buttocks and strong, straight legs. He was altogether beautiful, she decided, better made than the glorious statues in Greece. And, much warmer!

"If only . . ." she prompted him, thinking the silence had lasted long enough.

He turned back, his bearded face holding only a faint trace of smile. "If only the impossible were possible," he said. "I had been thinking how it might have been if I had met you when I was your age, and, of course if I had done so, you would have been a tiny child and interested me not at all." He laughed. "Do you realize, Laurie, that Vanessa Edrington is taking a maternal interest in you? And that both Vanessa and John are younger than I?"

She saw the direction of his thoughts, and it made her smile. "Indeed, you are very old," she said, sitting up and hugging her knees, "and feeling it sorely, aren't you? I shall have to refrain from taxing your strength in the early morning, I suppose."

He laughed, though the laugh was not particularly merry. Coming back to sit beside her on the bed, he said, "It is not that I am so very old, it is more that you are so very young."

She cocked her head at him. "A condition easily cured," she said amiably. "You have only to wait."

Laughing again, he put an arm around her. "A bright child," he said, "is always a joy." He tipped her face up and kissed her nose. "You have more answers than I have arguments."

She frowned and looked away. "There is too much teasing about my youth," she said. "I am a woman. If anyone should be aware of that, you should. I am bearing your child; therefore, *I* am not a child. You should treat me with more respect.'' She looked back at him, frowning again at his twitching lips. ''I admit to acting foolishly at times. I also admit to . . . to frolicking with you in a childish manner. But that is only because it seems to please you. I beg you to remember that in a matter of days I shall be eighteen.''

He groaned. ''And in a matter of two months I shall be precisely twice that old.''

''Surely,'' Laurie said stiffly, ''you knew that before we were wed.'' She was suddenly uncertain, wondering. Did he consider her boring and immature? Was that why he wanted her to leave?

''That is true.'' He sounded morose. ''I did know. I should have considered it more seriously. But I did not expect—I did not expect *you!* I expected a young and empty-headed Mayfair beauty, who would be satisfied with a beautiful home and a wardrobe of expensive gowns. Who would have suffered the embraces of a husband only in order to provide an heir. And who would have looked forward to a return to England as perhaps the wife or mother of a lord, and in the meantime would have contented herself with embroidery or the painting of china.''

''I could learn some of those ridiculous things,'' Laurie said passionately. ''Why have you not asked? I will do anything . . .'' She stopped abruptly, staring at him. ''You do not really care for such women,'' she added in a different tone. ''Why did you want one?''

''Because,'' he said, stiffly, ''she would not have engaged my . . . my interest. I still would have been as free as I have ever been, my life would not have been changed. I would have had a mistress for my home, had children and the conventions of a family. All of which I could have ignored when it suited me. You are impossible to ignore.''

Laurie felt a strange mixture of hurt and curiosity.

"You do not wish to love or be loved," she said slowly. "I find that odd. Very odd. Why do you fear it?"

He laughed. "How can one fear something that doesn't exist? Love, dear Laurie, is an illusion shared by the young. It is merely the mating instinct glossed into beauty by the sentimental. The only true love is parental or fraternal, for a parent will give his life for his child, and many a man has done the same for a friend. But the love between man and woman—ah, no! Half of it is desire, the other half a hidden antagonism."

She was silent, her expression introspective as she considered what he had said. She thought of the relationship between Lord Peter and her mother, and then remembered, suddenly, the way Annie and Breen were, together.

"I believe you are right in some cases," she said. "But in others . . ." She smiled at him, her eyes tender. "I have seen a man and woman, long married, who are knitted so tightly by love that they are one, even when separated by the width of my grandfather's moors."

David looked at her, his eyes amused and soft. "Ah, Laurie, it may be best that you believe in your illusion. It has made you even more beautiful. Your face glows when you speak of it." He drew her close and kissed shut the turquoise eyes, his hand caressing her bare breasts. Trailing from her eyes to her mouth, his lips warmed into seeking more. The arm around her tightened, and then he was urging her to lie down again on the bed. "It seems," he mumbled into her ear, "that you are taxing my strength again . . ."

Chapter Eleven

HAM WAS STILL ON WATCH. THERE WERE TWO OR three of the more stubborn slaves who had not given up the thought of revenge, and one night they succeeded in slipping past him by means of the ravine and started a fire in the skimpy ratoons of Bailey's field. Soon out, the fire brought an angry charge from Prentiss Bailey, who came to Silversea and demanded recompense.

David laughed at him, genuinely amused, and told him that an acre of ratoon would not make up for the provisions lost when Bailey's slaves had fired Silversea ground. He left, grumbling that there was no proof that his slaves were responsible, but unwilling to continue the discussion.

David was not as amused as he told Laurie about it. "They are savages yet," he said. "Even our young men who were born here. It takes so little to make them flame into anger."

"I should be constantly angry if I were a slave," said Laurie drily. "Undoubtedly my master would be exhausted from chastising me." She had been reading, and now sat up, her book forgotten. "Can you blame them, David?" They have so little, and cannot by their best efforts gain more. They are not free to use their minds or their strength for themselves—only to serve us."

"I don't need to be told," David said shortly. "Since I took over I am with them every day. And I no longer think slavery is an ideal state for a savage."

Laurie looked at him curiously. "Is that what your

father taught you? That the Africans were benefitted by being enslaved?''

"My father," David said distinctly, "thinks of our slaves as his flock. I told you—he is Moses, leading them into the Promised Land. Of course he believes they have benefitted."

"And you?" Laurie prompted. "Do you think the same?"

"I don't know," David said slowly. "Life in the jungle is undoubtedly precarious. But what good is the Promised Land if you can't own your own bit of it?''

Laurie lapsed into silence, afraid to say more. The first faint hope simmered; perhaps in time David would come to the other side of his own accord and realize that no man should own another man.

But as life went on in the luxury of Silversea, she still couldn't keep from thinking of the slaves and their problems. The maids of her household were now chattering away in English, and constantly learning new phrases and words. That proved Vanessa Edrington right. And when an overseer from Bailey's plantation came to the door with Grace's invitation to join her in a trip to see Vanessa's class, Laurie accepted with enthusiasm.

When she mentioned the trip to David, however, she did not mention the school. "I suppose," he said reluctantly, "that you are lonely for female companionship and wish to talk of babies and fashions and other feminine concerns. If you are sure the heat and travel will not indispose you, I have no objection."

Laurie's feeling of triumph was somewhat marred by the fact that she hadn't been open with him, but she forgot all her doubts in the morning when Grace called for her close to dawn, the horses trotting up the avenue pulling the shabby but serviceable Bailey carriage. Laurie ran from the house to get in, carrying a basket of fruit that also contained a pair of Octavia's meat pies and a container of tea. Grace laughed when she looked into it.

"That slender body must require more than one would think," she said. Her brown eyes were sparkling; she looked animated, without a trace of the dullness she had had when her father had accompanied her. Laurie smiled back at her.

"I am eating for two."

Grace's smile grew wider. "And no need to ask if it pleases you. I can see that it does. What does your husband say?"

"That it must be a boy," she said lightly, thinking how shocked Grace would be if she knew it was all part of a bargain. "And he expects to be obeyed."

"All men do," Grace said dourly, the smile leaving her face. The carriage, with one of Bailey's lanky Scotch overseers at the reins, had turned from the avenue and traveled at increasing speed along the main road. "My father foremost. I did not mention Vanessa's school, yet he had heard of it and guessed my interest. He told me last night that if I wished to make a fool of myself by attempting to educate savages, I would have to do it in some other place than his home."

Laurie was surprised, not by Prentiss Bailey's sentiment, but by Grace's frankness. But she was glad Grace felt she could share her problems with her.

"David also knows of the school, but he said nothing of it," she said slowly, and saw Grace's look of cynical wisdom.

"He does not expect you to rebel against him, Laurie. My father knows I will." She sighed, looking out across the fields at the first rays of sunlight. "I have put myself between him and an innocent slave he wished to punish, and taken the blows on my own back. He knows I will fight for the school if I decide it's worthwhile."

Laurie drew in her breath, shocked. "How can you?"

"The plantation is one-half mine," Grace said, grim with determination, "And I am twenty-two, with the rights of an owner. It should be all mine, since my mother owned it and left it to me. But my father managed to break the will and gain half . . ." She glanced at Laurie in wry shame. "I should not be telling you this, but I was so angry last night . . ."

"I shall not speak of it to anyone," Laurie said quickly. "Here!" She reached into the basket and gave Grace one of the meat pies. "Eat, and forget sorrow. The morning is beautiful and we're going to see Vanessa!"

Laughing, Grace took it and began to eat.

The Edrington home was a transplanted English cottage, half-timbered with stone below. The gardens around it held more vegetables than flowers, but when Vanessa led them inside it was homelike and cheerful. The air of welcome and love in the house reminded Laurie of Stepney Downs and she hugged young Barbara Lee with the feeling of being among old friends.

At the midday meal they met John Edrington, Jr., a ten-year-old replica of his father, and the reason, Vanessa said, that she had started her classes. John, Sr., smiled.

"Is that what we have here? Two prospective teachers?"

Grace answered for both of them. "One, at least. It will be some time before Laurie can join in."

Laurie met the Edringtons' speculative glances with a smile. "I am interested, however, and am here to learn how I can help."

"Good!" John pushed his plate aside. "It's the only answer to the future, if it's not too late." He leaned on the table, his thin face serious. "I will wager the slaves will be free in less than a generation. There is no legal trade now, and England is moving to stop the contraband slaves. The anti-slavery forces in London are gaining strength every day, and the sugar market is failing. In my opinion, Barbados will end with a great mass of freed slaves with no place to live or work. They will have their leaders, and God help them, and us, if the leaders are ignorant."

146

Laurie felt she was hearing the truth at last, and it was frightening. But later, seated in the small side room where Vanessa held her classes, she was fired with enthusiasm. Not only did the pupils speak in conversational English, they could read and do sums as well as any child. Vanessa's teaching was inspiring, and so was the light of intelligence in the small black faces as they recited.

"Wonderful! Miraculous!" Grace was pacing the room after the pupils had been dismissed, her hair loosened from its tight knot and curling moistly around her warm face. Her brown eyes were luminous, her cheeks pink with excitement. Laurie and Vanessa were smiling at her affectionately when the cook, a large and dignified woman, came to the door to announce a visitor.

"A man of God, Mistress," she said gravely, "called William Burdick."

"Why, yes," Vanessa said, perplexed, "I do remember he asked if he could call. Show him in, Anna."

"Reverend Burdick is also interested in the classes," she told them when the cook had left. "He wants to give religious instruction. What a pity he is too late to hear the class."

"No matter," Grace said firmly, "I can tell him everything. I won't forget a single syllable of what I have heard today." She was standing at the improvised teacher's desk, her hands full of papers. "I would have been content with half the results you have achieved, Vanessa. I understood the children of savages could learn no more than the rudiments. But your pupils have convinced me—they could learn anything!"

Burdick, somber in his dark suit, had appeared in the doorway halfway through Grace's remarks, and after Vanessa and Laurie had greeted him, his attention went back to her.

"You have answered the questions I came to ask, Miss Bailey," he said shyly, "and your presence here gives me new hope. If your father has mellowed enough to allow a school, then the tide has turned . . .''

Grace smiled grimly. "My father is unalterably opposed to education for the slaves, but I will find a way around him. I am determined to have a school of my own!"

Vanessa and Laurie exchanged startled glances, but William seemed caught up in Grace's enthusiasm and crossed the room toward her. She thrust the sheaf of papers into his hands. "Look at their writing! Examine the arithmetic problems they have solved, the questions they have answered! Small savages! Now, tell me they can't retain ideas."

His golden head bent to the papers, William read and nodded as Grace pointed out the excellence of the work.

"If Prentiss Bailey feels that strongly," Vanessa whispered to Laurie, "Grace may have much trouble."

Laurie nodded absently, temporarily engrossed in a problem of her own. She had promised David to be home early, and it was already too late to do that. Now, if Grace was embarking on a long conversation . . .

"We must go, I know," Grace said, raising her head and looking at Laurie. "But I do want to explain to Mr. Burdick what I have seen and heard." She turned to Vanessa. "Would you mind if I robbed you of your company? Mr. Burdick can ride with us as far as Silversea and I can tell him on the way."

Vanessa, with household duties waiting, said at once that it was an excellent idea, and they were shortly in the carriage, with Burdick's horse tied on behind.

On the way home Laurie had time to stare from the window and think her own thoughts. Opposite her, voices rose and fell, exclaimed and set forth ideas. Hands shuffled the papers, and William spoke at length on training young minds in Christianity. Laurie heartily approved of his aims, but found his habit of repeating himself tedious. She was glad when she saw in the distance the familiar row of trees that marked the avenue.

They stopped there to allow William to leave the carriage and retrieve his horse. He came back to the carriage window before he mounted.

"I beg leave to visit you, Miss Bailey," he said. "I am most interested in your ideas."

Grace smiled, sparkling. "I will be happy to receive you, any afternoon."

"Then I shall be there tomorrow," William said with uncharacteristic decision, and bowed to them both before riding away.

The carriage jolted into motion and turned into the avenue, where Laurie could see lamplight shining from windows. It was growing dark with that sudden fall of night common to the tropics and she was worried about David's feelings. Then, from behind them, a horse and rider appeared and passed, cantering toward the house. It was David, hatless as usual, his black beard and hair unmistakable. When they drew up to the carriage block and she alighted, he was waiting on the steps with the cool polite look that meant he was displeased. Still, he greeted Grace courteously and took Laurie's arm to help her from the block. But as the carriage creaked away he spoke coldly.

"You are late. And I noted from a distance that there was an extra guest in your party."

Laurie looked at him silently as they went up the steps. Surely, after all that had happened, he was not going to be silly again about William Burdick. She was tired and irritated enough.

"I could explain that to anyone's satisfaction," she said coldly, "but I do not consider it necessary."

He stopped beneath the portico, and since he still held her arm, she was forced to stop also. "I am not accusing you of misbehavior with William, Laurie. But knowing his interest—and that of Grace Bailey, which I have heard from her father—I know you were not chattering of babies and fashions. You were planning to interfere with my laborers, weren't you?"

She looked at him numbly, hoping the twilight hid the flush she could feel on her cheeks. "We . . . We did speak of education for the slaves," she said. "And John Edrington believes—"

"You went there for that purpose." His interruption was not a question. "Yet you kept your intention a secret from me." He was suddenly furious. "I am beginning to wonder just how devious you really are. If there is a taint of your mother in you—"

She gasped. "That is going too far! I am not at all like my mother! And you are . . . are hateful to say that. And heartless about the slaves!" She broke away from him and rushed into the house and up the stairs to their rooms.

David came to bed late and smelling of rum. Laurie pretended to be asleep. She lay on the edge of the bed, as far from him as possible, knowing she had been wrong not to tell him the true reason for the trip. But he might have kept her from going. It had been devious after all. But a taint of her mother! Surely, he shouldn't have said *that* . . .

In the morning she woke alone and lay there thinking about the quarrel. It was clear she owed him an apology, no matter his rudeness. She should have told him of her interest and, if necessary, argued for it. She rose, dressed quickly, and hurried downstairs, hoping to catch him at breakfast.

There was nothing of David in the house except a note beside her place at the table. Her heart sank as she read it.

He had left for Bridgetown, and would travel by a small sailing vessel to St. George, Grenada, on business. He would return in a fortnight, if not beset by bad weather. He had not signed the note nor added a personal word.

Grenada! Such a far island, on the southerly tip of the chain. And wasn't that where he had met the French

Creole woman? She put the thought immediately from her mind. *She* was not distrustful. He was an honorable man . . .

The house was as barren as any desert in spite of its beauty. Laurie told herself she was a fool to miss such a cantankerous and insulting man, and set about her duties so vigorously that the maids avoided her and Octavia cringed when she entered the kitchen.

On the third day following David's departure, a maid came to find her in the library and informed her in her new and less confusing English that the Reverend William Burdick had come to call. Hastily, Laurie sent her back to say that Mistress Covington was indisposed. Pondering the childish action later, she was ashamed. But it had an unexpected, desirable effect. The next day, Grace Bailey appeared.

"Willie says you've been ill," Grace said crossly, coming in without ceremony to where Laurie sat in the drawing room. "And I know from my father that David has gone to Grenada and you are alone. Why do you not call on a friend when you need one?"

Grace had not returned to her usual quietness, but was still full of fire and enthusiasm, even when cross. And, she had called William "Willie" in a most affectionate way. Even in her morose state, Laurie had to smile.

"I have not been ill," she confessed, "only lonely and bad company."

"Good!" Grace sat down, pushing windblown hair from her heated face. "I am glad you sent him away, for now I can have the pleasure of telling you our plans, which Willie had called to do. We are going to have our school, Laurie! My father is livid, but can do nothing to stop it."

Sitting forward, happy for the first time in days, Laurie was eager. "Wonderful! Tell me about it."

"You could not prevent me! First, we are building a structure with two classrooms, a washroom, a storage room for books, and . . ." She went on describing the plan, her face glowing.

"Of course, Willie will give religious instruction in the other classroom, and, since he is stronger in mathematics than I, he will teach that also." Her expression softened as she spoke of William, and Laurie smiled again.

"To think," she said, "that you two will be teaching in the first real schoolhouse for slave children in all of Barbados. I wish that I . . ." She stopped abruptly. The rift with David was wide enough, without causing another disagreement.

Understanding, Grace spoke quickly. "We are building very close to your property, Laurie, in the hope that the children from Silversea will attend. Do you think David could be persuaded?"

"That is very generous, Grace, but we couldn't think of it—your school would be overrun."

"On the contrary," Grace said, her smile disappearing, "without the children from Silversea we will not have enough to make it worthwhile. Our slaves are neither as healthy nor prolific as yours."

Unspoken between them, the knowledge of how her father starved and beat his slaves into submission hung in the air. After a moment, Laurie gasped. "Grace, I *can* help! I have income of my own from property in Scotland, and David never touches it. I can contribute handsomely, for I have spent none of it. And I will ask David as soon as he returns if our slaves can send their children, too."

"If your children can come, then you can contribute," Grace said firmly. "So be very persuasive." She stood up, adding that she did not want to keep William waiting. "He is to help me this evening in compiling a list of books to order. He is very well read and knowledgeable." Her smile flashed. "He is also very charming."

After she left Laurie found that she envied her. Grace was learning to love, and the man of her choice was using every opportunity to be with her, while this house was more barren than ever. David had been gone only four days, so it would be another ten—or more—before he came home.

Chapter Twelve

LESS THAN A WEEK LATER, DAVID CAME HOME. LAURIE saw him from the library windows, cantering his big gray saddlehorse up the avenue. Behind him was a gig with one man in it. Not stopping to wait to see who the other might be, Laurie ran through the house and out to the portico to stand waiting. Not until David heard the gig behind him and slowed, turning to look, did Laurie look, too, and discover Richard Allyn's broad face, beaming.

They came up the steps together and Laurie was forced to greet Allyn courteously, instead of flinging herself into David's arms. Allyn followed them into the hall, excited.

"I have wonderful news, David!" Allyn's Scot accent when excited grew almost unintelligible. "Lord Oldenburgh is coming to Barbados. He will tour the plantations to gather facts to refute the claims of the anti-slavery forces in England. I believe all the planters will appreciate his support in the House of Lords!"

"I am sure they will." David was amused by the flood of words from the usually taciturn Allyn. "And my father will be more than pleased. It is many years since he has seen his brother."

Then he began to question Allyn about what His Lordship had said of the situation in London. Laurie murmured an excuse and went up the stairs, her feelings swinging wildly between hope and despair. She sat down in the sitting room of their suite and wondered what David's mood would be when they were alone. She reminded herself firmly that she had done nothing really wrong and that he had been extremely rude. When the door opened she jumped to her feet.

"I was quite wrong not to tell you the purpose of that visit to Edrington's," she said, surprising herself. "But I have been properly punished. I have never been so lonely in all my life."

"Nor I," he said, and opened his arms.

Crushed against him she discovered that the mouth in the dusty beard was still eager, the hands still warm as they wandered. She urged him toward the bed, and when he insisted that he must bathe first, stripped and climbed into the big tub with him. David laughed helplessly and then stopped laughing as his eyes traveled over her. He reached to draw her closer, his hands caressing her wet breasts.

"They are growing," he whispered, "and growing even more beautiful. And so is the rest of you. You shine, Laurie. Your skin glows. . . ."

"Sh-h-h," she said, trying to hide the pleasure his praise brought her. "It's only the baby—and happiness . . ." Soaping a cloth, she began washing him determinedly. "We must get you clean, for I cannot wait much longer."

He laughed again and lay back in the tub, stretching luxuriously. "Have me here, then. I believe it is possible . . ."

"Possible, yes. I see that." Her lips twitched. "But the way you roar and rear and fling yourself about at the end, the water would leave the tub. We would have the maids running upstairs to find out why the ceilings were leaking!" She dodged his hands as he growled and reached for her, and, laughing, went on washing him.

In bed, their first joining was over in seconds and wildly successful. David laughed breathlessly, rolling to pull her against the curve of his still-damp body. "You were right about the water," he said hoarsely, "there wouldn't have been a drop left. But it would not have been my fault entirely . . ." He began to caress her, his dark eyes tender as they roved with his hands. "Now, allow me to take my time. I wish to examine each part of this body which is nurturing my child."

He pushed the pillows aside and turned her over, lifting the black, thick hair from her slender nape and fastening his mouth on the white skin, massaging her back with slow, kneading circles. Her surprised, muffled laughter faded into soft, sensual enjoyment as his skillful hands moved over her, his mouth kissing its way down her spine. He seemed to miss nothing, and by the time his kisses reached the soft flesh behind her knees she was shuddering with pleasure.

"David . . ." Her voice was half whimper as she moved, rolling up to curve her back against him. "This teasing is unbearable . . ."

"Teasing?" He had straightened, dragging her back tight against him, his breath fanning her ear. "I am *not* teasing . . ." Tilting her hips expertly, he entered her again, thrusting his loins against her soft buttocks, beginning a slow, easy rhythm. "This," he whispered, trying hard to keep his shaking voice calm, "will be very convenient . . . later . . ."

Her only answer was soft gasps.

In the morning, Laurie told David of her visit to the Edrington's, though he insisted she did not need to explain.

She smiled at him across the breakfast table. "But I wish to. I have plans that stem from that day."

"Then I see I must listen," he said wryly, "for I cannot refuse you." He stood, looking down at her with an expression that warmed her all the way through. "Come along then, where we can be comfortable."

She followed him into the library, thinking of that look and deciding that it was possible he was beginning to care more for her. It gave her confidence.

They sat together, the early breeze lofting the linen

draperies at the windows, and she told him everything beginning with John Edrington's talk of the future and ending with the school that Grace and William Burdick planned, and how it concerned Silversea's slave children. His face grew serious.

"John may well be right," he said slowly. "He thinks clearly. But I can't believe Prentiss Bailey will let Grace go through with her plans for a school. He is the last person who would agree to it."

"She says he cannot stop her. She has her own income, her own rights. Wait until you see her speak of it. She is transformed, full of fire and energy!"

"Grace?" He laughed, incredulous. "Perhaps. However, if she manages to have her school, I see no objection to providing her with extra pupils. Except that when the second gang is in the fields our older boys must go. Without them the work is too hard for the old men and women."

She had scarcely dared to hope. Now she slid from her chair and into his lap to kiss him. "And may I go to visit Grace this morning and tell her? She will be so happy."

He grinned at her, kissed her again, his brown eyes tender. "You may, for I will send Ham with you to see that you return on time."

Ham, she knew, was capable of carrying her off bodily if David told him to do so, and she was a bit offended that David wouldn't trust her to drive herself that short distance. But later on the strange road she felt safe with Ham on the box.

She was startled at the ugliness of the Bailey home. A narrow house, two storied, of plain, sun-bleached wood, a dearth of windows and a flat, disdainful entrance at the top of a flight of steps that creaked even with her slight weight. Inside, there was no reason to change her impression of dreariness, for the entry hall was gloomy and cheerless. Waiting, as the maid who had admitted her went in search of Grace, she looked around apprehensively, struck by a creeping sense of horror. What was the aura here? The place seemed heavy with fear and despair, a pervasive grief. It gnawed at her, stealing through even the sense of excitement about the news she brought to Grace . . .

"Laurie!" Grace clattered down the stairs, her face bright with joy. "I heard the carriage, but it never occurred to me that it could be you!"

The dark mood was dispelled immediately. Laurie laughed and said she brought good news. Grace knew at once what she meant, and took her up the stairs to her room to talk it over.

Her room suited her, Laurie thought. Scrupulously clean and neat, with a plain narrow bed and a desk, and books everywhere. They sat in straight chairs near the small window and talked steadily for a half hour about the school before Grace changed the subject.

"I have not even mentioned your own news! Even my father was glad to hear of Lord Oldenburgh's visit, since he is an important man and pro-slavery. Bartram Covington said that both you and your mother were acquainted with him, and I could not help wishing that it was your mother who was coming instead. How wonderful if she could be here for the birth of your baby."

Laurie looked at her. Honesty always shone from Grace, and it prevented a less than honest answer.

"It is my earnest hope that my mother never sets foot in my home," she said quietly. "The Lady Desirée is no more a parent than the male crocodile, which I hear devours its young."

"Laurie!"

Laurie told her, briefly, of her problems with the mother she barely knew. Grace gazed at her with disbelief and then a saddened sympathy. "And I have been envying you. I lost my mother when I was only a child. She was sweet, loving, and a friend to everyone. But she was murdered by one whom she had helped."

"Murdered!"

"Yes." The pain of the memory darkened Grace's

eyes. "I was attending a boarding school in Bridgetown, and my father came to fetch me, saying my mother wished my company for a few days. I was very happy riding home, for I missed her a good deal. But, when we entered the house we found her body in the hall. She had been strangled. A slave girl she had brought into the house to nurse back to health had disappeared, and a bangle she had worn was beneath my mother's body. The girl was never brought to justice, for no one could find her."

"Dear Lord in Heaven," Laurie whispered, cold with horror. "How could you stand such grief? And how can you now wish to help the slaves?"

The brown eyes looked at Laurie steadily. "The girl was wild with fear, Laurie. She understood nothing except that she was a captive. Even my mother's care could not get through ignorance. Had she understood our language it would have been far different. Do you not see?"

Laurie saw. Grace's love and pity for the slaves went straight to the heart of things and held no malice.

"In every way I can," Laurie said firmly, "I will help you in what you wish to do."

Laurie was on her way home, with Ham whistling on the box, when she remembered her feeling in the Bailey entry hall. She shivered, wondering at the spirit that had left such sorrow there . . .

Within a week Bartram Covington had come to announce his plans for Lord Oldenburgh's visit. He bowed Laurie ceremoniously to a chair in the drawing room and sat down beside her, his white beard jutting from a set chin, as he always looked when determined on a course of action.

"Naturally," he said, "Lord Peter will stay here at Silversea. His own plantation house was never meant to be more than a lodging for the manager's family and is not suited to entertaining. I am quite sure you will not mind, my dear, since it will be quite an honor." He stopped, looking at Laurie carefully, and she immediately assumed an air of meek compliance. It suited her very well to have Lord Peter as a guest.

"Also, considering your situation, I do not want to put you to any unnecessary trouble, so I intend to take Octavia as my housekeeper and cook, and give you Molenga." He sat back, satisfied that he had solved any lingering doubt she might have. Indeed he had, since Laurie could hardly believe her luck. To have Molenga, she would have agreed to any number of guests.

"Are you sure that arrangement will satisfy you?" She was sure that it would not, once he tasted Octavia's cooking, though by most standards Octavia was more than adequate.

"The sacrifice will be worthwhile," he said, sighing. "Not only will Lord Peter appreciate the excellent food, but Molenga will keep the servants up to the mark. I will instruct her to turn out the north suite, which contains two bedrooms. The smaller one can be used for a manservant if one is in the party." He rose nervously and paced the floor in front of her. "All must be correct, Laurie, for a member of the House of Lords."

Laurie was silent, wondering if perhaps she did not know his brother better than he did. That quiet, patient man, disappointed in his own life but wishing the best for David and her. She thought of him eating the simple repast at the home of the bishop of Wight, remembering how he had stood at the window with his face averted as the bishop had instructed them on the true meaning of marriage. Lord Peter's marriage was a parody, with his hopes of children denied and his only human connection a grasping, self-centered mistress. How bitter it must have been to listen. Yet he alone had made their own marriage possible.

"I agree wholeheartedly," she said to Bartram. "And all shall be correct. We will be more than happy to have him here, for as long as he cares to stay."

Bartram stopped pacing, the white beard shot out in

tufts from his broad smile. "Ah! I knew I could count on you, my dear. You know the ways of the nobility." He rubbed his hands together and resumed his pacing, but with a more relaxed air. "David told me he wouldn't have you bothered with details, but I knew you would wish to know. Now, do not worry about provisions. I am ordering in wines and liquors, a side of good beef. Molenga will order the other foods and make up the menus." He chuckled, beaming down at her. "You will enjoy my brother's visit as much as he does, for you will have leisure to spare. Molenga will take over completely."

Laurie started to protest that Molenga would be overburdened if she had to do everything, and then closed her mouth. Somehow she felt that not only could Molenga do it, but that the strange, ebony woman would resent any interference. And she remembered the feeling she had had of relief and happiness the day of the party, how she had turned away in perfect confidence and left everything to Molenga. She smiled back at Bartram, thinking it was likely she would be spoiled during the visit, and sorry to see Molenga leave afterward.

But later, when she told David of the conversation he was frowning before she was half finished.

"He is trying to live our lives for us," he said, with a bitterness that Laurie thought unjustified. "Of course I do not mind having Lord Peter as our guest. But to upset our home, plan the rooms and accommodations, roil the staff with a different cook! He is issuing commandments from Mount Sinai again. Why did you agree?"

"I will thoroughly enjoy Lord Peter as a guest and Molenga as my housekeeper," she said, "and I know that you also will enjoy the food. I remember what a difference her spices make."

He stared, and then the brown eyes flickered and left her face. "True . . . she cooked at the party. I had forgotten you liked her so well. Molenga is not well liked by most white women."

"Why?"

They were dining, and for a moment David played with his food, deep in thought. "At times she is most disrespectful," he said finally. "Perhaps because she is manumitted—freed." He looked up at Laurie. "If she is ever disrespectful or unpleasant to you, I wish to hear of it immediately. I will not have it."

"She will not be unpleasant to me," Laurie said, slowly. "I . . . I am sure that she likes me."

David smiled suddenly. "That is entirely possible. And Ham may have spoken of you to her. He told me once that you were the only white woman who had ever shaken his hand and treated him as a friend. If he told Molenga that, she would be more than pleased with you, for Ham is her son."

Laurie was surprised, though in a moment she realized she shouldn't have been. That look of arrogance, that look of an eagle that sometimes crossed Ham's face was always present in Molenga's expression. But Ham was more often calmly pleasant, while pride seemed to burn in Molenga's thin, elongated body, her small, high-held head. She was even more like an eagle, her black eyes cold, bright, dangerous. But not dangerous to me, Laurie thought. Somehow she knew that.

If Bartram Covington had one real fault, to Laurie's mind it was his inordinate love of the nobility. Perhaps because he had missed such distinction so narrowly, had been exposed to their grandeur at an early age and then been sent away, to spend the rest of his years remembering that grandeur and never discovering the decadence that lay beneath it. In any event, he now behaved as if a king would arrive momentarily.

Cases of expensive wines and crates of liquors arrived from Bridgetown, as well as new bed linens, table-clothes, napkins—even an ornate desk to replace a perfectly good one in the suite His Lordship was to occupy. Laurie protested good-naturedly that even Silversea House would not be able to hold all the things sent in anticipation of Lord Peter's visit. Bartram simply gazed down at her with smiling indulgence.

"Peter must see us at our best," he said grandly. "No expense is too great if it adds to his comfort and convenience." He strode around in the drawing room, fingering surfaces to detect the tiniest fleck of dust. "You must remember, dear Laurie, that a lord is accustomed to perfection."

Remembering a certain library in Mayfair, with well-worn leather chairs and a tumble of books, Laurie doubted it but said nothing. Her father-in-law was enjoying himself.

But David grew increasingly restless, and one day Laurie heard him tell his father that the constant monitoring of the state of preparation was wearisome.

"Try to remember," he added, "you agreed that when I married, you would cease trying to interfere in my life. Bring Molenga. Then you will not have to inspect us daily—she will do so!"

Laurie thought him rude, but his words had the desired effect. Molenga arrived the next day, and Octavia, her clothes and belongings bundled in her arms, departed with Bartram to take Molenga's place. Laurie noted with sympathy the frightened way Octavia rolled her eyes at her, climbing into the wagon.

As for Molenga, she walked in as if she owned the house, inclined her head at Laurie like a queen acknowledging a subject, and disappeared into the kitchen. By ten o'clock the following morning Laurie stood in the kitchen with a sheaf of her orders and menus in her hands where Molenga had placed them.

"You have left me nothing to do," she protested. "How am I to fill my hours? I cannot fold my hands and sit."

"Sew for your baby," Molenga said. "Read. Think. And walk in the garden often. You must use the body that is to bear a child."

She did not bother, even that first morning, to address Laurie as Mistress, or even Ma'am. Laurie knew David might consider that disrespectful, but she was comfortable with it. Annie and Breen were servants, yet they would not dream of calling her anything but Laurie. And she was indeed happy with Molenga, more amazed than ever at her perfect command of English, her perfect command of the house.

"You will spoil me," she told Molenga. "When Lord Oldenburgh goes I will have to learn my duties all over again."

Molenga gave her the usual half smile, the look of faint amusement. "I shall stay," she said in a tone that admitted no argument. "I have told the Master I will be needed here when your baby is born."

So, she called Bartram Covington Master, yet made her own decisions. It was all quite curious. Laurie wondered why Molenga believed she would be needed at the time of birth, but she was too contented to question it. She left Molenga standing in the kitchen like some brightly painted statue of an African goddess and went to her room to put on suitable shoes for walking in the garden. She had walked for some time before she realized that she was obeying Molenga's instructions as carefully as any of the maids.

These were some of Laurie's happiest days, with time to plan and dream of her child, and time to spend with David, for his work was not consuming his time now. She was content, waiting for Lord Peter's arrival, waiting for the slow turn of the seasons that would precede the other, more important arrival of the baby. She knew nothing of childbirth, but she believed she had become pregnant in June and expected the birth in March. David chaffered her about it, saying that the cane would be in full harvest and he wouldn't see his son for a month. Seasons were on his mind, too, for it was now the beginning of September and he fretted that Lord

Peter's visit might interfere with his full attention to the fall planting.

Laurie smiled and told him to "leave it to Molenga," which had become her favorite saying. At the mention, he gave her a critical, half-puzzled look which she recognized as the same look he had given her when they had spoken of Molenga before.

"You do not like her, do you?" Laurie was almost displeased. "I cannot think why."

"I do not dislike her," he said slowly. "Yet I wonder at your complete acceptance of her."

"Who knows?" Laurie shrugged carelessly. "Annie told me once that at times people come into your life and it is as though you have known them before, as if they had been your friend forever. It is like that with Molenga . . ." She smiled suddenly. "She is staying, even after Lord Peter goes home. She has told your father she must be here when the baby is born."

David stared. "Father already complains of Octavia's cooking. He will be very upset."

Laurie laughed, too happy to concern herself. "I will leave that to Molenga, also."

Chapter Thirteen

THE TEMPO OF LIFE QUICKENED. RICHARD ALLYN CAME with news that the ship that Lord Oldenburgh traveled on had been caught in a storm and forced to put in at Martinique, but had been repaired and would dock at Bridgetown in two days.

"The Governor himself sent me word," he said proudly. "And said that Lord Oldenburgh would be his guest on the night he arrived, but would travel on to Silversea the next day. So, it appears that at the end of three days our visitor will have arrived."

David looked both pleased and relieved, and Laurie knew he was thinking that the sooner the visit began the sooner ended, that he would have time then to put his energies where they belonged, in the fields. Laurie herself felt excited. Their first truly important guest, and one whom she knew and liked very much. She went immediately to tell Molenga.

For once, Molenga was hard to find. Laurie wandered from kitchen to pantry, then outside to the vegetable garden and back again to the laundry and linen rooms. Maids worked industriously around her, stepping aside with a quick little bow when she drew near. Finally, she asked one of them Molenga's whereabouts.

"She in her nest, Mistress," the girl said with a giggle, and when Laurie looked bewildered she pointed up the narrow service stairs. "Top high," she added, and this time she didn't giggle but looked solemn.

Laurie had never been up those stairs, and while she started off bravely enough she soon tired, and by the time she had reached the third floor she was panting. In the narrow hallway she saw a partially open door and headed toward it, her soft slippers making no sound on the bare boards. That it was Molenga's room she had no doubt, for through the door she caught glimpses of crimson and bright green, a strand of saffron yellow. Her silks, hanging. She paused, however, in the doorway. As the scene unfolded she was suddenly reluctant to disturb her.

Molenga sat, erect as always, but with her long, slender legs folded beneath her in a curious, convoluted manner. Her seat was an animal skin of some kind, mottled brown and gold, and beneath it only the floor. Her back was to Laurie, and smoke curled around the smooth contours of her head. One hand, resting on a knee, held a long-stemmed pipe. In her colorful wrapped silk of gold and green, with gold bangles hanging from tiny, close-set ears, she looked more foreign than ever.

Sure now that Molenga couldn't have heard her, Laurie turned to go, to leave her in peace. Molenga spoke without turning her head.

"Come in, young mother, since you have come so far."

Laurie walked forward silently, passing the seated form, and took a chair.

"I am disturbing you," she said. "And it is not at all necessary. My news can wait." She found Molenga's face intensely interesting, almost frightening. The eyes were wide but unseeing, as if she gazed into a profound distance. Beneath the ebony skin there was not a quiver, the muscles like stone. Then her lids dropped, and when they rose again she was looking at Laurie with her usual bright, cold awareness. At once Laurie was comfortable again, and smiled at her.

"Mr. Allyn has brought information," she said. "Peter Covington, Lord Oldenburgh, will arrive in three days." It pleased her, somehow, to give his full name and title, as if announcing him to royalty.

Molenga's head inclined, accepting. "His ship survived the storm. It is better, so." She rose in one fluid motion, her gown slithering around the long legs as she walked away, laying the pipe on a small table and then going to the window. She stood there, leaning gracefully against the sill, breathing deeply.

"His Lordship brings misery as well as happiness," she said slowly. "Are you prepared for both?"

The words startled Laurie, the more so because she did not doubt them. "Yes, at times he is unhappy . . ." Her voice trailed away as she realized belatedly that it was hardly proper to discuss Lord Peter with Molenga, no matter how close she felt to the woman. She rose, conscious now of a sweetish odor in the room that seemed to come from the small pipe on the table. For a wild moment she wondered if it could be opium, or some other dangerous substance. She took out a handkerchief and held it to her nose as Molenga watched her with distant amusement.

"I should be going," Laurie said hurriedly. "David will wonder where I am."

But as she started toward the door a dark gleam above attracted her eye and she looked upward. Hanging there, on the wall above the doorway, was a strange weapon. A black, polished shaft, long and thin, its dark blade gleaming dully. A spear, then, handmade and beautiful in design. It hung from feather-decorated thongs, the breeze touching it had made it quiver, the moving blade was what had attracted her eye. She stood rooted to the floor, unable to take her eyes from it, for her head was full of swirling images, indistinguishable and yet very frightening . . .

"You must go," Molenga said calmly. "Your husband is waiting . . ."

"Why, yes," Laurie said, seizing the words eagerly. "That is what I said, isn't it? And it is quite true . . ."

Outside the room she turned in the opposite direction from which she came and went forward along the hall until she came to the stairs to the gallery, and then into her rooms. She lay down on the bed, feeling dizzy and distracted. For the first time she was uncertain of Molenga. The thought of the spear was somehow terrifying, though she didn't know why. She lay thinking for some minutes before her logic returned and she laughed at herself. The spear was merely a tribal symbol, no more peculiar hanging on Molenga's wall than a ceremonial sword in an English home. Nor was it odd that she smoked a pipe, many of the Africans did. She began to feel a calm acceptance and rose to wash her face and go downstairs again.

Halfway down she stopped, her hand on the railing. Molenga had mentioned a storm; she had not. How had she known? Laurie shook her head to rid it of fancies. It was a time of year when storms were common, the ship was delayed—logical to assume that a storm had caused it.

Three days later, precisely as expected, a coach came rolling smoothly up the avenue. David and Laurie had both been on watch and went out together to stand at the portico and remark to each other on the glory of the equipage.

"Uncle Peter's title has won him the regard of the governor," David said wryly. "He has provided him with his own official transportation. What luxury, indeed."

A pair of matched grays pulled the carriage, which glowed with decorated panels of rosewood and glittered with gilded lamps. It rocked along gently on heavy springs, manned by two footmen perched on the rear as well as a coachman and guard in the box. Laurie thought once more of the foolish love of the English for their nobility, though she felt that if anyone deserved such treatment, Lord Peter did. Her heart leaped as the carriage drew up at the block and she took David's arm to go down to greet him.

Tall, gray haired and lean in his impeccable clothes,

Lord Peter stepped out smiling, seeming dearly familiar. Laurie felt a rush of grateful affection, of happiness, and then he turned and reached inside to assist his companion to alight and Laurie stopped, dead still, frozen in disbelief.

Even in late afternoon the clear, bright light of Barbados was not kind to the Lady Desirée. It was possible, Laurie thought irrelevantly, that she was over-tired from the voyage. In any event, the artificial coloring on her face stood out from pale, drawn skin and lusterless eyes; her burnished hair was limp and lifeless. But, her manner had not changed at all.

"My darling Laurie! How well you look, how happy! And David! Quite the lord of the manor in that handsome suit. I am so very glad to see you both." Her small hands grasped Laurie and pulled her close, the painted lips touching her cheek. Then she released her to take both David's hands in hers and exclaim over the beauty of the surroundings, the grandeur of the home.

Laurie was speechless, but it hardly mattered. She had forgotten how adept Desirée was at filling an awkward pause with flattery and grace. And then her mother had taken her arm and begun mounting the steps, continuing her chatter while behind them Lord Peter and David conversed in low tones. Laurie, turning to look back at them, gasped and snatched her arm from Desirée, running back down with sudden tears of joy in her eyes.

There had been another passenger in the depths of the large coach, and Laurie threw her arms around the bony body and kissed the thin cheek. Thérèse!

Laurie ignored the startled stare from Lord Peter, David's ill-concealed amusement and Desirée's indignation at being left so unceremoniously on the steps. It was Thérèse herself who brought her back to proper behavior.

"Thank you, Madame. How nice that you remembered me." Her tone was so formal, her white cap bobbing, and the glint in her eyes affectionate but

warning. Laurie let her go and stepped back, brushing
tears from her eyes, and reluctantly went back up to
rejoin Desirée. Some of the sting had gone from the
unwelcome surprise.

It became apparent in a very short time that Lord Peter
intended to leave the Lady Desirée in their company and
depart again for his own plantation. He was to have
dinner with the Allyns, he explained, and Bartram was to
be there also. He did not know when he would return and
they were not to wait for him, for if he found himself
tired he would stay over with the Allyns. He seemed
nervous and harried, and they did not argue with him.
David said there would be a servant waiting in the hall
that night to let him in and escort him to his rooms, and
Lord Peter said promptly that it would not be necessary.

During this discussion, which took place in the
drawing room, Lady Desirée sat smiling and silent. But
once Lord Peter had gone, she turned to Laurie with a
laugh.

"Poor Peter is sure that our trip will be considered
scandalous," she said gaily, "which of course is ridiculous. After all, what is more natural than a mother
visiting her daughter, and an old friend offering his
protection on the voyage?"

"Very natural in appearance," Laurie said stiffly. So,
Desirée had insisted on coming along, evidently over
Lord Peter's objections. It was easy to believe. "Since
we did not know you were coming," she added, "there
is no room prepared for you. However, we have a room
ready for a manservant which may be satisfactory to
you."

Desirée gave her a sharp glance, wondering if insult
was intended, but maintained her charm.

"If it is half as luxurious as what I see about me," she
said, "it will be more than adequate."

In the suite, garnished with bouquets of flowers and
swept by the afternoon breeze, Desirée exclaimed with
genuine pleasure over both bedrooms and the sitting

room between them. She declared the smaller bedroom perfect for herself.

"And for Thérèse," she added, "if there is a cot. Heaven knows I will need her near me to use her skills on my appearance in this climate."

"There are several cots," Laurie said quickly. "Come, Thérèse, and we shall choose one for you." She led Thérèse out, glad to have her alone, and once out of earshot she chattered, words tumbling. "It is worth having my mother as a visitor," she ended, "just to see you again."

"Lord Oldenburgh would not agree with you," Thérèse said, examining the cots in the storeroom. "She tricked him." Her eyes were full of wry humor as she looked up at Laurie. "I would not have believed even she could be so rash. She discovered the name of the ship he was to travel on, and booked passage for us as well. He did not know she was aboard until we were at sea."

"Was he very angry?" Laurie was amazed.

Thérèse nodded. "Furious. He had broken off their relationship shortly after you left. He was generous, arranging a trust fund to care for the house and give her a decent living. But she has been frantic, trying to resume her life with him. She believes it was brought about by her treatment of you, and hopes now to prove that she has a real affection for you and is neither greedy nor selfish."

"She is grasping at straws."

The white cap bobbed in a warmly familiar way. "Certainly. His Lordship knows her well, and has tired of her. Play acting will not fool him."

After that, Laurie was not surprised when Lord Peter failed to return that evening. Desirée, pleading exhaustion, asked that a simple supper be brought to her room instead of joining the rest of them for dinner, and stayed in the suite waiting, as Thérèse whispered to Laurie, like a spider in a web. But it was not until midmorning of the next day that Lord Oldenburgh appeared to explain that he had decided to remain in his own plantation house.

"Richard Allyn and I have much to discuss," he told Laurie, and hesitated. Her feelings must have been plain, for when he continued his tone was apologetic. "I will try to convince Desirée that her visit should be short. In any event, I will not allow her to stay here when I leave."

"Thank you." As David had remarked many times, there was little diplomacy in Laurie's nature. "I am grateful for that promise. And disappointed that you will not be our guest. But I do understand."

He smiled and left, and there was a good deal of relief in the way he waved from the front seat of Bartram's wagon.

Laurie went up the stairs reluctantly. Her mother was still in bed. Propped on pillows, she looked considerably better than she had on her arrival. The sparkling eyes and small, painted mouth, the carefully dressed hair were all set off by a lovely negligee.

"Lord Peter has just been here," Laurie said stiffly, "to say that he has decided to remain with the Allyns. You may wish to move into the larger bedroom."

For only a second the painted face was marred by angry frustration, then the smile dropped into place again. "Peter is always so considerate," Desirée said smoothly. "He wishes to give me time alone with my daughter, I presume. I do hope you thanked him? I shall do so at dinner, if not."

"I thanked him," Laurie said dryly. "And now, shall I send Thérèse to you? We will have luncheon in an hour." She turned to leave, but Desirée held out a hand, her face soft and pleading. "Wait, my darling. Come, sit on my bed for a moment. There is something I must say, and I have traveled far to do so."

Warily, Laurie did so, but sat out of reach of her hand. She could not forget the memory of Desirée's enraged face that last night, nor the heavy lamp she had hurled at her. She seemed even now to see that face behind the smile, though now it looked evil in triumph. The image faded as Desirée spoke.

"Dearest, I had hoped you would have forgotten our past differences in your happiness. You have so much now, a good and kind husband, a beautiful home. And I have regretted my selfish actions, my unnatural behavior! They were caused—believe me!—by the effects of brandy and my feeling of loss as you left me. I offer you my humblest apologies." She stopped and then put a hand to her eyes. "Please, do not look so cold and unforgiving. I can hardly believe it of you . . ."

Laurie trusted her no more than she would have a snake. But there was the faint possibility that she meant at least part of what she had said.

"I am sure we will get along quite well while you visit," Laurie said finally. "Do not trouble yourself over the past, for I do not. I . . . hope you'll enjoy your stay."

Even to her the words sounded stilted and meaningless. But the Lady Desirée accepted them as complete forgiveness. She beamed and swung her rounded body from bed. "You are wonderfully sweet, my dearest!" She hugged Laurie, the scent of her perfume cloying. "I know I will enjoy every minute here. Send Thérèse, by all means. I can hardly wait to join you and your husband!"

At luncheon she praised everything, from the mahogany furniture to the settings of fine china, and told David it surpassed Mayfair's best.

"How furious Madame Smith-Alderly would be," she said to Laurie slyly, "if she could see the home she thought could not be good enough for one of her unattractive daughters. You do remember, darling, how she laughed as she told us of David's offers?"

So, she meant to bait him. Avoiding David's eye, Laurie nodded and answered lightly that she did remember, and had always been glad that Adele was so young. "Otherwise," she added fondly, "I might have lost him."

David's eyes gleamed, understanding. "Adele was a delightful child. I was tempted to wait for her."

The Lady Desirée looked at them with disgusted disappointment and began to chat of parties and balls, weddings and other social events and, as they rose from the table, she told David she had hoped to meet his father. "Since he did not appear at table, I presume he is away. Naturally, I am anxious to meet the brother of my Lord Peter."

David smiled blandly at the obvious possessiveness.

"My father does not live here, Lady Desirée. He lives in the house he first built on the plantation, some miles from here. Still, I am sure he will be here this evening for dinner, in company with Lord Oldenburgh. He is very fond of his brother."

"How nice," Desirée said, her eyes glinting. "And how unusual. The families in London are quite different. Jealousy is rampant in the hearts of younger sons."

Silently, Laurie wondered how far Desirée dared to go. Her remark was far from subtle, suggesting that Bartram, titleless and forgotten on a far island, might well be jealous of Lord Peter. She expected at least a frown from David, but he merely looked bored.

"Perhaps you should cultivate a better class of families when you return," he said, leading Desirée from the dining room into the hall. "Now, I am sure you are still fatigued from your journey and would like to rest more. Laurie and I will not keep you." He released her arm at the foot of the stairs and gave her a faint smile. "We dine at twilight, ma'am."

Desirée gave him a glance of startled respect, wished them both a good afternoon, and went up the stairs obediently. Laurie knew her mother was quite aware she had been sent away because of her tactless, provocative remarks. Outside, walking in the garden, Laurie tucked her hand in David's arm and told him he was most comforting. "I do believe you have drawn her claws," she added, laughing. "Perhaps her visit will not be so bad after all."

He looked down at her wryly. "I wish I agreed. But the more I see of your mother the more I realize her infinite capacity for hurting others. I fear trouble."

Chapter Fourteen

LAURIE DISCOVERED DURING THE NEXT WEEK THAT HER mother, having found out it was not wise to bait David nor attempt to make Laurie uncomfortable, became charming, affable and sweet tempered. She insisted on lending Thérèse to teach Laurie the latest in hair styles and fashions and Laurie accepted quickly, since it afforded a chance to talk with Thérèse in privacy.

And Desirée was courteous when Grace Bailey and William Burdick called. She sat listening with apparent interest to the talk of the schoolhouse construction, which was nearly completed, and smiled rather wryly when Grace mentioned Laurie's contributions from the property in Scotland.

"And can you force the children from Silversea to attend?" she asked Laurie. "Or will they run off to play before they arrive?"

Laurie laughed. "At first they might wish to do that, but Ham will see that they go."

William chuckled. "I can believe that easily. The slaves on every plantation know of Ham, and speak of him with awe. They call him the Bonebreaker."

"He uses his strength only when necessary," Laurie said defensively. "Ham is most gentle and pleasant."

"*I* think him frightening," Desirée said suddenly, and shivered. "He is so quiet. It gives me such a start to look up and see him, so huge and black, like an avenging demon."

"Such fancies can come only from an empty stomach," Laurie said dryly. "I will ring for tea."

Surprisingly, Molenga brought the tray herself, and Laurie thought perhaps it had suited her fancy to come in and show off her gown. She wore crimson silk wrapped to leave one shoulder bare, and instead of her usual bangles she wore gold earrings, long tubes which held a pearl nested in the end. Her skin was like black satin against the glowing color and she carried the tray with easy grace, bending to set it on a low parquet table. Grace watched her, intent and sober, as she left the room with her flowing walk. Then, looking at Laurie with a faint smile, she remarked that if that was the new uniform for Silversea maids it was quite unusual.

"Oh, Molenga is queen of our household, Grace. She wears what she likes, cooks what she likes. Taste one of these tarts and learn why I do not object. I dread the day she leaves me."

"Leaves you? How could she do that?"

"She is free. Ordinarily she is Father Covington's housekeeper." As an afterthought, Laurie added, "She is also Ham's mother."

Tart poised in one hand, Grace shot her a startled glance. "So, that is why she is free." She began to eat slowly, savoring the tart. "Then Ham has the blood of the Rundi tribes. I should have known, if only from his height. But it is unusual to find a Rundi amongst the slaves. They live far to the southeast in Africa and seldom wander near the traders' outposts. Your Molenga is a perfect example of the Rundi. They are a handsome people, uniformly tall and slender, with a proud nature."

William was watching Grace with pride, and Laurie thought how much Grace had begun to resemble him in her speech, relating knowledge in the manner of a teacher. They were well suited, and now seemed to recognize that fact. But Desirée was beginning to move restlessly in her chair, ignoring the tarts and sipping her tea without interest.

"I have begun a headache," Desirée announced

suddenly, and turned her smile on William. "A turn in the garden, Mr. Burdick? I need a bit of fresh air, and would enjoy your company."

Always courteous, William rose immediately to usher her out, while Laurie thought how like Desirée to not only escape boredom but take along the only available man to amuse her. She was content, though, and turned back to Grace with renewed interest.

"You must have studied a great deal to know so much about an obscure African tribe. Do you know about all of them?"

"Oh, no. I wish I did. It is only that years ago my father was offered a group of Rundis at a very low price and bought them. They did not work out well at all, for their nature does not permit them to submit to slavery. No punishment could break their spirit and most of them ended as runaways. Much later, when I was grown, I studied their origins, trying to understand." She stopped, her eyes distant. "It was a Rundi girl who killed my mother."

Laurie wished Molenga had not brought the tea. Grace seemed haunted by the memory of the tragedy, and soon left to find William, saying she would send word when the school was finished and classes were to begin.

Entering the house alone, Desirée sighed with relief. "How boring a young man can be! However, he is a great admirer of yours, my dear. You were all he wished to talk of—your beauty, your charm, your goodness. Why did you not tell me you had your own abject slave?"

"William praises all, and criticizes none," Laurie told her. "An ideal minister. In your case, he undoubtedly thought you would be pleased by compliments to your daughter."

"And so I was," Desirée said prettily, and took Laurie's arm. "If he wished to praise a female to me, he could have made only one better choice."

For once Laurie laughed with her, seeing the light

eyes sparkling with humor. It was rare that Desirée was so frank.

Still, as time went on, Laurie began to see a side of her mother she had never seen before, a part of her personality that seemed very pleasant, almost endearing. Play acting, as Thérèse had described it, yet done very well and certainly easier to live with than her usual bitter sallies. It was all directed at Lord Peter, yet he remained distant, barely polite to her when they met each day at dinner.

By common consent the dinner table became the meeting place nightly for the whole family, augmented by either the Allyns or the visitors that came to see and talk with Lord Oldenburgh when the news spread of his interest in defeating the anti-slavery act. And another subject cropped up, for sugar prices were dropping rapidly in the face of competition.

But the gloomy talk was confined to pre-dinner meetings, for when the wine and brandy had flowed, the mood changed and became gay and sociable.

Desirée shone. Not only titled but beautiful and charming, she was the center of attraction. Small groups formed around her in the drawing room, to chat and flirt and hear the latest gossip from London. Laurie thought she would never forget how Desirée sparkled and glowed, standing in the midst of admiring men. At those times she seemed completely happy.

But then Laurie discovered that her mother had made one real conquest, a shocking conquest. Giving up at last on Lord Peter, Desirée had turned the full force of her charm on his brother and it was embarrassing to see how quickly Bartram became enamoured. Laurie couldn't believe her father-in-law was naive enough not to realize Desirée's former connection with his brother, but he came every day to see her, to hang about at her side and look woebegone when someone else captured her attention.

His adoration had a predictable effect on Desirée. Her confidence soared and she burned with bright gaiety, pleasant at all times until she took note of Laurie's pregnancy.

She had entered Laurie's room at midmorning, gravitating naturally to a mirror to pluck at a curl that swung behind her ear.

"I suppose that is a baby's garment," she said, glancing at the sewing in Laurie's hand. "I hoped at first that I was mistaken and you were merely fatter, but since you bulge larger each day I presume you are expecting."

Laurie was silent. While she had not expected joy, she had not expected criticism, either. Desirée turned from the mirror, laughing.

"Oh, my dear, do not be offended. Surely you cannot expect me to like becoming a grandmother. I feel for you, also—an infant to care for so soon. Had you asked, I could have told you how to prevent such a mischance."

Laurie said rather stiffly that she did not consider it a mischance, that David was happy also, and had reported that his father had been delighted by the news.

"Bartram? Of course. Good English blood, you know. Poor foolish man, promising David everything— house, control of slaves and plantation, all he had—if only David would seek a proper wife in England."

She was watching Laurie in the mirror in sly enjoyment as she added: "Of course, Bartram told me what a fright David gave him years ago, falling in love with a most unsuitable French Creole woman and wishing to marry her. Of course Bartram is pleased with *you*, pleased enough that he was furious a short time ago to find that David had gone off to Grenada again to see that woman!" She sighed theatrically. "She must be both beautiful and engaging, to stay in his heart so many years."

Laurie had lowered her head to her sewing, determined that Desirée would not see the pain that filled her.

She reeled under the impact of the last words. They could not be true! But, how else would Desirée know, had Bartram not told her?

Desirée was waiting, expectant. Pride rose in Laurie, pushing the pain down. She held up the little gown, looking at it critically.

"I had forgotten how fond you are of lurid gossip," she said carelessly. "Likely you found the story more interesting than I did." She laid the gown across her knees, smoothing it. "Tell me, do you think I should press out these wrinkles?"

Unsatisfied malice flashed in Desirée's eyes. "Well, if you wish to hold your handsome husband, you have chosen an odd way. I have noticed that when pregnant wives become ungainly and misshapen, a man frequently finds a former mistress more attractive than ever."

"This is not Mayfair," Laurie said tartly, losing her temper at last. "There is decency and faithfulness here."

Desirée left the room, laughing maliciously. She never mentioned the pregnancy again, nor did she refer to the woman in Grenada. But Laurie couldn't forget it. It seemed incredible to her that David had been unfaithful and then returned to her with such evident passion. Not that she was so stupid that she didn't know that men—and women, too—did such things, but . . .

But what? She asked the question silently but cynically, wandering the house. It seemed that David had made two bargains, one with his father and one with her, and had evidently regretted them both. He was tiring of Silversea and the life of the plantation, and he was tiring of her . . .

But she still had friends. Thérèse fussed over her, claiming her to be too pale, too silent. She blamed it on too many guests, too rich foods. Forever a maiden herself, she seemed to have a fund of endless advice.

And Molenga. Laurie sat with her in early mornings

and went over the list of guests expected, their likes and dislikes as reported to her by Bartram. And daily, Molenga's black eyes roved over her, noting progress. Her advice never concerned food, for she provided it and expected Laurie to eat it. But she talked constantly of exercise, and took Laurie up the steep back stairs again to show her the curious, folded-leg position she used to relax.

"So," she said, pushing Laurie's unwilling legs into position. "Stay as long as you can, twice a day. The times will lengthen and grow easy. Your body is small for childbirth, but it will be easy if you do as I show you."

Laurie mastered the position after a day or so, and as she grew larger it was the most comfortable way to sit.

She was avoiding David, since it was painful to be with him. Since Lord Peter's arrival the only times they had alone together had been late at night, in their rooms. They had talked, made gentle love, laughed at some of the foibles of their guests and complained of others. But now she slipped away early, pleading exhaustion, and if she was not asleep when he came up, she pretended to be. For some time he accepted her actions but finally one evening he sat on her side of the bed and took her hand.

"I know you are not asleep, Laurie. Open your eyes."

A habit of obedience is hard to break. She opened them, staring up at him silently.

"Tell me what is wrong. I have little enough pleasure in this house of strident voices and I won't have you behaving this way. Has someone annoyed you?"

Laurie had promised herself she would never mention the story her mother had told her, not to anyone, and particularly not to David. It was hard to believe the words that came from her mouth.

"When you went to Grenada did you go to see the French Creole woman?"

He looked as if she had slapped him. He got up,

straightening himself, and walked away from her as if he were very tired. "Someone has told you of Jeanne Marie," he said to the wall. "Who?"

"First, Vanessa—to explain your unreasonable jealousy at our first party. Then, the Lady Desirée, who informed me that Bartram had told her how angry he was that you went to see her last month."

"My father grows garrulous and foolish in his infatuation," David said bitterly. "And your mother stays true to her nature. What did you think of the tale?"

Laurie sat up, suddenly angry. "Do not question me. Answer *my* question. Did you go to Grenada to see her?"

He turned and came back to the bed, looking down at her. "Yes. Your deception led me to seek out the most deceiving woman of all my experience. I planned to make love to her and realize once more that the tender yielding of a woman means nothing more than her wish to bend you to her will. To know again that there is nothing valuable in a woman but the pleasure one receives from her body and the children she can bear. That they have no honor nor integrity." His voice shook and he paused, controlling it. "In the end, I did not go to her. I went to the Sparta Club instead, to drink more than I should and gamble with some old friends. Then I came home to you."

Her heart leaped with hope. "Why, David?"

"Because I knew I was wrong. You *are* honorable, in spite of your small deception. I know you would never truly betray me. And, you are living up to your bargain. Could I do less?"

It wasn't the answer she had hoped for, and she fought with disappointment and bitterness. In a way, Desirée had been right, for no matter what his reasons he had lusted after that woman, and only his own sense of honor had turned him back. She was almost sorry for him, thinking that now when she was becoming misshapen and unattractive, he would be forever struggling with his desires, wishing he could go back to Grenada . . .

"That bargain," she said, the words bitter. "You asked me once if I thought I would regret it, and I answered that I hoped neither of us would. Tonight, I think we both do."

"I'm sorry," he said stiffly. "Truly sorry. I will do whatever you wish me to do."

"Why, what can we do?" Laurie felt as if she were made of ice, cold and brittle. "We are fairly caught up in it now. We can not turn back or change our minds. I suppose we must simply congratulate each other on our admirable integrity and go on as we have, making the best of it."

"Yes, of course." Even his voice was weary, his broad shoulders slumped. She wished she could put her arms around him, comfort him. But it wasn't her arms he wanted, nor her comforting. She lay back on her pillow and closed her eyes, realizing that the Lady Desirée had done as she had once sworn to do, made her pay for her escape. She could see the enraged face, hear her say, "your heart will bleed!" And so it was, or felt like it . . .

She woke at dawn, to find that the chill had sent her creeping closer to David's warmth, as it always did. And her touch must have disturbed him, for he was watching her with a sober sadness that made her feel almost ashamed. He could not help his feelings any more than she could, and she felt she would have been wiser not to mention that cursed story. It had torn the delicate balance of their life together and made them both unhappy. She moved away, pulling up the coverlet, and as she did he moved, sitting up.

"For once there is silence in this house," he said, forcing cheerfulness. "If we hurry we can breakfast alone, out on the slope."

In answer she smiled, flung the coverlet back and ran

to dress. If they were to make the best of it, breakfast on the slope would be a good place to start.

David carried the basket she had filled with Molenga's cold chicken and tiny sausages, the long loaves of bread, the fruit and wine. In a golden sunrise they tramped through a copse of trees and shrubs and slid downward on the slope until they were hidden from the house.

Sitting, they were silent, for with the excellent food and the view there was no need to talk. Laurie watched the black shadows creep around behind the jagged rocks below them and imagined again that they were alive; queer, ragged creatures of the night, hiding from the sun.

They had finished, and momentarily she expected to hear David stirring, ready to go back. But instead he lay full length on the slope, shielding his eyes from the sun with a thick forearm.

"I have missed this," he said. "Our perpetual visitors have even stolen our mornings. I wish we could go back now and find the house empty. When will they all go home, Laurie?"

She had been looking east, knowing that just beyond the roll of the next field there was a small valley she had never seen but which now held the school that would soon open for the slave children. She had hoped to get a good view of it, but except for a corner of the gray roof and a red chimney, it was not visible.

"I do not know," she answered absently. "They never speak of leaving."

He propped himself on one elbow, his brown eyes slitted against the sun. "Then we must do something to remind them," he said. "I want your mother out of the house." He sat up, brushing dead grass from his hands with an expression of distaste not caused by the grass. "I asked Father yesterday when he thought we would be rid of them, and he was horrified. He was waiting then for your mother to finish her primping so he could take her on one of their interminable rides. He is acting like a lovesick young swain! I cannot understand such foolishness in a man his age.'' He lifted his eyes to Laurie's. ''Besides, she is vicious. She must go.''

Laurie knew it was not just that Desirée had carried a tale which he had admitted was true in part. It was that Desirée had known it would hurt her and had delighted in it. Vicious, she thought, was an excellent description. And, though David had not mentioned it, Laurie felt sure Desirée would eventually hurt Bartram, also. She pulled up her knees and leaned on them, thinking.

''Perhaps you could ask Lord Peter for help. He promised me he would suggest to her that her visit be short. If he finds out she is deliberately making trouble he will act, and if anyone can persuade her he can. He could threaten to take away the income he gives her.''

David sighed. ''It will not be easy, telling my uncle he has brought us a problem, even though inadvertently. But I suppose he will understand better than most. It is worth a try.'' He looked at Laurie, his face clearing somewhat. ''Once she is gone and our baby is born, we will be happier.''

''I hope so,'' Laurie said. Unable to stop herself, she added, ''At least, I will not be so unattractive to you.'' From the corner of her eye she saw him sit up, his face turn toward her. Glancing at him, she saw amazement.

''Unattractive? You are more beautiful, more desirable than ever to me! Your small body carries our life together, nurturing it with love. When I join with you now, my passion is greater than before, exalted by such a miracle.'' He reached for her, his arms trembling as he held her tightly against him. ''I feel so humble, and yet proud when you allow me to make love to you. But I do not blame you for being cool and withdrawn—surely, you are beginning to feel the burden.''

Her mouth searched blindly up his bearded cheek and found his lips, silencing them. She felt the heat of his hands through the silk of her blouse, moving over her sensitive breasts, so full and tight now that the merest touch set them throbbing.

"My only burden is loneliness," she whispered. "I want you so much, and I thought you didn't want me . . ."

"More, much more," he said hoarsely. "Constantly . . ." He moved her between his thighs and began on the buttons of her blouse, his fingers shaking as he pulled aside the folds of silk and slid his hand in, looking into her eyes as he cupped and caressed the tender heaviness. Her mouth opened in a soundless gasp, the soft lips exposing the tips of white teeth, the pink velvet of tongue, and he bent to cover it with a crushing kiss, wildly possessive, that sent shocks of sensation flaming down through her.

She was dazed by his passion and her own, lying against his aroused body, her arms around him, her hands caressing his back, loving the heat and tension of his muscles, the hard strength. But then he raised his head, and his body became motionless, oddly still. She opened her eyes and saw his gaze on the rocks below, wary and searching, felt him pull her gently upward and away from him.

"We will not make love here again," he said quietly. "One of your rock people has come to life."

She sat up, startled, and looked down. There on the other side of the ravine was a horse and rider, slowly leaving the shadows of the rocks and traveling up the steep slope, the horse laboring beneath the solid, black-clad man who rode him. Prentiss Bailey! He turned once and looked back toward them and she saw the thin slash of mouth, the untidy, stringy gray hair beneath his hat.

"What is *he* doing there?" Her voice held the revulsion she felt for the man.

David shrugged, getting to his feet. "The ravine is as much his as ours, I suppose. Neither plantation claims it." But David's mouth was flattened and stern as he picked up the remains of their breakfast and packed it away in the basket. "Still, I wonder," he added tightly, "if he has spied on us before."

Rising, Laurie straightened her gown, buttoning the blouse. "Surely not," she said, injecting the words with more certainty than she felt, "or we should have seen him."

"At times, we have been quite preoccupied with each other," David said wryly. "I doubt I would have noticed him today if he had not moved—to allow himself a better view."

Laurie's face reddened at the thought. "To watch our lovemaking? David! What kind of a man would do that?"

"A man like Prentiss Bailey," David said grimly. "But he will not have his vicarious pleasure again. Now, let's go home."

Chapter Fifteen

THE DAY WAS AS HECTIC AS EVER, THE HOUSE SEEMING to vibrate with action as Bartram arrived to list the dinner guests and talk interminably about their importance as Desirée appeared in a graceful morning gown to flirt outrageously with him. Without Molenga to take care of the routine of the household Laurie was sure she would have been exhausted. As it was, she simply nodded and smiled and made a note that the Edringtons would be there that evening—what a pleasure!—and that on the other hand Bartram's most pressing remarks concerned strangers, the Van Horns.

"He is a special attaché to the Governor," Bartram explained, "and is coming to gather information from my brother. It is most necessary to treat Mr. Van Horn with great respect and show him every courtesy."

Continuing to nod and smile, Laurie bit her tongue to keep from reminding him that she treated every guest with respect and courtesy, and wished they would all disappear. She could hardly wait for the day to end, the night to fall. David's eyes when he left her had spoken volumes, and she could think of nothing but the two of them, closing the door of their rooms, shutting out the world. It was a great relief when Bartram left off his instructions and warnings and took Desirée out for a stroll in the gardens. Laurie sighed and went to find Molenga.

Alone in the kitchen, Molenga wasn't much better company. Silent and snappish by turns, she took note of what Laurie had to say and shook her head. "A gathering you will long remember," she said enigmatically. "There are days on which life pivots, and I believe this is one of them." She turned away as Laurie, intrigued, began to question her. "I know no more than that," she said angrily. "Go and exercise. Leave me to my work."

In the afternoon, when Desirée had gone to her room for her usual rest, Lord Peter came riding up the avenue on horseback. When Laurie greeted him he asked immediately for the Lady Desirée and Laurie knew David must have spoken to him of their problems. Embarrassed, she left him standing in the entry hall and went up to fetch her mother, hating the thought that Lord Peter must again deal with the woman he now detested.

Desirée was nestled in her mound of small pillows, dreamily content but awake. She gave Laurie a brilliant smile beneath a somewhat startled gaze. It was not often her daughter sought her out.

"Lord Oldenburgh is here, asking for you," Laurie said coolly, and saw that she had startled her further.

"Indeed?"

Laurie nodded, watching the small smile come and go, malicious and amused.

"In that case," Desirée said pertly, "I suppose I should hurry down, shouldn't I?"

Predictably, she dawdled, choosing a gown and then tossing it aside for another. She called for Thérèse to dress her hair and was very demanding about the style. Laurie waited, shrugging as Thérèse gave her a questioning glance. Who could account for Desirée's actions? She had been sure her mother would make all haste, once she knew Lord Peter had called.

At long last Desirée was satisfied with her appearance, though she asked Laurie's opinion before she left the room. Coming close so that Laurie could examine her elaborately dressed hair, her eyes were too bright, and Laurie could detect a distinct odor of brandy. Perhaps it made her braver . . .

As Desirée's footsteps receded toward the staircase Thérèse again gave Laurie a curious glance, and Laurie, in a few quick words, told her why Lord Peter had called.

"It will not be that simple," Thérèse said quietly, a prophecy instantly proven true by raised voices from the hall below.

Laurie could not believe Lord Peter would bellow like that. Running out on the gallery, with Thérèse following, she grasped the railing and stared down in disbelief. Lord Peter's lean hands gripped Desirée's shoulders, his face close to hers, shouting in rage.

"You will not! I won't permit such a parody! You will tell Bartram at once that you are not fit to be his wife—or I will!"

"Oh, dear Lord," Laurie said faintly, and felt Thérèse's arm go about her. Then Desirée wrested herself free from Lord Peter and, holding her skirts high, came running up the stairs like a deer. She halted beside the two shocked faces, her eyes sparkling.

"The poor man has gone mad," she said, and burst into laughter. Laughter filled with bitter triumph, with singing malice. "Completely mad—with jealousy, of course! Now that I have found my own true love, My Lord wants me back again and hopes to keep us apart." She looked at Laurie with her eyes dancing, begging her to share the joke. "Is he not foolish? Bartram could not be persuaded to give me up now—we are to be wed within a month." She whirled past them, into her room again, and behind the closed door the laughter continued.

Nausea churning in her stomach, Laurie watched the gray, motionless man below. He had heard every word, and he met Laurie's eyes with angry despair. Then a movement directly below the gallery caught her attention and she saw the small, ebony head, the brilliantly wrapped body. Molenga's gaze swept the scene and there was a barely perceptible nod of the head before she was gone, and Lord Peter was gone also, the heavy door closing softly behind him.

Laurie allowed Thérèse to cajole her into going to her rooms to lie down, eyes closed, for a rest. But behind the closed lids she kept seeing the dancing eyes, hearing the laughter. Desirée would make life a hell for Bartram Covington, and Laurie could well imagine David's feelings when he heard that news.

Desirée was avenging herself. Against Lord Peter. Against the world! She would split our family apart but she would be a respected wife again. If Bartram outlived his brother, she might even become Lady Oldenburgh at last, for David, Laurie knew, wouldn't want to be a peer.

Why hadn't they seen the danger? Wise in some ways, David's father was a child when it came to understanding a woman like Desirée. Given his foolish reverence of the nobility, he undoubtedly believed he had won a prize.

She could hear Thérèse moving around the room, her steps seeming nervous, hurried. Then the door closed. Laurie knew she should be up preparing for the evening, but somehow she couldn't face it yet. She turned and burrowed her face into the pillow, making her mind blank and trying to gather her forces.

"You are ill? Laurie! What is it, darling?"

She jerked upward, stared at David and then the windows. "Can it be that late?" She looked back at him, large and strong, and put out her hands to him. "I am not ill, only upset. David, your father—my mother—she means to marry him!"

"Good God." He sat down, hugging her. "What is this unlikely story? She is only attempting to stir up more trouble, and it seems she has succeeded. My father is struck by her charm, but he would not take his brother's paramour as a wife."

She drew away from him. "Are you positive? Lord Peter believed her. He was furious when she told him."

"She told *him?* She went that far?"

Laurie nodded. "He came to speak to her—I supposed at your request. He shouted that she was not fit to be a wife, and he would tell Bartram so—"

She was alone on the bed. David had leaped to his feet, his face dark red. "Stay here," he said grimly, "I will speak to this *lady.*" The door slammed, and she could hear his angry stride pounding along the gallery.

Fright gave her energy. She got out of bed hurriedly and hands trembling, washed her face and combed her hair. She expected at any moment to hear David roaring even louder than Lord Peter, for she had never seen him so angry. But instead she heard only his pounding steps again on the gallery and then the stairs, hard and quick, going down. She rushed out, but he had disappeared, and the front door was opening as a maid admitted the first of the evening's dinner guests.

She went down, dressed as she was, distraught but courteous. It was the Van Horns from Bridgetown, both strangers to her and both dressed in the height of fashion, expecting a gracious welcome at Silversea House.

Ushering them into the drawing room, Laurie explained that her husband must continue looking for her mother, who seemed to have wandered away. She noted their expressions of embarrassed pity and rang for a maid to bring them wine and cheese. She felt faint, her mind whirling madly and then weak with relief as the door opened again and the Edringtons came in. She told them quickly and John nodded and left to join the search, while Vanessa calmly took over the duties of hostess.

Going up the stairs to put on more appropriate clothing, Laurie was struck by the hope that Desirée had returned unseen and went to her room. There the odor of brandy now seemed to overpower the scent of powders and perfumes, and she followed the odor, finding a bottle lying on its side beneath the bed, the last of its contents dribbled on the thick rug. Kneeling there,

Laurie was suddenly faint, the room seemed to darken. There were vague, moving forms shimmering against the darkness, engaged in some macabre task. Her heart pounded with fear and an indescribable pity. She pulled herself up with a supreme effort of will, closing her mind firmly to everything but the necessity of keeping calm, dressing, going down to her bewildered guests. Somewhere, Desirée was either hiding or wandering, drunken and triumphant. She would be found.

In her own rooms she dressed and went down again, expecting news. But Vanessa, chatting with the Van Horns, gave her red-gold head a hardly perceptible shake, her emerald eyes worried.

Lord Peter rose from a chair and came to meet Laurie, taking her hand. He had just arrived, he said, with Bartram. Bartram, of course, had joined the searchers, and Ham, who had been driving their carriage, also had gone to help.

"I, of course, would be useless," Lord Peter added, his eyes sliding away from Laurie's face, "for I do not know the grounds or where she might go."

They sat, making polite conversation, sipping wine, waiting. John Edrington came back to fetch lanterns and left again quietly. A warm wind came through the open windows, gusting occasionally against the draperies, bringing the shrilling of insects to their ears, and, at times, the distant calls of the searchers. Their voices faltered, fell silent, rose again hurriedly, and Laurie shivered in spite of the warmth of the night. The time seemed interminable, but at last, through the window to the west, she heard the noise of feet on the steps outside. She hurried to the door and looked out at the crowd of dim figures, the swinging lights of lanterns. Relief made her weak.

"They have found her," she called back into the room, "for they are all coming in!" She saw the waiting guests relax, their stiff faces begin to smile, and heard the buzz of relieved talk. Then she went back to the door.

Only then did she think of how oddly silent the searchers were, coming up to the portico. She froze, seeing the light of one of the lanterns shining on a trailing, muddy skirt, the arm hanging down from the limp body borne in David's arms. She closed her eyes momentarily, knowing there was no life in that body. Then Old Hugh's courage rose in her and she turned again toward the guests in the drawing room.

"I am afraid there has been an accident," she said evenly. "Please excuse us." She shut the door, softly.

Bartram had found her, and he took most of Laurie's concern. He was bowed with outraged grief, trembling with it, tears running from his eyes, as he told Laurie how he had discovered the body of the woman he planned to wed. He looked his age for the first time, and she sat with her arms around him as they laid Desirée's body on the bed and straightened her limbs.

She had fallen to the rocks at the bottom of the southeast slope, David said quietly. Her neck was broken. The evening dew, he supposed, had made the grass slippery. As she had never been there in daylight, she could not know the danger of the sudden precipice. Laurie gave him a warning glance over Bartram's head. The old man needed no more details, not now. After a time she was able to move Bartram into the little sitting room, to leave the body in peace. Then she called for Thérèse and had her bring rum.

At first the rum only made it worse as Bartram lost restraint and sobbed wildly. But Laurie kept pouring, and in the end David and John supported him down the hall into another room where he fell into a heavy sleep. Laurie was unsure if she had done the right thing, but David reassured her, saying that he was glad she had thought of it. He stood with his arms around her as John Edrington went down again to explain to the others.

"I am sorry," David said, muffled. "Poor woman. Poor, vain little woman. One misstep . . ."

More than one misstep in her life, Laurie thought. She had no tears, her heart was stone. She could still hear the cruel laughter and see Lord Peter's despair, and now she ached for Bartram. Bartram, she thought, did not know how lucky he was to have only her memory. But Lord Peter would know, for the chains had dropped from his neck. She sighed, her head against David's chest, listening to the strong, steady beat of his heart.

"I am very tired," she said.

"Of course you are." He lifted her and carried her to her rooms where Thérèse waited, her long face stricken and silent. He laid her gently on the bed and stood before her.

"There is more, my dear, and you may as well know now. Grace has lost her school building. It burned tonight. It was the dying glow in the sky that brought us to the slope and showed us the white dress on the rocks below. Otherwise, I am sure we would not have found her until morning."

Laurie burst into tears. She could cry for Grace's lost dream, and perhaps, a little, for her mother. She was sorry for Desirée, that strange, bittersweet little creature, for she was sure she hadn't wished to die. She hoped she had not suffered. But she didn't grieve, for grief is for oneself at the loss of a loved one, and she had lost no one she loved.

"Help her to undress," David said to Thérèse. "I will bring some food." He left quickly, as if Laurie's tears were something he could not bear.

Later, when she was calmer, she held Thérèse's hand as they said good-night.

"You will stay with me now, until you wish to return to France."

The white cap bobbed assent as Thérèse took the supper tray and left.

It was not until Laurie was drifting off into a restless

sleep that she realized how warm the wind was, soothing her face. Warm and dry, the wind told her there had been no evening dew to make the grass slippery.

As soon as the body had been found Ham had been sent to fetch the doctor from Speight's Town. He had not stopped to rest, and by midmorning the next day he and the doctor, who must determine the cause of death, were back at Silversea. They had brought a wagon, and in the back of it was a long, mahogany box, clean and bright, shining in the sun. David took the doctor up while Laurie remained at the breakfast table trying to make conversation with the Van Horns, who had slept very late. Mistress Van Horn, a plump pigeon of a woman, maternal and kind, appeared to think Laurie should be in bed, and made no secret of it.

"Your father-in-law is taking a much wiser course," she said firmly. She had visited the darkened room where Bartram remained with people tiptoeing and whispering around him. "Grief must be dealt with gently, especially in your condition . . ."

Mr. Van Horn was quiet, his spectacled face thin and oddly pale for this climate but showing an alert interest. Laurie had learned he had some special position with the governor, but did not understand it. He seemed intelligent and reserved. He had offered his sympathy, mentioning that he had known Desirée slightly in London, had found her charming and very much regretted Laurie's loss. Then he had patted her hand and never mentioned it again. Laurie wished his wife would follow his example.

Having heard the jostling footsteps of slaves carrying the long box upstairs, Laurie rose and shut the door into the hall before sitting down to begin a long conversation about Vanessa's school. Only when she heard the heavy tramp of feet on the stairs and then departing through the entry did she let the talk slow. It seemed less than delicate to watch Desirée leave in that manner when she had wished so desperately for her departure. Shortly afterward, David came in and gave her a swift, searching glance.

"I have told Dr. Townsend of your condition, my dear, and he wishes to examine you before he leaves."

"An excellent idea!" Mistress Van Horn's voice was firm. "Come, I will see you up the stairs."

Fortunately, Thérèse entered at that moment and took Laurie's arm. Upstairs, she still attended her. Sitting in a corner she was like a watchful crow in her black dress with her long nose.

Dr. Townsend was old, very old, Laurie thought. Likely in his seventies, but brisk and businesslike. He listened, poked and prodded, asked questions. She bore with it all, answered willingly, but still when he sat back he did not seem satisfied. Something other than her condition was bothering him.

"Your husband has told me you were not close to your mother," he said, "that in fact you barely knew her. He felt your grief would not be great enough to cause trouble with your pregnancy." His white brows were raised questioningly, and Laurie nodded.

"Then perhaps you will not mind a question or two. Did you consider your mother mentally stable?"

Laurie was amazed. "Indeed, I did. She had a quick and able mind."

"Overly emotional? Apt to think of taking her own life?"

"Never." Laurie could say that with absolute conviction. The doctor looked away from her, thoughtful, staring from a window.

"She wore slippers. Soft slippers. Surely she would not start out on such a long walk without putting on leather shoes to protect her feet. I thought perhaps she might have been upset, and rushed from the house unthinking." He looked back at Laurie. "Could that have happened?"

Thérèse spoke from the corner. "My mistress always

wore soft slippers, sir. She could not abide heavy footwear, and did not even own a pair of leather shoes."

He looked over at Thérèse with surprise. Thérèse had a faculty for making herself unnoticeable.

"That would explain it, then. My other question is not truly a question, I suppose. It is only that I wonder at her going out at all, so far from the house. I have not yet examined her thoroughly, but I could see she was slight and poorly muscled, as if unused to physical activity. Her face was . . . ah, got up, as if for an evening party, and her gown was a fragile, lacy affair. Not at all what one would wear for a long walk, with evening falling." He spoke slowly, hesitantly, as if thinking aloud, but when the light blue eyes came back to Laurie they were sharp with curiosity. "Was it a habit of hers to wander about alone at night?"

"No," Laurie said flatly, "it was not."

"Then why do you think she did so, last night?"

"She did not say, sir. None of us knew she contemplated it. In fact, we do not know when she left. The search started when we found she was missing. But I do know she was quite excited, exhilarated. Full of nervous energy." Laurie hesitated, knew he would ask, and went on. "She has been a widow for many years, as Bartram Covington has been a widower. She told us last evening that they were to wed. She was quite . . . happy about it."

She had stunned him. "Old Bartram?" He spoke without thinking, and a tinge of red crept up his cheeks. "You will pardon my informality. I have known Bartram for years, and now he planned to wed at last! Oh, my—and he was the one who found her body . . ." He sighed, leaning forward to fasten his capacious bag. "Tragic, indeed. On the eve of happiness, so to speak . . ." His blue eyes were old again, full of an old man's sympathy. Then he was gone, with a few instructions on diet for Laurie.

When the door closed behind him Thérèse sighed, a

long, slow exhalation. Then she rose and came to the bed, looking down at Laurie.

"She would never have gone that far, Madame."

Laurie was startled only by the "Madame." Thérèse had expressed her feelings exactly. She lay looking up at the bony face, realizing that the two of them were the only ones in the house who knew that the Lady Desirée never walked except on paving. It was a queer trait of hers. She despised the feel of grass, feared the thought of snakes or even insects around her. She nodded and sat up, swung her feet over the side of the bed.

" 'Madame'? Is that what you will call me now?"

"It is correct."

Laurie sighed, looking at her dangling toes. "You believe someone was with her."

"How else?"

Laurie looked up again. "Do you believe I should say so—to David, perhaps?"

"No! That is—I do not know . . ." Thérèse sat down suddenly, her gaunt face strained, her eyes red-rimmed from lack of sleep. She looked at Laurie, her mouth trembling. "God knows, Madame, enough of us had reason . . ."

Laurie put her arms around the bony shoulders and thought irrelevantly of Grace's mother, murdered by a frantic, fearful slave, and how outraged and sad she had felt when Grace told her of it. Yet all she felt now was a distant horror.

"It couldn't have been any of us," she said. "We were all here in the house. . . ."

"No. We were all outside except for you and Lord Oldenburgh. And I had seen him earlier when I searched for her in the gardens. He was there, rushing from the back of the house. Then he took Ham and they went to bring Mr. Covington here. His Lordship did not see me, nor do I know why he was there, for he had left the house some time before."

Laurie's flesh crawled. Lord Peter had been desperate.

Had he found her, wandering drunkenly . . . ? She straightened, releasing Thérèse, and forced a smile.

"We are becoming children," she said, "frightening each other with tall tales. My mother was full of triumph, drunk from brandy and drunk again with the power to hurt those who had hurt her. Who knows what she might have done? Perhaps she did wish to be alone, to savor her victory, and became lost in the twilight." She took Thérèse's hand. "I cannot believe such evil of any of our men."

Thérèse nodded, and brought out a weak smile, but her eyes did not change.

The body of Lady Desirée Stepney had not been taken to Speight's Town as they had supposed, but to Bridgetown. There, in honor of her title, she would be buried in a cemetery that held the remains of several other members of the nobility and various dignitaries of church and state. David told Laurie that it had all been arranged by Mr. Van Horn, who had intercepted Dr. Townsend as he left and insisted on it.

"Burial will take place as quickly as possible," he added. "But a memorial service will be held the day after tomorrow, to give us all time to attend. Then we are to spend the night at Government House, an honor I presume is due to Lord Peter."

Laurie noted the irony in his voice, the concern in his eyes as he looked down at her.

"Then it will be over," she said, "and you will be so busy in the fields you will soon forget it."

They were sitting in the dining room at breakfast, and Laurie thought of the mornings on the southeast slope and knew they would never go there again. She pushed the thought away.

"Then Lord Peter will leave Barbados, I suppose, and Richard Allyn also will be able to put his mind on his work," she added, hopefully.

"Not yet," David said absently. "I hear that Van

Horn has asked Uncle Peter to stay over for a time. Some problem he wishes to clear up.''

Laurie was silent, thinking. Lord Peter would not intrude on Silversea, not with his brother still in residence. Bartram had turned against Lord Peter to a marked degree and would scarcely speak to him. Laurie thought it possible that on that fateful day Lord Peter had made an attempt to dissuade Bartram from marriage to Desirée, and had said something that Bartram couldn't yet forgive. In any event, she was glad that her father-in-law had stayed with them, for he needed a family now—and he ate well, with Molenga in the kitchen.

That day Laurie made an attempt to return to normalcy. There was still the memorial service to get through, but in the meantime she went through the exercises Molenga had taught her and began again on her sewing. Vanessa came to call, bringing a pattern for a cradle coverlet, and stayed to tea, talking of cheerful news and children. But in the end she spoke of Grace's school.

"How terrible that the books burned," she said. "The knowledge that would have truly set the children free."

"I know how Grace must feel," Laurie said. "It was her life. Does she plan to begin again?"

Vanessa frowned. "I'm afraid not. She must have been completely overcome, for her father said she left the next morning, saying only that she was going away for awhile and would visit friends on Martinique."

"I hope she finds a place there to teach," Laurie said impetuously, "and never returns to her father!"

"John said the same thing," Vanessa told her. "He also remarked that the fire would make Mr. Bailey happy. What a peculiar man he must be."

Laurie thought peculiar hardly touched it, but nodded and began to talk of pleasanter things.

Later, when Vanessa was gone, Laurie went upstairs and through the now-empty rooms that Desirée had used. David had gathered up her jewels and given them back to Lord Peter; the maids had disposed of her clothing and paints. Standing there, Laurie thought of David's words: ". . . Poor, vain little woman," and knew he had been kinder than she had. But he had not heard that triumphant, malicious laughter . . . nor seen Lord Peter's despair. She went to the window, to raise it and dispel the last lingering scent of perfume.

Below, Molenga was walking back to the house from the vegetable garden with an overflowing basket of produce. She was a pleasant sight in her colorful silk and gold bangles. Laurie looked further east at the dark green of the lime trees, and then on, seeing a rider on a horse, motionless on top of a rolling, dunelike hill in the sugar cane fields there. Prentiss Bailey, again, with his head turned, watching. Watching the house? Laurie turned away, somehow apprehensive.

Chapter Sixteen

⌇

"I INSIST ON YOUR SERVICES," DAVID SAID. "YOU HAVE neglected me long enough. As your husband, you know, I have certain rights."

"I do know," Laurie said, trying to keep from smiling. "But where in the wedding ceremony does it state I must wash you?" She was standing in their bathroom, late that night, looking down at his long body in the big tub, the outline of most of it wavering and indistinct beneath the water.

"Right where it forces you to say you'll obey me," David replied. "I have told you to wash me, haven't I?"

In spite of herself, Laurie laughed. "You have," she admitted. "But . . . Oh, David, I do hate to expose myself now. I feel so ungainly and ugly—"

He interrupted her by the simple expedient of lurching upward and grabbing her arms, his movement sending water cascading over the rim to splash on her skirt. "You may have your choice," he said dangerously. "You may disrobe and get in, or get in as you are, whichever you prefer. In the last case, I will have the pleasure of removing your clothes myself."

She knew his playfulness was a sharp reaction against sadness and tragedy, a desperate affirmation of life and pleasure, and suddenly she gave in. Laughing, she began taking off her clothes, stripping herself efficiently. Yet climbing in with him, she was uncomfortable again as his gaze traveled warmly over her rounded belly. Watching her eyes, his own eyes softened.

"You are beautiful," he said, and urged her into his arms, turning her so she lay back against him. "We shall start our son learning our way of life," he said in her ear. "The first thing he must know is to never come between us." He was caressing her water-slick body, his hands shaping the growing abdomen tenderly, moving up to take the weight of her breasts in his palms and bending to kiss her ear and neck.

Laurie was helpless against the warmth and skill of his hands, the tantalizing kisses he was placing on her neck. She was shaken by a warm rush of desire, urged into erotic imaginings as his arousal became ever more evident against her back. Finally she could no longer lie still and sat up, busily taking a cloth and soaping it. Her turquoise eyes were dark and velvety as she turned, kneeling between his legs and beginning to wash him. She bathed him as she would a baby, her hands gentle and slow, washing and then rinsing each section of his upper body and avoiding his eyes for fear that he would see the desire in hers. It seemed impractical now to think of making love, with her body growing clumsy.

He lay back and watched her through half-closed eyes, looking at the tumble of black hair pinned up on her small head, the soft, parted lips, the lowered lashes. He could feel how she felt, how shy she was of her feelings now. Yet her tight, full breasts and the rounded belly that held his child brought his desire to full strength, took over his decision to be gentle and humor her. Then she sat back and looked at him, biting her lip.

"That is all *I* can do," she said, rather breathlessly. "The rest of you is under water."

He rose slowly, water streaming from his muscular body as he stood over her, fully aroused, his strong thighs quivering, his feet apart. He looked down at her, at the fascinated eyes that swept over him, at the way her breasts rose and fell with her quickened breathing.

"Now you may continue," he said grandly, the effect

somewhat marred by his shaking voice. "And be sure you miss nothing . . ."

She was torn between her aching sexual desire and a nearly equal desire to smile at his grandiloquence. Sitting on her heels, she lowered her eyes again to the washcloth and proceeded to soap it carefully. Then she set the soap aside and rose to her knees, her face close to his loins. Reaching behind him she began covering his hard buttocks with swirls of lather, then moving down the backs of his thighs with slow, soapy strokes. This brought her closer, her cheek brushing against him, and she hid a smile as she heard him take in a sharp breath.

Inexorably the small hands circled and made their way to the front of his thighs, smoothed upward carefully and began to move across his belly in featherlight strokes.

"Laurie . . ."

The strangled voice held that same tone she remembered, a mixture of male domination and urgent pleading. Beneath her hands his whole body was rock-hard with tension, waiting.

"Just a moment," she said softly, and leaned forward, her lips parted. Quickly and lightly, she kissed him where he wanted it most, and then sat back and methodically covered him with lather.

"Good God, what a tease you are!" He sat down, sending water flying, and grabbed her. "Now I'll show you how it feels to be tantalized."

She erupted with laughter, hugging him close. "Better yet," she whispered, "show me in bed . . ."

There were, she discovered, many and varied ways of making love without bothering the sleeping child within her. But David still insisted on ending with the way he called "spooning," entering her as she curled in the semicircle of his body.

"It is safe," he whispered. "And I do not feel complete unless our bodies are joined. I need it . . . I need you."

Delightfully satisfied, her whole body relaxed and glowing, she went to sleep in his arms, wondering drowsily if he ever would truly love her. And if he did, would he know it . . .

They left at dawn for Bridgetown and the memorial service that would end the gloomy aura that still seemed to hang in the rooms of Silversea House. They rode in silence, since Bartram was with them and seemed disinclined to talk, his face stern and thoughtful beneath the white beard. But it wasn't as bad as Laurie had feared it might be, for his grief seemed to have abated and he no longer seemed compelled to talk of Desirée's loveliness and charm, or the cruelty of fate.

The service was well attended. Officials of the island government and their wives, other members of Bridgetown society and old friends of the Covington family all came to pay homage to a member of the English nobility unfortunate enough to die outside of England. But the service itself was not impressive. The clergyman seemed uncomfortable, and contented himself with ritual and a few words about sudden, tragic death.

They came out into clear late afternoon sunlight, and knowing that Government House was only a few blocks from the parish church, Laurie would have preferred to walk, to breathe in fresh air and forget sadness. But Mr. Van Horn had provided dark funereal carriages for them all, and she obediently climbed in, along with David, the Edringtons and Thérèse.

Bartram, having regained control and a better regard for his brother, rode with Lord Peter and the Van Horns. They had learned that the Van Horns were officially their hosts, for the governor and his lady were at present visiting one of the other islands. Laurie was glad, for she looked forward to a quiet evening and an early bedtime. Today she felt heavy and listless.

It was a lovely building they entered. Government

House was low and painted white, with an air of permanence around it, as if it had grown in its own gardens. There was a portico, much larger than at Silversea, and inside a gentle, perpetual sound of clattering jalousies from the wind. There was a large, cruciform drawing room, with windows that curved against the constant wind. Even the chandeliers were protected from gusts, Laurie noted, with a separate, small glass vase protecting each candle.

Awaiting the dinner hour they sat in a group in the drawing room, a group dwarfed by the magnitude of space around them, the massive, magnificent furniture. Wine was served to them, along with an infinite variety of cheeses and fruit. The conversation was disjointed and full of awkward pauses, as if no one spoke of what was on his mind, but only of inconsequential, easily forgotten generalities.

Mr. Van Horn, Laurie saw, seemed particularly preoccupied. He moved constantly and restlessly in a big chair which hardly suited his small frame. She saw that David watched him with guarded interest and wondered at that, but could catch nothing of the conversation between them. She was distracted continually by the heroic effort of Mistress Van Horn, who seemed determined to tell her in one evening how to raise a child from birth to adulthood.

Dinner was served at last in a large dining room alive with the sheen of highly polished silver on table and sideboards and in glass-fronted cabinets. They were served by liveried black servants, silent and skillful. Laurie ate without interest, half-nodding. The tension of the last few days had slipped away, the relief of having it done with leaving her limp, and now she thought of sleep as a thirsty man thinks of water. David seemed amused when, dinner over, he took her arm and led her to the stairs.

"We will torture you no longer, dearest. You may go

to bed. I have been afraid to look at you this past half hour, for fear I would find you sleeping in your plate.''

Laurie smiled, too glad to be going to bed to wonder what conversation she might miss below. She asked David if he were sleepy also, hoping he would join her.

He shook his head. ''Van Horn has asked the men to join him in the library. He wishes to discuss a matter he believes will be important to us.''

The problems of Barbados, whether sugar prices or slavery, did not interest Laurie this night. When she reached the large bedroom allotted to them she saw Thérèse waiting in the doorway and a large, canopied bed behind her. At once she yearned for it, and quickly kissed David good-night.

He wakened her later, crawling in and settling his big body. He seemed restless, and toward morning she woke again, seeing him sitting in a chair near a window, staring out morosely. But she slept heavily afterward, and wakened to bright sunlight pouring through louvres and making striped patterns on the carpet. David was gone, and she dressed hastily, anxious to start home.

They were all in the dining room, cavernous now in dim, shuttered morning light. Laurie gratefully sat down to eat, hurrying because she felt they were waiting for her to finish. David looked wretchedly tired and John Edrington was silent, frowning, with Vanessa looking at him in puzzled concern. And they *were* waiting, for as soon as she laid down her fork David was on his feet.

''We are leaving for home,'' he said. ''I have told Thérèse, and she will have our baggage ready. Vanessa and John will ride with us, but Father and Lord Peter are to stay over another day and come home in the Edrington carriage.''

Laurie heard the strain in his voice and looked at him questioningly, but he shook his head and turned aside.

It made for a long ride home. Neither David nor John wished to talk and Thérèse sat silent in her corner.

Laurie and Vanessa attempted to ease the tension by chatting of books and her school, of weather and food. But it was hot, too hot for October, and finally, with perspiration streaming down their faces they too fell silent.

Finally they alighted at Silversea and were soon alone, since the Edringtons left immediately, anxious to return to their children. But it was not the homecoming to peace that they had imagined, for David told Laurie that the meeting with Van Horn had been of a serious nature.

"He is convinced that your mother's death was not accidental, and none of us could change his mind. He intends to investigate it and with the power of the governor behind him there is nothing we can do to stop him. I am sure he will discover in the end that he is wrong, but the investigation will be painful for you—for all of us. I am indeed sorry."

They had gone into the garden for their talk, since it was cooler there. Now Laurie stared at the lush, emerald grass around her feet while a feeling of cold nausea—a feeling that was to become very familiar in the days ahead—crept over her. David had expected her to be surprised, horrified, and after a moment his hand closed over her arm.

"You had expected this."

"No, not expected—feared." Looking up she saw that his gaze on her was sharp, and looked away again. "She would not have gone there alone. Both Thérèse and I knew that. She would not walk ten feet in the deep grass. She had a morbid fear of insects, snakes—nature itself . . ."

"Good God!" The words burst from him. "Then you believed from the first she had been murdered! Oh, Laurie . . . Laurie . . . you could not trust me enough to tell me?"

"I tried to believe it was not so. I hoped that her strong emotion that day had driven her, that like a triumphant child who runs and leaps, she had for once been without her fear and had gone to . . . to walk in the wind, to glory in her revenge against us all." She turned to him, her turquoise eyes brimming with tears. "I did not want to believe it! She had driven your uncle to desperation! And you, you were blindly angry with her. I did not want any of us punished . . ."

"You thought one of us had done it."

"Or Thérèse," she said faintly. It was true—Thérèse's feelings ran deep, and she was clever. Her words of suspicion could have been meant to blind them. She had been absent a long time that evening. She was strong, her hands like iron. And the Lady Desirée trusted Thérèse, yet Thérèse despised her.

David's face was very pale, his brown eyes opaque. He drew away from Laurie and stood up.

"I was almost afraid to tell you of Van Horn's suspicion, fearing how the news might affect you. Ridiculous of me, wasn't it? You had already accepted the idea that I might have murdered your mother myself."

"David!"

But he left her there, stalking away to the house without another word.

Laurie sat still while the knowledge came to her that no matter how much one loved someone, it was never possible to understand another person completely. The man she loved was a stranger at that moment. And she was a stranger to him, for he had not understood her feelings. She felt alone, more alone than she had ever been. Her mind sought out Old Hugh, who had taught all she knew of courage, and she leaned back on the garden bench remembering.

Before her the cane fields became rolling moors, dotted with grazing sheep, and Old Hugh stood there facing into a bitter wind. Broad and erect, he watched a storm approach. It had always seemed to Laurie that he loved the testing of a storm and the demands it put on him to meet it, to keep his animals safe and his world intact. Her world was now in storm. The Lady Desirée had set the storm in action and now it threatened to blow their lives apart. She felt a blaze of determination. Their lives would go on, they would live through this and all else that ever threatened them!

Her child chose that moment to move strongly, as if he stretched his small limbs and curled again to rest and grow. She was not alone, after all, and had much to fight for and keep safe. She rose and went carefully through the darkening twilight, over the uneven ground, conscious that she carried a life more precious than her own. And then she smiled faintly, for there in the gloom was David coming back for her. He took her arm silently and went up the steps with her. In the hall he spoke solemnly.

"I suppose your fears were natural. I was furious that night, I admit. And Lord Peter was upset. But you have forgotten one fact—he was not outside. He refused to aid in the search and was in the house from the time he arrived. You cannot consider him a suspect."

He sounded as if he were speaking to an errant child caught in some ridiculous flight of fancy. But she did not argue, nor tell him Thérèse had said Lord Peter was on the grounds after Desirée had disappeared. She had decided to wait until she knew more before she spoke again of suspicions.

Two days later Prentiss Bailey paid them a call. They had finished breakfast and David had gone upstairs for his field boots, so Laurie received Bailey and took him into the drawing room. She offered him a chair but he shook his head and stood, feet apart, his hands behind his back, rocking his thick body on its short legs. He said nothing, only stared at her with his bulging eyes.

She had sent Ham to tell David that Mr. Bailey had called, but David took his time coming. He was dressed for the fields when he arrived. Greeting Mr. Bailey with cold courtesy, he said he was on his way out and Bailey could accompany him.

"What I have to say is of interest to your wife also," Bailey said. "I shall say it here."

David's brows rose. "Are you sure, Prentiss? I can think of nothing you could have to say that would interest my wife. Her interests lie in her household, not the fields."

Bailey gave a short laugh. "Hardly true, sir! She has interested herself in the field laborers, at least to the extent of encouraging my daughter's insane scheme to educate them. However, that is not my reason for calling. Yesterday I was visited by a most inquisitive man, a Victor Van Horn of Bridgetown. He carried credentials from Governor Weatherby, or I wouldn't have given him the time of day. As it was, I learned that there has been a violent crime here. I think it most unneighborly of you not to pass a warning to me. Undoubtedly there is a renegade slave in the area and we should all know, and be on guard."

Laurie could not bear to look at him, so looked at David, who seemed not only furious but disgusted.

"The death of my wife's mother was a tragic accident," David said icily. "Your remarks are not only misinformed but cruel." He turned to Laurie. "There is no reason for you to be subjected to this. You may leave."

Laurie left, but she did not close the door tightly behind her. Something nagged at her mind, made her anxious to hear more. She went into the dining room and sat quietly, listening. Bailey's voice was penetrating and he was strangely insistent and loud.

"Whatever your belief, young Covington, Van Horn says she was murdered. And his visit was an embarrassment to me. I recently bought slaves—some twenty men and five women, to replace those who had sickened and died. Of course I bought them legally, from a planter in

Martinique. But Van Horn claimed he could see sores from ship's manacles on their limbs. I am sure that once he has finished with investigating your mother-in-law's murder, he will turn his talents to me.''

David's low answer was indistinguishable, but obviously impolite.

"Absurd! Of course I can prove it! I have friends in Martinique who will swear to it. Van Horn was simple enough to ask me if I could vouch for these "wild" slaves on the night of the murder, hoping, I suppose, to blame the deed on one of them. He is too ignorant to see that they are half-starved and weak. I doubt the strongest could walk as far as your house!''

He seemed to be rattling along with little regard for his original purpose, as if words flowed from his mouth to confuse and upset David, set him in the wrong. But David's voice was calm when he answered, and all Laurie caught was a phrase . . . "to the fields," then the sound of their feet as they departed. She supposed Bailey would now ride along, bombarding David with more of his obnoxious, insulting remarks. She sighed and rose to go outside. The house was lonely and oppressive, and the gardens cool.

She was still there when Bartram arrived. He had moved back into his house on his return from Bridgetown, and now he had come to thank her for her care of him.

She offered him a seat on the bench beside her and murmured that her care was little compared to his constant generosity, and added that they all should now put sorrow behind them.

"Yes, of course," he said briskly, surprising her. "Though it would be easier if that idiot Van Horn would listen to me. I have told him his ideas are outlandish and ridiculous, but he persists.''

She was even more surprised that his grief had been so quickly superseded by resentment, but felt it was a healthier emotion in this case. She told him of Van Horn's visit to Bailey's plantation and he grew even more indignant.

"Undoubtedly the man will make a nuisance of himself, and call on all our neighbors. As for Bailey's new slaves, of course they are contraband. He is in trouble there, having lost three of his overseers, also. One of them applied to me for work and said they were leaving because they feared an uprising amongst Bailey's maltreated slaves."

"A riot?" Laurie's thoughts flew to Grace. Perhaps it was as well that the school had burned and Grace gone away to a safer place.

"It is in the air," Bartram said reluctantly. "I have not mentioned it to David, but weeks ago I learned that several of Thatcher's overseers had been found dead, murdered by slaves."

Laurie drew her breath in sharply. "Did they find the slaves who had done it?"

"That is never possible," Bartram said absently, "for none of them will give information. They were punished as usual—ten slaves hanged for each man murdered."

"Dear Lord," Laurie whispered, shocked to the core. "And perhaps none of them guilty . . ."

Bartram shrugged. "At Thatcher's plantation a slave might well consider death a blessing. He is even more cruel than Bailey." He rose, looking down at her indulgently. "That is quite enough of such gloomy talk. Surely you shouldn't be worried by any of the problems we have, not at present. As for Bailey and those like him, they will end as they deserve."

At dinner she told David of his father's visit and what he had said, and watched a frown gather.

"Father takes such news too lightly," David said, troubled. "An uprising is like a contagion. We have not had a true riot here in years, but there is always the danger. Emotion rules at those times, for in every slave heart there lies the desire for freedom."

She looked at him with a faint smile, wondering if he realized how close he was to agreeing with her side of their arguments so long ago on the ship. He caught her gaze and grinned ruefully.

"Now you are thinking, 'Yes, yes! They should all be free!' Aren't you? But where would they go, what would they do? Most of our slaves here at Silversea are Creole, island born. They would find the jungles of Africa strange and inhospitable. Yet if they were all turned loose here, many of them would starve." He sighed, pushing his plate aside, putting his arms on the table and leaning on them heavily. "As I have hinted before, if I had not been born to this life I would never have chosen it. More and more, I despise the fact of slavery."

Laurie felt a dizzying surge of great hope, seeming to see a future in which David would come full circle to her own beliefs and they might live a different life. Their child, she thought, might grow up in a world where everyone was free, and no man owned another man.

It was clear in the next weeks that Van Horn meant to miss no chance of gaining information from anyone who had ever heard of the family at Silversea. One by one their neighbors either wrote or visited, some of them as concerned for their own safety as Prentiss Bailey had been with a renegade about; others, embarrassed, only wishing to tell them of Van Horn's suspicions and offer their help.

David and Bartram told them all that in their opinion the death had been an accident and they knew of no evidence to the contrary. But John Edrington, whom Van Horn had approached again, told them that the man believed he had good reason to call it murder.

"I am sure he does," David said disgustedly, "or he would not continue his probing. But he has refused to reveal his evidence, if he has any."

"I know something of it, though not all," John said slowly. "It is not strong evidence, perhaps, but raises a question." He glanced at Laurie, sitting nearby, and his thin face grew uncertain.

"I wish to know, John," she said. "It concerns me most of all, I believe."

He nodded, seeing how calm she looked. "Bruises. Naturally there were quite a few, though not as many as one would think since she had fallen on rocks. But bruises on her throat that did not appear to have been made by rocks. Van Horn took it upon himself to have the body examined by a medical officer, and the officer's opinion was that the bruises were indicative of . . . of strangling. He believes she was dead before she fell, or was thrown, into the ravine."

"Is the man insane?" Bartram was livid with sudden anger. "Has he *seen* the place where she fell? Those rocks are both large and small, smooth and jagged. They could cause bruises of any shape or any size. If that is all the evidence he has, I wonder that he continues this farce!"

David was silent, his eyes going to Laurie's stiff face. She looked away, knowing he was remembering her suspicion, and her reasons for it. All because Desirée despised walking in grass . . .

"I noticed no bruises on her throat," David said finally. "But it was dark when we found the body, and I did not examine it later. To us, it had been only a horrible accident and I still believe we were right." He smiled at John. "But thank you for the information. It may help us to prove the rumors wrong."

John nodded again and went on talking of other things.

Finally, Victor Van Horn came to Silversea. He came in a coach, not so grand as the one which had brought Lord Peter and Desirée to the door, but still luxurious and bearing the governor's insignia. Laurie saw him from an upstairs window and went to put on a dignified gown and brush her hair. When the maid came to announce that Mr. Van Horn was calling, she told the maid to find Ham and send him to the fields for David. Then she went down.

He did not look like a dangerous adversary. Thin, small, with his spectacles dominating his narrow face, he wore a wide-brimmed straw hat to protect his white skin from the sun. He was holding it, passing it from hand to hand, as Laurie came in. She took it from him and hung it on a wall rack and offered him a chair.

"I have come to ask you if you would mind a few questions, Mistress Covington," he said, taking the chair. "That is, if you don't mind . . ."

Laurie forced an amiable smile. "David will be here shortly," she said, "if you wish to wait until he is present." Her heart, she discovered, was beating rapidly from an odd feeling of guilt. As if she had already planned to keep this man from finding out anything that would lead to solving Desirée's murder. Surely, she thought, I cannot be that frightened. None of us could be hurt by the truth . . . unless . . .

"It is not necessary to wait," Van Horn replied. "Since I wish to ask about your mother it is likely you will have more knowledge than Mr. Covington. I hope I am not adding to your grief."

"I did not know my mother well," Laurie said, and then told him that she had been raised by her grandfather because her mother had been very ill following the death of her father in the Peninsular War. For once, she noted, it did not bother her at all to lie. "But the Lady Desirée had recovered by the time of my grandfather's death and it was then I went to live with her. Since I met and married Mr. Covington very soon afterwards, my mother and I were still virtually strangers. I am sad for her, naturally, yet there is not the grief a daughter would normally feel."

He looked at her doubtfully. "Then you know little of her life. I had hoped you could tell me if she had enemies."

Laurie thought him dense. "If she did, which I doubt," she said carelessly, "they would be in England. She had been here a very short time."

Van Horn smiled slightly. "She traveled here on the same ship as Lord Oldenburgh, I believe. Were they friends?"

"Very old friends."

"Yet the captain of the ship has told me that His Lordship was extremely surprised, even taken aback, when he met her on deck."

Laurie could feel the heat in her face. Perhaps he was not so dense, after all. "It was an amazing coincidence, I suppose. Or the captain a poor judge of expression."

"Perhaps." Van Horn stared at her, his pale face quietly alert. "Did His Lordship help in the search for her that night?"

"No, he did not." She spoke so hastily that she nearly stumbled over the words. "He was, of course, as worried by her disappearance as anyone, but he did not know the grounds well enough to be of assistance. He stayed in the house— But, why—you knew that! You were here when he arrived."

"That is true. But since he arrived in a carriage driven by your manservant I presumed he had been here earlier, before it grew dark. I thought he might have aided in the search then."

Laurie shook her head. "Only David and I knew she was missing then." More lies, and she wondered if her eyes gave her away. "As far as I know, David was looking in the gardens when you came."

Van Horn turned his head quickly, looking toward the east windows. Laurie did not have to look to know why. The sound of pounding hooves told her that David was arriving, and at a gallop. She was gaining respect for the inquiring mind in this man, and she felt that he would believe that David was in a hurry to stand between her and his questions. When he turned back she was sure of it, for he hurried a last question.

"Tell me, did Dr. Townsend question you carefully about the cause of your mother's death?"

"Oh, no. I am quite sure he knew her death was caused by a broken neck." Laurie was quite proud of the innocent stupidity of her answer.

David, leaving a lathered horse outside in full view, burst into the house and looked at Van Horn sharply. He was polite enough in his greeting, but his following question was critical.

"Is it your policy to question a bereft young woman without the protection of her husband? I am amazed, Van Horn. I would have thought better of a gentleman."

The small man seemed to shrink from David's bristling attitude. "I am indeed sorry if I have offended either of you," he said meekly. "Mistress Covington has been gracious and helpful. I would regret it exceedingly if I thought I had added to her pain."

"You have given me no pain," Laurie said calmly. "But you have aroused my curiosity. Now that Mr. Covington is here, I wonder if you would tell us both what has occasioned this to-do about my mother's accidental death?"

David stared at her in pure surprise, but Van Horn's expression was somehow admiring.

"Why, I— Well, you have a right to know. I had told your husband and presumed you knew. The fact is that your mother's death was not accidental. Someone killed her. And now I have a question for you both. Why are you fighting me? Don't you want your mother's murderer brought to justice?"

The question crystallized Laurie's attitude. She suddenly knew that if she answered her words would be *No! No . . . not if it is one of us . . .* Fortunately David answered.

"Neither of us wishes to obstruct justice, Van Horn.

But that does not give you leave to harass us or to harass our friends in order to advance some opinion of your own. We know the death was accidental and hope you will soon realize the truth."

"The truth is what I hope to find," said Van Horn enigmatically, and rose from his chair to retrieve his hat. "I will bid you good day." He turned to Laurie. "I hope I have not disturbed you, Mistress Covington."

He had not disturbed her half as much as David had. She knew David was nearly convinced that Lady Desirée had indeed been murdered, yet his manner had been so direct, so open as he spoke. He had hidden his feelings perfectly, and now she wondered what else might lie hidden beneath his mask of assurance.

Chapter Seventeen

"I DO BELIEVE," LAURIE SAID SLOWLY, WATCHING THE coach depart, "that Mr. Van Horn is suspicious of Lord Peter." She turned from the window and looked at David, who appeared unperturbed. "I am sure of it. He had talked to the captain of the ship, who told him that Lord Peter was taken aback by my mother's appearance on deck. Then he questioned me as to whether Lord Peter searched earlier in the day, when she was first missing. His tone was . . . very inquisitive." She sighed. "Perhaps he knows more than we think he does."

But David was still unperturbed; in fact, his expression had become amused, even relieved.

"If he means to try to prove my uncle a murderer," he said, laughing, "he will find it indeed difficult. He will be likely to lose his credentials, and even his position with the governor. He is either a fool or very new in government service to even consider it."

Laurie was silent. She hadn't thought ahead, but of course what David meant was apparent. The nobility was sacrosanct. A lord of the realm would have to be caught red-handed in these times to be blamed for a capital crime. She could hardly approve, but still she was grateful and listened with mixed feelings as David continued.

"If he brings up such a subject with the governor he is sure to be told to retire from the case or to publicly state that the killing was done by a renegade slave. It is a very popular conclusion. It relieves the white population to blame everything on the Negros.''

His tone was bitter, and Laurie, understanding, nodded. The slaves were used not only as laborers but also as scapegoats. Every theft, every crime of passion, was passed on to them. That had become clearer these last days, as not only Mr. Bailey but many of the other neighbors had mentioned a "renegade."

"I suppose that comes from the riots," she said reluctantly, "and in some cases experience. Grace Bailey told me of her mother's death—''

"Bailey's wife?" David's tone was still bitter. "I wouldn't put too much credence in that story, my dear." He stopped speaking abruptly and stood up, as if to end the discussion. "Forget such morbid thoughts. This will soon be over. In the meantime I am needed in the fields and I am sure there is some small garment you wish to bedeck with lace." He leaned to kiss her, smiling, and then went out to ride back down the avenue and turn toward the north fields, now covered with the bending bodies of slaves.

Laurie went back to her sewing with her mind troubled. Raised to believe in justice as firmly as in God, she could hardly credit her thoughts now. She wanted no justice that would hurt anyone she loved! And, over her other thoughts, what David had said of Grace's story about her mother kept haunting her. It was plain that he doubted the story, so perhaps the young Rundi slave had been innocent. She wondered what had become of her. Bartram had once said that near Speight's Town there was a deep gully, overgrown with trees and underbrush, that held an entrance to a series of caves and a subterranean river. Runaways lived there, he had said, creeping out at night to steal food from nearby plantations. He had told her that periodically they were hunted down with dogs and shot for sport. Thinking of an innocent girl under such a threat, she could stand her thoughts no longer and got up and went into the kitchen. Molenga might know something—members of the same tribes often fraternized across adjoining fields, taking comfort in a familiar language and background.

In a silk of tawny brown and gold Molenga was peeling mangos, slicing the bright orange pulp into a bowl of clotted cream. She smiled faintly as Laurie came in, deftly spooning some of the creamy slices into a small dish.

"Strength to your son," she said like a benediction and handed it to her.

Laurie found a small spoon and sat down at the kitchen table. Mango in cream was a favorite with her, as Molenga knew.

"He is strong enough," she said, eating and watching the black hands peeling and slicing. "He kicks like a horse." She was thinking how quick Molenga was, how she never wasted a motion. She looked so strong, and very beautiful. A strange face, but compelling.

"Molenga," she said finally, licking the last drop of cream from the spoon, "did you know any of the Rundis who lived years back on the Bailey plantation?"

She had been bent over her work but straightened swiftly, the small head held high, like a snake assessing the air for danger. Her jet black eyes were on Laurie's, holding her gaze.

"So, you have learned of my origin. From whom?"

Laurie smiled. "That is a question, not an answer," she said cheerfully, for as always she felt secure and happy with this woman. "But I will tell you. Grace Bailey. She said you were a typical Rundi; tall, handsome and proud."

Molenga was too much a woman not to be pleased by the description and her faint smile came again as she bent to the bowl and her work.

"I knew them all," she said, "though they were not there long. The ones who managed to survive the treatment they received all escaped."

"Did you know the young woman who was accused

of murdering Mrs. Bailey?'' Laurie knew the question would shock Molenga and watched her intently. The tall body became utterly still, even the fingertips holding the knife were frozen.

"Yes, I did.'' Molenga began again to slice a mango. "And now I have a question for you. Why did you describe the girl as 'accused'? Why not say, as everyone says, 'the young woman who murdered Mrs. Bailey'?''

Laurie looked away. She did not have the right to tell Molenga what David had said. "Why . . . I understood the girl was never found nor tried. Without proof I would call no one a murderer.''

Carefully Molenga put the dish aside, discarded the peelings and large seeds and washed the knife. Then she came to sit with Laurie at the narrow table.

"You are a caring woman,'' she said thoughtfully. "A daughter of lions.''

Laurie stared at her, amazement turning into a feeling, frightening in its intensity, of being drawn into a knowledge beyond her depth. People come into your life, she had said to David so carelessly, that you feel you have known forever . . . She shook her head, trying to laugh.

"Either you have heard me boasting to my husband,'' she said, "or your extravagant praise is a truly remarkable coincidence. My grandfather called me a daughter of lions whenever he thought I needed encouragement. I never knew where he found the phrase.''

Molenga smiled. "Perhaps he saw in you the same quality I see. A desire to protect the others around you. A female lion cares for the whole pride—all of the other lions; cubs, younger females and males. She is the bravest of animals and will attack even an elephant if necessary.'' Her gaze on Laurie was bright jet. "Your grandfather paid you a great compliment.''

"And quite undeserved,'' Laurie said, and this time

her laughter was genuine. "I am not brave at all. Quite timid in fact, and easily frightened by danger."

"But it is there," Molenga said quietly. "A strong spirit, struggling to grow. Its birth may cost you more pain than your son will. But, for now, I will answer the question you did not ask. The young Rundi did not murder Mrs. Bailey."

It did not occur to Laurie to doubt her. "Then, who did?"

"Bailey himself," Molenga said calmly. "His wife came home unexpectedly and caught him trying to rape the Rundi girl, and when she had rescued the girl and bound up her wounds as well as she could—for Bailey had used a knife in his attempts to subdue her—she told her husband to leave. The plantation was hers, not his, and she had put up with him long enough." She breathed deeply, her black eyes slitted in anger. "So, since he wished to keep the plantation, he killed her. The young Rundi tried to stop him, but she was weak from loss of blood. When she saw it was too late, she fled."

Laurie was sick with horror. "And he goes unpunished! Why haven't you told the authorities?"

"Think," Molenga said gently. "Would the Barbadian authorities take the word of a black woman against that of a white man?"

Laurie sank back into her chair. She knew they would not. Prentiss Bailey would swagger through the rest of his life without harm, beating his slaves, treating his daughter with hate and contempt.

"Did you ever hear what happened to her—to the girl? Was she hunted down and killed, as others have been?"

The carved ebony face did not change. "She lived long enough to tell the story but not a day longer. The wounds were too deep, there was too much blood lost. She died in my arms."

"How you must hate Prentiss Bailey," Laurie said slowly. "The girl was your friend—"

"She was my daughter." There was still no change in Molenga's expression. "In time, I will avenge her."

Later, as Laurie sat with David in the library, she noticed his gaze straying often from his book to her.

"You are very quiet," he said finally, laying the book down. "Are you well? I hope you wouldn't keep something from me . . ."

She smiled with a faint trace of irony. How much he kept from her! She could not stop thinking of Molenga's daughter and the bestiality of Prentiss Bailey. But somehow she didn't want to mention it to David. He might be angry at Molenga for telling her.

"Perhaps I am a bit sad," she said lightly. "It's a difficult time."

"If you are worried over Van Horn, I would advise you to forget it," David said. "His investigation has become laughable. I am sure he will be forced to let it die."

She hoped he was right, but more and more her thoughts were on the same question that interested Van Horn. She no longer tried to believe it had been an accident, but she still hoped it had been a stranger— perhaps a thief that Desirée had surprised in the dark, or an escaped prisoner . . .

But continually her mind went back to the three she knew had reasons to wish Desirée gone. Lord Peter, who was safe in his noble name; Thérèse, who—thank God—the police had ignored; and David.

David, whom she loved. David who kept things from her for her own good. And David who, only hours after their wedding, had shot one man and clubbed another, killing both. Strange that when she had thought of that night she had always thought only of Ham, huge and powerful, breaking bodies with his bare hands. Yet David had indeed done his part, on the other side of the coach.

She looked over at him, sprawled comfortably in his

leather chair, the lamplight falling on the book he had opened again, his face relaxed and interested as he read. But that night his pistol had rested on the window opening, and when she asked him if he would kill he had replied, "Only if necessary." Had he thought it necessary to kill the Lady Desirée?

Tossing her own book to the table beside her, she stood up. "I am tired, that is all." And she was. Tired of her thoughts. "I am going up to ask Thérèse to brush my hair before bed. It is very soothing." She leaned to kiss him and he put his arms around her and held her for a moment.

"Our child grows heavy for your small body," he said softly. "And that is one burden I cannot help you bear. I wish I could, my darling."

Laurie smiled as she climbed the stairs. How could such a man kill a defenseless woman? Her doubts were gone.

Lord Peter arrived the next morning to bid them good-bye. It was nearing the end of November, the weather was bright, the sun hanging in a cloudless sky. Thérèse and Laurie had been sewing together on the cradle coverlet when they heard the carriage below and then the sound of Lord Peter's pleasant, calm voice speaking to Ham. Laurie rose and went out on the gallery, looking down and seeing the tall, gray man in a far different mood than the last time she had gazed on him from that elevation. He and Ham were standing together near the door, talking, laughing, and His Lordship's face was alight with interest and happier than Laurie had ever seen him. Her own spirits rose as she hurried down.

"Laurie!" He held her hands and stood back to look at her. "Lovely, healthy—and happy, I am sure, with your prospect of motherhood. How very wise I was to see that you two married. And how lucky David is."

It was marvelous to see the change in him. She could

not stop smiling. "This time," she said, "You will stay with us! Ham, will you ride out and tell David his uncle has arrived?"

"No, no. Wait." Lord Peter released her hands. "Let me ride with Ham. It will give me a chance to see the plantings and to talk to David on the way back. I have little time, for I go back to Bridgetown tomorrow to board a ship for London."

"So soon?"

He laughed. "I have been in Barbados for months! My colleagues in London do not consider that I am coming home 'soon'." He leaned forward and kissed Laurie's cheek. "But I could not leave without an evening with the young Covingtons."

"Shall I send someone to tell Father Covington? With you here, he would wish to dine with us."

He smiled gently. "I will see him tomorrow, on my way back. I would prefer just the two of you tonight."

"As you wish," she said, lighthearted at his choice yet wondering if some ill feeling still stood between the brothers. "I shall tell Molenga our dinner must be superb."

He informed her that their dinners were always superb and left with Ham, striding out and down the steps like a young man. Laurie went immediately to tell Thérèse how wonderful he looked, how happy. Thérèse's long face broke into her rare smile.

"Of course. He is free." She bent again to the sewing, adding, "I believe he has wished for his freedom for many years. But he is a man of integrity and his feeling of responsibility for your mother long outlasted his infatuation."

She was very wise, Laurie thought, sitting down again and picking up her needle. The thought had never occurred to her, yet now she supposed that the Lady Desirée had known it. It was what made her so anxious to please him. And, when he had finally broken away, so anxious to hurt him in any way she could. That he no longer wanted her had been the supreme insult.

Lord Peter's high spirits were contagious. David came in in the same mood, laughing, his brown eyes sparkling. While they dressed for dinner he told Laurie the reason.

"As I thought, Van Horn is a fool! He did go to the governor with his suspicion of Lord Peter, and the governor was horrified. Van Horn was severely criticized and instructed to discontinue his efforts. So it appears that our clouds have drifted away."

"Wonderful!" Laurie meant it, it *was* wonderful, and she was angry at herself for the thoughts that came crowding into her mind as she put on one of the loose, flowing gowns she must wear now. It was a small voice saying that now another murderer had joined Prentiss Bailey, to stride free in the world enjoying his life after taking another. But this is different, she argued, far, far different from what *he* did. But was it? Murder was always murder, the voice said. If Abel had killed Cain, would God have applauded?

She went to join them at dinner in a sober frame of mind, but even the small voice was silenced by the joy and relief around the table. And there seemed no shadow of guilt or uneasiness in Lord Peter's lean face. Behind his smile and warm affection there was a new love of life. Laurie joined in a toast to the future, and then listened, speechless, as David told Lord Peter that they would be visiting him in London within a year, on their way to Scotland.

She turned and looked at him, her lips trembling, unable to believe that he actually meant to go *with* her. She had thought so many times of his offer to let her go, let her have her freedom in Scotland. To banish her— while the baby remained here. When had he changed his mind?

David smiled at her carelessly. "Why are you surprised, my dearest? As soon as our son is old enough to travel, you will be showing him to your Annie.''

"And Breen!'' Her words tumbled out, breathless. "Breen will be beside himself at the very thought of a boy! I was a great disappointment to Breen . . .'' She laughed, tears misting her eyes. "Perhaps just at the beginning—not after he taught me to row with him and fish the tarns.''

They laughed with her, and Lord Peter remarked he would like to meet the redoubtable Breen and fish the tarns also, and the rest of the evening was filled with planning visits in both London and Scotland.

"Did you truly mean it?'' she asked later. She was brushing her loosened hair and watching him in the mirror as he lay in bed behind her. "You will go to Scotland?''

He was smiling absently, his eyes on her full curve of belly so apparent in the thin silk gown, and thinking how agilely she moved around the room in spite of the weight. "Yes. Does it suit you?''

She put the brush down and came to him impetuously, leaning to kiss him. "It suits me very well. I shall have two handsome males to show off to Annie and Breen.''

He caught her as she began to straighten and held her, his face in her neck and hair. "Are you so certain?'' One large hand moved down and lay warmly on the curve, waiting to feel the life wriggling within. "This may be a daughter, with sea colored eyes and a fuzz of black hair. . . .''

She collapsed on him gently, laughing. "I would never dare! No, it shall be a son, for that was your order.'' Lying back against his arm, she studied him, the half-smile on his strong face, the warmth of his brown eyes. And he was, truly, going with her to Stepney Downs. A rush of love for him welled up and she leaned to kiss him again, finding the warm mouth in the soft beard incredibly, sensuously sweet. She made the most of it, lazily licking and nipping the firm lips, breathing in his scent luxuriously.

In a moment he pushed aside the covers and lifted her over to lie beside him. Raising himself on one arm, he slipped her gown up and then off. ''If this is the result of my promise to go with you to Scotland,'' he said, smiling down at her, ''then perhaps we will stay.'' His mouth covered hers, his hands gentle on her breasts, straying inevitably to stroke the swell of her abdomen. It no longer bothered Laurie that he could neither keep his eyes or his hands from that swell. She knew now how it fascinated him, how he loved to touch the tight skin and feel the rolling movement of his child inside. He had made her proud of her body and she was never embarrassed as they made love, as she had been when her body had first begun to change. How could she be, when his passion was so strong and evident?

''There is a very large and comfortable bed at Stepney Downs,'' she whispered, stroking his side, ''I will see that you enjoy your stay . . .'' Her hand had found the arrow of dark hair on his belly and her fingers threaded through it, their tips seeking the hard muscles beneath. He rolled on his back and drew her closer.

''Show me the method you plan to use,'' he commanded hoarsely. ''I am quite interested.''

She smiled, leaning on his chest, kissing him lightly. ''There are several.''

''Show me all of them.'' The brown eyes were shining. ''I'll choose my favorite.''

She shook back her long hair, laughing. ''David! You are so greedy . . .''

''For you, yes . . .'' He clutched her to him, pressing his body around the curve of belly, his hands kneading her back and hips hungrily. ''God, yes . . . I'll never have enough . . .''

She melted against him, dazed with love, and began slowly and intimately to thoroughly express that love.

She was quite sure she had never been quite as happy in her entire life.

Three days later, with Lord Peter on the high seas and all of them, even Bartram, full of contentment and confidence, a group of armed militia arrived at Silversea House and took Ham away with them. He had been charged with the murder of Lady Desirée Stepney.

Chapter Eighteen

"PROPER PROCEDURE OR NOT, VAN HORN, I DEMAND to know on what pretext you have charged Ham with murder!"

Laurie watched David's fist clench with the desire to hit the man. They sat again in Government House, but only Van Horn was present. The governor had fled as they were announced; unwilling, Laurie thought, to meet with angry members of Lord Oldenburgh's family. She was sure the governor had agreed to Ham as a suspect solely because he did not think they would object. Ham's color made him suitable as a criminal, his presence as one of the searchers made him convenient. What could be more logical than to clear up the well-advertised investigation with a proper suspect? Her thoughts, she realized, had grown as cynical as David's.

Van Horn sighed, and sat back in the chair behind his wide desk, staring at them owlishly through his spectacles.

"I do not have to tell you, you know. According to law and precedent, I should not tell you. Charges are explained during the trial, at which time the accused is given opportunity to prove his innocence."

"I put to you that your reason for accusing Ham is his color." David's voice was savage. "I put to you that you know very well he is not guilty but are attempting to sacrifice him to save face."

"I could have you for slander for that."

"But you will not. For you would have to publicize what I said and the public would know it was true!"

"No." Van Horn sighed again, leaned forward to pick up a piece of paper, crumple it and throw it back on the desk top. He was conscious only of his thoughts. "They would be glad to think him guilty and themselves out of danger."

"Then sue," David said dangerously, "and discover if you are right." His control was slipping. In a moment it would be gone, and Laurie, looking carefully at Van Horn, thought the man knew that.

"Perhaps you do have a right to know," Van Horn said placatingly. "It was a member of your family who was murdered. Ordinarily, you would be on my side in this, helping me find the guilty man." He glanced at Laurie. "Unfortunately, some of what I have discovered may well be painful for Mistress Covington."

"She will remain," David said, to Laurie's satisfaction. "Her concern is as great as mine, and her courage also. What you have done is more painful to her than anything you could say."

"It is your decision," Van Horn pointed out coldly, and settled himself to talk.

"Our investigation of Lady Stepney's murder was not confined to Barbados, Mr. Covington. A parallel investigation of her life, and the life of Lord Oldenburgh, took place in London. We discovered the connection between them, and the kind of life Lady Stepney had lived for many years. My men went even to Scotland, for I was puzzled by the long separation between mother and daughter." He paused, looking at Laurie. "The information from Stepney Downs was illuminating. You were fortunate to escape her guardianship."

Laurie was astounded at the thoroughness of the man. A ferret, she thought, staring at the thin face and slender body. And she had once thought him dense! She pulled herself together with an effort.

"You have dragged skeletons from closets and rattled their bones at us," she said. "But where is a motive for murder? I did escape, as you have noted. I no longer bore my mother any ill will.''

''I have only begun to describe my knowledge— knowledge that eventually led to my conclusion,'' he said carefully. ''Bear with me.''

''Then get on with it,'' David said roughly. He hated this, Laurie knew. He would have much preferred to pick Van Horn up and shake it out of him. But Van Horn merely looked at him calmly and went on.

''As we were thorough in England, we were thorough here. My agents included both men and women, both white and black. We talked to slaves, to freedmen, to your neighbors. We went to the older merchants in Bridgetown, to the doctor in Speight's Town. Every bit of information, even gossip, was recorded. I venture to say that Barbados has never seen a more perfect examination of a crime.''

There it was, Laurie thought. His reason for this. He could not hide how proud he was of his ability and what he had accomplished. He *had* to have a suspect. Everyone must know of his efforts, and if he admitted after all that work that he had no answer, they would laugh at him.

David, too, was silent. But whether he was shaken or not by the extent of the investigation Laurie couldn't tell. His expression was still that of barely controlled anger. He stared at Van Horn, waiting for more, and finally Van Horn continued.

''Then we began to put together the results from my agents in England and those from the men here. We learned—you will pardon me, Mistress Covington—that the Lady Desirée was blatantly immoral, a woman who chose bedmates with less care than she did her gowns. But, at the same time, she pursued a long and intimate relationship with Lord Oldenburgh. His Lordship had finally cast her aside, and it is evident that she was trying to capture his interest again, going so far as to follow him aboard a ship bound for Barbados. With the excuse of visiting you, she forced herself into the home in which she expected him to stay. And, he escaped her only by taking up residence in another place.''

He knew everything. Laurie couldn't believe it. How much was due to the bits and pieces, how much had he divined by thought alone? She heard David move restlessly, as if to speak, and Van Horn quickly began again.

"Naturally, the evening I visited your home I knew none of this. Yet I am always an observer.'' The pride was again evident in his voice.

"It is my nature to study the behavior of others, to try to understand their thoughts. And I could see that Lord Oldenburgh was extremely anxious. Even though he refused to join the search, I thought his anxiety was for her, that perhaps they were old friends. Then, I discovered that Bartam Covington's excessive grief was for the loss of his intended wife. When I later learned Lady Stepney's reputation, I realized that Lord Oldenburgh's anxiety was for his brother, about to be saddled with a woman noted for both greed and immorality. My suspicion, therefore, fell first on Lord Oldenburgh's shoulders.''

David's chin jutted forward. "And was lifted from those noble shoulders by Governor Weatherby, was it not? And did the governor at that time also advise you to find a black man to blame it on?'' David was fighting again, unimpressed by Van Horn's self-praise.

"You do me an injustice.'' The pale eyes blinked behind the glasses. "It is true the governor objected to my suspicion of Lord Oldenburgh, but it was new evidence that pointed to Ham. Through both slaves and freedmen we learned of his reputation. All are in awe of his strength.'' Incredibly, he stopped and smiled broadly. "We originally assigned two militia men to arrest him, but they insisted on a party of ten. They had heard he killed on the slightest provocation.''

"That is not true!'' David leaned forward, half-rising

from his chair. "Ham has never killed except in defense, of himself or others. He saved many lives in the Grenada riots, including my own. He saved my wife from certain death in London when we were attacked by cutthroats. But he has never killed anyone who was not a threat to him or to us." He sank back, his face pale. "Nor would he. He is a man I find preferable to most white men, Van Horn, for his absolute honesty and loyalty."

Van Horn, who had seemed to shrink in his chair as David leaned toward him, now sat up and cleared his throat.

"Of course," he said, placating again, "such stories are always exaggerated. I have no doubt you speak the truth. But you have listed the very qualities that provide a motive for Ham. So close to all of you, he must have known of Lady Stepney's character and her intentions. He must have known all of you were upset by her forthcoming marriage to Bartram Covington. And he, himself, would have found the idea extremely distasteful. He killed, to be exact, to protect his father."

His father. The words should have been a hammer blow to Laurie. From the way Van Horn's eyes slid to her face, she knew he expected her to be terribly shocked. But somehow it seemed she had sensed it long ago—in Bartram's dependence on Molenga, in the close affection between David and Ham. She looked at David and found his eyes on her. The words had hit him, instead. A secret he had not meant her to discover. She smiled at him.

"You must forgive Van Horn," she said calmly. "He doesn't know Ham as we do." She turned to the spectacled face. "Ham would kill if necessary for any of us. But the Lady Desirée was not really a threat. We regretted my father-in-law's innocent affection for her, but he would not have married her. Once we told him of her past, he would have let her go. He is a proud man."

She could see he had counted on an entirely different effect; his eyes blinked at her in bewilderment. She took advantage of his stunned silence to add: "If that is your only excuse for a motive, your case is lost. Who would believe you?"

Blood rose in the white face. "They will believe me. They must believe the evidence of the medical officer, if nothing else. The bruises—the broken neck. That is Ham's style. He had his motive—since he is black he cannot reason as you do. And he had opportunity. The jury will ask for no more." He stood up, his hands trembling as he gathered up his papers, growing more furious as they sat and stared at him. "That will be all," he added stiffly. "You may go."

They rose, but Laurie had more to say. "Ham reasons as well as you do, Mr. Van Horn. In fact, he reasons better! He does not make up his mind what conclusion he wishes to come to, and then force his reason to that point. That is what you have done, only because you fear your colleagues will laugh at you if you haven't found a victim!"

Not only Van Horn's hands trembled now, his lips shook with rage. "Your ridiculous confidence needs deflating, Mistress Covington. I planned to save the real evidence for the trial, but I'd like you to know now that I am right! Ham was seen that night, standing on the slope with Lady Stepney. And there was one piece of the medical report that can be laid only to the primitive sexual nature of the blacks! Your mother was brutally raped before she was killed."

David whirled, his face stunned and then black with fury. "Bailey!" He stared at Laurie. "My God! It was Bailey who murdered her!"

"Mr. Bailey is not the murderer," Van Horn said smugly. "He is the witness."

"He is lying to protect himself! Believe me, Van Horn, he did it. Bailey has murdered before, and is known as a rapist."

"You seem to be determined to slander everyone,"

Van Horn said coldly. "Mr. Bailey is a respected, if unpleasant, citizen. He has absolutely no criminal record. And even if he did, your accusation is absurd. The man had no motive. He had never even met Lady Stepney."

"Bailey would need no motive," David said contemptuously. "He killed and raped for pleasure."

Van Horn shook his head. "I will take your emotion into consideration and not report your words to Mr. Bailey. How do you expect me to believe your accusations? Surely, someone would have reported such crimes."

Laurie, speechless with shock, touched David's arm. He turned and looked down at her, his eyes losing their angry glaze. "Come," he said, taking her arm. "We will go home." He turned at the door and looked back at Van Horn.

"So Bailey says he saw Ham on the slope? The slope is a distance from his land, and it was a dark night."

The thin face split in a triumphant smile. "There was a fire, Mr. Covington. The flames lit the scene perfectly. And Mr. Bailey was not anxious to bring out his evidence. He only recollected it when I reminded him he was in the area of the crime, fighting the fire."

Laurie waited until they were in the carriage, until they were out of sight from Government House, before she cried. Huddled in David's arms she wept bitterly, hating the world of ambitious little men like Victor Van Horn, of vindictive, evil men like Prentiss Bailey. When she finally sat up and wiped her swollen, pink face they were well out of the small town and traveling rapidly north. She clutched David's arm.

"We have not talked to Ham . . . nor found legal counsel for him. We cannot go home."

"*You* are going home, Laurie. And I will go back and stay until I can bring Ham home with me."

It took only a glance to realize there was no argument

that would sway him. She turned away to the window, where the coolness of the breeze took the heat from her face. "Ham is my friend, also."

"And my half brother." He looked at her, his face set. "Will you want Molenga to leave our home?"

"No! And no again! They have always seemed like part of our family, even before I knew . . ." She hesitated, and then added, "I cannot judge your father, David. At least he did not do as others do—set them free and drive them away to live as they could."

"Father could never do that," David said wryly. "Molenga is necessary to him. My mother discovered that, and discovered that Ham was his son. She was horrified. She no longer wanted to live, and that is the guilt my father carries yet."

She looked at him wonderingly. "Then, why did he marry? Why did he wish to marry again—with Desirée?"

David sighed. "You misunderstand. The sexual relationship between them lasted only long enough to conceive Ham. Molenga wished a half-white child to ensure her freedom, that was all. Since then, her role in his life has been that of a witch, not a wife, though she is intensely loyal to him."

"I see." Laurie leaned back, feeling that she *did* see. There was a fire of purpose in Molenga that could not be denied. It seemed that if she wanted something from someone, from their heart or mind, it would grow within them, seeded from her desire. Perhaps she was a witch. She thought again of Ham.

"I wanted to see Ham," she said, "to be sure he is all right."

"You would not be allowed to enter the jail," David said firmly. "And in any event, I will not allow you to endanger the life of our child with this upheaval."

"Our child is not endangered! He is not some weak, puling babe to be affected by troubles. I am of strong Scots blood—"

"A daughter of lions," David finished, softly. He put an arm around her. "I now believe it. I could have burst with pride when you stood up to Van Horn. How you rattled him! I know he regrets it—he never meant to tell us so much. At least, we know now who committed that crime."

Laurie flinched. She could not think of that without horror. Impossible that her mother—even that vain and malicious woman—could have suffered such an agonizing ordeal and death. "There is room for doubt, David, surely. Perhaps . . . perhaps the medical officer was mistaken . . ."

"But why would Bailey lie, if not to protect himself?"

"To hurt us," Laurie said, knowing all the while she was looking for some other reason. The thought of Desirée in Bailey's clutches was too horrible to believe. "I believe he would like to hurt us, though I don't know why."

"Perhaps that was his motive for murder," David said quietly. "He must have known your mother was here, for his daughter would have told him and described her."

Laurie shuddered, and David pulled her close, spreading his greatcoat around her. "Put it from your mind, my darling. I will take care of everything. . . ."

They arrived at Silversea long after midnight, with the great house black and looming at the end of the avenue. They let themselves in and made their way to the kitchen where David lit a lamp and Laurie found bread, cheese and wine.

They ate in the flickering glow of the single lamp, tired and silent, and then David carried the lamp to light their way up to their rooms. The house had never seemed so immense nor so empty, the unseen spaces around them echoing to their footsteps on the gallery.

In bed they curled together for comfort and Laurie dropped into exhausted sleep, her last memory of

David's soft voice: "I will bring him home. There will be a way . . ."

David was gone when Laurie awoke the next morning, though she found he had spread a light blanket over her before he left. To take the place of his warmth, she supposed, and thought it entirely inadequate. She lay there thinking of him entering the stone building where Ham was held. She imagined the dreary corridors he would travel, passing guards pacing with their guns. She tried to think of Ham behind bars and could not imagine it. Oh, he would go into a cell, she felt sure, if someone in authority told him to do so. But she thought that when he tired of it he would walk out again. Push the bars aside and walk out into sunshine, under blue skies, and come back to Silversea. Anything else was unthinkable.

The door opened, and in a moment Thérèse appeared in the arch, her eyes anxious. Laurie smiled at her.

"I'm glad you came. I have been lying here in a welter of ridiculous fancies."

"You look exhausted," Thérèse said. "Stay in bed and I will bring you a tray."

Laurie swung her feet to the floor. "Lying in bed only makes one weaker. And I must talk to Molenga." She saw the question in Thérèse's eyes, and added, "You are worried, too. Mr. Van Horn is convinced that Ham is guilty—but David swears he will see that Ham goes free. He has returned to hire a counsellor."

Thérèse's face settled into grim lines. "It is most unfair, Madame. It's only his color."

"Yes, I am glad you understand that." She smiled to herself as Thérèse went to draw a bath for her. Thérèse had been extremely wary of huge Ham when she first arrived, but that seemed to have changed.

Later in the kitchen she told Molenga all she knew. She sat at the table while Molenga listened, asking a question now and then. Laurie had thought that for once she might see fear in Molenga's eyes, but the hard, bright jet gaze was the same, her face as proud as ever. If she was frightened for her son it did not show. But when she heard of Bailey's evidence, the eyes flickered.

"He lies."

Laurie nodded. "Yes, of course. David believes Bailey committed the crime and is lying to protect himself."

Molenga shrugged and rose, walking away with her curious, flowing motion. Then she turned back, questioning.

"Does the Master know?"

There was only one Master in Molenga's eyes. Laurie shook her head. "He wished to go with us to Bridgetown, but David thought it better if he did not."

Molenga considered that for a moment and then gave her quick nod of acceptance. "Your husband was right. The Master would have grown angry, spoken too quickly. You would not have found out the man's intentions."

It was time to tell her, Laurie knew, though not easy. "Mr. Van Horn knows that Ham is the Master's son," she said bluntly. At least, it was easier to tell Molenga than it would be to say it to Bartram, but David had said she must tell them both, so they would be prepared.

Molenga looked at her curiously. "Does Mr. Van Horn consider that to be of importance?"

Laurie marveled, and thought she would always marvel, at Molenga's self-possession.

"He does. He thinks Ham killed Lady Desirée to keep her from marrying his father and ruining his life."

Molenga stared at her in disbelief and then shrugged again. "I have lived among the English for many years," she said thoughtfully, "yet I still do not understand them. I did not understand why the Master would wish to mate with such a weak and useless woman, nor did Ham. But we know men must choose their own women. No one should interfere. Life will tell a man if he has chosen wisely."

Laurie said she supposed that was right, but that the

English often did interfere. Molenga ignored that and told her rather tartly that she had missed her exercises yesterday and should be doing them now. Laurie agreed and rose heavily to go to her room. She had found that when she sat in that odd, crosslegged position she could concentrate clearly. Today, she used the time in considering how best to tell her father-in-law that Victor Van Horn had discovered Ham's parentage. She realized that it would be a painful session. Not so much because Van Horn knew it, but because *she* did. She now knew that both David and his father had done their best to keep it from her.

But when she came back down the staircase it was not Bartram who awaited her, but one of the overseers. He was a freedman, one with very light skin and reddish hair, and he stood in the entry hall in an agony of embarrassment, twisting his wide-brimmed straw hat in his hands. When Laurie told him that her husband was in Bridgetown he looked at her helplessly and asked if the "Old Master" might be available.

"Certainly," Laurie said, "but first you must tell me the problem. Then, if necessary, I will see that Mr. Covington is told."

He hesitated and then plunged into words. "Ma'am, there is trouble with the workers! In the fields now they gather up, talk. On Bailey's fields the workers lie down and even his whip won't raise 'em. I look for bad times. A week, two week maybe—then, bloody hell!"

She stared at him, uncomprehending, and he stared back miserably. Bloody hell, he had said.

"You expect a riot."

He nodded quickly. "Maybe a big one. We caught two of Master Allyn's gang in ours today, slippin' in to talk. Three days past, one here from Thatcher's—that's twenty mile! I let him slip away. Thatcher burns 'em if he catches 'em, and I don't hold with that."

Laurie, nauseated, turned away. The scene outside the windows was peaceful, beautiful. Maybe he was wrong.

"Why?" she asked slowly. "What has caused such discontent?"

"Some white men from Bridgetown," he said bitterly, "been trampin' around, tellin' this man, that man, 'You be free soon.' They got the idea they already free and we just won't tell 'em. 'We *free,*' they say to me, 'King George set us free. Let us go.' I don't know what to say."

Laurie wondered what he would think if she said in that case, let them go. She sighed. "I will send for Master Bartram."

"Good! Good!" He looked immeasurably relieved. "He will calm them down better than any. Maybe he can talk sense into Master Bailey, too. That man will set it all off! Gone crazy, ma'am, beatin' all of 'em. Two of his new bunch died already . . ." He was gone, charging the heavy front door like the wall of an enemy bastion.

She thought of Prentiss Bailey, walking the world with blood on his hands. He can kill his slaves with no fear of consequences, she thought bitterly. They are his. She went to the kitchen, for there was no man to send for Bartram, nor could she send a maid, for they were easily frightened.

Molenga was nodding before Laurie was half through. "It has been there, bubbling beneath the surface," she said, and went to tell the gardener to harness a horse to the gig. She rattled away in less than five minutes, her straight figure brilliant and erect in the small seat, her whip flicking in the air over the horse's back.

Laurie was waiting on the portico when the gig returned, but they did not stop. Instead the gig turned into the deep, soft grass and went swaying across the end of the gardens and down the steep slope that led to the barracas. Laurie ran to the garden wall, gripping it in fear and staring over it, watching Molenga handle the gig down, bring it to a stop in the middle of the beaten paths around the barracas. In moments there was a milling crowd around it as slaves poured from doorways, came running from near fields.

Stepping down from the gig like a minor god, his white hair and beard glinting in the sun, Bartram stood half a head above most of them as he strode through the crowd to a central building and mounted the steps to turn and face them. Laurie could see his arms wave as he began to talk, but of course she could not hear him.

But they were listening, she could see that. The excited movement of the crowd lessened. They began to stand quietly, their faces toward him, and in a few minutes they began dropping to their haunches or sitting on the ground. Once a wave of laughter came to her distantly, she saw heads nodding. Then children began to play around the fringes of the crowd and she relaxed, leaning against the stone wall in weak relief. Bartram Covington had not lost his skill in managing his slaves.

Then, with one final, grand gesture of outstretched arms Bartram stepped down and the crowd began to disperse. There were men who gathered around him, others who drifted back toward the fields. Laurie watched him make his way slowly back to the gig, the men with him. Then he sat for awhile beside Molenga, listening, some times nodding, some times shaking the snow-white head. Then the gig moved, driving laboriously up the slope. Laurie ran to it and put out a hand to help Bartram down.

"No, my dear. Molenga will take me on to the Allyn's, and then I presume I will have to speak to Prentiss Bailey. The danger is greatest there." He hesitated. "What news of Ham?"

"He . . . David is there," Laurie said, and saw motion behind him as Molenga flickered a message. "Molenga knows," she added in a rush of new relief. "She will tell you everything."

"Very good. We will return soon. But you may rest assured there will be no trouble here." His smile brought tufts of beard up and out triumphantly. "You have nothing to fear from our men. They only needed a word or two from someone they trust."

Laurie watched them leave. The thin, straight back, the broad, heavy back, seated together in the tiny gig, disappearing down the avenue of trees. Bartram, recently so broken in spirit, was a man again, purposeful, self-assured. She went back into the house, deeply thoughtful.

That afternoon she told Thèrése of the talk with Van Horn and of David's determination not to let Ham come to trial. She also told her of the threat of riot, and watched the thin shoulders tense. But Thèrése did not speak of her fear, only of Ham.

They were sewing while they talked, and Thèrése was watching her tiny stitches. "Ham could never have killed her, even if ordered," she said, and lifted her gaze to Laurie to add drily, "He didn't know her well enough." She bit off a thread and shook the completed coverlet out, examining it. Her thin mouth softened. "This will do handsomely, even for our heir apparent!"

Laurie smiled and thought about the time remaining before the birth. The months she must wait had seemed endless, yet, she suddenly remembered, this was the first of December.

"Christmas!"

Thèrése looked at her in surprise and Laurie laughed. "How odd it will seem to have Christmas in this climate. But I suppose we must plan . . ."

Thèrése nodded thoughtfully. "Perhaps gifts and a celebration of some kind will distract the workers from their discontent."

So she had been thinking of the threat of riot, after all. But the idea had merit, Laurie decided, though it would be a muted, sad celebration unless Ham was free again.

Bartram arrived in the evening to talk of what he had seen and what the other planters were doing to ease the threat of an insurrection. He had found Richard Allyn concerned, though Allyn feared little from his own slaves and was most perturbed about Thatcher. He had told Bartram he would visit Thatcher and other plantations on the north end of the island during the next week. Bartram had also gone to Bailey's home. Bailey, he said, was handling the problem in his usual fashion, floggings and half rations for the malcontents, and had sneered that he needed no advice.

"His daughter is still away," Bartram added, "and I questioned him about her, knowing you would be interested. He told me he believed she would be home any day now." He frowned. "I doubt she will be pleased, however, for the house is as filthy as Bailey himself."

"*I* will be glad to see her," Laurie said quietly, but inside she wished that Grace would stay in whatever home she had found. As much as she wished to deny to herself that Grace's father had murdered again, she was very much afraid that David was right. And to have Grace there with him . . . She shook the thought away and went on listening to what Bartram had to say. She was very glad to hear that Molenga had had the task of telling him that Van Horn had rooted out the secret that he and David had hid from her. But then he mentioned Ham himself, and in a manner she would not have expected. He had moved restlessly in his chair, and now he sat forward, his hands on his knees, ready to rise.

"I will pray for Ham," he said abruptly, and stood up. "Other than that, I shall stay out of the case. You may tell David that, for I believe it will ease his mind." He stood there, his hands behind his back, his striking head of white hair and beard again looking like an ancient prophet, and his next words were startlingly appropriate. "In the Bible," he said slowly, "it is said that the sins of the fathers are visited on the sons. Hardly a comforting thought, is it?"

"Ham will be all right!" Laurie rose and went to him, taking his hands. "Please believe that, for I know it."

When he was gone, Laurie wondered why she had made such a rash statement. But at the time she had been so sure.

Chapter Nineteen

A WEEK PASSED, TEN DAYS, AND STILL NO WORD FROM David except through Richard Allyn, who had been to Bridgetown to confer with the governor on the threat of insurrection. Allyn came to tell Laurie that he had seen David but they had had time for only a hurried conversation in the portico of Government House. David had been going in for a meeting with Governor Weatherby and Allyn had been coming out.

"He is most determined," Allyn told Laurie. "But it is a bad time. With the insurrection threatening, all blacks—even the freedmen—seem under suspicion. However, if anyone can influence Weatherby, I am sure David can."

It was not particularly heartening news, but Laurie thanked him and held on to her courage. David would win. She was sure of it.

The next day she and Thèrése folded and put away the completed layette for her child and began—at first half-heartedly—to prepare for the holiday season. But the thought of the glory and hope of Christmas took over, and they grew enthusiastic. The great house was soon transformed with wreaths of dark green, shining lime leaves, with the brilliant gold of small oranges set into them like jewels. They invaded the fields for the silver swords of new cane leaves to make standing bouquets, holding in their centers the great, drooping heads of ginger blossoms like small cups of handpainted china. And ribbons, ribbons everywhere, dangling fluted paper bells. The house glowed, for the maids cleaned every day in a frenzy of good will. And over all, the tantalizing odor of spices and fruit as Molenga baked.

In a storeroom Laurie found two standing candelabra. Six-feet-tall, made of heavy brass, each had places for eight candles. She brought them out and polished them until they shone. Filling them with candles, she set them on each side of the staircase and lighted them every evening, filling the hall with rich welcome.

"They will come," she told Therese. "They must."

Finally one evening, as she lit the last candle and blew out the flame on the twist she carried, she heard the sound of pounding hooves and gasped. Running to the heavy door in spite of the weight she carried now, she flung it open. Even in the dark she recognized David and the towering dark figure beside him. Weak, she wrapped an arm around a pillar and stood there, outlined by the glow of candles from the doorway behind her, her heart pounding like the hooves, her eyes misting.

Both of them appeared thinner as they came up the steps; both looked tired, but they were smiling. After embracing David, she turned and took both of Ham's hands.

"They will never take you back," she said fiercely. "Never! We shall spirit you away if necessary, and take you to Scotland."

Behind her David laughed. "Then you should have to spirit me away to Scotland, also, for Ham is bonded out to me only until Van Horn brings him to trial."

"There is more than enough room at Stepney Downs for both of you," Laurie retorted, "and it would suit me very well to do so."

The next day David went to the barracas and declared holiday. No more work until after Christmas. On the still, cool nights they could hear the distant sound of singing and laughter from below, while in the empty fields the cane grew rapidly. Kneehigh to waisthigh, David said, satisfied. The provision grounds had produced surprisingly well in spite of the damage the fire had produced, the slave pockets were full, and David sent overseers to take them by the wagonload to Speight's Town, to buy their bright cloth and gifts for their young. They came back in high excitement, Ham reported, all thoughts of rioting forgotten.

But Laurie was increasingly uncomfortable physically. And worried about Grace Bailey. Undoubtedly she had come home by now to that filthy house where she would be more miserable than ever with her father. The thought nagged her continually, and finally, picking a time when she was sure Bailey would be in his fields, she asked Ham to drive her to Bailey's home.

Ham eyed her dubiously. David was in Speight's Town, or Laurie knew Ham would seek him out for advice. Since he couldn't, he questioned her. "Are you sure, Mistress? If Bailey is at home, you may not care for your reception."

Laurie noted his omission of Bailey's title and smiled at him. "I have known since I first met him that Mr. Bailey is a very rude man. However, he will be in the fields. I do wish to see Grace."

As they drove up to the ugly, neglected home Laurie saw that the gardens were overgrown with weeds, that the fields that could be seen were mostly bare, eroded and pale with only a sprinkling of drooping cane plants. A few slaves were working in a field they passed, with a listless overseer standing by, glancing at them incuriously as they went along.

She went up the creaking steps and knocked as Ham led the horses away. A maid let her in, her face sullen, and told her that Miss Grace was not at home. Laurie was enquiring as to when she was expected when Prentiss Bailey emerged from the shadows of the dank hallway.

"Go," he said harshly to the maid. "Rid the kitchen of some of the trash you have accumulated."

She scurried away, and Bailey stood staring at Laurie, rocking slightly on cracked, dirty boots. She was amazed at the worsening of his appearance, for the clothes flapping on his shrunken frame were thick with grime, the gray patches of hair on the sides of his head had grown to his shoulders, lank with grease. He was odorous of sweat and rum, even at that distance.

"I came to see if Grace had come home," Laurie said, breaking the silence. "The maid tells me she has not arrived, and I would like to know when she is expected." She spoke steadily enough, though her skin crawled with revulsion, and inside a distant fear trailed cold tentacles around her heart. *Was* she standing in this filthy hallway with her mother's murderer? She wanted so much to doubt it . . .

He was staring at her, his gaze wandering over her small body with its burden, the white face with the huge turquoise eyes that reflected, in spite of her, the doubt and fear she felt. He smiled, and she could not imagine a more revolting expression.

"Very soon, Mistress Covington, very soon. I expect her daily. However, I cannot tell you exactly." He came closer as he spoke, and now the odor he emanated was almost overpowering. "Would you like to leave a message for her? I would be glad to do a favor for such a pretty lady. . . ."

She drew away from him, barely resisting an impulse to turn and run for the door. "Oh, no. No real message . . . only that I miss her company and would like to see her. I will bid you good-day."

"Not yet . . ." He reached suddenly and his hand closed like a vise on her arm. "I myself miss company these days. I am a very lonely man. Surely you will spend a few moments with me . . ." His face was close, so close Laurie could see the grime in the pores of his skin, see the loose lips wet and hanging, the sick, growing excitement in his eyes. "We shall have some wine . . . I know many ways to please ladies . . ."

She jerked her arm from his grasp, desperation lending her strength. "I have nothing to say to you, Prentiss

Bailey!'' Her voice rose, wavering upward toward a shriek. ''Nor do I want your hand on me! I should think you would know what I think of you!''

The door flew open behind her and Ham was there, outlined in the glare of sunlight, filling the opening. Bailey froze, his eyes widening in shock, his hands dropping to his sides.

''Did you call, Mistress?'' Ham's voice was pleasant, his eyes on Bailey were not. They were Molenga's eyes; cold, bright, dangerous.

''Yes,'' Laurie said, weak with relief. ''I wish to leave immediately.'' She went toward him, knowing she was now completely safe.

Behind her, Bailey found his voice. ''So, your husband has managed to free his dark brother. Does it not frighten you, my dear lady, to ride alone with a murderer?''

Laurie rounded on him, courageous now with the huge figure beside her.

''How dare you! You well know only your vicious lies put suspicion on him. Look to your own black secrets! I promise you, if Ham is even tried, you will be in worse trouble than his.''

Bailey flinched, a look compounded of fear and hate flaring in his red-rimmed eyes. ''Do not threaten *me*, Mistress. You will regret it—'' He broke off abruptly as Ham moved toward him.

''Ham!'' Laurie was suddenly terrified at what he might do, the danger he would be in if he hurt Bailey, the witness against him. ''Come. I wish to leave this filthy place.''

Ham turned reluctantly, his curved hands relaxing, and followed her outside. The door slammed behind them as he handed her into the carriage. He was silent as they drove away, but halfway down the rutted driveway he stopped the carriage and jumped down.

''I will have a word with this overseer,'' he said

calmly, and walked into the field. Laurie watched the pale, apathetic overseer turn and start visibly as he recognized Ham. He looked for a moment as if he would break and run, and then stood his ground as Ham spoke to him. He seemed, she thought, quite eager to answer Ham's questions.

Coming back, Ham's face was grim. "It is as I thought," he said as he climbed into his seat. "Bailey set the fire, himself. This man was with him, and they made an attempt to keep it from spreading into the fields by slashing the plants near the school with cane knives."

"I find it easy to believe," Laurie said bitterly. "The man is entirely evil. It is no wonder that Grace does not wish to return."

"The overseer does not think she will," Ham told her. "He said Miss Grace and William Burdick ran down from the house, alerted by the fire's glow. There was a quarrel, and Miss Grace told her father she was leaving and would sell her part of the land. He heard no more, for Bailey sent him to fetch slaves to help save the fields."

"I am glad," Laurie said, her throat constricting as she thought how Grace must have felt. "She will be happier anywhere else but here." She hesitated, and then added, almost apologetically, "I was a fool to go there."

"Your husband," Ham said, "will agree with you. And think me a fool for allowing it."

Laurie was silent the rest of the way back to Silversea.

Ham had not been wrong in his prediction of David's reaction. Laurie waited until after dinner, and then, in the library, she told him the whole story. He was pale, from fright or anger or a combination of both, when she finished.

She listened meekly to what he had to say about *his* wife, bearing *his* child, deliberately exposing herself to a murderer and rapist. When he said he would have a word or two with Ham, she reminded him that she had insisted on going over Ham's objections, and that, in fact, it was Ham who had made her safe with his constant watch over her, outside the door.

"But I do admit my own fault," she said, wandering restlessly back and forth. "It was indeed unwise. I have no excuse other than my desire to see Grace and tell her I want to help her rebuild. But now I know she won't, not in Barbados. I wish I could write to her."

"William Burdick will have her address," David said, calmer. "When next I go to Speight's Town I will look him up and ask for it." He smiled at her suddenly radiant face and pulled her down on his lap. "We should have shown more concern for your friend, except that our own problems have absorbed us."

She kissed him and then hugged him as well as she could with the ever increasing bulk of the baby between them. It seemed that the weight now doubled every day and she longed for the months to pass.

There were no clouds on Christmas Day. David surprised Laurie with an extra gift besides the string of matched pearls she wore around her neck as she came down the stairs in what seemed a veritable tent of pale blue chiffon silk. He had invited the Edringtons for Christmas dinner and as young Barbara Lee ran to her to be hugged Laurie's eyes misted with happiness. She straightened, glowing, as Vanessa came toward her, her red-gold hair sparkling with the light from the candelabra, her lovely face gentle as she looked at Laurie.

"Not long to wait, now," she whispered, bending to kiss a flushed cheek.

"March. It seems long to me."

Vanessa's brows arched and she laughed softly. "Count again, Laurie. Much sooner than that, I am sure." She swept past her, going to greet David and Bartram, while Laurie, wondering, took John's hand and that of John, Jr.

Talk was light that evening, gaiety paramount, though after dinner Laurie and Vanessa withdrew to the drawing room and discussed not only Vanessa's school but Grace's whereabouts. Laurie told Vanessa what she had learned, and of David's plans to obtain Grace's address.

"We shall both write to her," Vanessa promised, smiling. "In honor of the season. I am sure she will be teaching, somewhere in the islands. Her desire to do so was too great to ignore." She paused and then added, softly, "There has been a great change in David, Laurie. His trust and love for you shines from his face. You have removed the bitterness he always wore."

Laurie gazed at her, astounded. "He has changed, yes. In . . . in his attitude toward the slaves, and, yes, toward me. But it is only because I am bearing his child, Vanessa. He is very protective of the baby's well-being."

Vanessa shook her head, looking tender and amused. "You are blind, Laurie. As blind as he was, when he doubted you." She looked up, smiling, as David and John entered the room. "Here are our husbands. Now we shall have to stop sharing feminine secrets."

When the Edringtons had gone home and they were sitting alone David told Laurie that John had convinced him that the sugar plantations were doomed.

"The feeling against slavery is strong now in England," he said, "though I didn't need John to tell me that. And the plantations cannot survive without the labor, especially now that the price of sugar has fallen. John is turning to other crops now, and I believe it is wise." He looked at Laurie and smiled faintly. "I told him something I had discovered recently. A slaveowner is as much a slave as the man he owns. The chain around a slave's neck must be held firmly, and when a chain stretched between two men tightens, one is held as firmly as the other."

Laurie nodded, her eyes large and dark. "No man

should own another man," she said as she had said before. "Perhaps you will feel as free as they will, once the law is passed."

He laughed. "I fully expect it." He rose, stretching. "Now I will escort you to our bed. I wish to hold our future in my arms."

The joy of Christmas was remembered, but the carefree feeling faded with the lime leaf wreaths, and as they took them down, along with the ribbons and bells, the cares came back. Going up and down the staircase with the boxes of ribbons, Laurie panted. She could no longer run to the door when she heard David arriving, but must walk sedately like a matron. She began to wonder if Vanessa had been right, and finally she mentioned it to Thèrése.

"I admit you do look well along." she said uncertainly. "Yet I do not know. Perhaps we should ask Molenga."

Laurie agreed. It pleased her that the two other women had become so close. They often were together, talking. Still in her morning robe she followed Thèrése to the kitchen.

Molenga did not seem surprised at Laurie's request for her opinion. She took the morning robe off with a sweep of her long arms and Laurie stood shivering before her in nothing but her thin shift. Molenga put her hands on the swelling curve that now seemed immense to Laurie and Laurie looked down, fascinated by the slender black fingers against the gauzy white. Gently, Molenga drew the shape of the swell from midriff to hipbone, the fingers slow and deliberate, the jet eyes staring as if she could see through the skin to the baby beneath. Then, silent, she picked up the robe and handed it to Laurie, her eyes distant and intent, staring off into space as Laurie slipped the robe on and tied it again.

"Well?" Laurie was impatient.

"Soon," Molenga said abruptly. "If you are going to Bridgetown and the English doctor, it would be safest to go within a few days."

"I will have my child at home," Laurie said firmly. "I am not ill, to need a hospital."

Molenga nodded, unsurprised. "There is no better midwife in all Barbados than the one in your own dispensary," she said. "Her name is Anyola."

Laurie was suddenly, ecstatically pleased. As always, she had no doubt that Molenga was right. "I must tell David," she said, and began to laugh. "He will think my counting most unaccountable! But how wonderful to meet my son so soon." She went hurriedly off to dress.

David did not laugh. The news galvanized him into instant concern. He paced around Laurie's chair nervously.

"I will ride to Speight's Town tomorrow," he said, "and ask Dr. Townsend to recommend the best midwife. I would like to have her in residence here immediately." He looked at her carefully. "Have you any pain?"

"None. And you do not need to be so precipitate. Molenga said soon, but that could mean a month."

"It could also mean a week, or tomorrow." He stood staring at her, his brows knitted, and then his face cleared, his mouth softening into a smile. Dropping to sit on the arm of her chair, he put his arms around her. "You must have conceived on the brig," he said softly, "Possibly the first time . . . when you finally understood why the young ewes didn't run from the ram."

They were both silent, remembering, and then Laurie sighed. "You were so wonderfully nice," she whispered, "and have ever been . . ."

"You have no regret?"

"Never!"

He laughed wryly and released her. "At this moment, I believe I have. I hate to think of you undergoing the ordeal of childbirth.'' He stood and walked back and forth again. ''Possibly I should leave now. I could see Dr. Townsend early, and—''

''David!''

He laughed sheepishly and sat down. ''All right. I leave in the morning. And, to satisfy other of your interests, I will seek out William Burdick while I am there.''

''Fine. Then, while I am waiting for 'soon,' I can write to Grace Bailey.'' She was smiling at him, a smile that exposed her small, perfect teeth and crinkled her amused eyes. ''Which might be some time.''

''I saw Bailey today,'' he said, reminded. ''He looks much as you described. He must be taking the loss of his crops badly. Something has broken him.'' He frowned slightly. ''He must have been simply wandering, for he was riding along the barren land between us, behind the lime grove. Nothing has been grown there for years.''

''At least,'' Laurie said, ''you will not receive another lecture from him on your soft and wasteful ways.''

''No. Our fields would silence him. His own are not half planted and his few miserable slaves cannot keep up with cultivating that much. Ham tells me Bailey spends more time hunting runaways than he does tending the work.''

Laurie remembered she had never told him of the day when the overseer had come, frightened, and she had called his father. She told him, describing how Molenga had handled the gig, and how his father had gone unhesitatingly among the discontented slaves.

''He went with such confidence, David. And from the moment he began to speak you could see the trouble melting away.''

''He is still the Master, to them.'' David smiled faintly. ''Moses and his flock. Here and there, there are other men like my father—paternalistic slaveowners who treat the men like their children.''

''That is how it was, precisely. But what pleased me

most was the change in *him*. When he came back up the slope he was a man again, with pride in his abilities.''

David looked at her sharply. ''Have I robbed him, Laurie? Taken away his importance? Is that what you are saying?''

She looked at him helplessly. ''It was his choice, wasn't it? I do not think he could work the hours you now do.''

''It was his choice,'' David assented. ''Surely not mine. Thank God it is a dying way of life. Our son will not be forced to be a slave master, but free to choose—''

''And you?'' Laurie forced the words out daringly. ''You cannot choose? Is there no other way you could make money?''

David laughed without humor. ''That would be the least of my problems, darling. My mother's fortune is mine and I have no need of money. But what would *they* do? If I free them they will drift away from us, for we have been their masters too long. I am caught by the chain I mentioned—tightly bound to them, if only to keep them from starving . . .'' He shook his head. ''Please, talk of something else. I have gone over this in my mind too often.''

Laurie was silent, surprised by his depth of feeling. He had grown to care about the slaves, and certainly he thought of them more practically than she had, considering fully what would happen to them after freedom. She was conscious of a dawning pride in her husband. He would work it out, if anyone could.

Chapter Twenty

WHILE THE SILVERSEA SLAVES WERE HAPPY AND PEACE-
ful, the threat of massive revolt was still growing to the
north of them, as Laurie discovered the next morning
from a most unlikely messenger. David and Ham had left
for Speight's Town when a maid came to tell her that Mr.
Van Horn was in the drawing room and requesting her
company. The maid said he had asked first for David and
then for Ham, and had seemed quite upset when she had
told him neither of them was at home.

Laurie went down in cold dignity, prepared to tell Van
Horn that he needn't worry, Ham had not run away. But
that was not the reason for the man's perturbation.
Instead, he told her quickly that it was not wise for her to
remain in this isolated plantation without male protection
since an uprising was expected daily.

"Evidently you have again been listening to our
neighbor," she said coldly. "Prentiss Bailey's slaves are
forever on the verge of an uprising, and with good
reason."

Behind his spectacles his eyes blinked at her and slid
away. "Mr. Bailey was one of my informants," he
admitted, "but I have heard the same fears expressed by
several others. What of your own slaves? You must have
two hundred or more."

"Except for the very old, they are Creoles," Laurie
told him. "Island born. Born on this plantation, as a
matter of fact. Therefore they are much more contented
than most."

"How fortunate." He did not look particularly
pleased and Laurie wondered if this thin, small man

wished for excitement, for the "bloody hell" of a riot.
To watch from a safe distance only, she decided. "I
thought I would call," he went on, "since I was in this
district. Governor Weatherby has asked me to meet with
Bartram Covington, your husband's father. I am to ask
him to call upon the governor at his convenience. Can
you give me directions to his home?"

Laurie did so, wondering. Not until Van Horn took his
leave did he mention Ham, and then it was to say that the
earliest date possible for his trial would be in February,
and to ask what Ham's surname was. Laurie told him she
hoped that by February everyone would have come to
their senses and there would be no trial. She added that
as far as she knew Ham had no surname. Van Horn had a
nasty little smile for that.

William Burdick was not in Speight's Town. David
told Laurie that as soon as he returned home the next
day.

"He has moved? I am surprised he has not told
us . . ." She stopped, smiling. "David, they have left
together. They may be planning a school on another
island. They may be married by now . . ."

"I hope you are right. But Burdick's landlady is quite
upset. She showed me his room, and his clothes and
books are still there. If he did leave with Grace it was
purely impulsive, and that is not Burdick's usual style."

Laurie drew away from him, her heart sinking. "You
think something has happened to him, don't you? But,
what could happen that we—or his landlady—wouldn't
have heard by now? News of accidents travels fast,
always."

"Yes, I am sure you are right." David turned away,
hanging up his coat. "Perhaps he *was* impulsive for
once. Grace was undoubtedly distraught, wishing to
leave immediately."

"I am sure she would feel so. *I* would!"

"And I would go with you." He was laughing

indulgently. "However, at this moment I am starving. May we stay long enough to have lunch?"

At the table she asked him what Dr. Townsend had said, and once again he looked sheepish.

"He told me if I wanted the best midwife available to go back to Silversea and look in the dispensary."

"Anyola. Molenga told me."

"A slave," David said thoughtfully. "I wonder what other planter's wife would allow a slave to bring her child into the world? None, I suppose, since all of them go into Bridgetown well ahead of time and stay for their confinement. Wouldn't you like to do that?"

"I will bear our child in our home. And, since Molenga and Dr. Townsend agree, I will be glad to have Anyola as midwife."

He nodded reluctantly. "Then I will send her up this afternoon and Molenga can get her settled in a room. I will tell her she must stay until the baby is born. And, after tonight, I will not leave home."

"Tonight?"

"A meeting at Allyn's house. There is still trouble in the air, more trouble than Bailey's constant problem. Another overseer has been killed at Thatcher's, and many of his slaves are missing. Thatcher has a huge plantation and many slaves, over seven hundred, I believe. If they riot . . ." He sighed. "Twenty miles away is not far when they begin to plunder."

Now Laurie gave credence to Van Horn's remarks, and proceeded to tell him of the visit. When she finished he was frowning.

"Did Van Horn give a reason for the governor wishing to meet with Father?"

"He did not. But perhaps it was not important. He specified that it would be at your father's convenience."

"That is only form. Father will be expected to go immediately. He is probably in Bridgetown now." He was still frowning. "I cannot imagine what the governor would want with him."

Nor could Laurie, but she was sure they would learn. Bartram was not a man to be secretive. In the meantime, she left the table and went to find Molenga to tell her to make arrangements for Anyola. She was not in the kitchen, nor in the kitchen garden, for Laurie wandered out to look.

The air was cool and fresh, the cleared, cultivated ground between the rows soft to walk upon. She went on, coming at last to the small grove of wild limes. She had never entered the grove before and the sharp, clean scent of the leaves lured her on. It was pleasant in there, with the sun dappling the bare packed earth, the thick branches muffling sound and the air quiet and peaceful. It did not occur to her that she might be wandering too far to suit her husband.

She came to the edge of the grove, and, stepping out on a rocky outcropping, she looked down into a shallow gully that held only a dry stream bed and a few weeds that clung to the sides. From the direction in which it led, she was sure that it ended at the deep ravine beneath the south slope. The thought depressed her, and she raised her eyes and examined the land beyond. Undoubtedly Bailey's acres, for they were barren except for a few dusty ratoons in the distance. The ground had not even been prepared for planting, though an attempt had been made to start, an area had been turned over near the edge of the gully. But only a very small area and abandoned, for the clods of earth left by the shovel were rain-washed and crumbling. Laurie thought that if the rest of Bailey's fields were like this one there would be no crop for him this year.

She turned, looking north, examining the Silversea side of the winding gully. The cane shone, silver green and nearly as high now as a man's head. She wondered at Bailey's feelings, watching that cane from his own barren land. And at that moment she saw the man himself, riding an old, thin horse and coming along the bed of the gully from the north. She stepped back into the shelter of the grove, instantly repelled, and stood motionless waiting for him to pass.

He came on, sitting the horse like a crumpled pile of dirty clothes, for once hatless, his grotesque head bent against the glare. But before he drew abreast of the grove he put the old horse at the slope of the gully and rode up into his field, stopping near the mound of crumbling clods.

As Bailey dismounted Laurie shrank back, moving further into the shelter of the trees, afraid if he glanced around he might discover her there. But Bailey's attention was on the ground and he walked forward until he came to the turned earth and then stood there, his head still bent, his arms hanging at his side with the powerful, callused hands twitching.

Did he stand there, Laurie wondered, thinking of the slaves who had begun the work and then, perhaps, run away while the overseer's back was turned? Was it his angry thoughts that now infected the air and had created the feeling of sickness that was creeping over her?

Some such emotion must have risen inside him, for as she watched him his short legs tensed and then kicked at the clods, breaking them, stamping them down level with the rest of the field. Laurie gasped for air and reached to hold the limb of a tree to steady herself, for the nausea threatened to overcome her. With relief she saw that he had turned away and was walking back toward his horse.

"Laurie!"

She turned, looking back through the trees toward the glimmer of garden and the house in the distance. David's voice, and as he called again the sound was nearer. Then, through a gap in the branches she saw him, appearing and disappearing as he walked through the vegetable rows, his head down. She smiled, knowing he was tracking her by her footsteps in the soft earth.

"I am here," she called without thinking, and then looked around quickly, seeing that Bailey had heard her and stopped, sitting on his horse and searching the grove with a penetrating gaze. Then, as David's big body came striding into view, for he made no effort to stay hidden, Bailey turned his horse and rode away.

David grasped her arm, his eyes following Bailey. "What in God's name are you doing here, Laurie?" His voice was furious and frightened. "I told you Bailey had been riding these barren acres!"

His fingers were hurting her arm and she pulled away in pain and surprise.

"I was only walking. That is, I was searching for Molenga in the garden and wandered on. I have never been inside the grove before and it was so pleasant . . ."

His only answer was to take her arm again and turn her around roughly. He hurried her back the way she had come, much too fast for her comfort. She was stumbling and panting by the time they arrived at the house, but not until they were inside and had made their way to the hall did he loosen his hold. He started to speak and then stopped as she whirled away from him and went rapidly up the stairs.

Laurie was angry beyond reason, but she knew as angry as she was, he was angrier. And unfair. Dictatorial. Dragging her through the kitchen, past the open mouthed maids! How was she to know that Bailey would come riding along at just that moment? Submissiveness was far from her mind as she flung open the door of their rooms and went in, to find a large, portly Negress sitting in the bedroom waiting for her. As Laurie entered the woman rose from her chair, smiling.

"Anyola." It was a statement, and she said no more.

David had indeed made haste to bring the midwife. It took a few moments for Laurie to compose herself and offer a weak smile. Then she greeted her and asked her if she had been shown her room and if it pleased her.

Anyola stared at her for a time and then answered, at length, in a low, pleasant and totally incomprehensible series of remarks.

Dropping on the edge of the bed, Laurie struggled with an impulse to break into hysterical laughter. Her midwife—who spoke no English! She was silent, trying to become calm, but when the woman continued to stand she motioned to her to take the chair again and she sat down obediently, still smiling. A solution occurred to Laurie.

"Molenga?"

Anyola nodded, rose, and left the room. Laurie began to seriously consider the thought of Bridgetown with its hospital and English doctor. When the woman returned with Molenga, she addressed the ebony face anxiously.

"This will be impossible! I cannot communicate with her. How are we to manage?"

"There will be no trouble, my dear." Never had Laurie thought that faint, amused smile so out of place. "The language of your body will speak more clearly to Anyola than could your inexperienced mind. And I will be here to talk between you when it is necessary."

"Then tell her," Laurie said angrily, "that she is to go to her own room unless there is something she wants, or something she wants me to do."

Molenga gave her a sharp glance, but turned and spoke for some time in the woman's language, after which the woman nodded and smiled broadly at Laurie again and went out.

"I have told her," Molenga said, "that you gladly welcome her to your home and that you are most happy to have her help because you have heard she is a baby-bringer of utmost skill. I have also said that when she wishes to speak to you or to examine you, she is to call upon me so that I may tell you of her wishes. I also thanked her."

Molenga's proudly held head was, if possible, more arrogant than ever, her black eyes colder. She had shamed Laurie, and Laurie knew it.

"And I thank you," she said humbly. "I am very

angry, but that is not an excuse. She did not cause the anger, and I should have remembered to be courteous.''

Molenga inclined her head and left her. Lying back on the bed, Laurie wondered miserably if she was becoming a shrew. She felt oddly unstable, her stomach still churning and her head beginning to ache. For some reason her mind flew back to the library in Lord Peter's Mayfair home. David stood there, looking down at her, doubtful. ''Intelligence in a wife is a virtue,'' he had said. ''But—a lack of feminine graces, a lack of softness . . .''

He had made his wants clear, then. Had she ever met them? Oh, she had met his passion. But had she ever satisfied his desire for a submissive, feminine wife? She stared at the ceiling unhappily, afraid that the answer was no.

There were footsteps in the outer room and Thérèse was beside the bed, her long face longer still with some new anxiety.

''Are you all right, Madame?''

''I am fine,'' Laurie said shortly. ''Wonderfully fine.'' Then she sat up and flung her arms tightly around the spare figure. ''In truth, Thérèse, I am utterly miserable! I could wish us both back on Grosvenor Square, dealing with nothing more distressing than my mother's greediness!''

''Sh-h!'' Therese's sibilant hiss was quick but too late. Laurie looked, seeing that David stood in the archway, stern and quiet. Blood rose in her cheeks as he came forward and spoke.

''You may go, Thérèse.''

Thérèse hurried out and Laurie wished she could go with her and hide in her room. David was no longer red with anger as he had been when she whirled and left him. He was now quite pale and very still.

''Tomorrow,'' he said, ''Ham will drive you to Bridgetown. You will stay there in the hospital until your child is born. Thérèse will accompany you." He hesitated, clearing his throat. "I will admit to no argument on that plan."

He was waiting for an answer, but what could she say? Sitting there, huge in her pregnancy and blotched by tears, there was no courage in Laurie at all. She wanted to refuse to go, to tell him that she wanted him near when their child was born because she loved him with all her heart. But she thought now that he would turn away, that the stiff, pale face would show his repugnance. She could not continue to look at him, so sat staring at the floor in miserable acceptance of dismissal.

"You will stay here in this room," he was saying, "and rest for your trip. I will have Thérèse bring your dinner to you, and stay with you all night."

Even the thought of food added to her nausea, but she was silent, accepting his orders, nodding her head. He stayed for another moment and then was gone, the door closing behind him. Laurie thought bleakly that she need no longer wonder if she had satisfied him in her role as his wife. She had not. He did not even wish to spend this last night with her in their rooms.

She lay back again and slept. When Thérèse came in with a steaming tray of food she wakened long enough to look at it and swallow hard before she turned away, closing her eyes again and ignoring Thérèse's pleas to eat, if only a little.

When next she woke it seemed very late. The windows were black with the night sky, the room dark except for a circle of light from a lamp beside a chair. Thérèse sat there, half asleep over a book. Laurie saw all this without interest, for her attention had centered on a strange and uncomfortable urgency within her belly. It was slow, gradual and gripping, and it grew until at the end until she was forced to reach upward and cling to the round spindles at the head of the bed, gasping and feeling perspiration dampening her face.

The sound of her gasp brought Thérèse to her feet and

then to the side of the bed. Still gripped by the pain, Laurie stared up at her in helpless silence and Thérèse drew in her breath and turned, running from the room.

The pain was gone. Laurie loosened her hands from the spindles and relaxed, drawing in great breaths of relief. It was nothing, then. There for a moment she had wondered, thinking her child was too impatient to wait for the trip to . . . There was a faint stirring, a gathering of forces . . .

Anyola was there. She had examined Laurie gently and was now doing something quite incomprehensible. She was raising her with her big arms, urging her toward the side of the bed. Her voice, soft and yet commanding, seemed to go on and on.

"She is saying you must walk." Molenga, from a place near the window.

They know more than you do, Laurie reminded herself, and was glad of one clear thought. She slid from the bed, standing shakily while Anyola raised one of her quivering arms and placed it over her own fat shoulders. They walked, into the other room, back again. The pains still came, but they were bearable. Laurie looked into the dark face beside her and nodded, tried to smile. They walked, back and forth.

Thérèse stared in amazement and then went to the wardrobe and came back with a shift and wrapper. Laurie looked down at herself, discovering that she was still in the dress she had worn all day. She stood alone while they undressed her, and once, though they were quick, she was faint with pain. Then they began walking again. Anyola's eyes slid to Molenga and the latter spoke, her voice mellow and satisfied.

"She says you will do well." The ebony head watched her. There was no pity in the black eyes but there was an understanding.

There was sound, a faint, rapping noise, and Thérèse was gone, through the sitting room, sliding into the hall and closing the door behind her. As they walked, Laurie could hear Thérèse talking, her voice trembling, and then David's voice, deep and harsh.

"Too late, then. I should have sent her away earlier."

Laurie stored away heartbreak to be examined later. Too late. Yes, too late for anything but this. Her child had reached some mysterious goal of strength and readiness and now was more powerful than she was. He would leave her body and begin his own life and nothing would stop him.

Thérèse came back into the room and stood watching with tears in her eyes.

"She is exhausted! *Mon Dieu,* let her lie in her bed!"

"It is not good to remain in bed," Molenga said, but then spoke to Anyola, the dialect smooth and effortless, with a lift at the end like a question. Anyola shrugged and then nodded and Molenga went to them, taking Laurie's other arm.

"Sit as I have taught you," she said, "and rest for a few moments. If a pain comes, lean forward and breath deep and fast."

Her hand supported Laurie as she sank to the floor. Leaning forward, panting, Laurie waited now with some patience, for she had learned the pain would give her time before it began again.

"It is not so bad," she said to Thérèse. "It is not constant."

Molenga's eyes grew bright, she spoke again to Anyola and Anyola laughed. Laurie smiled at her and leaned forward again to pant and wait. She was no longer frightened, but grateful to all of them. Feeling for them filled her and overflowed. Four women we are, she thought, together, knowing what women know, have always known. When they reached to pull her up again she went willingly, and put her arm across Anyola's shoulders to walk.

Thérèse was preparing the bed. She took the silk coverlet and the blankets from it and stretched a sheet tightly. She brought a stack of towels and padding, and last of all the small blue receiving clothes which together they had sewed. Laurie looked at them and they seemed magical, promising an end to pain, a beginning of happiness.

Three times more she sat to rest, panting and waiting. But the last time they had to lift her, for the pain was very strong. They helped her into bed and Anyola examined her, speaking rapidly to Molenga. Then she left the room and came back with a cup to hold to Laurie's lips. She drank, finding it bitter, tasting of green leaves.

"It will ease you into dreams," Molenga said with her faint smile. She moved away and Thérèse took her place, holding Laurie's hand and whispering encouragement.

"I will be fine," Laurie said, and her faint voice surprised her. The pain began and she knew it would be very strong, for even at first it gripped with incredible power. But there was also a sensation of numbness, of unreality, that came from the bitter green leaves. The pain encroached, building like a wave, and she stopped thinking to wait for it to end. Her mind slipped and fell into darkness where a macabre vision swirled, floating toward her. The vision, she knew, that had come as she knelt by Desirée's bed that terrible night, the vision she had refused to see. Nor did she wish to see it now as it floated nearer, ballooning to fill the dark space. David, she saw, and Ham, standing together in a dim field, a wide hole between them. They stared downward, and the light of their lanterns shone on their faces, revealing horror. And she knew why, she knew what they saw and tried to scream, and tried again, and only dropped deeper into total night.

Molenga spoke to her from far away. She struggled upward toward light, swimming in clouds. Then she opened her eyes and saw the ebony figure, outlined in lamp glow, tall and proud with a bundle in her arms.

Laurie's hands flew to her flattened belly and she believed, reaching instantly for the bundle, smiling.

"I saw you standing so, with him in your arms, the day we met."

"I know," Molenga said, and laid the bundle beside her, opening the edges of blue flannel. "Now, look at your son."

She did, and there were no words for it. She could not look enough. His eyes blinked, squeezed shut against light. An arm came thrusting upward, free and reaching. The others gathered around and spoke of his remarkable beauty and strength. Then Thérèse hurried out and came back in with David.

He was rumpled and sleepless, and his eyes were on Laurie, which puzzled her. He had wanted a son for so long. He stood beside the bed and stared at her silently until she smiled and pulled the blue cloth aside again. Then he knelt, his face pale, and looked at his child.

"A boy. Perfectly formed, but so small . . ."

Anyola's voice came from the background, the indignation needing no translator. David glanced around at her and smiled, looked back again at Laurie.

"She says I am a dolt and the baby is quite large." He reached gently and put the blue flannel over the baby, covering all but the grimacing little face. Then he stood up and looked at Molenga.

"Did the Mistress come through this well? Well enough to travel within a day?"

"If she must."

"She must," he said gravely. "Thérèse will go with her."

Molenga nodded, and he bent again to look at his son, to smile at Laurie. Then he rose and turned to leave the room.

"Wait," Laurie said. "There is something I must say." She looked at the women. Molenga's eyes glittered suddenly, she spoke to Anyola and they left, Thérèse with them, closing the door outside.

Hesitant, David came back to the side of the bed, his

brows drawn down. "Please, Laurie, do not ask to stay."

"I will not," she said, willing control. The words were like arrows. "I must tell you that I know what happened to Grace and William." She knew she must say it all very quickly now or she would not be able to say it at all. "Take Ham, and go across the gully behind the lime grove. There, on Bailey's land, you will find a place where the surface has been disturbed . . ." Now, she could no longer hold back tears. "It is their grave . . ." She sobbed helplessly.

David drew in his breath sharply and dropped again to his knees, putting an arm across Laurie, across his son, as if to shield them both.

"Why have you said that? What do you know?"

She clung to his arm, still sobbing. "I cannot tell you . . . only promise me you will do what I said, now! Please, David! They are there . . ."

"You have my promise," he said heavily, and held her, stroking back the hair from her forehead until she could stop her weeping.

Chapter Twenty-one

Wakened at dawn by the soft closing of a door, Laurie found she was alone with her son for the first time. Hidden in the cradle which had been placed beside the rocking chair where Thérèse had spent the night, the baby was making small waking noises, sighs and bubbling sounds that were far different from the desperate howls he had made twice during the night.

Those howls had been silenced by Laurie's full breasts. Feeling his tiny but ferocious mouth fasten and suck, seeing the small body relax into contentment, had brought her a suffusing warmth and satisfaction that she could hardly wait to experience again. She swung her feet to the floor and stood, bracing herself for a moment with one hand on the bed.

Shaky, yes, and very sore, but not truly weak. Her breasts ached worse than ever, but she had learned the cure for that. She made her way to the cradle and picked up the blue bundle with a pang of pure, reverent joy. Thérèse had been tending him, for he was clean and dry, but at her touch his eyes opened, his mouth moved, pursed as if seeking, and his voice came, demanding. She laughed softly and sat down in the rocking chair, offering him a tight, throbbing breast.

Feeding him, leaning back and rocking gently, Laurie felt enveloped by a love that included not only the baby but all others of her household. There were no problems while she gazed down at the soft fuzz of black hair, the curve of forehead and springing brow line so much like David's. When the baby slept he was David's miniature, but when his eyes opened she could see the brilliant blue already tinged with green. Her father had passed on his eyes through her, and that could be a mixed blessing. For a moment, watching the eyes blink with their misty blue-green gaze, her smile faded as she thought of the scene that had invaded the darkness before his birth. Surely it had been but a nightmare, and she had sent David on a fool's errand . . .

The door opened again and Thérèse tiptoed in, gasping as she saw Laurie sitting there. Laurie waved off her protests and reminded her that no one gained strength by lying in bed. "Nor starving, either," she added pointedly, and then laughed. "Is this baby the only one entitled to breakfast?"

Thérèse scurried out and returned in minutes with a full tray. She sat quietly while Laurie ate, her long face soft as she gazed into the cradle where the satisfied baby crooned, waved an arm and settled back into sleep.

"I will pack everything," she said as she took the tray again, "except what we will need in the coach. Your husband chose the largest equipage and has had it drawn out and cleaned thoroughly. It is large and heavy, but there are four good horses to pull it."

Laurie's heart turned over. "You must tell him I am weak and cannot leave today. Oh, Thérèse, I know I was a shrew yesterday and he is very angry, I suppose, at what I said. But surely, now that the baby is born—"

Thérèse interrupted, most uncharacteristically. "Madame! It is not anger that makes your husband want you and the baby in Bridgetown, it is fear for your safety. No one has thought to tell you, I suppose, or to worry you, but the insurrection they have feared has begun. All who lived in the manor house at Thatcher's plantation are dead and the house burned! A huge army of slaves are plundering their way south, and the Allyns have already left for Bridgetown, fearful for their lives!"

Laurie stared at her. She had ignored Van Horn's warning, but even David had thought the situation serious, and yet she had not given it another thought!

How could she be so blind? Her eyes flew to the cradle. They would not hesitate to kill a white baby! She was rising from her chair, ready to dress and tell David she was more than strong enough to travel.

"Then of course we are all going! Go, tell David I shall be ready."

"We are not all going," Thérèse said grimly, "though I have been most forward about arguing with your husband. He, his father, Molenga and Ham are staying, except that Ham, who is driving us to Bridgetown, will have to make his way back here later."

Laurie looked at her pitifully. "They will all be killed, Thérèse. We cannot let them stay!"

Thérèse put the tray down and urged Laurie's trembling body back into her chair. "Mr. Covington believes our slaves are loyal and will help them. He says there is a way to save Silversea and they must try. He is adamant! I do not believe anyone could convince him to leave."

Desperate and frightened, Laurie watched Thérèse take the tray again and leave the room. Thérèse would wish to go, and she could not blame her. She, too, had heard the stories of cane knives flashing, of murdered and mutilated women and children. Laurie wondered if there was any way she could persuade David to go with them.

David did not come to her room until almost noon, and then he brought Bartram with him. Dusty and travel-worn, they explained quickly that David had gone to Bridgetown during the night and had brought Bartram back with him. There was pride on both bearded faces as they leaned over the cradle, and then Bartram came with a glow on his face to take Laurie's hand.

"Handsome and well-formed, an image of his father! You have reason to be proud, daughter. And you? You look surprisingly fit."

She thrust aside her fears and told him her strength was returning rapidly. Then, perversely, she added that when the baby opened his eyes there would be evidence of her own part in creation. "The other grandfather," she said, smiling, "looks from his eyes."

Bartram promptly replied that it was well to have two noble families represented, which was so characteristic of him that she laughed. But her laughter died as she saw David sit down to wait for his father to leave. David looked unhappy.

And he spoke as soon as the door closed behind Bartram. Taking Laurie's hands, he looked at her steadily.

"The bodies were there, Laurie."

The words hit her hard. She had cherished her obstinate hope that the scene had been only a nightmare brought on by Anyola's bitter brew, and now she struggled for control and lost. Now she could see Grace so clearly. Luminous and happy, with a heart that encompassed all mankind. And William, so sweet and studious, so well meaning— She bent forward with more pain than she remembered from the night.

"Dear God in Heaven . . . Grace, and William, too . . ." Grief clutched her and shook her savagely, releasing a torrent of tears and wracking sobs, and David leaped to snatch her from her chair and sit down again with her held tightly against him.

"Don't . . . please, Laurie, don't grieve so. I cannot stand to see your heart breaking . . ." His arms were so tight she could hardly breathe, so comforting it didn't matter. She clung to him until she could stop, could move away and wipe her face and see that his cheeks were wet with his own tears and that his face looked lost and sad.

"I'm sorry," she said. "I knew. Yet I had to hope . . . they were such good people. And so newly happy together . . ." Her soft mouth quivered as she brushed the tears from his cheeks with a comforting small hand. "You grieve for them, too."

"No. I do deeply regret their loss," David said grimly, "and am appalled at the evil nature of the man who caused it. But I am very much afraid that my grieving is due only to you. I find I cannot bear to have you suffer.'' His arms tightened around her and he stood up, carrying her to the bed and putting her down gently, settling the pillow beneath her head and pulling the covers around her.

"You must rest, my darling. The trip to Bridgetown will be very hard on you, and you must leave within an hour.''

She rose on one elbow, the clear turquoise depths of her brilliant eyes full of pleading, her black hair streaming like satin over white shoulders. "I do not want to be parted from you, David. If you must stay, then let me stay, too.''

"No!'' His mouth twisted as if he hated to deny her, but the hard determination in his eyes never wavered. "Another thing I cannot bear is to have you in danger.'' He eased down on the edge of the bed and took her hands in his, turning them to lie in his broad palms and looking down at them. She watched him, knowing he had something he wanted to say and was struggling to find the words.

"Before you go,'' he said finally, "I must apologize to you. I laughed at you once, and made sport of your illusions. I said you were a child.'' He glanced at her, his face full of emotion. "You are a woman. Beautiful, strong and full of love. Last night, while you were bearing the child I so lightly bargained for, I was in agony. I could think of nothing but your pain and the possibility of losing you. That illusion of love between a man and a woman is not an illusion at all. I would have gladly given my life for yours, and I know now that I love you with all my heart and soul.''

She was crying again. How could she help it? She reached for him and he came very willingly into her arms, his bearded face in her neck, his hands sliding beneath her to hold her gently.

"That would have been a useless exchange,'' she whispered shakily. "My life would have no meaning without you. I have loved you from the first, I will love you forever . . .''

He was kissing the white neck, his arms tightening. "I hope so," he said, muffled, "for my offer of freedom has been withdrawn. You must now stay with me, also forever."

She laughed through her tears and hugged him. "I would have refused to accept that offer in any case." She turned her head and met his lips with hers, her mouth making rash promises for the future. "I have waited so long for you to love me," she said softly, "and now that you do, you are sending me away. . . ."

"Not for long, my darling." He sat up, his whole face glowing. "In a very few days we will be back together again, and—I promise you—we will have a new and better life."

She looked at him questioningly and started to speak, but he cut off her words with another, very possessive, kiss.

Later, he had questions for her, and one she could not answer, for she had a strange conviction that she should not tell him how it was that she had seen that yawning grave and had known what it meant. When he asked her how she had guessed the truth, she said only that Bailey's peculiar actions when he stood there had puzzled her, for he seemed to be trying to hide the fact that the ground had been disturbed. Then, of course, William's disappearance, and the fact that Grace had not written to her and no one had seen her . . .

David accepted her faltering explanation and said he must lay it to women's intuition.

"In spite of the tragedy, which we could not have prevented," he added, "one good thing has come from the discovery. Van Horn has dropped all charges against Ham."

So that was why David had gone to Bridgetown before dawn. Laurie nodded. "He believes you, now, doesn't he?" She spoke sadly, trying not to think of the horror of

Desirée's agonized death. "He too thinks Bailey is the murderer."

"He is convinced of it. He reasons that she must have witnessed some part of Bailey's crime against Grace and William, and that Bailey killed her to keep it secret."

"Yes." Laurie's gaze was tortured. "But *why* did he take her to that slope and . . . and rape her?"

David sighed. "I believe in some way the man is insane. He is a man of violence, of perverted desires. He may have been reenacting the lovemaking he had seen there . . . and envied."

Laurie shuddered. "From this day forward, we shall make love inside our home. With curtains drawn! How horrible to think of—"

"Do not think," David commanded. "And do not make plans right now, for we haven't the time. I know Thérèse must have finished her packing and it is late. I will send Thérèse to you, and see if Ham has harnessed the horses."

"David . . ."

He had risen, but he turned back and gripped her arms. "It will be all right, darling. You must be brave for a little while. If our plan fails, then Father and I can escape with Ham and Molenga. But to add you, our newborn son and Thérèse—we could not manage it all."

She was a danger to him, to them all. "I will go," she said quickly. "Send Thérèse."

The huge coach was full of the things Thérèse had thought necessary for the journey. Baskets of food and wine, a bed made up across the narrow seat for Laurie, a makeshift cradle in a padded box, a jug of water and stacks of cloth squares to cleanse and dry the baby. Only a small corner was left for Thérèse to sit in, but it seemed more than enough as she shrank back, white lipped, as the whip cracked over the backs of the four horses and the coach jolted into motion. The white lips were moving, Laurie noted, in silent prayer.

Laurie's only worry was Ham, sitting outside on the

box. He would be many hours on the way, and more coming back, and she wished him at David's side. But David would trust no other man to drive them. Ham, he said, would leave the coach in Bridgetown at the inn where they were to stay. He could come back much faster on horseback.

Laurie had asked fearfully if it was possible that coming back Ham might be caught by the rioting slaves, and David had given her a grim smile.

"If the slaves are particularly unfortunate, yes, it is possible," he had said. "Ham will return."

Now, as they bowled along toward Bridgetown Laurie lay back in the nest that Thérèse had fashioned and cradled her son in her arms. He was sleeping, and she shut her eyes too, fastening her thoughts on her hopes but still engaging in wordless prayer. Somehow she felt that their leaving had been a mistake, and every roll of the wheels on the heavy old coach increased her misgivings. If only we could have stayed, she thought rebelliously. If only they *knew* their plan would work, so that there was no reason to worry about escaping. . . .

They had traveled close to an hour without incident, without a word from Thérèse or a cry from the baby, when all at once the coach slowed and lurched to a stop. Surprised, Laurie sat up, her first sight Thérèse's horrified face.

"What is it?"

Thérèse pointed through the window. A mushrooming cloud of black smoke, tipped with gray, lay east of them. Laurie thrust her head through the window and looked up at Ham, motionless on the box and looking down at her.

"We are late, Mistress. Perhaps too late. That is Bailey's house burning, and it means the rioters have traveled east of us much faster than we thought possible."

"What should we do?"

"If it is only a few, we might get past them . . ." His

head flew up at some sound Laurie did not hear and she looked in the direction of his gaze. A mass of dark bodies, ragged clothing fluttering, moved down an embankment ahead of them. They were like a herd of animals, and the sound of their hoarse cries blended into an angry roar. Laurie fell back into the coach as Ham, laying on the whip like lightning striking, turned the team in the narrow road and shouted, heading them back for Silversea.

There were times on that ride that Laurie clutched two pillows around her baby, sure that the coach would turn over, crashing into the wall of earth beside them. There were times when she feared Thérèse would lose consciousness, for her face was bloodless, her eyes blind with fear. She wondered why Ham kept the horses at such speed, for they had far outstripped the savage mob behind them.

Then they turned at last into the avenue that led to Silversea and Laurie understood. There, to the north, there were fires burning in the distance. They were all around them, and Ham had known it would be so.

They left everything in the coach and stumbled hastily up the steps while Ham unloosened the horses and slapped them away, knowing they would head for the stables. But the door was locked, and Ham came running and flung himself against it. The lock shattered, and they were inside. Inside an empty, echoing house! Ham shut the door and, turning to look, grasped an immense, marble-topped chest away from the wall and shoved it against the door.

"It will hold," he said grimly. "Come, Thérèse . . ."

Gray still with fright but obedient, Thérèse followed his rapid stride toward the back of the house. When she came back Laurie was still standing, bewildered, her son crying from hunger in her arms.

"Where has everyone gone?"

From somewhere, Thérèse had found courage. She

put her arms around Laurie for a moment and then took the baby.

"They are all at the barracas," she said quietly. "And Ham has gone to join them. He said that later—perhaps much later—they would come back here. I must be ready to open the back door for them." She held the crying baby on her shoulder, patting him. "Compose yourself, Madame. You must feed this boy before he thinks you mean to starve him."

Laurie looked at the baby, at the thrusting arms and red, indignant face, and took him, going into the drawing room. I will not know if they kill him, she thought, for they will have to kill me first.

Laurie learned, that day, the true meaning of fear and the ultimate necessity of courage. She had thought before that courage was wrapped in pride, a virtue of the wellborn, and not to be confused with the cornered small animal that turns because he must to snap chattering teeth at his pursuer.

But she had never been beset by such fear before, fear that did not resolve itself, but stayed like a fog surrounding them. Thérèse, always so nervous and fearful, had become that cornered animal. Her long face was stiff with determination and she had armed herself with a huge knife from the kitchen. Laurie could see its handle protruding above the apron band. Thérèse would bite before she died.

When the baby had finished nursing he slept, and Laurie put him in a large chair, held in by pillows. Then, wondering why Molenga had gone with the men, she went through the house and found fruit and cheese in the kitchen and took them back to the drawing room for them to eat. They did not think of leaving the room; it had become their station, with the large windows to give them a view on what might come, perhaps with an angry roar such as the sound Laurie had heard, or perhaps stealthily, creeping through the gardens . . .

Laurie went often to gaze out, seeing nothing, hearing

no unusual sound. The peaceful scene became ominous. Silversea was too large and wealthy a plantation to be ignored by the looters and murderers, and she could only believe that the rioters thought it too strong for casual action by the vanguards of the army. They were hanging back, she thought fearfully, until they could gather the whole force and plan their attack. She wished now that she and Thérèse had taken time to bring in the clothes, the baby's clothes and garments and the food from the coach. She said so, and Thérèse nodded grimly.

"I shall fetch them," she said, and nothing Laurie could say shook her determination. Even pushing together they could not budge the immense chest Ham had pushed against the front door, so Thérèse led Laurie to the kitchen and went out, insisting that the door be locked behind her. Laurie rushed to watch from the drawing room as Thérèse gathered the necessary things from the coach, then rushed to the kitchen to let her in again.

Thérèse entered with a tight smile. "We have guards," she said, putting her burdens down with a sigh of relief. "Guards everywhere, may *le bon Dieu* bless them all. Your husband must have sent them when he heard you were here. They are hidden in the gardens, armed with cane knives." She shuddered, but not for herself, for she added: "They nodded at me, quite . . . quite pl– pleasantly." She threw her arms suddenly around Laurie and gasped with half laughter, half cry. "When I saw the first one, Madame, I thought I was lost!"

Laurie hugged her back. They clung for a moment in tearful laughter, and then gathered the bundles to take them back to their place, instantly creating a useful clutter in the stately room. Now, knowing where to look, Laurie saw one of the guards from the window, a young, strong man with his wicked long knife at his side, motionless behind a screen of leaves. Glancing from the window at the west she saw more, a thin line of slaves mounting the far end of the slope and disappearing into the tall sugar cane field that led to the main road. She pointed wordlessly, and Thérèse came to look.

"More of ours?"

Laurie nodded and sat down, realizing that she was, after all, quite weak. Somewhere down at the slave quarters, she thought, David and his father were working out their plan to save the plantation. And David would now be worried and distracted, knowing that she and his son were helpless in the great house. He might have needed the men he sent to guard them. And she, herself, was useless. Even Thérèse had a knife . . .

She rose and went into the kitchen, looking for a weapon. Through the kitchen window she saw smoke billowing to the northeast, and with a throb of terror realized that it had to be at Lord Peter's plantation. The Allyn's house—thank God they had deserted it! They were safe in Bridgetown.

None of the knives left in the kitchen were large enough or wicked enough in appearance to suit her, and she thought suddenly of Molenga's spear. That long, thin and deadly looking weapon seemed most appropriate to this day.

The stairs were longer than ever, her body ached all over when she reached the top floor. It was a useless effort after all, for the spear was gone. She looked around the room, wishing for Molenga's presence and the sense of security and ease she felt with her. Her colorful lengths of silk were hung neatly in a row, and she saw that the crimson one was missing. Molenga was dressed for battle, she thought wryly, in her brilliant crimson and carrying that spear.

It was now habit to peer through windows, and before she left she parted the curtains and looked down. The view from up here took in a great distance, even to the edge that led down to the southeast slope she had once loved and now could not go near. And, as she watched, three half-naked dark figures, rags fluttering from their

loins, passed swiftly from the slope into the copse of
trees near by. She turned and went down the front
staircase and into the drawing room.

"There are strangers coming from the southeast," she
said breathlessly. "I saw them from the top floor!"

Instantly Thérèse was at the window to the garden.
She threw it open. "There are rioters coming from the
other side," she called, and one of the guards answered
her in dialect, adding awkwardly:

"Man there, here."

Thérèse shut the window, puzzled.

Laurie smiled at her. "I suspect," she said, relieved,
"that he meant to say there are guards on both sides of
the house." As she spoke there was a new noise, a
rattling and then a strong knocking. They went quickly
and half fearfully to the kitchen.

"Let us in!"

David. Laurie's hands shook as she grabbed and
turned the key and flung the door open. David picked her
up and swung her aside, allowing Molenga, Bartram and
Ham to enter behind him. The door swung shut as she
gazed at all of them, knowing she loved them all and for
the moment they were all safe. Molenga, splendid in her
crimson silk and gold earrings, grasped the spear in one
hand as casually as ever she had held a kitchen spoon.
Ham, standing back behind Bartram, towered even over
that snowy head, a shadow of them all, darkly protective. She sighed, and loosed David unwillingly. He gave
her a tight, reassuring smile that did not reach his eyes.

"It is going well, so far. It is time we were all here
together."

Laurie told him quickly of the three men she had seen
and he nodded, unsurprised.

"They are gathering from every side. In an hour or so,
I believe the whole mass of them will ring this house,
called here by their leader. Only then will we find if our
plan has worked."

They went, silent, to the drawing room. Molenga's

head darted like a snake as she saw the baby, sweating in the pile of pillows. She went to him and picked him up, so skillfully that he did not waken.

"There is a cradle," she said to Laurie indignantly. "I will put him in it, where he can stretch his limbs and grow." She left, carrying him, with the long spear hanging by its thongs from her shoulder, the blade above her head and the thin line of the shaft no straighter than her long legs.

"You, also," David said to Laurie firmly. "Go and rest for awhile. You are swaying on your feet from exhaustion."

Laurie nodded, knowing that if there were trouble, if they were forced in the end to try for escape, she must be able to do her part. Rest would help. She followed Molenga up the stairs and watched her lay the sleeping baby in his cradle and move it close to the bed.

"You will not need to rise when he is hungry," she said. "Only reach for him."

Laurie sat down on the edge of the bed and looked at Molenga searchingly. "Stay with me for a time," she said. "I have questions."

Molenga looked into the brilliant eyes and her faint smile appeared.

"You wish to ask me about the gift we share," she said slowly. "I am not sure I can tell you what you wish to know."

"I am frightened," Laurie said simply. "I do not understand, nor do I wish to see these scenes."

Molenga sighed, and dropped to the floor in the easy motion that left her in that position she had taught Laurie. Her eyes changed, became unseeing, as if they saw through what appeared before them and scanned the distance beyond.

"There is a gift which is not always a gift, given to few, who then see what others cannot see. In the beginning the gift is capricious, coming and going. But some who receive it learn to use it at will. If then they seek to see all, the gift is a curse instead. For what you see you cannot change, and the heart may suffer."

Laurie understood and shuddered, thinking of seeing tragedy ahead for a loved one. "A curse indeed," she said softly. "May I never—"

"Wait! There are times when your heart itself will insist that you look. Then you may slide your sight into time without fear. What you see then will bring you one of three things—knowledge that may aid another, strength to meet an obstacle, or, best of all, happiness that will last." She smiled; not the faint, amused curve of chiseled lips Laurie knew, but a wide, brilliant smile that glowed triumphantly on her dark face.

"I saw you," she went on, "On the ship that brought you here. Young and untried, needing my help. But still I knew your presence would change our world . . ." Her voice trailed off, suddenly hoarse and tired, and her eyes saw Laurie again, losing the distant world she had been examining.

"There are things you need not know yet. I also must rest." She came to her feet as smoothly as she had sat down, and went quickly from the room.

Laurie lay back on her bed, dazed. She believed only half of what Molenga had said, and wished heartily that she believed none of it. She wanted no more than the baby, who lay sleeping in the cradle beside her, and the man she loved, who kept guard for them below. I do not, she thought sleepily, want to be a witch at all.

Chapter Twenty-two

LAURIE JERKED UPWARD, EVERY MUSCLE TENSE, LIStening in a silence so complete that she could hear the frantic thumping of her own heart. There had been a scream, she was sure of it. A scream that had dragged her from deep sleep, had set the blood rushing through her veins.

The baby still slept peacefully, not a quiver or movement. She breathed deeply, eased backward . . .

A shot rang out, reverberating through the house, and she was up and running, through the rooms and along the gallery, unsteady and grabbing at the balustrade as she turned down the staircase and plunged on, half falling and recovering as she dashed into the drawing room.

David was on the floor, writhing, there was blood on his shirt, on the rug. She flung herself down beside him and he pushed at her futilely.

"Go, Laurie . . . get out of here . . ."

She stared up at the others. Bartram, Ham, Thérèse . . . frozen, staring . . .

"*Help* him!" She was screaming in fright and anger. "He is bleeding! Can't you *see?*"

"They see," said a voice behind her, a voice drunkenly malicious, full of hate. "*You* are the one who is blind, my dear . . ."

She whirled, still kneeling, seeing first the cracked boots and filthy trousers, then raising her eyes to Prentiss Bailey's blotched, leering face, to the barrel of the pistol in his hand. In the other hand a pistol hung down, a wisp of smoke still curling lazily from it.

293

"They see," he repeated, "and they wait—to find out who will receive the other bullet. Perhaps they are glad to see you here, since it raises the odds . . ."

Ham moved, a deep, inarticulate sound in his chest, and the barrel of the gun swung swiftly. On the floor, David raised his head.

"No, Ham," he said hoarsely, "the plan . . . rests on you . . ."

Fear had Laurie by the throat. They had thought the danger was outside, in hundreds of raging black bodies seeking freedom and revenge, and that had been understandable. But here was the danger, in their midst. A white man, a neighbor . . . and evil incarnate. She swallowed, knowing she had never been truly afraid before. She was paralyzed with it, staring at him as if the grotesque head had hypnotized her.

"How did you get in here?" A stupid question, asked in a cracking whisper she couldn't recognize as her own voice.

He laughed, his eyes gleaming. "My, the little firebrand is frightened, isn't she? Through the ravine, my dear—a spot of pleasant memories for me. And up through the gully, escaping the men who pursued me. And through your back door, so conveniently unlocked."

She closed her eyes, thinking of that moment of high joy when they had all trooped in and none had remembered to lock the door behind them. But at least she had him talking . . . gaining time . . . She forced herself to look at him again.

"Why use your guns on us? There are hundreds of rioters to use as targets." Her whisper was gaining strength.

His mouth twisted bitterly. "Why should I fight the rioters? To live, and dangle at the end of a rope? I have no future, thanks to you . . . to your husband there with his life leaking out and to that savage that stands waiting for my bullet! I have seen the open grave, I know I will be hunted down!'' He laughed, close to hysteria.

"Perhaps the bullet will be for you, Mistress Covington. I killed the other woman who spied on me. But *you*—you watched me and knew, didn't you?'' He was losing control, his voice shaking. "You with your love of slaves, you pushed my daughter to disobey me . . .''

Death stared into Laurie's face, and, unable to move, she stared back. But still a flicker of motion caught the corner of her wide eyes. Something flashing darkly near the open doorway. Molenga. And Bailey had noticed nothing, his eyes were riveted on her. She *must* move. She willed her frozen body into action and rose slowly to her feet.

"You may be right,'' she said, trying to keep her voice even. "I cannot see how the others are at fault . . .'' She moved her unwilling feet, moved away from David, her eyes fastened on Bailey's face. "I did encourage Grace. I even gave her money . . . to . . . to buy books . . .'' She swallowed. "I suppose you could say it was my fault . . . my fault entirely . . . that . . . that you were forced to kill her.'' He was turning, as she had willed him to turn, following her with his gun, the barrel like an evil black eye. In the other end of the room the three still standing were motionless and silent, and she knew they must have sensed Molenga's presence. But David was inching after her, trying to rise, his hoarse, frantic voice protesting . . . she ignored him, knowing she must, seeing Bailey's angry gaze drop momentarily and then come back to her. She moved farther, as if to escape the grasp of David's reaching hands, and Bailey swiftly followed her with the gun.

"Yes,'' he said harshly, "that is all true. You forced me . . .''

His back was square to the door as she had wanted it. She raised her head, her eyes blazing. "What forced you, Prentiss Bailey, was your own evil, filthy nature, your consuming greed! The same despicable qualities that forced you to kill your wife—and blame it on a Rundi girl.''

With a hoarse, guttural sound of rage he raised the gun, pointing it directly at her breast, his finger tightening. . . .

Laurie saw crimson in the doorway, an upthrust black arm, a dark blade winging. She felt David's shoulder lunge heavily against her knees, heard the gunshot blasting. She was on the floor, held down by David's still, heavy body, and Bailey, his eyes stretched wide, his mouth open, was slowly toppling over on his face, exposing the thin, black shaft of Molenga's spear quivering above his back.

Ham moved fast, lifting David to the couch, tearing his shirt off, pressing it, wadded, against the wound to stop the flow of blood. Thérèse had gone running to the kitchen and storeroom, bringing back a basin of water and cloths. They worked over David together, so closely that Laurie could not see the wound for their flickering hands. She knelt by the couch, holding his hand and watching him breath. He was so white, so silent.

"He is not conscious," she whispered to Ham fearfully.

Ham grunted. "Good. Then what I am doing will not hurt him." He glanced at her. "He will heal, Mistress. A broken rib, that is all. And a great loss of blood, which has weakened him considerably. But that will mend." He sat back, holding a lead ball in bloody fingers for her to see. "A poor load, to be stopped by a rib. And a drunken fool with poor aim. Your husband will be up in two days."

Life ran through her, gladness. She was suddenly dizzy with it. She slumped against the couch, watching them deftly bandaging, for Molenga had found strips of white linen.

Behind her, Bartram spoke. "Laurie."

She turned and looked up at him, at the face as white

as the beard and hair, and then stood up, smoothing down her skirt, now patched with blood from David's wound.

"He will be fine," she said reassuringly. "Ham says he is not badly hurt."

Bartram's mouth trembled. "I have seen few men with your courage, Laurie. You deliberately drew his fire. How did you dare?"

She looked at him, surprised. "I knew I must. Molenga was there, waiting her chance. I knew she could save us all." She looked around, finding Molenga's jet eyes looking at her. "You did well," she added to her softly. "Thank you."

Molenga's eyes glittered. "I join the Master in saluting your courage. But now you must go to your son. In the hall I heard him shaking the roof top with his angry yells, and no one else can feed him."

It was not until she sat in the rocking chair, with the baby silenced at last by her breast, that Laurie thought of the threat yet to come and glanced fearfully through the window.

Below her, beneath a mahogany tree, two Silversea slaves were talking to four or five others, strangers to Laurie. They were thin, ill-dressed men she had not seen around the place before. Allyn's slaves, escaped from the insurrectionists and here to help? Certainly they were not the enemy, though all of them, their own men included, were armed with the swordlike knives stuck through their belts. But they were friendly, talking with the wide gestures of African communication. Laughing, their white teeth shining in the shade of the big tree. She turned away, hopefully. Any assistance was welcome.

Later, she washed the baby and wrapped him in a clean blanket. His blue-green eyes blinked at her as she took him downstairs. Thérèse, wan and serious, met her at the foot of the staircase and automatically reached for the baby.

"There is hot food in the dining room," she said.

"And your husband is sleeping, and does not need you. Eat, you may need your strength."

Bartram, still white and silent, was at the table. He rose, immediately, and poured a glass of wine, filling a plate at the buffet to bring to her. He sat down, heavily.

"David was conscious for a few minutes while you were gone," he said. "I believe his sleep now is normal. We are fortunate the wound is no worse."

"Was he in great pain?" Laurie was eating rapidly, wishing to be with David, to reassure herself.

"He did not seem to be. Weak, and I'm afraid confused. He asked about you at once, and we assured him you were not hurt and were with your infant. He replied with an odd phrase . . . 'a daughter of lions.' His mind wanders, I fear."

Laurie smiled. "No, I think not. I believe he will be fine."

"I trust you are right . . ." he began, and then stopped, his eyes going to the door. Molenga stood there, with Ham.

"It is time, Master," she said to Bartram. "The leader is here."

Her look of high pride was again paramount. Laurie saw that she had her spear again, hanging from her shoulder, the blade clean and shining above her head.

Bartram nodded. "Go," he said, a tremor in his aged voice. "May God guide your words as he did your spear."

"Molenga!" Laurie was on her feet, alarmed. "You will not go into danger. . . ."

"It is all right, Mistress." Ham was calm, pleasant as always. "We go together."

Dismayed, Laurie left the rest of her food and followed them, watching Ham move the huge chest from the door, saw them open it and go out, pulling it shut behind them. She went on, into the drawing room where Thérèse sat with the baby in her lap, watching over both him and David, asleep on the couch. Laurie glanced aside, half fearing to see Bailey's body still there, relieved to find it gone.

"Ham took him away," Thérèse whispered. "I do not know where, nor do I think it matters. A murderous beast!"

Laurie nodded, irresistibly drawn to the couch, where she knelt and examined David's face, still pale, but relaxed. She looked up to smile with satisfaction at Thérèse, but Thérèse, her face frightened, was staring at the front windows. Laurie, her heart beginning to pound, rose and went to look.

It was the scene that had come into her mind, unbidden, the first time she had seen Silversea. A flowing black mass of bodies converging on the house. Men, women, half-grown children, all in constant motion and surging forward. And more of them, ranks that came from the horizon it seemed, for there was no end in sight. They kept coming, heads bobbing, bodies weaving, their combined voices a low rumble, as if the earth beneath them swayed to their feet. In the foreground there were some of the Silversea slaves and Laurie stepped back, frightened by the sheer immensity of the crowd and the thought that even their slaves had joined them. It seemed a nation of its own, a force that would move with one mind, one purpose. *And Molenga and Ham had gone out there.* Laurie went swiftly out into the hall and opened the door quietly.

The noise came in like a solid blow, a roar that subsided as Molenga, standing on the portico, raised her spear high over her head and spoke, her voice a clear, ringing shout of melodic dialect. When she had finished Ham stepped out before her and began, his deep voice booming out over the mass of moving, excited blacks.

Shaken, Laurie stepped back, shutting the door. Amazed and puzzled, she went back into the drawing room, meeting Thérèse's horrified gaze.

"What are they doing?"

"*Talking,*" Laurie said stupidly. "I cannot imagine . . ." She went again to the window, still drawn by the scene. Some of the Silversea men had mounted the two sets of steps and were facing the crowd, talking, their arms gesturing. Finally, from the center of the mass, a man made his way forward. A tall man, as black as Molenga, wearing boots on his bare legs, a pair of torn trousers that ended at his knees. Dangling on his chest was an elaborate necklace of gold and jewels. The crowd fell back, making a path for him.

Not fear, thought Laurie, dazed. Deference. The leader. When the man reached the carriage block he stepped up on it, facing the portico, staring at Molenga and Ham. Laurie heard his voice in the new silence that fell when he spoke. He talked, and it sounded like questions, the inflections rising. Ham answered, in easy confidence, and though Laurie couldn't see him from the window, she could hear his smile in his voice.

Laurie jumped, startled as the man on the carriage block suddenly threw his arms high and wide, his heavy face split in a grin. He whirled, shouting to the crowd, and all over the great mass hands shot up, fists clenched, and a new roar of sound vibrated against the glass of the window. The man jumped down from the block, strong and agile, and strode back through the path they had made. And, as he went, the ones he passed turned with him, following. *Following.*

Disbelieving, Laurie watched them go, melting into a river of bodies, flowing away down the avenue, draining the space around the house, until there were none left but the Silversea men, gathering in laughing, excited groups.

"They are going," Laurie said softly. "Thérèse, they are leaving this plantation!"

Thérèse rose with an exclamation and came to Laurie's side, holding the baby.

"Where? Why did they go?" Her long face was childlike, anxious with hope.

Laurie shook her head. "Someone has worked a miracle," she said. "But I do not know how."

David was awake, feverish and in some little pain. But once the slave army had disappeared Ham had gone to the dispensary and returned with a container of Anyola's bitter brew. He gave David a small amount that eased the pain but left him awake. Laurie sat on the floor and held his hand, watching his grin as he looked from Ham to Molenga. In spite of the fever and pain, he had never looked so young, so happy.

"So you managed it all without incident," he said. "I am proud of you both. I do not believe any other two could have done it."

"We had reason to do our best," Ham said quietly. "The reward is great."

"For us all," David said, and tightened the hand that held Laurie's. "Perhaps greatest for me. Thank you for our lives."

Molenga's faint smile appeared. "You could have run, like the rest. They are all safe in Bridgetown."

David's grin grew wider. "I prefer this method. God bless you both."

They both nodded solemnly and left the room, the last to do so, for Bartram had gone to see if his house still stood, and Thérèse had taken the baby up to his cradle and was watching over him, herself still shaken by what had happened. It had been decided it was best to leave David on the wide, comfortable couch for a time and Laurie could not bear to leave him.

Now that they were alone the questions she had came immediately.

"*How*, David? What could Molenga and Ham possibly say to turn that army of rioters? They kill loyal slaves more quickly than the whites, I have always heard, and a mob at the door of Silversea should be as wolves near a sheep pen."

"Wait," David said gently. His eyes, glazed by fever,

were still tender as he looked at her. "Tell me again what you have impressed on me so many times. What does a slave want?"

"Freedom," Laurie said promptly. "But what has that to do—"

"What else do they want?" His interruption was also gentle, but firm.

She sat back, folding slender legs into the position she had come to prefer. "A chance to make their own lives. To use their strength for themselves . . . to have a place of their own . . ." She was trying to go along with his game, but the turquoise eyes were snapping. She wanted her own question answered. He looked amused as she ended with some violence: "They want what we all want, David! To live free."

He nodded. "That is their dream. They never quite believe it, Laurie, but still they dream. And today they saw the dream come true. They saw a huge plantation owned by a black Rundi woman and her son. And all the workers were free, to come and go as they wished. How could they destroy their own dream?"

She stared at him. "You asked Molenga and Ham to lie . . . to put themselves in danger? What if one of our slaves had gone over to them and told the truth—"

"We have no slaves, darling." His eyes were tender, watching it dawn on her, changing first to awe and then to incredulous joy. "I persuaded my father to give it all to his firstborn son and the woman who bore him. It was not at all difficult, he is closer to them than anyone realizes." He smiled. "And of course as soon as it was theirs, they freed the slaves, as we knew they would."

Laurie let out her breath in a great, gusting sigh of happiness. "So that's what they were telling the rioters, there on the portico . . ."

"And for hours before. As the slaves were freed they went out to meet the vanguards and bring them back one by one to witness what was happening. By the time the mass of them arrived there were many amongst them, explaining.''

Laurie leaned forward, careful not to touch his side, and kissed him almost reverently. "Oh, David . . ." Her voice broke. "If they are free, then . . . then *we* are, too!"

"Precisely." He laughed and then winced, his hand going involuntarily to his side. "God, how I wish I could put my arms around you!"

"Soon," she said, and took his hand to hold against his cheek, kissing the broad palm. "Soon, darling." Her brilliant eyes brooded over him tenderly, her love for him glowing in their depths. "And will we still go to Scotland?"

"Certainly."

"And live there?"

"No, my darling. We shall visit often, for we will not be far away. In France there is a certain estate with large vineyards, very old and very beautiful, with a large chateau suitable for a family. It was my mother's, handed down from her family, and is now mine. Since the manager is retiring . . ."

Laurie's smile held no regret. "Where you are, I will be happy—and think how pleased Thérèse will be!"

Chapter Twenty-three

IT WAS WEEKS BEFORE ANYOLA PRONOUNCED DAVID fit to travel, and a month of rough sailing to reach France. There they made their way to the south where the estate lay and were welcomed by the estate manager, who put them up in his own comfortable house. They spent days examining the chateau and the luxuriant vines, loaded in this spring weather with great bunches of small, pale grapes.

Laurie found the chateau ideal, a large country house surrounded by charming gardens. But, after a generation of being unoccupied, it required care. They hired carpenters and painters, bought furniture to be delivered following the repairs, and traveled to the coast to embark for England and a visit to Lord Peter.

Thérèse was adamant in her refusal to accompany them. Her thrifty French soul was aghast at the thought of leaving the chateau in the hands of strangers, who, she said violently, would charge them a fortune and cart off every treasure in the house.

"I will stay," she said, "and they shall work for their money."

Laurie only smiled, knowing how happy Thérèse was to be in her native country. She had no intention of dragging her away.

In Mayfair they had an enjoyable visit with Lord Peter, who, though amazed that they had given up Silversea, ended by saying wryly that it was inevitable that slavery would be abolished, so it was just as well.

He had already heard from Bartram and knew he intended to stay, to live out his years with Molenga and Ham. Ham, Bartram had reported with pride, was already experimenting with different crops, and the land seemed admirably suited to various fruits. The former slaves, he had written, had been given an area in which to build houses.

Laurie and David avoided the subject of Desirée and her death, but during their last evening, as they sat in the well-remembered library and drank a bottle of wine brought from their French vineyard, Lord Peter brought the subject up himself.

"You have undoubtedly wondered what part I played, that night of Desirée's death," he said heavily. "And I would like to tell you of it, and perhaps rid it from my mind. I began the series of events that led to her murder, and I feel great guilt when I think of it. You saw me leave, Laurie, but I don't believe anyone saw me come back through that door." He stopped, pouring another glass of wine, a muscle quivering in his lean cheek. "I was on my way to Bartram to tell him of Desirée's character, but as I drove away I knew he wouldn't believe me. I remembered her drunken temper as I left, and I thought if I took her with me, her own actions would convince him. So, I went back for her. It was . . . very foolish of me." He got to his feet and paced away from them and then back again.

"This," he said quietly, "is harder than I thought it would be. I was very angry. I dragged her from her room and down the staircase, and my violence frightened her. She broke away and ran, disappearing toward the back of the house. I followed, and discovered that she had gone outside. I found footprints in the vegetable garden and started after her. Then, suddenly, I knew if I caught her I would kill her. I *wanted* to kill her! The knowledge frightened me, and I turned and rushed back around the house, got into the carriage with Ham and went to

305

the Allyns'." He took a deep breath. "Desirée's maid saw me. I was sure she would speak of it to you later, perhaps suspect me . . ."

"Odd," David said, "she never mentioned it." His gaze slid to Laurie, who was examining her shoes. "However, none of the rest of us noticed the footprints, or perhaps we would have found her—in time."

"I have wondered," Lord Peter said, "why she stayed there so long."

"It is very pleasant in the lime grove," Laurie said reflectively, "and she was very drunk. Perhaps she found a place to hide, and went to sleep . . . to waken later and wander the wrong way in the darkness . . ." She stopped, remembering again the horror of what had followed.

David saw the memory in her eyes. He rose, taking her hand. "If we are off to Scotland tomorrow you should be in bed, my love. Your Annie will believe I have exhausted you."

He was leading her thoughts again, but in this case she was grateful. She bid them both a good night and hurried up to relieve the maid who was watching over young David.

The scent of heather, of wild sea, of Scotland, came breathing farewell again, drifting on a soft breeze that stirred deep meadow grass around them. They had stayed a long, lazy and luxurious month, stuffing themselves with Annie's hearty Scotch soups, the mutton roasts and oat cakes, until forced to tramp miles on the moors to rid themselves of the weight they gained.

But now it was time, Laurie thought. She was anxious to return to the chateau, could barely wait to see it shining and ready for them to begin their new life. A far different parting than the last one, she thought, and Annie and Breen so happy with her choice of husband that they didn't grieve at all. She rose from the blanket and began putting the remains of their enormous picnic back into the basket.

Propped on one elbow, David watched the blue glitter of the afternoon sun on the tarn before them, the snowy fleece of the sheep that had wandered down to drink. He noted the rough shape of the small boat drawn up on the bank, its oars askew and awkward, as roughly made as the shaggy hull.

He glanced at his wife as she repacked the basket, and noted with considerably more pleasure the shape of her, slim as a water reed again, but with the more generous breasts that motherhood had given her.

"It is difficult to believe that those small hands ever handled such oars as I see here," he said lazily. "I doubt your fingers would fit around them. In spite of your tall stories, I am quite sure Breen did the rowing."

Laurie turned to look at him, shaking back the black hair that had loosened in the breeze and fallen to her shoulders. Her eyes gathered sunlight and sent it forth again, sparkling with more brilliance than the waters of the tarn, and David thought her more beautiful than ever. But her soft mouth was now compressed.

"Tall stories, my love? I tell no tall stories. I rowed. And I did it well."

He grinned at her, the black beard giving him a more devilish look than the teasing brown eyes needed. "Childhood memories," he said solemnly, "are often exaggerated by time."

She rose to the bait like a salmon in summer, dropping the basket and standing straight in the loose linen gown she wore.

"Then, come," she snapped, "and I shall show you. I have not forgotten the skill."

Grinning, he followed her down to the shore and helped her push the clumsy craft into the water. Bending, she took off her shoes and stockings, hiked up her skirt and stepped through shallow water into the boat. He sloshed after her in his boots and sat in the stern, regarding her with pretended doubt.

"You will not capsize us, my dear?"

She gave him a blue-green flame of a glance and settled herself on the seat, picking up the oars.

"You cannot swim?"

He laughed. "I swim, but I would not care to sport in such cold water." He began enjoying himself thoroughly as she rowed out into the middle of the small lake. Her full breasts were thrust against the loose gown as she pulled the heavy oars, her bare feet braced wide apart on the bottom of the boat for balance. Her skirt fell limply between her knees, revealing the contours of her softly curved thighs, the neat, small belly above them.

"You are doing quite well," he said patronizingly, "for someone your size. And you say that in those days you actually caught fish, my love?"

The turquoise eyes had been watching him closely, and Laurie was now quite aware of his teasing and his blatant examination of her form. She stopped, panting, and leaned on the oars.

"I did," she assented, her voice soft. "It is very unfortunate that we have no pole, or I would also prove *that* point. However, I could catch a crab for you, if you think that would be amusing."

David laughed, surprised. "A crab? In a mountain lake? Surely, that would be a miracle. Do so, by all means."

She nodded, hiding a smile, and set her oars again. "Watch closely," she said, "or you may miss it . . ." She leaned into her rowing, her eyes on his face as he bent to look, pretending an interest. With a swift turn of a wrist on the side where he watched, she sent a silvery flood of icy water through the air, drenching him.

David gasped and leaned back, wiping his streaming face, brushing at his soaked shirt, listening to her clear, delighted laughter as she rowed toward shore. Rowed *slowly* toward shore, he noted, since she was helpless with amusement. The laughter kept dying away and then bubbling up again, her white throat throbbing with it. Her eyes were wet with tears of mirth, her cheeks pink as she finally sent the prow of the old boat grinding onto the shore. Stepping out, her bare feet white and delicate beneath the water, she offered him a hand.

"I will assist you to land," she said, still chuckling. "It isn't everyone who leans into a crab quite so eagerly—you must still be blinded."

Far from blinded, his eyes gleamed. He wrapped his arms around himself and shivered as he trudged toward the blanket. "I am frozen," he said dolefully. "I do believe my wound is aching from the cold."

"Oh!" She stopped, staring at him, at the thin shirt wet and clinging to his chest. "Oh, David . . ." Her hands were swift, unbuttoning the shirt. "Sit on the blanket and I will pull the corners up around you. Let me dry this shirt in the sun . . . I never considered such an ending."

He sat, shivering exaggeratedly, and let her pull the blanket around him, watched her rush to spread the shirt over a bush and come back to him.

"Lie back, darling. The sun will help to warm you." She dropped beside him and began rubbing his skin, careful not to touch the long scar on his side. "I am so very sorry."

A long arm slid around her, pulling her closer. "Lie against me, Laurie. The warmth of your body will be comforting, I am sure."

She obeyed quickly, settling over his bare chest, her full breasts in the loose gown warm on his skin, her fragrant hair brushing his face as she kneaded and massaged his shoulders, her eyes worried as she gazed into the face so close to hers. His eyes were closed, and she wondered frantically if he was in great pain and trying to hide it.

"Do you feel warmer? Is the pain going away?" Her voice was tremulous, full of guilt. His eyes remained closed.

"I am warmer," he said slowly. "But there is still a slight pain . . . not entirely unpleasant."

There was something in the timbre of his deep voice that made her grow suddenly still, and then turn her head to glance down the length of his body, seeing the telltale bulge of his loins. She drew in her breath and flattened her hands on his chest, pushing futilely as his arm tightened.

"You are cruel! You made me feel so guilty . . ."

Both arms around her now, he pulled her resisting body down again, and, as she twisted her face from his angrily, he caught the mass of silky hair and turned her back again to look into her eyes, his own gaze amused but laced with tenderness.

"Not cruel, Laurie," he said huskily, "I could never be cruel to you."

He was so close, his familiar scent so evocative of sensual memories, the firm mouth so enticing within the soft beard. The sunlight glistened on the touches of silver at his temples and brought her an aching realization of how short life was, and how much she needed an eternity with him. She sighed and yielded, bending to put suddenly soft, parted lips on his, to search within the firm mouth with the tip of her tongue.

Gasping, rolling with his catlike grace, David covered her body with his, thrusting a hand through the neckline of her gown to close tightly on a breast. A muscular thigh moved swiftly across her hips and clenched, dragging her against his throbbing loins.

"Laurie . . ." His eyes on hers were black velvet, his face tense with passion that quivered on the edge of control. "God, how I want you . . . your very touch inflames me . . ."

She was almost frightened by his intensity, by the flaming response that ran through her. This was not the place . . . not here, in the open. Remembering, horror ran through her, and she strained to look around, fancying leering faces behind every bush. She pushed against his shoulders, wriggling beneath his weight. "No, not here . . ."

His mouth covered her protest, his tongue sliding in as she gasped, thrusting strongly, searching . . . possessing. He moved, his hand leaving her breast to raise the hem of her skirt, slipping beneath it to caress her thighs, moving warmly upward.

She was suddenly limp, her loins on fire. In a moment she felt the involuntary movement of her thighs, widening. Of her body, arching, pressing against his hand. Sound rose in her throat, purring, as his fingers found the center of her desire.

"Ah, Laurie . . . my lovely Laurie . . ." He was panting, pulling the gown up, leaving her white thighs glistening in the sun. The gown was off, over her head, his hands trembled as he removed her undergarments and left her, naked and soft, on the rough blanket.

"So beautiful," he whispered. "So full of passion . . ." His bearded face bent to her breasts, his mouth hotly devouring, his hand stroked and teased, expertly bringing her desire to full flood. He seemed completely unconscious of her frantic hands on him, until she began making small, urgent sounds, her hands intensifying their efforts.

"Sh-h-h, my love," he murmured. "It is truly all right. There is no one around us, nor has been for hours . . ." He paused, looking into her face, at the fire in the blue-green eyes, at the soft open mouth and pink velvet of tongue. "I must have you or burst . . ."

"Then, please," she said huskily, "*please* . . . will you rid yourself of those damnable breeches?"

His shirt was dry enough by the time he wanted it, and as they walked back across the moors with their basket and the carefully folded blanket, it was twilight. In the huge kitchen of Stephney Downs Manor the rocking chair was creaking and Davey was asleep in Annie's capacious lap.

Laurie smiled as Annie touched her lips with a finger and motioned them on. Annie would want the boy in the trundle bed beside her this last night before they left, and Breen would be in when he finished in the barn, wanting a last look himself. She nodded, taking David's arm and heading for the dining room, where she knew their supper would be spread.

Later, climbing onto the huge, goosefeather mattress, she sank warmly into the yielding hollow at David's broad back and ran her fingers lightly over the long scar where the lead ball had ploughed a furrow.

"You'll not fool me again," she whispered. "Your strenuous activity in the meadow has proved you completely healed."

He laughed softly and rolled over, taking her in his arms. "And you have made love again under the open sky. We are both healed and whole, my darling."

She nodded, her cheek brushing the crisp hair on his chest. She was not at all sleepy, though perfectly relaxed and content, smiling a few minutes later as she felt the chest rise and fall with the deep, slow breathing of sleep.

France. She could see the chateau in the acres of vineyard and the thought of it enthralled her. Her mind ranged dreamily over the future, visualizing David's work in the vines, out in the open air where he loved to be, and thought hopefully of the children she might have to help fill the rooms of the chateau. Then, there would be the visits to Scotland . . .

Her heart nudged her, and frightened, she drew her mind away swiftly. It nudged her again . . . look. *Look.*

Warily, staring up into the vast darkness of the high stone ceiling, she let her mind slide forward in time.

Scotland. And what she saw was the scene from the kitchen window of Stepney Downs Manor, for she recognized the familiar roll of the moors seen from there, and a sheep dog frisking, playing . . . and running back to a motionless figure standing and looking out over the land. It was . . . Bartram? No, not Bartram, for the man was taller than he, though the beard and hair were as snowy-white . . .

Then the man turned and seemed to look into her face, smiling and coming toward her briskly. David. David old, very old, but still healthy and hearty, with that look in his eyes reserved for her alone.

Her heart leaped and then pounded as the scene faded in the darkness. She thought of what Molenga had told her. How had the words gone? *Knowledge to aid another. . . . Strength to meet an obstacle. . . . Happiness that lasts . . .*

She turned her head and looked at the vigorous man beside her, at the thick, black beard and strong features softened by sleep. *Happiness that lasts.* The gift that is not always a gift was a gift indeed tonight, for it had shown her the happiest of futures. She would have her love with her for a long, a very long time . . .

Tapestry

HISTORICAL ROMANCES

**Next Month From
Tapestry Romances**

WILLOW
by Linda Lael Miller
PRIDE AND PROMISES
by Adrienne Scott

Home delivery from Pocket Books

Here's your opportunity to have fabulous bestsellers delivered right to you. Our free catalog is filled to the brim with the newest titles plus the finest in mysteries, science fiction, westerns, cookbooks, romances, biographies, health, psychology, humor—every subject under the sun. Order this today and a world of pleasure will arrive at your door.

POCKET BOOKS, Department ORD
1230 Avenue of the Americas, New York, N.Y. 10020

Please send me a free Pocket Books catalog for home delivery

NAME _____

ADDRESS _____

CITY _____ STATE/ZIP _____

If you have friends who would like to order books at home, we'll send them a catalog too—

NAME _____

ADDRESS _____

CITY _____ STATE/ZIP _____

NAME _____

ADDRESS _____

CITY _____ STATE/ZIP _____